THE
FIRST
PATIENT

.

ALSO BY MICHAEL PALMER

THE
FIRST
PATIENT

·

MICHAEL
PALMER

St. Martin's Press 🌊 New York

This is a work of fiction. All of the characters, organizations, and events portrayed in this novel are either products of the author's imagination or are used fictitiously.

www.stmartins.com

Library of Congress Cataloging-in-Publication Data

Palmer, Michael, 1942–
The first patient / Michael Palmer.—1st ed.
        p. cm.
    ISBN-13: 978-0-312-34353-8
    ISBN-10: 0-312-34353-1
    1. Physicians—Fiction. 2. Presidents—United States—Health—Fiction. 3. Physician and patient—Fiction. I. Title.

PS3566.A539 F57 2008
813'.54—dc22

                                                              2007040443

First Edition: February 2008

10 9 8 7 6 5 4 3 2 1

To Dr. E. Connie Mariano, Rear Admiral (Ret.),
Renaissance woman,
physician to presidents:
Without you, this book would never have been.

And
to Matthew, Daniel, and Luke,
for making it all worthwhile

ACKNOWLEDGMENTS

First and always, thanks to Jennifer Enderlin, my extraordinary, brilliant, compassionate, and hard-working editor at St. Martin's Press. You are and always will be my kind of bookkeeper.

Jane Berkey and Meg Ruley of the Jane Rotrosen Agency are everything literary agents should be and more.

Talented singer, musician, novelist, computer wizard, songwriter Daniel James Palmer is responsible for lots of good and helpful things surrounding this book, including Alison's blues.

In addition:

Dr. David Grass shared his strength and vast neurological knowledge.

Remarkably talented artist and children's book author Dara Golden shared her considerable understanding and love of horses.

Robin Broady read and read and read some more.

Chef Bill Collins (www.chefbill.com) reasoned out problems with me while putting together one award-winning meal after another.

Bless you, Sally Richardson, Matthew Shear, and Matthew Baldacci at St. Martin's.

Attorney Bill Crowe taught me how to shoot straight, Jay Esposito taught me how to buy a used car, and Dr. Ruth Solomon gave me veterinary advice.

Thanks to the staff at the White House Medical Unit for your hospitality, and to the Big Book for always having the right answers.

And finally, thanks to Luke for suggesting nanotechnology when I told him I was stuck.

Anyone I overlooked, I promise to get you next time.

THE
FIRST
PATIENT

.

CHAPTER 1

The rotors of Marine One slowed, then stopped. Dust clouds billowed into the still air. Minutes later, a second, identical helicopter landed twenty yards away. A short staircase lowered to the parched ground. A Marine sergeant in formal dress left the shelter of the first chopper and took a position at attention at the base of the staircase. The door of the chunky Sikorsky Sea King swung open.

And with no more fanfare than that, the most powerful man on Earth, his ubiquitous, well-publicized dog at heel, stepped out into the warm Wyoming evening.

Fifty feet away, still in the saddle, Gabe Singleton calmed his horse with a few pats behind the ear. The mid-morning appearance of a Secret Service agent at the Ambrose Regional Medical Center had given Gabe warning that the presidential drop-in was going to take place, but the man hadn't been specific about the time and, following an exhausting all-nighter caring for two patients in the ICU, even a visitor of this magnitude couldn't keep Gabe from his customary ride out into the desert and back.

"Hey, cowboy," President Andrew Stoddard called out, descending the stairs and sincerely saluting the lone Marine as he passed, "whattaya say?"

"I say you and your choppers scared the crap out of this world-weary old nag. . . . Frightened my horse, too."

The two men shook hands, then embraced. Stoddard, who Gabe felt looked presidential even when they were first-year roommates at the Naval Academy, showed the stress of three and a half years in office. Silver highlighted his razor-cut dark brown hair, and deep crow's-feet had appeared at the corners of his iridescent blue eyes. Still, he was every bit the man in charge—the decorated Desert Storm pilot and former governor of North Carolina, whose star had been on the ascendancy since the day he took his first privileged breath.

"One of the downsides of the job," Stoddard said, gesturing toward his entourage. "Twin helicopters so that any whacko who decides to take a bazooka shot at one of them has only a fifty-fifty chance of blowing me away, Secret Service studs checking out every inch that's gonna be stepped on by these size elevens and every toilet seat that's gonna be graced by these presidential cheeks, plus a medical team trained to know that it's not *if* something terrible happens to their boss, it's *when*."

"If you're looking to make a job change, I could use a wrangler on my ranch."

"How many do you have working for you now?" Stoddard asked, glancing about.

"You would be the first. I'm afraid our benefits package is a little thin, too, starting with that you'd have to pay me to work here."

"Hey, put me on the list. I don't know if you follow the polls or not, but I haven't got a hell of a lot of job security at the moment. Got some time to talk with an old pal?"

"If you'll let me put my other old pal Condor, here, in the stables."

"Fine-looking horse."

"And that's a fine-looking pooch. Liberty, right?" Gabe patted the dog's rock-solid flank.

"Good memory," Stoddard said. "Liberty's making quite a name for himself, tagging along with me and changing people's misperceptions about pit bulls, just like we're changing people's misconceptions about America. I've had dogs all my life, Gabe, but Liberty, here, is the best. Strong as a tiger, wise as an owl, and as gentle and dependable as that horse of yours."

"Maybe you should have named him Simile."

The president laughed out loud. "I love it. This here's my trusty dog, Simile. He's tough as a Tennessee hickory nut, but gentle as baby powder. Carol will think that's very funny, too, especially since, unlike her husband, she's actually likely to know the difference between a simile and a metaphor. Hey, Griz."

A thick-necked, barrel-chested, balding Secret Service man wearing the obligatory black suit and reflective shades seemed to materialize from nowhere.

"You rang?"

"Griz, this is my old college roomie Gabe Singleton. *Doctor* Gabe Singleton. It's been five years or so since we last saw one another, but it seems like yesterday. Gabe, this here's Treat Griswold, my number-one protector and probably the number-two man in the whole Secret Service. Obsessive to a fault. Swears he's telling the truth when he says he'll take that proverbial bullet for me, but with that crooked smile and those beady little eyes of his, I just don't believe him."

"In that case, sir, you'll just have to wait and see," Griswold said, stopping just short of pulverizing the bones in Gabe's hand at the same time. "I'll be happy to get Condor settled in, Doctor. I used to muck out stables and ride warm-ups when I was a kid."

Gabe liked the Secret Service agent immediately.

"In that case you've come a long way," he said, handing over the reins. "Tack room's in the barn. Maybe we can go for a ride sometime."

"Maybe we can, sir," Griswold said. "Come on, Liberty, let's put this big ol' fellow to bed."

Stoddard took Gabe by the arm and led him to the back door. The house, seven rustic rooms that still had the feel of the cabin it was before some additions, was Gabe's cut from the end of his five-year marriage to Cynthia Townes, a bright, vivacious nurse from the hospital who loved him to pieces from day one to day last. Her mistake.

Cinnie's last words to him before she handed over her keys and took off for a teaching job in Cheyenne were to beg him to finish dealing with his past before he made any further attempts to build a future with anyone. For seven more years he had taken her at her word, and so had carefully avoided another in-depth connection. He might be done dealing with his past, but he had serious doubt it was ever going to be done dealing with him.

"Sorry I haven't gotten out here for so long," Stoddard said. "I used to really enjoy the evening rides and our fishing trips up into those mountains."

"The Laramies. There's no place on earth quite like them. But stow the apologies, matie. From what I've heard, you've had a few other things on your plate—like saving the world."

Stoddard grinned wistfully.

"It's a little bigger a job than I once thought," he said, settling in at the round oak table in the kitchen, "but I still intend to make a dent in it."

"I remember you talking like that during our first or second night of bar-hopping together at the Academy. I kept trying to stay cynical and believe that you were an idealistic jerk, but this little voice inside me kept saying that this was a guy who might actually be able to do it. Then, when you drank me under the table, I really decided to give you the benefit of the doubt."

"That was beginner's luck, and you know it. You must have had a virus or something."

"Speaking of which, it should come as no surprise that I can't offer you a beer, but I can brew you some coffee, or—or some tea."

"Tea would be great," the president said, placing a manila folder in front of him. "While I'm in apology mode, sorry I couldn't make it in for your dad's funeral. I appreciated your letting me know he had passed."

"And I appreciated that you would take the time to call from South America."

"Your dad was a bit . . . quirky, but I always did like him."

"He was very proud of you, Drew, you being a fellow Annapolis grad and all."

The instant he spoke the words, Gabe wished he hadn't. Cinnie's pleas notwithstanding, he had done what he could to deal with Fairhaven and his father's reaction to it. He hadn't meant the statement to come out the way it did.

"I'm sure he was very proud of you, too, Gabe," Stoddard said, a bit uncomfortably, "what with your M.D. degree and all those medical missions you've been on, and that youth foundation you're running."

"Thanks. Hey, speaking of sires, how's yours doing?"

"Same old LeMar. Still trying to micromanage everything, including me. He tells me he's bought his way onto a Russian space shot. Fifteen million and he becomes the first seventy-five-year-old to soak his hemorrhoids in the international space station tub."

"Fifteen million. God bless him."

"Hey, come on. When we're talking about my father, it's like Monopoly money. Just do the math. The ten billion or so he's worth minus the fifteen million or so he spent is . . . um . . . take away three, carry the one—still ten billion or so. I wouldn't be surprised if he paid in cash with bills he pulled out of his sock drawer."

Gabe smiled. If, over the years, he had suffered from too little father, Drew Stoddard had suffered from too much. From his days in diapers, Stoddard had been molded by the charismatic, wildly successful industrialist. The heartache Buzz Singleton endured when Gabe was drummed out of the Naval Academy had to pale next to LeMar Stoddard's having to explain to his pals at the hunt club or the polo pitch or wherever that Drew had become a Democrat—and one of the shining stars of the party at that.

Did Drew's remarkable transformation from elitist Republican to populist Democrat have its roots in the accident at Fairhaven all those years ago? Gabe often wondered. In such an inestimable tragedy, not even the bystanders and innocents like Drew Stoddard escaped unchanged.

Gabe set a pot of Earl Grey tea and some shortbread on the table. There was a time before the last presidential election when the two of them got together once or twice a year to hike and fish in the Smokies or Laramies, and exchange news and stories, but now, despite their long-standing friendship,

Gabe felt strangely edgy about taking up the time of the most powerful man in the solar system with small talk. Still, this last-minute trip to Tyler was Stoddard's doing, so it seemed right to let him set the agenda.

Gabe didn't have long to wait.

"Did you know that in addition to the comprehensive medical facility on the first floor of the Eisenhower Office Building we have our own medical clinic right in the White House?" Stoddard began.

"You said something about it in one of our conversations, yes."

"It's run by the White House Medical Unit. Which, for reasons lost in antiquity, is actually a division of the White House Military Office. Pretty nice setup, too—recently renovated, state-of-the-art equipment, top-notch nurses and paramedics, and the best doctors from all branches of the service. Twenty-five or thirty staff altogether. They take care of me and Carol and the boys when they're home from school, as well as Vice President Cooper and his family, and anyone else who happens to need medical care while they're at the White House."

"The boys—they doing well?"

"Terrific. Andrew's going into eleventh; Rick'll be in ninth. Both are at school in Connecticut. Right now they're at soccer camp. Andrew's an all-star goalie. Rick plays because he thinks he should. He wants to go to the Academy and be an astronaut."

"Think you can get him in?"

"I think he can get in on his own, but I may keep an eye on his application."

"Eleventh and ninth—that's amazing."

"They're happy and healthy. That's all that really matters."

"Speaking of healthy, you had your doc from North Carolina come up to D.C. to care for you, yes?"

"Jim Ferendelli. He's been a great doctor for me and the family. The best. Kind, knowledgeable, empathetic. Plays beautiful classical piano, too."

"I'm really glad to hear all that, Drew. Having a doctor one can trust is a huge weight off of anyone's shoulders."

"I agree, but I'm glad to hear you verbalize it just the same."

"Well, that's how I feel, although when it comes to caring for the President of the United States, I assume you know I'm just stating the obvious. Your well-being and good health have an effect, one way or another, on every person on the planet."

Stoddard laughed with no great glee. "I understand what you're saying, but I still get the willies thinking about things that way."

"It's a hell of a job you signed on for. I don't envy that responsibility in the least."

"But I still have your support?"

"Of course."

"In that case, it should come as no surprise that I didn't break away to fly here in the midst of a heated campaign just because I missed your smiling face. I need something from you, Gabe. Something important."

"Name it."

"I need you to come to Washington and be my doctor."

Gabe sank back in his chair and stared at his onetime roommate in utter disbelief.

"But . . . you said this Jim Ferendelli is a terrific doctor."

"He is . . . was."

Gabe felt as if a band were tightening around his chest.

"I don't understand," he finally managed.

"Gabe," Stoddard said. "Jim Ferendelli's gone. . . . Vanished."

CHAPTER 2

*W*hat about the FBI?"

"You don't think they're all over this? Hundreds of agents have been on the case for almost two weeks. Nothing."

Evening had settled in, and a steady breeze from the north had dispelled the last of the day's warmth. Gabe had listened in stunned silence to the description of a fifty-six-year-old widower, devoted father of a grown daughter, personable and diligent, churchgoing and humble, who one day simply failed to show up at work. A search of his apartment in Georgetown and his Chapel Hill home revealed nothing out of the ordinary, and a check of his phone and e-mails had also been of no help.

With the presidential campaign just heating up, Andrew Stoddard's advisors had managed to keep the potentially distracting disappearance out of the news until they were certain the search was not going to be successful. For more than a week, now, that was clearly the case, and what scant details there were had just been released to the press.

"They've all been told that for now the White House Medical Unit would handle any problems I might have, but as competent as the unit is, I really want my own physician."

"This is absolutely incredible," Gabe said. "The doctor to the President of the United States has vanished without a trace. What about his family? Have they heard anything?"

"As I said, Jim's wife died of cancer about five years ago. His mother's in a nursing home, and two older sisters haven't heard a word from him."

"But you also said he had a daughter. Has she heard anything?"

"Actually, Jennifer's disappeared, too."

"What?"

"She's a graduate film student at NYU. The evening of the day Jim disappeared, Jennifer's roommate came home from a date and Jennifer wasn't there, but the FBI already was. There was no evidence she had packed anything, no note, nothing. They tried every number the roommate could think of, but just like her father, the girl had simply . . . vanished."

Gabe could only shake his head.

"Jesus," he muttered. "Do you make any sense of this, Drew? Any sense at all? Do you think this is politically related? Maybe it's just a coincidence of some sort, like an accident, or . . . or a mental crisis. Was the daughter stable?"

"A terrific kid. Some therapy after her mother died, but none for years as far as we can tell. No drugs, minimal drinker. No current boyfriend, but her last one had only good things to say."

"Was Ferendelli seeing anyone?"

"Not that we've been able to determine."

Gabe rubbed his eyes and studied the vaulted redwood ceiling.

"I wish I could help you, Drew," he said at last. "Really I do. But there's just too much going on here."

"Actually," Stoddard said, "Magnus Lattimore, my chief of staff, has been here in Tyler for a few days nosing about. He's discreet and very, very efficient, and he can move very quietly when he needs to."

"Like the guys in the suits and sunglasses out there."

"Just like them, yes."

"Terrific. I'm not sure I want to know what he learned."

"Well, let's see. Both of your partners say they can hold down the fort for the time between now and the election in November. Apparently you guys just hired a new physician's assistant named Lillian Lawrence, who's in a position to absorb a lot of the load that sending you off on a working sabbatical would generate. One of your partners said Lillian is probably smarter than you are anyway."

Gabe was unable to stifle a grin.

"Which one?" he asked.

"Sorry. He swore Magnus to secrecy."

"It's not that simple, Drew. In addition to my patients I have a commitment to my foundation."

"You mean Lariat?"

"Uh-oh. What'd Magnus learn about that?"

"He learned that over the years you've kept more than a few kids from heading down the wrong path by getting them involved in rodeo and other riding projects."

"So he must have learned how important it is to me . . . and me to it."

"What he learned is that there isn't a soul in southeast Wyoming with money to donate that you haven't successfully squeezed—most of them more than once."

"I've always been a determined little beaver when I set my mind to it."

"Well, yesterday Magnus had lunch with"—Stoddard opened the folder and scanned one of the pages—"Irene deJesus. She told him you never do much work around Lariat anyway."

"If Irene said that, she's toast, but I know she didn't."

"Okay, okay, she said she would have to recruit three or four people to match what you do with the kids each week."

"That's better."

"She also said that a lot of your efforts lately have gone into planning and raising money for an indoor riding facility."

"We're getting there."

"Gabe, take this job for me and you *are* there."

Gabe felt his pulse leap. Sooner or later, the new stables and riding arena were going to happen, but at the moment they were still little more than an ambitious dream.

"You would do that?" he asked.

"The day you set foot in the White House medical office, an anonymous angel will donate fifty thousand dollars to Lariat. If that isn't enough to finish the job, I know another angel or two who will want to help."

Another volley of skipped heartbeats. Bake sales and silent auctions could only take things so far, so fast, and other Lariat projects had all but tapped out their regular boosters. Fund-raising for this dream had been surprisingly slow, and there were at least a dozen boys and girls on the waiting list who could be brought on board along with the staff to deal with them, the moment the arena and stables were finished.

Gabe paced across the kitchen and back. He had no doubt that if Drew Stoddard promised money for Lariat, money there would be.

"I can't believe," Gabe said, "that with a machine as efficient as this Magnus working for you, you're worried about getting elected."

"Well I *am* worried. This campaign's going to be a marathon. Brad Dunleavy is a warrior, who has already served a term as president. Our two parties are poised and ready to claw one another to shreds. Control of both houses of Congress could hang on a single seat. But you know what, Gabe? I just heard what I was saying about arranging for your project to be funded if you come to D.C., and I'm taking it all back. You don't deserve to have me sit here bribing you. That was Magnus's idea, but now that I've done it I don't like the way it sounds and I don't like the way I feel. After all you've been through and the way you've bounced back, and all the people you've helped, you just don't deserve it. So I give you my word that regardless of what you decide about coming to Washington, the money you need will be here for you and all the kids you serve."

Gabe knew he was surrounded—outflanked, outmaneuvered. No wonder the man had never lost an election. Was the sudden commitment to fund Lariat's expansion irrespective of Gabe's decision part of Magnus Lattimore's carefully designed strategy, or was Drew being legitimately spontaneous and sincere? And most important, did it really matter?

How can you tell a politician is lying? His lips are moving!
Who first said that?

If Drew was being the politician, he deserved to have Gabe simply say, "Okay, I'll take the money and you find another replacement doctor."

But that wasn't going to happen.

Gabe sighed and sat down across from his friend.

"The accident at Fairhaven is bound to come up," he said. "How would you plan to deal with what happened there?"

"Thanks to you and what you've accomplished with your life since your release, that's not going to be as big a deal as you might think."

"Says Magnus Lattimore."

"And others."

Gabe gazed through the rear window at the violet sky and the silhouette of Marine One. As always, his mind balked at dredging up the accident and the terrible aftermath, and as always, the images—as far as they went—were inexorable. He and Drew, like many of the second-year midshipmen, were celebrating the end of the term with a veritable Olympiad of drinking games conducted at a variety of bars. Rockfish . . . Acme . . . McGarvey's. The Boatyard was the last stop Gabe remembered, but according to court records, there were several more. As almost always on what they called drinkathons, Drew Stoddard was at Gabe's side, if not matching him glass for glass and bottle for bottle, as he once could do, at least making a respectable effort.

Fairhaven wasn't the first time Gabe had drunken himself into a blackout. In fact, since high school he had been somewhat notorious for them. He took pride in describing himself as a hard-ridin', hard-studyin', hard-fightin', hard-lovin', hard-drinkin' sonofagun, and few of those who knew him well would dispute any of those claims. Nor could anyone argue with a high school valedictorian and rodeo champ, who was also coveted by the football coach at Navy as a running back, although Gabe never bothered to try out for the team.

"An alcoholic doesn't usually start off as a failure," Gabe's AA sponsor would tell him one day. "He often has to work and drink very hard to become one."

Gabe's blood alcohol level—.34—could have been lethal in a body less adapted to heavy drinking, even a twenty-year-old's body. His blackout came and went over the hours following the accident. He remembered the rain-soaked ground at the bottom of the steep embankment, and pawing at the blood cascading down into his eyes. He remembered Drew's quavering voice, calling to him from somewhere in the darkness, asking him over and over if he was all right. And he remembered the police . . . and the handcuffs.

It was hours after he lost control of the borrowed car, jumped the median, and plowed head-on into the subcompact being driven by a young pregnant woman before his mind began permanently to clear, but he never remembered any details of the accident—not one. And he remembered absolutely nothing of the young woman he had killed, along with her unborn child.

"Gabe?"

The president's voice cut into his thoughts but did not dispel them entirely.

"Huh? Oh, sorry."

"It's still hard, isn't it."

"It's not the sort of thing I was put together to deal with, if that's what you mean. I just can't imagine the Washington press corps won't dredge up every lurid detail. A year in prison isn't exactly what the American public would consider a ringing endorsement for the man taking care of their leader."

"My people assure me it won't be that bad. You took the punishment society gave you and you went on with a life of service to others. Even the nastiest of reporters knows it could have been them behind the wheel that night, and even the most jaded can appreciate what you've accomplished since then."

"Thanks for saying that."

"We both know it hasn't been easy."

"Or really all that successful. That kid would be over thirty now. Sometimes I find myself wondering what he might have grown up to be."

The statement, though absolutely true, seemed to catch Stoddard by surprise. For a time, the decorated Desert Storm fighter pilot, now commander in chief of the most powerful armed forces ever assembled, seemed unable to respond. Thirty-two years had passed since Fairhaven, and still Gabe's wounds were raw and, at times, festering.

"Gabe, I mean it," Stoddard said finally. "I came all the way out here personally because I really need you. The campaign is already taking its toll on my health. Headaches, stomach pains, insomnia, intermittent diarrhea. Name a symptom, I've had it. Jim's been secretly having neurologic tests run for headaches I've been having—migraines, he's been calling them. I need someone I can trust—someone who is above the Washington gossipmongers, someone I can bank the future of this country on."

"The FBI is still going full bore to find Ferendelli?"

"And the investigative arm of the Secret Service."

"If he's found and wants his job back, I'm coming home."

"You have my word."

"Damn, but I'm not excited about this, Drew."

"I know."

"I'm a frigging homebody. Except for the missions to Central America, the closest I come to going anyplace is reading *Travel and Leisure* magazine at the dentist's office. My partners love me because I'm always around to cover for them in case of any emergency."

"So they said."

"Dammit, Stoddard, why are you looking and acting like you already know I'm gonna cave in?"

Stoddard's boyish smile had probably won him 10 or 20 million votes in the last election.

"Because you're a good man, Dr. Singleton, and you know this is the right thing to do."

"How much time do I have to get ready?"

"According to Magnus's inquiries, two days should be enough."

"I'm looking forward to meeting up with this Magnus of yours."

"In D.C.?" Stoddard asked.

"In D.C., Mr. President."

CHAPTER 3

The White House Physician's clinic was situated directly across the corridor from the elevator to the First Family's residence. Standing before the bathroom mirror in the elegant three-room office, Gabe sensed he would have been more at ease had he been stationed in a clinic in downtown Baghdad.

It was just after seven in the evening. As promised, the tuxedo, complete with shoes, had arrived at the office at precisely six. The size was perfect in every respect—not surprisingly, since the arrangements had been made through the Social Office of the President by Magnus Lattimore. Unfortunately, the garment bag failed to include either a clip-on or instructions on how to knot the enclosed bow tie—a rare, if understandable, Lattimore oversight.

Gabe watched as the hands that had lassoed steers, hung on to bucking broncos, and sutured innumerable lacerations struggled to create even a passable knot. The directions he had printed out from the Internet were propped up on the sink. In addition to his limited dexterity, he looked tired and strained. The zygomatic arches above his cheeks were even more pronounced than usual, and his dark eyes, which Cinnie had called his sexiest feature, seemed lost. No surprise. Four whirlwind days in a new apartment, new city, and new job were taking their toll.

The formal dinner reception, scheduled for eight in the State Dining

Room, was ostensibly to welcome the recently reelected President of Botswana. According to the Africa expert sent by Lattimore to brief Gabe, the country was a staunch ally of the United States and one of the enduring democracies on the continent. In truth, the guest list had carefully been stacked with dignitaries and cabinet members who were interested in meeting the man the president had selected to bring stability to the White House medical office.

Another try at the knot, another morbid failure.

The muscles in Gabe's neck and shoulders, always the physical receptacle in his body for stress and emotional fatigue, were drumhead tight, and a throbbing headache was developing beneath his temples. Some sort of medicine would help make the evening more bearable, he decided—maybe a couple of Tylenols with codeine.

Since Fairhaven he had sworn off alcohol forever, and for his first few years out of prison he had expanded that pledge to boycott all manner of drugs as well. But with an array of orthopedic maladies dating back to his rodeo and football days, and stress-related head- and neck aches, Tylenol and ibuprofen had intermittently begun surrendering to Darvon and Tylenol No. 3, with whatever happened to be in the medicine cabinet thrown in from time to time for those discomforts that crossed the imaginary line between dull ache and disruptive pain.

He knew relying on pain pills and even the antidepressants he resorted to from time to time wasn't the smartest behavior for an alcoholic in recovery, and he knew that there was always the danger he would be conjuring up the pains to justify taking the drugs, but he had gone about as far in life as he could go in terms of doing the right thing.

He set the tie and the instructions in the sink, brought a glass of water to the exquisite cherrywood desk the White House decorators had determined was appropriate for the inner office of the physician to the president, and fished out two Tylenols with codeine from the thirty or so he had transferred to a bottle that read simply: TYLENOL. If anyone found out about the deception, or discovered the envelopes of Demerol and antidepressants in the eyeglass case in the back of his drawer, so be it. If Drew had asked him about pills, he would have told him the truth. Probably should have said something anyhow. If he had, he might still be back in Tyler taking care of folks with calluses on their hands and teaching kids how to throw a lasso. But in the end, he decided it was his business and his business only. The world knew quite enough about him as it was.

The codeine had just begun its journey from stomach to brain when, with a firm knock, the door to the receptionist's office opened.

"Hello?" a man's voice, not one that Gabe recognized, called out.

"I'm in here," Gabe replied.

The admiral's dress whites seemed to throw off at least as much light as the desk lamp, and the golden "scrambled eggs" insignia on the brim of his cover appeared possessed of its own inner glow. He stepped across the threshold and, with his gaze fixed on Gabe, reached back and closed the door.

"Ellis Wright," he said, giving Gabe's hand a perfunctory pump. "My apologies for not having come by sooner, but I was overseas when you came on board. I assume you know who I am."

The two photos of the man Lattimore had shared with Gabe did not do the imposing officer full credit, nor did *craggy* and *steely,* the adjectives that had first come to Gabe's mind when he saw them. Ellis Wright was every fiber a military commander—ramrod straight and rock jawed, with gunmetal eyes and shoulders that seemed mitered at perfect ninety-degree angles. Given just one guess as to what he did for a living, few would ever be wrong. Gabe wondered if Wright's eyes were always this cold or the look had been reserved for him.

"Ellis Wright holds sway over virtually everything that moves or breathes around the president," Lattimore had said during his briefing, "except you, and to a much lesser extent, me. Nobody has any control over you other than the POTUS himself, and even he had better be careful trying to order you about. Before President Stoddard took office, his predecessor Brad Dunleavy allowed Wright to choose a military M.D. to be his personal physician, so it should come as no surprise that Wright resented having a civilian assume this position when Jim Ferendelli was appointed.

I think it's safe to anticipate that he'll have issues with you for the same reason. Around here everything boils down to proximity and access to the POTUS, and first Ferendelli and now you nudge Wright back a notch in that regard."

"I'm the head of the White House Military Office," Wright, still standing, was saying. "The military's involvement with the smooth, efficient running of the presidency dates back to George Washington. We're responsible for communications, emergency operations, the airlift group, Helicopter Squadron One, Camp David, the White House Transportation Agency, the White House Mess, and"—he paused unsubtly for emphasis—"the White House Medical Unit. We're Military with a capital *M*. If the president so much as thinks of something he wants done, our people will have already started doing it. Is that clear?"

"Pretty clear, yes. You . . . um . . . want to sit down?"

Gabe stopped himself at the last possible moment from asking if the admiral also headed a department that knew anything about bow ties.

"I intend to say what I have to say and leave," Wright went on. "I can do both standing. You sound like something of a wiseass, Singleton. Are you a wiseass?"

Gabe cocked his head and hoped his expression said that he was open to any frank discussion, but he was not going to be easily pushed around.

"Admiral," he said, "I've been brought here to take care of the president. I'm board certified in internal medicine, and I've worked in big, gleaming hospitals and in Central American jungles. Most people who know me and know medicine think I'm pretty competent at what I do. If that's your definition of a wiseass, then maybe we have a problem."

"I told the president when he was considering a replacement for Dr. Ferendelli, and I'm telling you now: We have doctors in every branch of the military who are so knowledgeable, precise, and clinically competent that I doubt most doctors, including you, could carry their instrument bags. This is a military operation, and you are needed here about as much as a bull needs tits."

"The president doesn't seem to think so."

"I know all about what happened to you at the Academy, Singleton. Kicked out for being a drunk and killing a couple of people. You still a drunk? Pill popper?"

It was time, Gabe decided, to meet his new nemesis eye-to-eye. He exhaled as he stood, wondering how the president's spin doctors would deal with a fistfight between the president's private physician and the head of the White House Military Office. At just a shade under six feet, Gabe was still looking up at the admiral. He had the fleeting cartoon image of his fist slamming against the man's angular jaw and shattering into a million pieces.

"Exactly what do you want, Admiral?" he asked.

"I wonder, Dr. Singleton, if you have taken the time to learn anything about this job you have signed on to do." Wright's metallic eyes sparked. "For instance, the details of the Twenty-fifth Amendment to the United States Constitution."

"Presidential succession," Gabe said, grateful to have that much knowledge, although he remembered at the same instant that Wright had asked for details.

"Actually," Wright said with unbridled disdain, "presidential succession was dealt with in the Presidential Succession Law of 1886, and modified in 1947 to include the succession following the vice president of two elected officials—the president pro tempore of the Senate and the Speaker of the House."

"Oh."

Gabe felt the slight calming effect of the codeine kick in, and welcomed the sensation. In the short time between Drew's trip to Wyoming and his own flight on Air Force One to Washington, no one had discussed the provisions of the Twenty-fifth Amendment with him. Assuming that not doing so was an oversight on Magnus Lattimore's part, the seriousness of the lack of bow tie instructions had just been supplanted.

"The Twenty-fifth Amendment," Wright went on, "deals with the inability of the president to reliably conduct the duties of his office. It took years to hammer out the precise wording, and the most junior of my

White House medical officers could summarize the amendment section by section. Many of them know the whole thing verbatim."

"The ones I've met have certainly seemed very bright."

"As the president's personal physician, I want you to review the presidential law of succession and memorize the Twenty-fifth Amendment," Wright demanded.

"And I want you to stop barking orders at a civilian," was Gabe's knee-jerk reply, "especially one who has been chosen by the president to *be* his personal physician."

Gabe transiently felt as if he were going to melt before the man's gaze and power.

"They put their pants on one leg at a time, just like the rest of us," his high school football coach used to say about an intimidating opponent. At that moment, Gabe could not imagine Admiral Ellis Wright ever being out of uniform.

"I am the head of this medical unit," Wright said with controlled fury. "If anything unusual goes on here and I am not informed, I promise I will squash you like a bug. You could never qualify to be considered military, my friend, but that doesn't mean for one second that you are not vulnerable. If you wish to learn *how* vulnerable, simply let me find out that you have been withholding information about the president from me. I will see you at dinner."

Wright executed a perfect turn, opened the door, and had taken one step into the reception area when he stopped.

"Cromartie, what in the hell are you doing here?" he snapped.

"I . . . I'm the covering nurse tonight, sir," a woman's quavering voice replied. "Seven until midnight."

For several seconds there was only silence.

"Well," Wright said finally, "if anything Dr. Singleton and I just discussed gets back to me, you're the first one I am going to come looking for."

"Yes, sir. I mean the door was closed, sir. I mean I didn't hear very much."

"Civilians," Wright grumbled as the outer door opened and slammed shut.

Cromartie. The name meant nothing to Gabe, but there were still a number of unit nurses and physician's assistants and even a couple of doctors he had yet to meet.

"Well, come on in, Nurse Cromartie," he called out. "The Admiral Wright fan club is now in session."

Gabe heard a magazine being dropped onto the table, and moments later Alison Cromartie appeared in the doorway to his office.

CHAPTER 4

*R*adiant. The word filled Gabe's thoughts the instant he saw Alison Cromartie for the first time. Absolutely radiant. What Admiral Ellis Wright's starched whites did to light up a room Alison accomplished wearing nothing more imposing than a crisply tailored green pants suit—maybe jade green, Gabe decided—and a muted yellow top. No jewelry. And if she wore makeup at all, it was precious little and impeccably applied. Gabe flashed on his reaction to first meeting Cinnie in the hospital ER, when he vowed on the spot that this was the woman he was going to marry.

No such pledges here, but he did sense immediately that this was someone he was going to enjoy being around. Her looks were unusual and exotic—mixed nationalities of some sort, he guessed—with smooth, light mocha skin and a trim athlete's body. Her jet hair was cut short, and her face, dominated by dark, curious eyes, seemed ready to laugh at the slightest provocation. She shook his hand firmly and introduced herself, keeping her gaze fixed on him just long enough to express interest.

"From what I just heard out there," Gabe said, motioning her to the chair opposite his, "you're not an Admiral Wright appointee. Yet here you are."

"Here I am," she replied matter-of-factly.

"So, how'd you manage that?"

"I used to work with a surgeon who's a friend of President Stoddard. He recommended me. I think he's a big-time fund-raiser as well."

No accent whatsoever—if anything, a hint of the South. Alison Cromartie either was American born or had one hell of an English teacher.

"So, have you had to take care of the POTUS?"

"POTUS?"

Gabe grinned. "When I got here, I thought I was the only one in the city who had never heard the acronym."

"Acronym? . . . Oh! President Of The United States. No, I met him once, but I haven't been involved in his care. I like the acronym, though. I'm always the last one to hear about anything that's in."

"There's even *FLOTUS* for the First Lady, for those who absolutely can't live without abbreviating things."

"Well, when the POTUS recommended me to the admiral—*insisted he hire me* would probably say it better—Dr. Ferendelli was still here. Then, soon after I arrived to begin work, he was gone. It's a measure of my personal growth that I didn't feel responsible."

"Aha, one of those! Another club we both belong to—the Loyal and Honored Order of I Would Have Been the Cause of World War Two If I Had Only Been Alive When It Started."

Gabe added Alison's smile and laugh to the list of attributes he felt drawn to.

"So, how's it been going for you so far?" she asked.

"This is only, like, my fourth day, but so far so good—except for all the protocol I've had to absorb, and that little exchange with Admiral Starch."

"That doesn't count."

"Did you hear the part about how I couldn't carry the military docs' medical bags?"

"I did hear that, yes."

"Actually, as far as I can tell, the military docs and nurses and PAs working in this unit are pretty damn good."

"I've been impressed with the same thing, but I'll bet you're a pretty darn good doc yourself."

"As far as I know, most of my patients and colleagues back in Wyoming think so. How about the stuff about my drinking, did you hear that, too?"

"I . . . um . . . tried not to."

Alison's blush was genuine.

"No big deal. It's been years—decades, even—since my last one."

"You don't have to justify yourself to me. My dad was in AA. He was Creole. Drinking was a way of life where he was raised. Besides, I'm in the habit of forming my own opinion about people."

"How'm I doing so far?"

"You were doing perfect . . . until you asked."

Again, that smile.

"Well, don't worry, I'm much less insecure when I'm running a code."

"Let's hope you never have to prove that to me here. But I have a feeling that in crunch time you can handle yourself pretty well."

Her expression gave the statement a thousand layers. Gabe was working, probably too hard, at formulating a response when his radio sounded.

"This is Piper," Magnus Lattimore's detached voice said. "Has anyone seen the doc?"

"This is Dr. Singleton. . . . I copy direct."

"Doc, it's Magnus. You still in the office?"

How did you know where I was?

"Yes. Yes, I am."

"I'll be by to escort you to dinner in ten minutes."

"Roger."

"And Doc?"

"Yes?"

"Whatever the admiral had to say, pay no attention. He's just spraying to mark off his territory."

"Just spraying. Roger that."

"Your first state dinner," Alison said as Gabe set the radio down. "How exciting."

"I'll tell you what—you go to the dinner and I'll man the fort here. I'm a wrangler, not a mingler—especially not sober."

"Who's the dinner for?"

"Um . . . depending on who you ask, that would be either the President of Botswana or, to a lesser extent, me."

"The guest of honor!"

"More like an auxiliary guest of honor. People are jittery over Dr. Ferendelli's disappearance, so President Stoddard wanted everyone to get a look at the man who was taking his place, and to know he was in reliable medical hands."

"Makes sense. Well, in that case, I think some sort of tie is called for to go along with the rest of that tux—perhaps the one I noticed casually resting in the bathroom sink."

"It's being punished—a time-out for insubordination."

"Nothing worse than a surly, disrespectful bow tie. I've dealt with its kind before."

"Well, make this one behave and you get a year's supply of tongue depressors."

"Plus a rubber glove blown up and decorated like a rooster?"

"You drive a hard bargain."

"You got that right."

Alison retrieved the tie and took less than a minute up on her tiptoes, inches away from him, to knot it. Wishing it had taken longer, Gabe breathed in what might have been her shampoo or a microdot of subtle perfume. He decided as she stepped back to appraise her handiwork that he would try for a Guinness record for breath holding before he had to exhale.

"There you are, Doc," she said. "Not bad. Not bad at all."

"Congratulations, Nurse. You have been of great service to the United States of America."

"I want my rooster smiling and autographed," she replied.

CHAPTER 5

Direct sunlight never found its way into the three-hundred-foot-long underpass beneath Levalee Street. The tunnel, just a few miles from the seats of justice and government of the most powerful nation on Earth, was a living, teeming monument to the have-nots in this richest of societies. In fact, in many ways the rules of this microcosm were as complex and constricting as those of the civilization that surrounded it. And chief among those rules was never to deal with outsiders.

The man appeared at the south opening of the squalid corridor just as dusk was settling in over the city. He wore a light brown suit over a dark knit shirt and looked average in every way, at least until he extracted a powerful flashlight and a noise-suppressed .45-caliber Heckler & Koch pistol from loops on his belt. He had learned to kill game as a child in Mississippi and humans as a sniper in the Army and then had honed his skills over the dozen years since his discharge. The name he used most was Carl—Carl Eric Porter—but there were many others. As usual, he was being well paid, and as usual he was relishing every aspect of his job.

For a time Porter stood motionless, his eyes adjusting to the gloom. With no great effort, he closed his senses to the stench of garbage, filth, urine, whiskey, and vermin. He had encountered worse. Stretched out before him, spaced on either side, was a gauntlet of cardboard appliance containers and makeshift lean-tos.

Every four years, as the world descended on Washington for the inauguration of a new or returning American president, police would swoop down and roust the denizens of the Levalee underpass and other such places from their fetid homes, at times even putting the makeshift villages to the torch. But within a short while, like a forest recovering from a volcano, the space would begin to fill with life once again until soon it was indistinguishable from the village that had preceded it. With a presidential election just a few months away, it would not be long before the cycle commenced once more. But at the moment, no one in the Levalee underpass was concerned with anything but the intruder.

Aware of the dozens of eyes following him, Porter pinned his pistol and flashlight beneath his arm and pulled on a pair of rubber gloves. Steve Crackowski, a security chief for some sort of company—Porter didn't particularly care which one—had hired him to find and eliminate a man named Ferendelli. Now Crackowski had gotten a tip that the mark, a doctor, was hiding out with the down-and-outers he had once taken care of in a nearby free clinic. This was the second hobo village Porter had visited. He strongly sensed this might be the one.

Certain the denizens of the tunnel had gotten a good look at the gun, Porter replaced it in his belt and took a five-by-seven photo of Ferendelli from his jacket. Then he made his way purposefully down the squalid gauntlet, panning the beam from one side to the other, pausing each time the light struck a face to ask about the photo.

"A hundred bucks," Porter was saying to one of the men, loudly enough for everyone to hear. "Tell me where this here man is and a hundred is yours. Don't tell me, and one of you is gonna get hurt real bad."

Over the years, Porter had taken great pains to keep his heavy Mississippi drawl intact. There had been times when his dense accent had actually fed into a mark's southern stereotype and put them at ease. Their mistake.

"White man, five ten, dark hair, fifty-five, thin body, narrow face. Speak up now. I'm losin' my patience, and believe me, you don't want that to happen."

Nothing.

Porter inched ahead, shifting his focus from one side of the tunnel to the other. The eerie, intense silence was broken only by staccato coughing and the clearing of inflamed throats. The killer stopped now and again to kick the soles of tattered shoes to get their owners to look up into the light.

"You there, you seen this man? . . . A hundred bucks is a pile a money."

The gnarled, wizened man, kneeling placidly beside his refrigerator carton home, stared at Porter with vacant, rheumy eyes and shook his head. Then he coughed up a dense wad of phlegm and spit it in Porter's direction.

Without a moment's hesitation, Porter pulled out his pistol and from less than ten feet away shot the old man through the eye.

Silence.

"I'm gonna wait one minute. If I don't hear something, I'm going to pay a visit to another one of you. . . . Last chance."

"He's gone!" someone called out.

Porter whirled to the voice and fixed the intense beam on the man it belonged to. The hobo blocked the brightness with his hands.

"When?" Porter demanded.

"J-just now when you got here. Out—out that way."

"Fuck you, Frank," someone called out. "The doc was good to us."

"Here, Frank," Porter said, throwing a bill at him. "Go nuts."

Porter raced to the end of the tunnel and scanned the area beyond it. Then he put the flash back in his belt and took a device from his jacket pocket—a remote of some kind. He aimed it down the rows of the cardboard village and depressed a button on it several times.

Nothing.

Finally, without a glance back at the old man he had just killed, Carl Eric Porter disappeared up the embankment.

For ten minutes beneath the Levalee overpass the only sounds were the rasping breathing of forty men and women, the clearing of inflamed throats, and the occasional lighting of a cigarette. Then, from deep within a makeshift duct-taped cardboard home at the end of the tunnel farthest from where the killer had left, Jim Ferendelli, physician to the president, worked his way out from where he had been hiding, huddled beneath a damp, mildewed Harry Potter sleeping bag, and crawled to the opening of the box. Drawn and filthy, Ferendelli looked no different from any of the others in the hobo village.

"What do you think, Santiago?" he asked of the cachectic man sitting on the dirt outside the opening.

"I think he is gone," the man said with a heavy Spanish accent, "but I also think he might come back."

"Did he hurt someone?"

"He killed old Gordon. Just like that. Shot him like he was nothing."

"Damn. I'm sorry, Santiago."

"Frank saved you, I think."

"I heard him. That was quick thinking—by all of you."

"You were always good to us in the clinic."

"I need to go, Santiago. Thank you for sheltering me. I'm so sorry about Gordon. Thank Frank and the others for me, too."

"We wish you well, Doctor."

Still on all fours, Ferendelli crawled cautiously to the tunnel entrance, then ran as best he could down the deep swale toward the next road.

CHAPTER 6

*G*abe stood near the doorway leading from the stylish Red Room to the glittering State Dining Room. To his right, a string quartet was playing what might have been Mozart. To his left, popular Vice President Tom Cooper III and his wife were chatting with the Secretary of State. Scattered throughout the room were leaders of both parties as well as members of Drew's cabinet. Calvyn Berriman, the President of Botswana, was across the room, shaking hands with a steady stream of dignitaries and simultaneously nodding politely at any number of passersby.

Gabe was unable to suppress a sardonic smile. He strongly suspected that only he of all those present at the formal dinner was thinking about Ricky "The Shiv" Gentille or Razor Tufts, or any of the other inmates who had once joined him shuffling along in the food line at the Maryland Correctional Institution in Hagerstown. The interminable lines, the dehumanizing inspections, the payoffs, the gangs, the smuggling, the egos, the violence, the ignorance, even the scattered acts of heroism—he hated every second of the year he spent at MCI, every single second he spent trying to avoid eye contact, to keep his back to a wall, and to remain invisible. Thirty-six hundred seconds an hour, eighty-six thousand four hundred seconds a day. They were numbers burned into his consciousness like death camp tattoos.

Still, although even he had to acknowledge he had come far since his days in an orange prison jumpsuit, it was possible that, in some ways, he felt more at ease among the murderers and other felons than he did right now. He had voiced his concern to the president and the White House social secretary, begging to be left off the guest list for the dinner altogether, let alone the two-man list of those being introduced to the Washington glitterati. But the dinner was already scheduled and there was still a great deal of restlessness in D.C. surrounding the disappearance of Jim Ferendelli. The president wanted to assure the politicians and the voters that he was in good hands medically.

"You're handling yourself well, Doctor."

Chief of Staff Magnus Lattimore had materialized at Gabe's elbow. He was a slightly built, kinetic man with a boyish face, carrot hair, and the vestiges of a brogue. Of all the president's men, Gabe had learned the most about him—Scottish immigrant, Harvard grad, tireless, smart in many senses of the word, decisive, meticulous, not the least afraid of stepping on toes, and blessed with a rapier wit that at times could be devastating. He was also, it was clear to Gabe, absolutely devoted to Andrew Stoddard, his presidency, and his reelection.

"It's the monkey suit," Gabe replied. "Throw a tux on me and you've got instant socialite."

"I can tell. Your bow tie is a dead giveaway that there's more to you than the backwoods buckaroo you claim."

"How's that?"

"Tying a bow tie is an absolutely individual affair. It should never be knotted perfectly. Yours is tied with perfect imperfection. Says a lot about your level of sophistication—gruff saddle tramp image or not."

"Is that why you didn't have the rental people include a clip-on?"

"I suppose you could conclude that, yes. I was prepared to help you if necessary. In dealing with people, data is worth collecting regardless of the source. If I ever did have the urge to underestimate you, which I most certainly do not, I need only remind myself of your skill with a bow tie."

Gabe flashed on Alison Cromartie, her brow knit as she focused on the task at hand. Had she left the knot just slightly askew on purpose? The truth was he hadn't even noticed. Gruff saddle tramp, indeed.

"Was that article in the *Post* about my arrival on the scene your doing?" he asked.

"We have a friend or two on the staff there," was Lattimore's typically oblique reply.

"I had sort of planned to keep a low profile until I was done with the job."

"In Wyoming you get to keep a low profile. Here you keep whatever profile most benefits the president."

"So I gathered. Speaking of the man, where is he?"

"Actually"—Lattimore checked his Omega—"he's late."

His expression had darkened.

"Any problem?"

"No, no. He's usually fairly prompt, though, and Calvyn Berriman is a man he actually likes and admires. He went out of his way to have me ask Joe Malzone, the pastry chef, to do a cake in the form of the presidential flag of Botswana, and a wild flag it is, too, complete with zebras, African shield, elephant tusks, and even a bas-relief bull's head, perfectly rendered in black frosting. Makes our flag look sedate."

"Save me the bull's head; I've gone after them at birthday parties since I was a tyke. And also, let me know if Drew needs me to do a physical exam on anyone in the next couple of hours. This would be the perfect time for me to have to leave. Back home I used to bribe the hospital operator to page me when I couldn't find another way of getting out of a cocktail party, or worse, a formal dinner. Perfectly imperfect bow tie or not, I'm sure it's only a matter of time at this soiree before I go Emily Postal and commit some huge social gaffe."

"Don't use your fingers except for the bread, don't slurp your soup directly from the bowl, and avoid throwing up on the person next to you. That's all you need to know."

"Slurp my bread, finger my soup, throw up on the guest of honor. Got it."

"Oh, and most important of all, don't think for a moment that any-one here is more interested in hearing what you have to say than in hearing what *they* have to say. In this town a good listener is like a one-eyed man in the land of the blind."

"Mouth shut, ears open. I can do that."

"Good. Speaking of socialites, there's one more person I'd like you to meet before we all go trooping on in there. You ever heard of Lily Sexton?"

Gabe shook his head.

"Should I have?"

"When we get reelected, one of the president's first moves will be the creation of a new cabinet post—the Secretary of Science and Technology. Dr. Lily Sexton will be it."

"An M.D.?"

"Ph.D. Molecular physics or some such. She was a professor of Carol's at Princeton."

Although he had been at Carol and Drew Stoddard's wedding and had spent a fair amount of time with her over the years, Gabe really knew very little about the First Lady. He knew she was bright—exceedingly so, in fact—but nothing she had ever said suggested that she might have studied molecular physics in college.

"Secretary of Science and Technology," he mused out loud. "I wonder where that will rank on the presidential succession list."

"Bite your tongue."

"You're right. See? I told you it was only a matter of time before I said something stupid."

"You're doing fine. Just remember about the one-eyed man. There's Lily over there. She's not too hard to spot, given that every woman in this room is wearing a designer evening gown and she's wearing a tux."

Lattimore led Gabe by the arm across the Red Room and introduced him to the second interesting and attractive woman he had met in just an hour. Lily Sexton had a dazzling, ageless aura, starting from her pure sil-ver hair, cut elegantly short. Her face, virtually unlined, was sharp and in-telligent, highlighted by piercing blue-green eyes. Her black tuxedo was perfectly tailored to her tall, slender figure, and just above the top button of her jacket, where a shirt would have been, had she been wearing one, rested a spectacular turquoise pendant on a silver chain.

Protruding from beneath her pants were top-of-the-line alligator cowboy boots. The stylish western look made a clear statement about the woman's willingness to fly in the face of fashion, but Gabe guessed that, with the addition of the inlaid turquoise ring and earrings that matched her necklace, the price of her outfit came to as much or more than that of many of the evening gowns in the room.

"Excuse me if I'm out of line," Gabe said after Lattimore had completed the introduction and moved on, "but Magnus told me you were one of Carol's college professors. I don't know exactly how old the First Lady is, but I have trouble doing the math around that relationship."

"Why, thank you, Dr. Singleton," Lily said with an easy drawl—maybe Arizona, Gabe thought. "What a flattering thing to say. But I'm afraid my friend Magnus hasn't got his facts quite right. I was a graduate assistant of Carol's, not a professor. We've been dear friends since the day we met. There's not much more than five or six years' difference in our ages. She would have made a terrific scientist, but she had other plans."

"The dilemma of Carol Stoddard," he said, "test tubes, Bunsen burners, and white mice, or the chance to marry an absolutely brilliant war hero, hunk of a man, and change the world for the better. Hmmmm. Let . . . me . . . think."

"Believe me," she said, "if a man like Drew Stoddard had dropped into my life, I would have made the same choice Carol did. Actually, somewhere along the way, a few men did come along with enough going for them to marry, but none of them ended up having Drew's staying power. . . . So, Doctor, how has your Washington medical experience been so far?"

"A few visiting dignitaries have been sent to the clinic for various bumps and bruises and upset stomachs, but thankfully, the First Patient hasn't dialed my number except to tell me that there were a lot of people anxious to meet me tonight and so I'd better show up."

"Oh yes, speaking as one of those people, congratulations."

"Thanks. You're the one deserving of congratulations, though. Magnus tells me you are destined for a cabinet post."

"If we win."

"We're going to win."

"In that case, I'll be the first Secretary of Science and Technology."

"Pardon me for sounding uninformed, but what is the president's position on science and technology that he would need a new cabinet post to implement it?"

"Actually, it's built into the party platform. The president feels that the federal government needs to take a more proactive position regarding control of scientific research and development—stem cells, cloning, nanotechnology, fuel alternatives, reproductive physiology, cyberspace utilization, and the like. The FDA is overwhelmed as it is, and no cabinet post is specifically set up to coordinate the research necessary to put together some legislation with teeth."

"I didn't realize that Drew had taken such a hard-line approach to government control of science and technology."

"First of all, it's neither hard-line nor control, and second of all, it's more Carol's concerns than Drew's. The administration is not opposed to research and development in any field of science, but they want the people to have the right to know what's going on, and to monitor if any particular product or line of research has the potential to do harm or to cost the taxpayer in some as yet unseen way."

"It sounds like they've picked the perfect person for the job."

"That's very kind of you to say. Oh, Dr. Singleton, I'm sorry to be monopolizing you so. As a guest of distinction, you must have many more important people to meet than me."

No, actually I have no one more important to meet than you.

"The truth is, I was grateful to you for protecting me from the masses. The last thing I remember clearly was riding one of my horses through the desert. Then the president showed up at my doorstep, and now this. I feel like Alice floating down the rabbit's hole."

He gestured to the room.

"That's right!" Lily exclaimed. "You're a high plains drifter. Wyoming, yes?" She took a thin silver case from her jacket pocket and removed a pale lavender business card. "I can do without a gown or even an evening bag, but a rule of survival in this town is never, ever go out without your business cards."

"Magnus had mine waiting in my desk drawer when I arrived. Now I know why. Alas, they're still there."

LILY PAD STABLES, the card read simply, along with an address in Virginia and an ornate LPS in one corner.

"I'm West Texas born and bred, " she said, "and where I come from, people say that the number-one reason for making piles of money is to have horses."

"In Wyoming we like to say that a horse is nothing more, *or less,* than a four-legged shrink."

"Same thing, really." Her laugh was unforced and totally appealing. "Well, at Lily Pad we have some of the finest saddle horses anyplace, unless you like to jump. We've got those, too."

"Jumping things on a horse makes no more sense to me than jumping things not on a horse. When in doubt, go around. That's my motto."

"In that case, give me a call. I'll show you some of my adopted state from a western saddle."

"I'd be happy to. I'm already having saddle soap withdrawal."

"In that case, the sooner the better."

Her enigmatic expression at that moment would, he knew, stay with him until they hit the trail together—whenever that was.

No sooner had he and Lily moved apart when the admiral, Ellis Wright, stepped in to introduce Gabe to a general as "my man in the White House." There was no hint whatsoever of the rancor that had so recently marked Wright's visit to Gabe's office.

The outer face, the inner face, Gabe mused as the general and the admiral turned to greet Calvyn Berriman. Did anyone in this town actually say what they meant, or mean what they said?

It was at that instant Gabe noticed Lattimore, standing by the doorway to the hall, motioning him over with his eyes and a minute shake of his head, even as he smiled and nodded at various passing guests. His expression, at least to Gabe's reckoning, was grim.

Slowly, deliberately, feeling very much like the other guests as he masked his purpose with a cheerful expression, he worked his way across to the chief of staff, joining him in acknowledging the Secretary of Defense and his wife, then the chief of the National Security Council.

"Is there a problem?" Gabe asked softly, taking pains not to look directly at Lattimore.

"Perhaps. Wait two minutes, then make your way to your office and get your medical bag. The president's Secret Service man, Treat Griswold, will be waiting to take you upstairs to the residence."

"Do I need to bring anything special?" Gabe asked.

"Just an open mind," was the reply.

CHAPTER 7

Battling to look nonchalant, Gabe retrieved his medical bag from the floor by his desk.

"An open mind."

What in the hell had Lattimore meant by that?

By the time Gabe reentered his office reception area, Treat Griswold was waiting, motioning with an upraised hand for him to stay quiet and stay where he was. Cautiously, the Secret Service agent checked the corridor, then beckoned Gabe across to the elevator, which another waiting agent keyed electronically.

"Is the president in trouble?" Gabe asked as they rode.

"I guess that's for you to determine, sir," Griswold said.

A floor above, the elevator opened into a small anteroom, with double doors to the broad, elegantly furnished foyer of the First Family's residence. Griswold motioned Gabe down the hall to the master bedroom, then retreated to a position not far from the elevator.

"Just call if you need me, sir," he said, his expression severe.

Magnus Lattimore stepped into the foyer.

"Anyone see you?" he asked Griswold.

"No one."

"Good. I've sent for the mil aide with The Football. Keep him right there in the landing."

"Will do."

The Football!

During his orientation, Gabe had been told that "The Football" was the name given to the communications case containing the codes and other necessary equipment for the quarterback, the president, to trigger a retaliatory or preemptive nuclear strike anywhere in the world—quite possibly the prelude to Armageddon. Whenever the chief executive was traveling away from the White House, the case was brought along by a military aide rotating from one of the five services. Also contained in The Football, Lattimore had told Gabe, were the papers of presidential succession.

Now the chief of staff turned to him, his intensity threatening to burn a hole between Gabe's eyes.

"Go on in, Doctor," he said.

He followed Gabe into the bedroom, stepped inside, and quietly closed the door behind them.

Legs out straight, the President of the United States sat bolt upright, his back pressed against the massive brass headboard. His eyes were wide and feral, his gaze darting—an expression of absolute fear. His fingers were in constant motion, like waving fronds of kelp. The corners of his mouth pulled back repetitively, then relaxed. To his left, standing close by the bed, was the First Lady, stunning in a simple black strapless gown. Her expression was an odd mixture of concern and embarrassment.

"He's been like this for twenty minutes now," she said, eschewing any greeting.

"I know about his asthma and his migraines," Gabe said. "Are the meds he takes up here?"

"Yes. Plus some Tylenol sometimes and ibuprofen for some back pain."

"See if you can find those bottles, Carol. Bring me any pills you come across. Anything at all. Also the inhaler he uses."

The First Lady hurried into the bathroom.

Suddenly Stoddard began rocking forward and back like an Orthodox Jew reciting his prayers. After a minute or two, he seemed to notice Gabe for the first time.

"Gabe, Gabe, my old friend, what in the Sam Hill are you doing here?" he asked, still rocking. His voice was strained and higher pitched than usual, his speech pressured. "You've got work to do, work to do, my man, my man. People to meet and greet and work to do."

"Mr. President, I'm here because you suddenly aren't acting like yourself."

"Mr. President, Mr. President . . . they all call me that. Mr. Frigging President. But not you, Gabe Singleton, not you my old friend. My roomie. You must call me Drew. Call me Drew and I'll trust you. Hey, a rhyme. Call me Drew and I'll trust you. Not like the others. I don't trust any of the others. Just my lovely Carol. Isn't she lovely? Hey, where is she? Where'd she go? And of course sweet Magnus. Sweet, think-of-everything Magnus. How could anyone not trust him? But Tom Frigging Vice President Cooper the Frigging Third—him I don't trust any farther than I can throw him. And Bradford Frigging Dunleavy can't be trusted. He wants to beat my ass in the next election and take this house away from us. Have us evicted. And the frigging Chinese. When it comes to trust, they are just the worst of all. . . . I can't stop rocking, Dr. Gabe . . . back and forth . . . forth and back. Help me stop rocking and I'll double your salary. You know who you really can't trust? It's the Arabs you really can't trust, that's who. The *A-R-A-B-S*. . . . Maybe we should just take a little old nuclear device—that's what we call them, devices—and waste the whole lot of them. That'd solve the frigging Middle East crisis once and for all. Might as well take out Israel while we're at it and start all over again. . . ."

Carol Stoddard returned with her hands full of pill bottles, plus an inhaler, and passed them over. Gabe scanned them one by one, setting each on the bedside table. None of them differed from what he already knew Stoddard was taking.

With Ellis Wright's words booming in stereo in his brain, Gabe moved cautiously toward the bedside opposite where Carol was standing.

"The Twenty-fifth Amendment deals with the inability of the president to reliably conduct the duties of his office. . . . I want you to review the presidential law of succession and memorize the Twenty-fifth Amendment."

"Drew," Gabe said gently but firmly, "there's something going on here with you that's not quite right."

"Not quite right . . . not quite right." Stoddard sang the words to the tune of "lit-tle lamb, lit-tle lamb."

Gabe felt an ice-water chill. Somewhere in the building, a military aide was approaching, bearing The Football—the buttons and codes that could, effectively, end all life on Earth, codes that could be triggered by one man and one man only. His mind struggled with only minimal success to wrap itself around the enormity of the situation. He glanced at Carol and then at Lattimore to confirm that they, too, were aware of the awesome implications of what was transpiring before them, but their expressions validated nothing.

"Drew, is it okay if I do a little examination of you? I want to get to the bottom of this."

"I see the answers."

"Drew, is it okay if I check you over?"

"The answers to all questions."

"Is there some sort of shot you can give him?" Magnus Lattimore asked.

Gabe stopped himself at the last possible instant from snapping at the chief of staff.

"As soon as I know what's going on, I'll treat him," Gabe said instead. "Right now, as long as he's not in immediate danger, masking these symptoms is the last thing I want to do."

Stoddard was perspiring profusely now, his face cardinal red. But the rocking had stopped. Still, he continued a rapid, disjointed chatter, jumping from topic to topic, laughing inappropriately, and mixing in often bizarre opinions on issues of public concern—opinions that Gabe knew were not typically held by the man. The Andrew Stoddard he had known since college was Dr. Jekyll. This was Mr. Hyde. Gabe wondered in passing what would happen if the nation's commander in chief suddenly started calling out for the military aide with The Football.

Moving slowly but deliberately, Gabe checked his patient's blood pressure in each arm and his pulse in the neck, arms, and feet. The pressure was up—160 over 100—in each arm, and the pulse was also up at 105. Years of training and practice had kicked in the moment Gabe entered the room, and with each second he was observing, avoiding assumptions, and considering dozens of diagnostic possibilities—rejecting some, filing others away as possible, moving still others to the forefront of probability.

Ignoring the steady stream of pressured babble, Gabe did as rapid a physical exam as he dared. There would be time for more detailed examination and testing when the immediate crisis had been dealt with. As matters stood, two things were apparent to him: The President of the United States was not having a cerebral hemorrhage or a cardiac episode and so was in no immediate danger, but also, at the moment, the man was quite mad.

CHAPTER 8

*F*or the twenty minutes that followed and the twenty minutes just past, Gabe knew that the United States was without reliable leadership. He continued his evaluation of Andrew Stoddard, but Gabe's mind was spinning. Someone had to be notified, probably the vice president. Ellis Wright was an ass, but he had been absolutely justified in saying that Gabe had to become an expert on presidential illness and succession.

But why hadn't Lattimore stepped forward—or even Carol? Why were they standing by almost calmly as one of the greatest crises imaginable evolved before them? Why had the only even slightly emotional thing either of them uttered been Lattimore's request—a request that Gabe brushed aside as bordering on malpractice—that the president be given some sort of shot to settle him down? It didn't take a formal medical education to reason out that unless a diagnosis was either known or quite obvious, giving any sort of mind-altering medication to someone with acute brain dysfunction, from either trauma, stroke, or chemical imbalance, was contraindicated.

The president's continuous rocking had slowed, then finally stopped, and the tenor of his speech had softened somewhat. Gabe propped a pillow behind him and took advantage of the relative calm to focus his ophthalmoscope beam onto the retinas of Stoddard's eyes—the only place in the body where arteries, veins, and nerves, specifically the large optic nerves, could be directly observed.

The arteries appeared healthy, with minimal, if any, signs of arteriosclerosis. The veins, too, seemed normal and were free from nicking where the arteries crossed on top of them—a finding that would have hinted at prolonged high blood pressure. But most important, the margins of the optic nerve in each eye were sharply demarcated. Blurring of those edges, known medically as papilledema, would have suggested a buildup of pressure on the brain from swelling, hemorrhage, or infection.

Reflexes normal. Extremities normal. Strength and range of motion good. Cranial nerves intact. Carotid pulses strong and free of bruits—the churning sound made by blood rushing past an obstruction. Heart rate down to 88—still high, but improved. Blood pressure down to 130 over 80. Lungs clear. Respiratory rate down from 40 to 24. Abdomen soft.

Stoddard's perspiring had slowed and the redness in his face had begun to abate.

"Drew, are you with me?"

"You're the best, pal. The salt of the earth."

"Drew, I want to ask you some questions. Will you answer them no matter how silly they might seem?"

"Go for it."

"What city are we in?"

"Why would you ask me something as—"

"Please, Drew, humor me."

"Washington, District-o of Columbi-o."

"The day?"

"Thursday. Doc, this is—"

"Please—"

"August the something. Maybe the seventeenth. Isn't that right, Carol, baby? The seventeenth?"

"That's right. You're doing great, honey." She looked over at Gabe. "He's coming around."

"Drew, how much is forty times twenty?"

"Eight hundred, of course. I was always good in math."

"A hundred minus thirty four."

"Sixty-six."

The answers came out almost before the questions were finished.

"Name the first eight presidents."

"Washington, Adams, Jefferson, Madison, Monroe, the other Adams, Jackson, how many is that?"

"Enough."

"Van Buren, the first Harrison, the one who croaked after thirty days, Tyler—"

"That's plenty, Drew."

"I can do them all. The latest one is me."

"I'm glad of that. The capital of Uruguay?"

"Montevideo. What do I win?"

"Most home runs by someone who never took steroids?"

"Aaron. You thought I'd say Ruth, didn't you?"

"No, Drew. I knew you'd get it right. You're doing better, my friend. Much better."

"Doc? I have one question."

"What is it?"

"The beasties that have been flying around here—the fairies and those round hairy things with the long tails—what do you make of them?"

Gabe looked to see if Stoddard was toying with him, but there was nothing in the president's expression to suggest that was the case. He checked Stoddard's pupils again. They had initially been midsize and a bit sluggishly reactive to light. Now they were smaller and more briskly reactive. Another sign that things were getting better.

Hyperactive cardiovascular system, uncontrolled rocking, disjointed, pressured speech, excessive perspiration, inappropriate affect, visual hallucinations. What in the hell was going on?

Gabe desperately needed to speak with both Carol Stoddard and Magnus Lattimore, but there was no way at this point that he would leave his patient to do so. Lattimore saved him the anguish.

"Whatever you need to say to us, Doctor, you can say before the president."

There was no panic in his voice and little, if any, anxiety. Gabe wondered if Lattimore's odd demeanor was at least in part due to the fact that Drew Stoddard now appeared to be rapidly improving. Lattimore moved over to where Carol Stoddard stood, stroking her husband's hand. Her expression was odd—more one of annoyance, perhaps, than concern.

"Okay," Gabe said, "it's your call." He calmed himself with a deep breath and slow exhale. "To begin with, it looks like whatever is going on here is beginning to resolve. Drew's life doesn't appear to be in immediate danger. But we all know that for the last hour or so, he has not been in control of his faculties. The implications of that are obvious."

"Go on," Lattimore said, his expression unchanged.

To Gabe's left, the president had sunk down on his bed, eyes closed. His breathing was still somewhat rapid and shallow. The redness had drained from his face, which now looked drawn, pale, and utterly spent. Concerned, Gabe checked Drew's pulse and blood pressure once more.

"Fairly normal," Gabe said, shaking his head in bewilderment. "Give me a minute to draw a few tubes of blood."

"What for?" Lattimore asked.

"I'm not sure yet, but it's better to have them and not need them than to realize tomorrow I should have gotten them."

"Do you need to put them on ice?" Carol asked calmly.

"I don't think so. I'll refrigerate them in the clinic until I'm ready to send them off."

"You won't put his name on them, will you?"

"No, I promise. I'll identify them some other way."

"Honey," the First Lady said gently, her lips brushing her husband's ear, "Gabe's going to draw some blood. Is that okay?"

"Go for it," Stoddard managed, through lips that were stiff and dry.

Gabe drew three vials of blood and set them in his bag. The president barely reacted to the procedure.

"Well, there's still an impressive collection of diagnostic possibilities,"

Gabe said when he was done. "Some sort of atypical seizure or even un-usual migraine is on the list along with a small hemorrhage in some strate-gic area of his brain, or a tumor—possibly one in a part of his body away from the brain that is secreting some sort of hormone or other psychoac-tive chemical. There are a number of possible organs in this regard. He certainly seems toxic, but unless he has some pills hidden away that we don't know about, I don't have an explanation for how that toxicity could have happened. Then there's the diagnosis that is at or near to top of the list at this point."

"Namely?" Lattimore asked.

"Namely, that the stress of the job and the reelection campaign has pushed his emotional and mental faculties past the breaking point."

"You have no idea the hours he puts in," Carol said.

"Well, it's not a physician's job to guess. So, at the moment, the field of possibilities is wide open, and we've got to get him to the hospital for an MRI and some other tests. At this moment I am quite concerned about a tumor or a small hemorrhage."

"It's not a tumor," Lattimore said. "And it's not a hemorrhage."

"How could you possibly know that?"

"Because," the chief of staff said, meeting Gabe's gaze intently, "the president's already been recently checked for those by Dr. Ferendelli. He's run every test in the book."

"I don't understand."

"Gabe," Carol said evenly, still massaging her husband's hand, "this isn't the first episode like this that Drew has had. . . . It's at least the fourth."

CHAPTER 9

Incredulous, Gabe stared across the bed at Carol Stoddard and Magnus Lattimore.

"I can't believe this," he said, barely maintaining control. "How many episodes?"

"Four," Carol said. "All within the last three months. Jim Ferendelli was actually with us when the first attack occurred. It was right here in the residence. He was up here for dinner. All of a sudden Drew began shaking his head as if he were trying to clear something out of it. It turns out he was hearing voices."

"I just can't believe this," Gabe said again, making no attempt to lower his voice. "How in the hell could Drew come all the way out to Wyoming to ask me to take over as his doctor and manage not to tell me about this? And you two. Carol, we've known each other for years. Magnus, you had plenty of chances to talk to me before I flew out here. Who in the hell do you think this man is—an organ-grinder? How can you ask me to uproot my life and come here to take care of him and then withhold information like this?"

"Gabe, please," Carol replied. "I understand why you're upset. We debated how and when to tell you what had been happening, but with all the tests coming out negative, and no attacks for a few weeks, Drew thought

48

we'd be better off hoping the whole matter was a thing of the past. He really needed you, Gabe. Then and now."

"So that's why he lied to me? That's why *you* lied to me? Because you all needed me?"

Gabe glanced down to see the president's reaction, but Andrew Stoddard, eyes closed, was lying motionless, breathing coarsely, and had clearly not heard a word. Reflexively, Gabe reached down and checked his pulse. One hundred and regular.

Then suddenly Gabe found himself reflecting upon the meeting with Drew in Wyoming. There was time then, plenty of time, for Gabe to tell his longtime friend about the self-prescribing he had been doing—about the pain pills and the antidepressants. He hadn't said anything to the president for the same reason he had never said anything to his former AA sponsor—the same reason he had gradually cut back on his meetings until he stopped going altogether. He was ashamed—not frightened, not worried he was heading for an alcohol relapse like so many warned at the meetings—just ashamed of his weakness and maybe of his foolhardiness and denial as well.

Whatever the reason, he had lied by omission just as Carol and Lattimore had been lying since his arrival in D.C. Just as Drew had done back in Tyler. Different stripes, same zebras.

"The episodes haven't all been the same," Carol said, maintaining her composure against Gabe's onslaught. "The second one happened at a press conference. Jim was there, and so was Magnus. The moment Drew's color changed and his speech became disjointed, they got him off the stage. The whole thing didn't last half an hour. There were more audio and visual hallucinations than there were today, but no rocking. That was when Jim had him brought to the presidential suite at Bethesda Naval. After all the tests were negative, including an evaluation by a team of neurologists, the diagnosis was made of atypical migraine. I'm surprised you didn't read about the whole thing in the papers or else hear about it on TV."

Gabe's smile was mirthless.

"I don't own a TV that works with any reliability, and the only newspaper I ever read is the *Tyler Times*. Life has been much easier that way."

"I guess that's why you never asked us about the atypical migraines," Lattimore said.

"I guess," Gabe replied acidly. "Drew mentioned something about migraines when he was in Tyler. Listen, you two, I don't know what's going on with him, but I do know this man is in no position to function as the President of the United States. We've got to do something, and quickly. I haven't had the chance to study up on the Twenty-fifth Amendment, but I would imagine a call downstairs to the vice president is in order."

"Wait," Lattimore said sharply. "Please, Gabe, just wait . . . and listen. . . . Please?"

Gabe flashed on the desert behind his ranch. The sun would be setting just about now. The perfect time for a ride.

What in the hell was he doing here?

"Go ahead," he said. "But you should know that I have no reason at this point to trust anything you tell me."

"I understand. With lobbyists and spin doctors and hidden agendas on every corner, this town is justifiably famous for people playing fast and loose with the truth, and I'm afraid that as a political advisor, I'm hardly blameless in that regard myself. Even now, the guests downstairs have been apologized to and told that the president has a migraine headache, some asthma, and some sort of gastric upset, and that you're attending to him. The press will be next."

"Go on," Gabe said, picturing the truth being batted about like a badminton shuttlecock.

"First of all," Lattimore went on, "remember that when you first came upstairs, I asked Agent Griswold to send for the military aide who is entrusted with The Football. We talked about The Football when you first arrived in town."

"Believe me, I was paying attention. That sort of stuff is not easy to ignore."

"Then I may have told you that among other things, the briefcase contains the papers necessary to hand over control of the government to Vice President Cooper. The military aide is waiting out there in the foyer right now, Gabe. Ultimately the decision as to what is best for your patient and for the country will be up to you."

"Go on."

"I'm sorry, truly sorry, that we weren't more forthcoming about these episodes in the first place. We had come to an uneasy agreement with Jim Ferendelli that so long as the situation didn't worsen, he would continue to try and come up with a diagnosis. Then, when he disappeared the way he did, we three have been in a quandary about what to do next. The president and First Lady felt that you were the only one who would step in and continue Jim's investigation into the situation, while at the same time giving the president the chance to be reelected."

"Gabe, the country needs him," Carol said. "The world needs him. But not if the price of that service is his mental health."

"Carol, if Drew was an exam question, and there was only one right answer, I would have to say that his neurological presentation today and the history you've given me add up to some sort of stress disorder. That is not a desirable condition in the man with his finger on the big, red button. It seems like with each episode he's drifting farther and farther from reality."

"But in between these episodes," Lattimore said, "the president has been as focused and energetic as he's ever been, and I mean that. He's gotten the Koreans and Iran to back off and allow nuclear inspections. That's major. The new trade agreements with Mexico and China have already brought us the lowest unemployment in a dozen years. He knows that the only solution to the drug problem in our cities is to deliver hope for the future in the form of education, and already he's gotten more money for schools than the last two administrations combined. He's pushed through more legislation, more of the pieces of his populist agenda, than anyone ever thought he could, and with the polls predicting the shift to a friendly Congress, there's no telling what he could accomplish in the next four years. This is no ordinary man, Gabe."

"Magnus, this man"—Gabe gestured down at Stoddard, who had yet to move except for the rise and fall of his chest—"has the authority and the power to destroy everything. *Everything!* And he may be losing his mind."

"There's got to be something causing this besides stress," Carol said. "I'm certain of it. You heard him answer your questions. He's absolutely brilliant. You had barely asked the questions before he produced the answers. Gabe, you're worried that Drew has the power to destroy everything, but he also has the power and the vision to change the world for the better as no president—no *person*—ever has."

"This upcoming election is by no means a lock," Lattimore added. "Dunleavy still has a lead in most of the red states, and the religious right is starting to get mobilized and organized again. Their political machine weakened when Dunleavy lost the last election, but there's strong evidence they're regrouping. Do you remember Thomas Eagleton?"

"No. . . . Wait, maybe. Yes, yes, I do. He was McGovern's vice presidential nominee in, what, seventy?"

"Seventy-two. McGovern wasn't going to beat Nixon no matter what, so none of the Democratic biggies would run with him. So he picked Eagleton, a nice enough senator from Missouri. Only McGovern's half-baked research didn't uncover that the man had several psychiatric hospitalizations for depression, which included electroshock therapy. The negative press made McGovern seem like anything but fit to lead this country, and forced Eagleton to quit."

"He was replaced by Sargent Shriver, the Peace Corps guy. I remember now."

"It was even worse with Dukakis. He was ahead in the polls when all of a sudden word started to circulate that he had been treated for depression. Rumor. Pure unsubstantiated rumor. But the result was a dramatic shift in the polls, and that scene in the tank notwithstanding, he could never catch up."

"I understand what you're saying."

"If word gets out about these episodes of the president's, all the king's horses and all the king's men aren't going to be able to help us. And the

most important thing, as Carol said, is that in between episodes, he's as sharp and in command as ever."

At that instant, as if on cue, Andrew Stoddard's eyes fluttered open. He looked to his left at his wife and chief of staff, then to his right at Gabe.

"Dr. Singleton, I presume," he said, sweeping his tongue across his parched lips.

"Hey there. Welcome to our world."

"This doesn't look good. Another episode?"

Gabe nodded.

"Honey," Carol said, "are you okay?"

"Doin' fine. Doin' fine. A little bit of a throbbing up here in my temples, but otherwise I feel great. I confess, though, that seeing the doc here like this is a little disconcerting—especially when he's supposed to be having dinner and Botswana flag cake with Calvyn Berriman."

"Do you remember anything about what happened?" Gabe asked.

"Not really. I vaguely remember not feeling well. Mostly in my stomach. Why? Did I insult someone we're supposed to be friends with?"

"No, nothing like that," Carol said. "We're just glad you're okay. Honey, Gabe's really upset that we didn't—"

"Carol, I can do this myself," Gabe said, with more snap to his voice than he had intended.

He looked from Carol to Lattimore and back, and considered whether or not to send the two of them out of the room so he could speak to his patient in private. Finally, though, he pulled a brocade chair over next to Stoddard, who had pushed himself up on one elbow.

"Drew, have you been totally aware of these episodes all along?"

"I have . . . except when I'm having them, of course."

"But you chose not to tell me about them before I agreed to come to Washington to care for you."

"That may have been a mistake."

"Drew, I appreciate your owning this, and not deluging me—at least not up front—with rationalizations for why you chose to keep me in the dark. And I understand why you and Carol and Magnus might have chosen that course. But it was a mistake. It was a lie. I know, I know, omission of something isn't technically a lie. But where I come from we don't draw that line."

"I'm sorry, Gabe. I truly am. There was so much going on, and so much pressure to stabilize the situation surrounding Jim's disappearance, and I so desperately needed you with me. Jim told me the episodes were probably some form of atypical migraines. He started me on Imitrex and told me they might never happen again. Meanwhile, he did all the tests and called in consultants."

"What kind of consultants?"

"Neurologists, I guess."

"Any psychologists? Psychiatrists?"

Stoddard shook his head.

"I . . . I don't think so. Gabe, if word gets out about these things, I'm finished."

"Drew, as things stand, I feel as if I only have two choices: to call in that military aide who's out there so that you and I can turn over the government to Vice President Cooper, or to quit and jump on the next flight back to Wyoming."

Lattimore leaned forward and seemed as if he were about to enter the discussion, but Stoddard, whose back was turned directly toward him, stopped him with a raised hand and then sat up in bed, still facing toward Gabe and away from the chief of staff. In that instant, every vestige of Drew Stoddard had vanished and was completely replaced by the President of the United States.

"Gabe," he said, "Jim Ferendelli had to deal with the same crisis of conscience as you are right now. I ached for him then just as I ache for you now. Ultimately, he rejected both possibilities you suggest. He didn't quit and he didn't insist I turn over the government of this country to Tom Cooper. He put me on medication for what he felt was causing my problem, and he promised not to rest until he knew what was the matter with me and what we should do about it. Please believe that."

"I do."

"Gabe, working with a Republican Congress, my jobs programs have taken more than six hundred thousand workers off unemployment. Communities have joined with me and private business to add two hundred thousand computers to our schools. Drug use in the inner cities has begun a serious decline. A decline, Gabe. The polls say that if I win, I'll likely have a friendly Congress next term. Give me that and there's no limit to what we can accomplish for the people of this country. I'm begging you, Gabe. Stay close to me. Find out what's the matter with me. Treat me with any medication you want. Bring any specialists in to evaluate me. But please, for God's sake please don't pull the plug on me. Not now. Not when we're so close."

In the silence that followed, Gabe felt much of his anger at being deceived and much of his zeal to take immediate action deflate. He didn't have the statistics that Lattimore and the president had cited, but he did know that there was a spirit of hope and optimism in the country that hadn't existed for a generation or more. And best of all, there were no American soldiers losing their lives on foreign soil. Drew Stoddard, scholar, intellectual, war hero, humanist, populist, was the real deal.

"I need some time," Gabe heard himself say. "I need some time to sort things out. That was a very frightening scene in here."

"I'm sure it was, Gabe. Take all the time you need."

"And I need Jim Ferendelli's records about his findings and his conclusions so far."

"Wherever they are," Lattimore said, "we can't find them, except for some very thin records at Bethesda Naval. The FBI and the investigative arm of the Secret Service have gone over every inch of the medical office, Jim's house in Georgetown, and his home in North Carolina. Dozens of agents are still on the job. Maybe a couple of hundred."

"Well, I want access to his place."

"No problem."

"And if I decide to go along with what you're asking, I need at least one other doctor to be my assistant in this case and to be close to you when I can't be."

"Do we have to tell him everything?" Carol asked.

"I need to decide that. First, though, I have to feel more certain that this is a secret I want to keep."

"Just tell me what you need," Stoddard said. "Tell me what you want me to do."

"Stay close to home. Here or Camp David. I want to know precisely where you are every minute until I've made my decision."

"What about Texas?" Lattimore asked the president.

"Cancel it," Stoddard ordered brusquely.

"Finally, I want your word, Drew, and yours, too, Carol and Magnus, that if I opt to bail on this whole deal and involve Vice President Cooper, you won't try anymore to convince me otherwise."

"You have our word," the president said.

The other two hesitated, then reluctantly nodded in assent.

"In that case," Gabe said, "get ready for bed and then crawl back under the covers. I'm going to be here tonight for as long as it takes to convince myself you're stable."

"Fine. The Lincoln Bedroom is right down the hall if you want to rest there," Carol said. "I can get you a robe and pajamas. Griz will arrange for some food if you're hungry."

"That's all right. A few quiet hours and I'll go home. For now, after I check you over again, Mr. President, I want to do some reading. You have a library up here, yes?"

"Not a huge one, but yes, yes, we do. And Griz can get you into the main library in the East Wing."

"Good."

"Exactly what do you want to read about, Doctor?"

Gabe reached over to again check Stoddard's pulses. Then he tested the man's eye movements and the response of his pupils to light.

"The Twenty-fifth Amendment," Gabe said.

CHAPTER 10

*M*idnight came and went. By 2:00 A.M., when Gabe decided it was safe to leave, the president had been sleeping soundly for an hour and a half. At Lattimore's request, Gabe watched from a distance as the military aide carrying The Football was dismissed. Then Gabe gathered his things, including two books on presidential illness, succession, and the Twenty-fifth Amendment.

He was about to notify Treat Griswold he was leaving when Carol Stoddard knocked softly on the open door. She had removed her makeup and changed into pajamas and a robe but still looked no less elegant than she had in her evening dress. Her doe's eyes were slightly reddened, leading Gabe to suspect she had been crying.

"Ready to leave?" she asked, taking a step into the room.

"I think it's safe. No matter what, I'm just a mile or so away."

"He'll be all right, I think—at least for now. Do you know what you're going to do about all this?"

"I need a little time—maybe just until later this morning."

"Gabe, the job is taking a heavy toll on him—on us. Heavier than either of us imagined, I think. Drew's been working seven-day weeks, often as many as sixteen, even twenty hours a day. We hardly ever go to sleep at the same time and . . . and our personal life has dwindled until . . . well . . . until there just isn't much of it left."

"I'm sorry to hear that."

"Gabe, I'm begging you, if you think for the sake of his health Drew should drop out of the campaign and let Tom Cooper take over, please tell him. He thinks he can be all things to all people. But someone has to help him see that nobody can—not even him."

Tears began to well in Carol's eyes. Gabe hesitated, then crossed to her and held her quietly until her composure returned.

"Whatever I decide will be what's best for my patient," he said finally.

"I understand. Maybe you can convince him to just cut down—take a nonworking vacation, spend more time with me and the boys, spend some time each day doing nothing, accept the fact that everyone has limits."

"I'll try, Carol. Really I will."

"Thank you. Thank you so much for what you're doing. I'll send Treat Griswold over to walk you out."

Before Gabe could respond, the First Lady was gone. He flashed on the envy he had felt when he arrived in D.C. and first saw her and Drew together—the perfect, beautiful First Couple, leading the country together into a cultural, political, and social renaissance. Now he reflected on one of many wise observations by his original AA sponsor—this one dealing with the dangers inherent in going through life comparing your insides to everyone else's outsides.

He took the elevator down to the first floor, where he identified the tubes of blood he had drawn by using his Tyler phone number in reverse and set them in the small refrigerator in the clinic.

One fascinating vignette he had come across in his reading involved President Bill Clinton's knee injury and subsequent surgery. The president was on a golfing vacation in Florida when his knee buckled while he was walking down a short flight of stairs. His quadriceps muscle had torn in two and snapped off the patellar tendon. A White House Medical Unit physician, on duty nearby, immobilized the leg and arranged for immediate transportation to the nearest hospital. Already waiting there was Clinton's personal physician, who, as usual, was part of the medical team caring for the chief executive when he was away from the White House.

From that moment until Clinton's surgery at Bethesda Naval Hospital in Maryland, and even after the muscle and tendon repair was completed, his physician had two major decisions to make—pain control and anesthesia.

Never far from Clinton throughout the ordeal was the military aide bearing the codes for unleashing nuclear missiles as well as an agreement forged between Clinton and Vice President Al Gore regarding situations in which the reins of government would be turned over to Gore.

Together, Clinton and his doctor decided that the only pain medication he would receive would be anti-inflammatories with no central nervous system effects. In addition, with the approval of the orthopedic surgeons at Bethesda Naval, he would receive epidural anesthesia, and so would be awake and alert throughout his surgery. The two-hour procedure and Clinton's recovery went off without a hitch.

In print it all sounded so straightforward, so simple. Gabe wondered how Clinton's personal physician would have handled a situation like the one he was enduring now. It seemed doubtful that if Drew Stoddard had a doc other than his friend and college roommate he would still be president. Then Gabe remembered that, in fact, until just a couple of weeks ago, Stoddard *did* have a different doc and he *was* still the president. Gabe also realized that at no point had he been told the precise nature of the agreement between Stoddard and Thomas Cooper III.

Because of the large number of dignitaries attending the state dinner, the Navy captain who was covering the medical office had elected to stay in-house. Gabe dropped off his medical bag and gave the man the line Lattimore and he had concocted and disseminated first to the dinner guests, then to the press, that the president had been seized by a combination of his asthma, migraine, and severe gastroenteritis and had specifically asked his personal physician to attend to him until the attacks were resolved.

More lies.

Edgy and uncertain about the decisions he had made throughout the night, medical *and* political, Gabe allowed Treat Griswold to accompany him down the elevator and out of the White House to the senior staff parking area on West Executive Boulevard. The Eighteen Acres, as the White House compound was known, was eerily quiet. The two of them made the trip in pensive silence, bound by the enormity of the drama in which they each had played a part.

Bull-necked Griswold, a loyal veteran of many years in the Secret Service, had signed on to take a bullet for Andrew Stoddard if necessary. Was the man raving incomprehensibly and rocking as if trying to shake demons from his mind a person he would want to die for? Gabe wanted to ask that question of the agent but knew he never would.

If they only knew, Gabe was thinking. *The press, the cabinet, the Congress, the Chinese, the Israelis, the Arabs, the terrorists, the American people—if they only knew what had transpired this night in the presidential residence.*

He wondered about those men who had preceded Drew Stoddard into the presidency. How many secrets had been kept on their behalf? How many lies had been told?

"You gonna be all right?" Griswold asked as they reached Gabe's car.

"Thanks for caring, Griz. Yeah, I think I'll be okay. I'm assuming you know most of what went on in there."

"I know as much as I need to know," the agent said. "He's a very special man, Doctor. We should do what we can to keep him around."

"I hear you. I'm not a hundred percent certain I agree with you, but I hear you."

"We've all got to do what we've got to do. Take care, sir. At the moment I don't envy you."

Gabe patted Griswold's massive shoulder. It was like patting a boulder.

"At the moment I don't blame you. Listen, let's not forget about taking that ride in the desert someday."

"I won't. Good luck, sir."

Griswold retreated the way they had come, leaving Gabe alone in the quiet.

The silver Buick Riviera Gabe was driving was, like his furnished four-room suite in the Watergate Apartments, an open-ended loan from LeMar Stoddard. The First Father wouldn't have it any other way. From the day

Drew and Gabe came together at the Academy, the senior Stoddard had embraced Gabe and his parents as family, inviting them to his North Carolina estate as well as to his Virginia hunting lodge. Even though the accident and Gabe's subsequent expulsion from school and imprisonment proved more than Buzz Singleton could handle, LeMar had remained a dependable friend and supporter, providing him with a top-notch defense team and visiting him more than once at MCI. Years later, LeMar even pulled some strings to make sure Gabe's past didn't keep him from being accepted into medical school.

Gabe started the Buick and for a few minutes simply sat behind the wheel, letting the air-conditioning get up to speed and continuing the process of sorting out his thoughts and feelings. Over the years, when faced with a medical puzzle, he tried to keep all diagnostic possibilities in play until they were weeded out by either a negative lab test, a positive lab test, or a new physical finding. But always he had an early suspicion as to where the answer lay. The trick was not to be ruled or even influenced by that suspicion until the weeding out had left little, or better still *no,* choice.

"He's a very special man. . . . We should do what we can to keep him around."

With Griswold's words reverberating in his head, Gabe pulled out of the White House compound onto Sixteenth Street and then made his way to G Street for the mile-long drive to the Watergate Complex. The night was thickly overcast, warm, and humid, even for August in D.C. Essentially lost in thoughts about the evening just past, Gabe rolled along with the languid early morning traffic. As he stopped at a red light at Twenty-second Street, the dark sedan that had been following him since he left the compound pulled into the empty lane to his left and drew up precisely even with him.

What happened then was nothing but a blur.

Aware only of slight movement in the car next to him, Gabe turned his head to the left. The driver of the other car, his face obscured by a baseball cap pulled low, and by dense shadow, had opened his passenger window and had raised a large handgun, pointing the menacing barrel straight at

Gabe's face from a distance of no more than five or six feet. An instant before the killer fired, Gabe's car was struck firmly from behind, sending it forward several feet.

With the muzzle flash etched into his vision and the shot ringing in his ears, Gabe's head snapped back. The rear side window of the Buick spiderwebbed from the errant bullet. There was no second shot. Instead, tires screeching amid the smoke and stench of burning rubber, the sedan vaulted forward, spun on two wheels onto Twenty-second, and disappeared.

Still unable to piece together exactly what had happened, Gabe was limp, held in place by his seat belt, gasping for air and for composure.

No time. There had been no time even to react. A man had just tried to kill him!

From somewhere behind him a car door opened and closed. Then there were rapid footsteps, and seconds later his own car door flew open.

"Are you all right?"

The voice was familiar.

It took a moment for Gabe's vision to clear.

Standing there, looking down at him with undisguised concern, was Alison Cromartie.

CHAPTER 11

*I*s he all right?" a motorist called out from across the street. "Do you want me to call an ambulance?"

"Do you?" Alison asked Gabe.

Still stunned, he managed to shake his head.

"No, he's fine," Alison called out. "Just a little fender bender."

The motorist, the only one around, hesitated and then drove off.

"A guy in that car next to mine tried to kill me," Gabe said, fumbling for the words. "He . . . he shot at me from . . . Jesus, I can't believe this. I . . . I don't know if it was some sort of random drive-by or . . . or—"

"Easy, Doctor, easy. Are you sure you're not hurt? Can you stand up?"

"I think so. I . . . I froze. All I could see was the muzzle of that gun, and . . . and all I could think was, 'This is it.' I don't even know what happened next."

"I hit you from behind. That's what happened next," she said. "I saw what was about to happen and I rammed you. It was the only thing I could think of to do."

Gabe glanced back at the shattered rear window of the Buick.

"Nice move," he said.

Slowly, with help, he managed to stand and brace himself against the roof of his car. Alison, wearing black jeans and a black tank top, kept a supportive arm around his waist until it was clear he could manage on his own. As before, he became instantly engrossed in her closeness and the scent of her.

"Uh-oh," she said.

A D.C. black-and-white pulled up and stopped directly over the burnt rubber from the assassin's car. The strobes flicked on, and the cop in the passenger's seat, a lean black man, lowered his window.

"What's the deal here?" he asked.

"Oh, am I glad to—"

"Nothing big," Alison said, pointedly cutting Gabe off. "He did the right thing and stopped for a light, and I did the wrong thing and bumped into him. I'm guilty as charged."

They could see the policeman eyeing the rear window, clearly trying to put the odd damage together with a rear-end collision.

"You all right?" he asked Gabe.

Unseen by the cops, Alison's expression was strongly cautionary.

"I . . . I'm a little shaken up. That's all."

"And that window?"

"Two days ago, while it was parked, vandals probably. I'm getting it fixed tomorrow."

"Want us to call an ambulance? Sometimes the adrenaline from an accident can mask serious injury."

Again the look from her warning Gabe to say nothing about the shooting. What in the hell was going on?

"No, no ambulance," he heard himself say.

"Listen, guys," Alison said to the cops, "do whatever you have to do, but I really *do* intend to take full responsibility for this, and I really *do* have to get home. I just finished doing three hours of overtime in the ER at D.C. General and I have to be back for the day shift in just a little while."

"You a doc?"

"Nurse. I know way too much ER medicine to be a doc."

"You got that right," the cop said, and exchanged approving glances with his partner.

Just then the radio in the cruiser crackled out something that sounded urgent. Alison watched benignly as the officer behind the wheel took the call, but Gabe, bewildered as much at her handling the situation as he was at the situation itself, saw the keenness in her eyes and sensed that she was on top of the action, if not well ahead of it.

"Another second and they're gone," she whispered before the conversation was complete.

"Listen," the cop closest to them said. "We gotta go. You sure you're okay, fella?"

"I'm fine . . . fine," Gabe replied. "If you don't have to, there's no need to write this up."

"Okay. Suit yourself. You got an ER nurse there just in case you have any delayed reaction."

"That I do," Gabe said as the cruiser squealed away.

He watched until the taillights had vanished up Twenty-second Street, and then looked down at Alison.

"What? What?" she asked. "The license plate on the killer's three- or four-year-old dark blue Taurus was covered, and with that baseball cap, there was no way whatsoever for me to get a look at his face. And staring down the barrel of a gun, I would strongly doubt that you got any kind of a look at him, either. By the time the police got the story straight from you and made their calls for backup help, the odds that the shooter's still driving around out there would be slim to none. What good would telling them do? There would be hours of interrogation and paperwork, and piles of unwanted publicity—especially given Dr. Ferendelli's disappearance."

Gabe had no quick response. Alison Cromartie sounded incredibly certain and confident of what she was saying and absolutely comfortable with the lies she had told to deal with the police. She was anything but the trim, professional nurse who had tiptoed up to tie his bow tie just seven hours ago.

"Wouldn't they at least have gotten a crime team to find and examine the bullet?" he finally managed. "It's got to be back there someplace."

Alison sighed.

"I'll tell you what," she said. "Trade cars with me for a day and I'll arrange to have the damage fixed on yours and the bullet checked out as well."

"Who are you?" Gabe asked, no longer willing to trust anyone in that city.

Alison drew a thin leather case from the pocket of her jeans and flipped it open for him. Gabe flashed on Lily Sexton and her elegant folder of business cards. But there were no business cards inside this case. There was a gold shield and a photo identification card.

CROMARTIE, Alison M.
United States Secret Service

"People were worried about you," she said.

CHAPTER 12

I'm sorry not to have told you who I was back in the office, but the higher-up who placed me in the clinic asked me not to."

Alison sounded sincere enough and Gabe wanted to believe her, but at that moment—nearly four in the morning—he really couldn't focus well enough to sort very much out.

A man, his face hidden in shadow, had driven up next to Gabe's car and taken a shot at him from almost point-blank range.

Four days in D.C. and in one evening he had been browbeaten by a Navy admiral, lied to big-time by the President of the United States, his wife, and his chief of staff, deceived by one of his office nurses, and now nearly assassinated by—by whom? Someone who was systematically killing White House docs? Why? A whacko random drive-by? That hypothesis made as much sense as any. It was simply a roll of the dice that a madman with the need to kill happened to reach the intersection of G and Twenty-second at the same moment Gabe did, and another roll that Alison Cromartie, with the instincts and reflexes of a Secret Service agent, just happened to be in the car behind his, following him.

"The Secret Service doesn't like things that don't make sense," Alison was saying, "and right now, Jim Ferendelli's disappearance makes no sense at all. I'm one of the few RNs in the service, so they plucked me off a backwater desk job in San Antonio and arranged for me to become part of the White House Medical Unit. My instructions were to keep my eyes and ears open for anything regarding Dr. Ferendelli and to keep an eye on whoever got brought in to succeed him. That's what I was doing tonight."

Gabe rubbed at the grit in his eyes and tried to focus on what Alison had just said—that she had been placed in the White House medical office *after* Ferendelli's disappearance. Hadn't she told him earlier in the day that she had started working there *before* Ferendelli vanished? Gabe tried, through the deepening fog of fatigue, to re-create the exchange between them but sensed he might not be recalling it exactly. Why would she bother lying to him about when she started working at the White House? Then again, why would anyone have been lying to him about anything?

He thought about trying to pin down which version of her story was the real one, but this just didn't seem like the time or place to get into an irresolvable yes-you-said-it, no-I-didn't discussion.

"Well," he said, "whatever the reason for why you were there, thanks again for saving my life."

"The alternative would have made a hell of a mess of the interior in that snazzy Buick of yours."

Earlier in the evening, as she was working on his tie, Gabe would have offered his ranch for them to be sitting together at four in the morning on a bench behind the Watergate, overlooking the silent, ebony Potomac. Yet here he was in just that situation, distracted, edgy, and totally ill at ease.

"Tell your boss that your secret is safe with me."

"I'm not sure that will do the trick, but I'll try."

"I always wondered why they called it the Secret Service when those agents in their dark suits and shades made no effort whatsoever to be secret."

"They're meant to be seen and recognized. A lot of us aren't."

"And there are Secret Service offices outside of D.C.?"

"There are field offices all over. We do investigational stuff and also prepare for any presidential or major diplomatic visit."

"And our good friend the admiral doesn't know he's got a Secret Service agent working for him?" Gabe asked.

"Almost no one knows."

"Treat Griswold?"

"Nope. I report only to one man—the head of internal affairs."

"Internal affairs?"

"Gabe, I really can't tell you any more right now. First thing in the morning I'm going to have to report to my boss that I've blown my cover."

The hour caught up with Gabe, and he tried unsuccessfully to stifle a yawn.

"Listen," Alison said. "Why don't you go on in. I can do all my explaining sometime later. I'll get this bullet to the lab and arrange for your car to be fixed. Just leave it on the street where you parked it. It'll be taken away within the hour, and it won't take more than a day to be good as new."

"Better be. It's on loan from the First Father."

"I know."

"Of course. Everybody here knows everything, or at least tries to. So, what are you going to tell your boss?"

"The truth," she answered matter-of-factly.

"Ach, truth. Such a word. I would have never thought it was one of them words that meant different things in different parts of the country, like *soda* and *pop* or *pancakes* and *flapjacks*. Is that what you told me back in the office about how you came to be at the White House? The truth?"

"I'm sorry. You have every right to be irritated, but I was just doing what I had been ordered to do."

"And what should I tell my boss?" he asked.

"That's up to you, but I'm not sure what's to be gained."

"Secret Service protection?"

"Depends on how badly cramped you want to be."

Gabe again pawed at his eyes. He felt worn down by the events surrounding the president and utterly bewildered by this woman and by the attempt on his life, but he was also strangely unwilling to head up to his apartment. Below them, the surface of the river had begun subtly reflecting the first changes of the new day. Gabe found himself absurdly wondering which dignitary had gotten the bull's head on President Calvyn Berriman's Botswana flag cake. Maybe it was Lily Sexton.

"So tell me," he asked finally, "how did a nurse end up with a badge and a gun and a desk job in San Antonio?"

"You sure you don't want to do this later in the—"

"No, no. I'm really interested. Besides, I feel a second wind coming on."

"I can't tell if you're being facetious or not."

"*Defensive* might be a better word. Or maybe I'm just testy. I was busy taking care of the president's gastroenteritis and migraine, and missed out on dessert."

Gastroenteritis and migraine. The untruth rolled out effortlessly. Perhaps he had a future in D.C. after all.

"Well, okay," she said with a shrug. "The story I told you is pretty close to what is. I was born in Louisiana and raised in New York—Queens. My dad, I think I told you about him, is . . . was, I mean, part Creole, part southern cracker—very handsome, very charming, rarely employed for long. My mom is part Japanese, part other things. She's a nurse. Still works in a nursing home. I became a nurse because of her, and got my master's."

"When we first met, I tried to piece together your background from your looks."

"I doubt you would have come close."

"I didn't. But it's a combination that works pretty well."

"Thanks. More?"

"If you want?"

"Let's see, then. A brief fling at marriage took me to L.A., where I worked in a surgical ICU. Like many hospitals, it was more or less ruled by the surgeons—one group in particular, busy beyond imagination, wealthy, and arrogant, all male, all well connected. The Cognac and Cuban Cigar Club, we used to call them—the Four Cs. The problem was that while most of them were top-notch and maybe deserving of the big bucks, a few of them weren't that good."

"Go on."

"Well, I won't go into the details, but there was a death in the unit. An order that should never have been given, written by a surgeon who was well aware of the patient's history and should have known better. He was one of the founding partners of the group, and drank too much. He also had neglected to inform the nurses about past events with their patient. Then there was a ridiculous delay in his getting in touch with the unit after he was paged, followed by a botched attempt to open the poor woman up right there in the ICU."

"Sounds gruesome."

"Even more gruesome was the way the group railroaded blame for everything onto one of the nurses. It was done with the ruthlessness and efficiency of a commando unit. Sheets disappeared from the patient's chart; doctors came forth with blatant lies. Unfortunately for her, they picked on a nurse who was going through a bitter divorce and was on a bunch of meds for depression, and who wasn't really that clinically strong anyhow. Janie got suspended from work, and then she overdosed. She didn't die, but I think sometimes she wished she had. Eventually, her ex got their kids and she moved away."

"Were you two close?"

"Not *that* close, but we considered one another friends. I couldn't stand to see what they had done to her, and I was on duty when all this happened, so I decided to blow the whistle on the surgeon and those who covered up for him."

"Uh-oh."

"Uh-oh is right. They went after me the same way they went after her. It was a total mismatch. Evidence began to surface that suggested I had assisted Janie in diverting drugs and was just trying to defend my partner in crime. I began getting weird phone calls. A year before, I had broken off a three-year relationship with a man who decided that, despite what he and I had agreed upon all along, he didn't want kids. A new guy I had just started dating, who seemed very promising, without any real explanation suddenly wanted nothing to do with me. My record at work had been spotless, but out of the blue several groundless incident reports were filed against me by supervisors who had connections to the surgical group. It seemed as if the doctors were actually enjoying the challenge of systematically dismantling my life."

Gabe studied her face. Even through the gloom, he could see the tension and hurt. They seemed real. Then he reminded himself that he had already bought her story once tonight. These people were good at manipulating the truth—very good. He turned back to the river. She was so attractive to him that it was hard to hang on to the notion that she might not be someone he could trust. At the same time, it was odd to think that while he was sitting there, listening to her this way, he was managing to avoid the issue of whether or not he should be instituting measures to remove the President of the United States from office.

Tough night.

"So what happened?" he asked.

"Well, because in reality I had done nothing wrong, the conflict became sort of a Mexican standoff, even though I knew that sooner or later, the surgeons would increase their attack and I'd lose. Finally, in a secret meeting, the head of the hospital offered me a deal. If I left the hospital and stopped making trouble, he would see to it that I got an unconditionally strong recommendation. If I stayed, I was on my own."

"And?"

"And so I swallowed my whistle and gave up. It hurt then to make what seemed like a cowardly choice, and it hurts every day now knowing that I did. I guess I'm just not hero material."

"I don't know if I'd say that. Remember, you just saved my life at the expense of blowing your cover."

"Reflex actions don't get processed by the brain."

"Sometimes living to fight again is just as heroic as getting destroyed for your cause, and often a hell of a lot smarter."

"I have no intention of fighting again. I'm afraid I'm just not cut out to be a crusader."

"Now *there's* something we have in common."

"The rest is essentially what I told you in the office. A doctor I worked for before his retirement was a big supporter of the president, and helped me get into the Secret Service. The irony is, here I am back working as a nurse—something I promised I would never do again. And sadly, that step back is a step up from the paper pushing I was doing in San Antonio."

"Well," he said, "I really appreciate your sharing all that with me. I'm getting a little chafed from the Washington version of the truth." He yawned again. "Okay, it's time. To steal a movie title from one of our former chief executives, I think it's Bedtime for Bonzo."

"Appropriate choice of films. So, what was it that kept you in the White House so late tonight? Was the president that sick?"

Instantly Gabe felt himself tense. On the surface, the woman's question was innocent enough, but the transition to it seemed awkward and given that he had just announced he was going to sleep, the timing felt forced. Was she trying to take advantage of the hour, and the rescue, and the intimacy generated by telling her story in order to pump him for information about Drew, or was he just sensitized and overreading the situation?

What if the whole scenario with the gunman was a setup—a nifty maneuver to gain his trust? What if Alison had been placed in the White House clinic not because she was a nurse, but because she was an attractive, beguiling nurse? What if this whole affair was nothing more than further proof that Dr. Gabe Singleton was playing out of his league and should never have left Wyoming?

"I've got to go now," he said abruptly.

And before Alison could react, he was gone.

CHAPTER 13

*G**abe* lay facedown on LeMar Stoddard's king-size bed, trying unsuccessfully to will himself to sleep. He had come to D.C. to replace a physician who had disappeared, and now he himself had almost been killed. At least that was the way it looked. Eyes closed, he envisioned Alison Cromartie's expression as he stood abruptly and left her by the river. She was clearly surprised, but was that because she expected him to tell her what was going on with the president? Was she or whoever she was working for trying to expand on some rumors—some half-truths they might have learned about the chief executive's health?

What she said about the futility and possible negative fallout of reporting the drive-by attack to the police made perfect sense. Still, it seemed, he had to do something more than merely allow her to get LeMar's car fixed and have the bullet examined. He had to share what had happened with someone. Lattimore? Treat Griswold? Admiral Wright? The president himself?

Even more important, he had to decide what to do about the recurrent attacks of insanity in the commander in chief of the most powerful armed force in history. For a time he tried to imagine what Nixon's final days in office had really been like—pacing the empty halls of the White House, allegedly holding animated conversations with the ghosts of Lincoln, Wilson, and other presidents past; down on his knees, blubbering like a child to

Secretary of State Henry Kissinger. From all Gabe could tell, Nixon had lost his grip well before that last, fateful walk to the waiting helicopter. How long had the finger of that madman rested on the button that could have killed hundreds of millions? Days? . . . Weeks? . . . Even longer?

Had Kissinger, Ford, and others somehow banded together and formulated a plan to bypass any orders from Nixon that they felt were not in the best interests of the country . . . and of the rest of mankind?

He rolled over once again, this time replaying the remarkable accomplishments of Andrew Stoddard's first three and a half years in office and the potential of the four years ahead—especially if the man was working with a friendly Congress. Gabe had never had much faith in the political process being able to make a huge improvement in the quality of life of the average American—and especially in the lives of those less fortunate than the average. He often mused about how much could be accomplished if the billions spent on political campaigns, most of them unsuccessful, could be applied to public works projects, or to reversing global warming, or to cancer research, or to providing computers for inner-city schools.

Yet here the man was—a president with a true vision for America, not someone frantically navigating the country from one crisis to another; a president of the people, with the courage to go nose-to-nose with big business, and big oil, and big pharma, as well as with the architects of terror; a president with the charisma to bring people together. Would it be right at this time to invoke the Twenty-fifth Amendment, effectively pulling the plug on Drew's presidency, when it was just getting rolling? The decision wasn't one he could put off much longer.

At quarter after six, still unable even to doze, Gabe showered and shaved, then gave serious consideration to taking a Xanax.

"You still a drunk? Pill popper?"

Ellis Wright's words kept Gabe from immediately reaching into the bottom bureau drawer for the plastic bottle and its varied contents. Few would argue that after the day he had just endured, a little sleeping aid was both necessary and deserved. But there were others who would point out that sooner or later, the reasons for taking pills would mutate into reasons *to* take them. Maybe they already had, he wondered briefly. Maybe this particular fallout from Fairhaven would be part of his life for keeps, enduring as long as he did.

He considered putting LeMar's elegant coffeemaker to work with something high-octane. Loading up on caffeine would be the final capitulation to his inability to sleep. Then, as if in a trance, he searched out a Xanax from his stash of pills and washed it down.

Whether it was the act of taking the drug or the drug itself, fifteen minutes later he floated off to a fitful sleep. When the ringing phone woke him at eight forty-five, he had decided, with an edgy certainty, what he was going to do about the crisis in the White House. For the time being, he would do what he could to keep Drew in office and in as strong a position as possible for reelection, while at the same time doing everything he could to follow up on Jim Ferendelli's investigations into what might be causing the president's episodic mental imbalance.

Hopefully, sometime in the future, when the reason for the president's episodes had been diagnosed and properly treated and any of the countless potential disasters had simply failed to materialize, he and Drew and Carol would look back and laugh at the role the tranquilizer Xanax had played in saving the country.

The ringing persisted.

At some point during the hours since he had returned to the room, he had managed to pull the room-darkening drapes. A scant amount of sunlight from between them made it possible to find the bedside lamp, which he turned on, and a half-empty glass of water, which he finished before picking up the receiver.

"H'lo?"

"Dr. Singleton?" a woman's voice asked.

"Yes. Who's calling?"

"Doctor, please hold for Mr. LeMar Stoddard."

Gabe reflected that if *he* were worth 10 billion or more, he probably wouldn't be making his own calls, either. Hopefully the First Father wasn't calling to take his Buick back.

"Gabe? LeMar Stoddard here."

Gabe pictured the surpassingly handsome man in a penthouse office somewhere, seated at a desk the size of his bed, gazing out across the city.

"It's me, sir."

"Drop the 'sir' stuff, cowboy. We've all grown up now. It's LeMar."

"I'll try."

"Everything okay? The place? The car?"

"Everything's fine. I'm very grateful to you for all this."

"Good. I like having people feel grateful to me. It'll go that much better for me when my damn high blood pressure or bad cholesterol or whatever catches up with me and I have to check into the great office building in the sky."

His laugh was hearty and self-deprecating, but Gabe had little doubt that the remark about having people beholding to him was serious. For a multibillionaire, LeMar had always seemed to Gabe to be reasonably right sized, although Drew, of course, had other thoughts about that. Whatever negotiations had landed Gabe the Watergate suite and the Riviera had been between the First Father and his son. The last time Gabe had met the man face-to-face had been early in the campaign when the Stoddards flew into Salt Lake City on LeMar's jet and Gabe drove down from Tyler. LeMar, a year or two short of seventy then, with dark hair graying at the temples and electric gray-blue eyes, was as fit and dashing as any Hollywood swashbuckler.

"Well," Gabe said, "all that this incredible place and the car have done is dig me deeper and deeper in the gratitude hole."

"Nonsense. You're a good guy, Gabe—a good guy who had a lousy break and has had the character to overcome it. Having you up here taking care of Drew makes us more than even. In fact, not to toot my own horn, but it was me who originally put the bee in his bonnet about bringing you on board."

"Well, thank you for that. I'll be here as long as he needs me."

Gabe stopped himself at the last instant from adding *sir*.

"Excellent. So, I was wondering if you might have a little time today for me, say lunch?"

"Provided my patient doesn't need me, I can do that."

"Wonderful. We're moored at the Capital Yacht Club downriver from you. I'll send a driver to pick you up at noon. Once you get a look at *Aphrodite*, I don't think you'll feel too guilty about nudging me out of the Watergate."

Given how much everyone in D.C. seemed to know everyone else's business, Gabe half-expected the tycoon to mention the shattered rear window in his Buick.

"I'll be waiting in front," Gabe said.

"Perfect. Bring your appetite."

Gabe set the receiver down and then pushed open the drapes, flooding LeMar's wondrous apartment with morning light. Four stories below, the Potomac sparkled. Somewhere downriver, the apartment's owner was probably sitting on the deck of the boat named for the Greek goddess of love and beauty, sipping some exotic blend of Arabian coffees, while his companies continued churning away, adding to his net worth at a rate far faster than he could ever spend.

Nice life, sir . . . except for a little problem with your son.

Gabe chose some Kenyan beans from the wide variety in the freezer and spooned them into the built-in Coffee Master. The single push of a button took the selection from beans to brew. Not surprisingly, the result was perfect.

Nice life.

Cup in hand, he retrieved his address book from the desk, opened it to the *B*s, and set it by the phone.

He had made his decision regarding Drew Stoddard. Now it was time to put this aspect of his plan in motion. He dialed and listened to the ringing of Kyle Blackthorn's private line, picturing the small office fifteen hundred miles away, warmly decorated with Indian weavings and artifacts, mostly Arapaho, Blackthorn's tribe.

"Dr. Blackthorn."

"Kyle, it's Gabe."

"Hey, brother. I feel like I should break into a rendition of 'Hail to the Chief.' But I really only use that one at tribal councils."

"Hey, that's pretty funny. And here I thought you guys had no sense of humor at all."

"You doing okay in the big city?"

"Pretty much. I miss everyone back there, but they allow cowboy boots in the White House, so I'm managing."

"What can I do for you, my friend?"

"You can let me send you first-class tickets and fly out here to do what you do."

"The patient?"

"I'd rather brief you when you get here."

"Does it have to be soon?"

"Very. Can you juggle your schedule?"

"I know you wouldn't be calling like this if it wasn't important, and you know that after you saved my mother's life there's nothing that I wouldn't do for you."

"Someone will call you later today with travel details."

"It will be good to see you, my friend."

"Don't forget to bring your testing stuff."

"I never leave home without it."

CHAPTER 14

The windowless white van had B&D DRYWALL painted on the side along with a D.C. number that, had anyone dialed it, would have routed their call to an answering machine that had never been checked. Inside, Carl Porter adjusted his headphones and continued to listen to a conversation between Dr. Gabe Singleton and another doctor named Blackthorn.

Despite less than three hours of sleep in the last twenty-four, Porter was completely alert. He had always responded to anger and frustration that way and at the moment he was consumed by both. For the second time, he had come within just a minute or two of completing his mission, but somehow Dr. James Ferendelli had managed to elude him.

When he took the contract, Porter had expected to have his mark in a few days—a week at the most. Crackowski had hired a small army of PIs and had sent word out of a fifty-grand reward for anyone who fingered the man. But after Porter had just missed him at his Georgetown place, Ferendelli had proven wily and resourceful, and as one lead after another had dried up, Porter's frustration had begun to mount. Now there had been another near miss.

Singleton's conversation ended, and Porter set the headphones aside. He knew very little of the man who was paying him, but what was clear was that Crackowski had unlimited resources and access to professionals who knew how to use them. The surveillance equipment he had gotten installed in Singleton's apartment was sophisticated and top-of-the-line. In addition, a Starcraft GPS tracking system had been clamped onto the chassis of Singleton's car and wired for power into the electrical system.

Porter was stretching away some of the stiffness from his neck and back when there were knocks on the rear door—three, then two. Crackowski.

With his silenced pistol drawn and the interior lights cut, Porter undid the lock.

Steve Crackowski pulled open the doors and quickly climbed inside. He was at least as tall as Porter, with broader shoulders, a narrower waist, and a large, perfectly shaved head. Wire-rimmed glasses helped make his overall appearance something of a cross between a college professor and a stevedore.

"Anything?" he asked, with no more greeting than that.

"The president's daddy invited Singleton to lunch. Then there 'uz just a guy named Blackthorn, Kyle or Lyle I think he said. Singleton made the call. They just finished talkin'. Singleton asked him to fly out here as soon as possible and to bring his testing stuff."

"That's what he said? Testing stuff?"

"I think so. I think he's a doctor, too."

"All these doctors," Crackowski muttered. "I'll check it. You tired? Want me to take over?"

"I want Ferendelli."

"I've got the word out. Sooner or later he's going to surface. You tried using the remote in the tunnel?"

"Several times, just in case the animals living there were pulling my chain about Ferendelli taking off."

"I don't think it has much of a range. You sure you're okay here?"

"You jes' find him for me."

"Ferendelli's got to be feeling the pressure. He knows if he comes in, he's dead. He knows that if he stays hidden, he'll never find out what he's up against or what he can do about it. His best bet is to contact someone and try to work something out with them. I'm betting that someone is gonna be Singleton."

"The car?"

"It's in that body shop, right? Just keep it on the screen, and when it moves you move."

"Go check with your people. Just get me something to work with and I'll do the rest."

"Just be ready, Porter. We're going to find him. I'll be back to check on you in four hours."

"Make it six," Porter said.

He watched until the door had closed, then turned on a small light and repositioned the headphones. In the past, he had spent more than a day wedged high in a tree in the jungle just waiting for a mark. Six more hours here was nothing. Time well spent if it meant putting a bullet in Dr. James Ferendelli's eye—his favorite shot. It was time the man's photo joined the other two hundred or so in the gallery on the wall of his study.

High time.

CHAPTER 15

She's a Fendship F-45. A hundred forty-six feet fore to aft, thirty-foot beam. Steel hull. . . ."

If Gabe felt like Alice in Wonderland before his lunch with LeMar Stoddard, his tour of *Aphrodite* sent him spiraling well beyond the rabbit hole. The yacht was embarrassingly luxurious, with Oriental carpets, leather furnishings, crystal light fixtures, and three full baths with deep Jacuzzis. The other two staterooms merely had elegant shower stalls.

It was odd being escorted on a private tour around the spectacular boat by Drew's father when Drew himself was just a few miles away. In fact, before LeMar's driver came to pick him up, Gabe had taken a cab to the White House and met in the residence with the man's son and daughter-in-law, as well as Magnus Lattimore.

The news that Gabe had decided to stay the course charted by Jim Ferendelli—at least for the time being—was accepted by the trio with quiet gratitude and what seemed like forthright determination to do whatever Gabe asked of them.

In exchange for the reprieve, Drew would have to agree to work with Dr. Kyle Blackthorn for as long as the forensic psychologist needed to formulate a diagnosis and treatment plan. And finally, they would all have to understand that another episode involving the president, just one, would likely result in Gabe's pulling the plug and calling in Vice President Tom Cooper for a crash course in the Twenty-fifth Amendment.

"Where was this beauty made?" Gabe asked, grateful that he had actually thought of a question.

"Holland. The Dutch and the Italians are the very best at this sort of thing. I've only had *Aphrodite* for six or seven months, but she puts any other boat I've ever owned to shame."

"What's her range?" Gabe asked next, reconnecting with some of his Naval Academy roots.

Stoddard, wearing a dress shirt, no tie, charcoal slacks, and a navy blue blazer, looked pleased.

"Transatlantic. Maybe even to the end of the Mediterranean traveling fourteen or fifteen knots. Not the swiftest lady on the seas, but certainly one of the sleekest and most relaxing. I won't mind an extra half a day crossing the Atlantic. Maybe someday you'd like to join me on the trip."

"First things first. Let's get your son reelected."

"Well put."

Gabe marveled at the utter comfort and relative lack of pretension with which the president's father enjoyed and presented his wealth. Of course, Gabe reminded himself, when you had everything, and billions in the bank in case you discovered something you didn't, it had to be fairly easy to act as if it were all no big deal. Still, he also reminded himself as they settled in across from one another at a glass-topped table on the lower deck, this was a man who had founded and supported a number of charities devoted primarily to cancer research and reducing infant mortality. And he was also the man who had supplied Gabe with emotional and financial support, and an attorney, at a time when his own father had all but turned his back. Whoever had looked at wealth without class or style and had coined the term *nouveau riche* clearly did not have LeMar Stoddard in mind.

The table was set with crystal and fine china. There was a small silver pillbox to the left of LeMar's place. He noticed Gabe glancing at it and answered the unasked question by dropping three tablets onto his tongue and washing them down with a long draft of lemon water.

"See what you have to look forward to? Two blood pressure pills and one to stop my stomach from making acid. And that's just the noon box. My doctor's going to get my blood pressure down to a hundred and twenty or kill me in the process."

"Sounds like you have a good doc. I shoot for numbers like that in my patients, too. And they complain just as much. Is your pressure responding?"

"Don't ask." Stoddard ended the exchange by motioning to the young white-coated waiter that they were ready to be served. "I hope you like salmon."

"We don't get a lot of good seafood in Wyoming," Gabe replied. "The aroma clashes with that of the cattle being driven down the center of Main Street."

Stoddard grinned.

"It's good to see you after so long, Gabe," he said. "I always liked your sense of humor."

"Laughing at oneself is said to be an advanced form of wit, and it's especially easy when the one happens to be me."

"Stow that talk. I was there, remember? You have certainly overcome the tragedy and the odds and made something of yourself."

"Thank you, sir. Rumor has it that your son is well on his way to making something of himself, too."

Stoddard's face crinkled in an arresting way when he smiled, but Gabe also noticed that the tycoon's remarkably intelligent eyes remained leveled at him, as if taking in every nuance of his expressions.

Stay sharp, he cautioned himself. In all likelihood, this was not a man who relished immersion in idle chitchat—at least not for very long. Gabe guessed that, when it came to lunch with Stoddard, whether at his club or his suite at the Watergate or his lodge or here aboard *Aphrodite*, the courses on the menu were seldom served without an agenda.

"So," Stoddard said as Waldorf salads were placed before them, "I understand that you were a special guest at the dinner honoring the President of Botswana last night."

Gabe wondered briefly how often the president's father was invited to such affairs. He guessed that despite being the most powerful leader in the world, Drew was and always would be intimidated by the man. It seemed quite possible that omitting him from guest lists was one way of dealing with that dynamic. Gabe also decided that if Stoddard knew about the black-tie affair, he also knew that both his son and his son's physician were conspicuous by their absences.

Even for a man with considerably less acumen than his host, the implications of such a concurrence would be obvious. Gabe gripped the sides of his chair as if it were a flotation device. Five minutes into lunch, with *Aphrodite* tied fast to the pier, and they were already on choppy seas.

"I . . . um . . . at the last minute I wasn't able to attend," he tried.

"But you were there for a while."

The assault on what had transpired in the White House was close at hand. Gabe knew it was time for a preemptive strike.

"Sir—"

"LeMar."

"LeMar, you know that I would never violate the trust any of my patients place in me. My belief in patient/physician confidentiality is second only to my belief in my horse."

"I'm worried about my son. That's all."

"I understand."

"Gabe, even though Drew has had asthma for a number of years and has mentioned migraine headaches to me in the past, I couldn't help feeling that there was more to the story than what the public was being fed. I didn't accumulate all of this"—he gestured to *Aphrodite*—"without a built-in bullshit detector, and when I saw a tape of that press conference last night, every light on my detector panel lit up."

"I don't know what to say," Gabe replied, unwilling to lend even the slightest credence to Stoddard's belief that there was something medically wrong with his son beyond what the public was being told. "There's nothing I can or would tell you other than what you already know."

To Gabe's utter surprise, the billionaire forged ahead.

"Gabe, is there something the matter with Drew?" he asked. "I mean seriously the matter."

Gabe hesitated, then pushed back from the table.

"LeMar, don't force me to leave," he said. "And please, don't play the card of all that you did for me way back when. I've already told you, many times, how grateful I am for that."

"Easy, easy," Stoddard said, hands raised. "I'm a very worried parent. That's all. My son starts getting migraine headaches he never had before; then all of a sudden his personal physician vanishes, along with the man's daughter. Do you blame me for being concerned?"

"No, sir—LeMar. I don't blame you a bit." He chose his next words carefully. "If Drew ever tells me there's something about his health he wants me to share with you, I'll contact you in a heartbeat. But until that happens, you'll just have to get used to some frustration."

Stoddard sighed and motioned to the waiter that he had no further interest in his salmon. Anxious for the inquisition to end, Gabe did the same. For the next ten minutes, through coffee and a chocolate soufflé that Gabe suspected was close to perfect, the conversation lightened considerably—an amusing tale out of school about the president's childhood, some questions about Gabe's medical practice and Lariat, and an anecdote about Magnus Lattimore containing a veiled suggestion of the man's sexual preference for men, a possibility that Gabe had wondered about in passing but didn't particularly care about one way or the other.

"So," Stoddard said, with no more transition than that, "have you had much contact with Thomas Cooper the Third?"

"Very little, actually."

"He insists on using 'the Third' whenever possible—doesn't want to be just another Tom Cooper. You don't have a physician/patient relationship with him, do you?"

"Not unless he comes to see me for medical help, and so far that hasn't happened. He has his own doctor—a Navy man."

Gabe felt uncomfortable speaking about anyone else to Stoddard, but it was quite clear that the president's father, like most of those people he had met since arriving in D.C., traded in gossip, speculation, and information the way folks in Tyler traded in horses. It wasn't necessarily anything sinister or immoral; it was just the nature of the Washington beast. Gossip, speculation, and information—the coin of the realm.

Gabe knew that even the most casual, offhand remark, such as the one he had just made about Tom Cooper *not* having come to him as a patient, could have useful implications to the right person. Once again, Gabe cautioned himself to be careful. He was no better equipped to be playing in this game than he would have been in Olympic ice dancing. He flexed his neck and became aware of the all too familiar discomfort of tightly knotted muscles.

"I know you're being very careful with what you share with me," Stoddard was saying, "possibly with anyone. But I want you to know that if you hear or encounter anything about the vice president, anything at all, you will be doing a great service to your friend and my son by reporting it to me."

"I don't understand," Gabe replied. "I thought the vice president and Drew were linked emotionally and politically."

"Nonsense," Stoddard shot. "Simply put, and contrary to the pap his PR men have fed to the public, Thomas Cooper the Third is no friend of Drew's. He would like nothing more than to set his butt down behind that desk in the Oval Office, and it kills him every day that he's going to have to wait another four years to get there, if in fact he gets there at all."

Gabe was shocked at the virulence of Stoddard's attack.

"Well, nothing I've heard supports that view," was the best he could manage.

"During the primaries four years ago, Cooper started every manner of rumor about Drew. When confronted, of course, he denied everything, and my son actually believed him. But I know better. I warned Drew against choosing him for a running mate, but he wouldn't listen. Tom Cooper is a Brutus, and as things stand, he's just waiting until after the election to begin to assert himself and to take credit for Drew's achievements."

Gabe shook his head in dismay. One of the many things credited to the president was adding a public importance and credibility to the office of second in command that hadn't existed in prior administrations. The explanation in the press, of course, was that Drew was grooming Cooper for eight more years of Democratic control of the office. Was there something behind LeMar's vitriolic attack on the man? Gabe wondered now. Did LeMar have suspicion or information that something might be wrong—that his son's presidency might be in trouble? Was that what was behind the invitation to lunch? Did he know more than he was letting on about Drew's illness?

"Well," Gabe said, "I'll be certain to keep my eyes and ears open."

Without warning, the billionaire's countenance softened dramatically. He reached across the elegant table and took Gabe's hand in both of his, suddenly looking vulnerable and very much like a man in his seventies.

"Gabe, please," he said, his earnestness unquestionable. "Please don't let anything happen to my boy."

CHAPTER 16

*G*abe, please. Please don't let anything happen to my boy."

With LeMar Stoddard's oddly compelling display of vulnerability still reverberating in his mind, Gabe entered the White House through the West Wing checkpoint and headed directly to the clinic. The president and First Lady had promised him they would spend the day at home, leaving the residence only for a luncheon meeting with his campaign advisors in the small White House dining room, and after that a carefully orchestrated press conference in the press-briefing room, which Gabe was to attend.

By and large, the polls were holding between an eight- and eleven-point lead for Drew and Tom Cooper over Bradford Dunleavy and Charlie Christman, a four-term representative from Texas, whose politics were clearly and purposefully further to the right than those of Dunleavy, a self-proclaimed moderate conservative.

Eight to eleven points—certainly not a landslide, but an encouraging margin at this stage of the campaign. Still, Lattimore had reminded Gabe just a few hours ago, even an eleven-point lead was unlikely to survive any credible evidence that the chief executive was undergoing diagnostic evaluation or, even more damaging, treatment for mental illness of any sort. Rumors of treatment for depression had been enough to start the Dukakis campaign spinning out of orbit. There had been other errors by the Democratic strategists in that election, Lattimore admitted, but a Dukakis twelve-point lead after the convention had turned into a ten-point deficit with jackrabbit quickness.

Of passing interest to Gabe was a poll reported in that morning's *Post* that he had read during the car ride from *Aphrodite* to the White House. In it, Thomas Cooper III held a fourteen-point lead over Charlie Christman if the two of them were running against one another for the top spot. Experience and public trust were the two main issues to those voters who were polled. Nowhere did the poll pit the vice president against Bradford Dunleavy, but the analyst of the survey did opine that Cooper might win that race as well.

"Tom Cooper is a Brutus."

The small waiting area in the physician's office was empty save for Heather Estee, the young, ultra-efficient office manager cum receptionist. By her account, over the three-plus years she and Jim Ferendelli had worked together they had become quite close, and she was devastated not only by his disappearance but by his daughter's as well.

"Jennifer and I had lunch together several times," Heather had told Gabe, "and once we even went clothes shopping. She's a brilliant, talented, wonderful person. I can't believe she's missing. I pray every day that she's all right."

As Gabe entered the modest space, Heather, on the phone, glanced up from the notes she was taking, smiled, and waved. Gabe motioned to the partially opened door to the physicians' office, and she waved him to knock, that the covering doc was in.

Gabe had just done so when she said, "Gretchen, just a second, please. Dr. Singleton, this was on my desk when I came back from running some errands a little while ago."

She handed him a plain white business envelope with DR. GABRIEL SINGLETON typed on the front but no address. At that moment, the inner office door was pulled open. He slipped the envelope into his jacket pocket as he was greeted with a noncommittal smile, curt nod, and brief handshake by the doc on duty this day, a Navy captain named Nick McCall.

The greeting wasn't the least bit disconcerting to Gabe. There was still a coolness and formality toward him on the part of most of the other physicians assigned to the White House Medical Unit—no surprise, especially with Admiral Ellis Wright running the show from his position as chief of the White House Military Office and boss of everyone on the unit staff . . . except for the president's personal, civilian physician.

"Any word from the POTUS?" Gabe asked, closing the office door gently behind him.

"Not since you were here earlier. Not a word. He's been in a meeting in the dining room for about an hour. Magnus just called and said he'd be up here to get you in a few minutes."

"Fine."

"Gabe, I'm really sorry we haven't had much chance to talk. I've been scrambling to catch up with everything I let drop after Jim Ferendelli vanished."

"Any theories about that?"

McCall shook his head.

"It makes no sense. Jim seemed like a pretty low-key guy, totally devoted to the president and to doing a good job. There are still a slew of FBI and Secret Service people beating the bushes for him, and rumors are still flying."

"Well, there's nothing I'd like better than to see him walk through that door right now."

"How's it been going for *you* so far?"

"I went from seeing like thirty patients a day in my practice back in Wyoming to seeing one here, and I'm totally exhausted. What do you make of that?"

"The strain of having your one patient be the most powerful man on Earth will tend to do that to you. Don't worry, you'll be seeing more cases as time goes by. An hour or so ago I had a maintenance man with chest pain and hyperacute changes of an MI on his EKG. That was sort of exciting. We just finished cleaning up."

"You have everything you needed?"

"Pretty much, except maybe a couple of more hands and a dozen or so more square feet of treatment room space, but we did okay. IV, nitrates, oxygen, morphine, aspirin, bloods drawn. He was pretty stable by the time the ambulance arrived."

Bloods!

Shortly after drawing the three vials of blood from the president, Gabe had brought them down to the office, labeled them with the reverse of his home phone in Tyler, placed them in a sealed specimen bag, and set them on the back of a shelf in the under-counter refrigerator until he could decide what tests to order and where the samples should be sent. It wasn't done according to a legal, chain-of-custody protocol, but he wasn't handling evidence, and the fewer things Drew Stoddard's name was physically attached to, the better. Fatigue, the hour, the lack of a specific plan, and subsequent events had temporarily driven thoughts of the samples from Gabe's mind.

"Sounds like you did great," he said, wondering if there was anything wrong with sharing the fact that he had drawn the vials. The memory of LeMar Stoddard pumping him for information and the vision of Ellis Wright staring him down and calling his medical ability to question gave him enough pause to hold back. Lattimore would probably be able to answer his questions about where the blood chemistry studies should be run.

For effect, he cleared his throat twice and then asked if McCall wanted to grab a glass and split the Diet Coke he had sequestered in the fridge. There would be none there to split, but he had plenty of fallback explanations for that, centering about his absentmindedness. The captain begged off, and Gabe entered the treatment room prepared to continue the charade.

The refrigerator was empty.

No Diet Coke. No tubes of blood.

Nothing.

Gabe mentally retraced his steps from the eventful evening. Somewhere around two, he had taken the elevator down to the clinic, labeled the tubes, and placed them on the rack in the back of the refrigerator. Then he and Treat Griswold had left the White House.

Gabe was certain of it.

"Nick, has anyone been in the fridge that you know of? My Diet Coke is gone."

"I can only tell you since seven thirty this morning when I got here. I haven't even left for lunch. Heather had a wrap sent up for me. There was a lot of chaos when the MI was here, and about as many people as that room will hold, so someone might have come across it and maybe helped themselves."

Damn! Okay, Singleton. A Diet Coke is one thing. The blood samples you drew are another. Come up with some scenario to explain how they might have gone MIA.

Speaking through the intercom, Heather's voice sliced into the moment.

"Dr. Singleton, Mr. Lattimore is here."

"Tell him I'll be right out."

Come on! his mind urged. *How did it happen?*

Gabe left Nick McCall and crossed through the examining room to the small bathroom where, a lifetime ago, he had engaged in near-mortal combat with a bow tie. The brief note in the envelope was typed.

Doc,
I have the keys to J.F.'s place. Meet me at your parking space
at six.

A.

PS: Your car looks great.

Alison.

Gabe flushed the toilet for effect and washed his hands. He was drying them when he returned to McCall.

"Nick, tell me something," he asked, sensing the answer before he had even voiced the question. "What nurse was assisting you during the MI?"

"It was the new one, Alison. She rushed over from the clinic in the Eisenhower Building. She's really excellent. Like having another M.D. Have you met her?"

"Yeah," Gabe replied, the tension gathering in his chest. "I've met her."

CHAPTER 17

*G*abe left the White House at five and headed to the Watergate by cab. Following the realization that the bloods he had drawn on the president were missing and that Alison had been in the clinic assisting in the cardiac resuscitation, he had visited with the First Family and checked his patient over. Drew Stoddard was cheerful, alert, and energetic. He had some significant amnesia surrounding the events of the previous night, but his long-term memory was sharp, and his mental status testing showed no real holes.

"Admiral Ramrod thinks he runs this place," Drew said. "And to some extent he does. But sometimes I have to find a way to remind him that despite all the authority he has, I am still numero uno. Bringing you to Washington instead of taking Wright's suggestion that I go for a military doc was one way of keeping him in his place. You know, I don't think I mentioned it back in Tyler, but the initial idea to bring you on board was my father's. He really thinks a great deal of you."

"And I do of him."

"You think you can handle the admiral okay?"

"With your support, I can handle him as much as I need to."

"So I get another day as the Big Kahuna?"

The question was asked with some lightness, but there was no mistaking the seriousness behind it.

"You get another day," Gabe said.

"How long a leash?"

"For the time being, short—very short."

For a moment, the president seemed ready for debate.

"Maybe after tomorrow, I can start doing a little campaigning?" he ventured, finally. "You know, to keep my job?"

"Let's do this a day at a time, Drew. I've lined up a consultant who should be here sometime tomorrow. I need to share some of the burden you've heaped onto these stooped shoulders. He's the one I've chosen."

It wasn't until Gabe was in a cab headed back to the Watergate that he sorted through the significance of his decision to say nothing to the president about having had lunch with his father. It wasn't an oversight, Gabe admitted to himself, but now just didn't seem like the time to wade into the deluge of questions that were sure to follow. Perhaps he was merely catching onto the Washington game of Less Is More—It Can't Be a Lie If You Never Said It.

Another unresolved issue was who to speak with regarding having a point-blank shot taken at him as he was headed home from the White House. The last thing he wanted, next to being shot, was a Secret Service contingent following him around, and the next thing to that was any sort of leak and the massive publicity that was certain to follow. Until his best response became clear, he had decided, he would just leave things be.

It would be a huge relief to have Kyle Blackthorn on the scene. The psychologist, whose logic sometimes reminded Gabe of Mr. Spock on *Star Trek,* had an earthy wisdom and perspective unlike anyone else he knew.

First, though, there was the matter of Alison Cromartie—who she was really working for, why she had lied to Gabe, and how she came to steal the blood he had drawn on the president.

At quarter of six, when Gabe arrived at the Watergate garage, the Buick was back in its space with a new rear window and a clean interior. If there had been any damage to the rear bumper, it had been touched up. If the upholstery had been torn by the would-be assassin's bullet, it had been repaired. If nothing else, Alison most definitely had some clout.

Gabe leaned against the car and tried to put together what he knew and what he sensed of the woman. A continuing-ed course he had once attended on psychiatry for primary-care docs had spent an hour on sociopaths— people with little or no innate ability to separate truth from lies, right from wrong. Glib, often charismatic, usually believable, always dangerous. The condition had a formal, for insurance purposes, name—antisocial personality disorder, or something like that. He wasn't sure of the precise wording. Could Alison be one of those? Gabe wished he had paid more attention at the course.

"So, cowboy, what do you think of your new wheels?"

Alison, wearing jeans and a light, zip-up-the-front San Antonio sweatshirt, was leaning against a Volvo, appraising him from no more than ten feet away.

"Can you arrange for one-hour tailoring, too?"

"I can be resourceful, if that's what you mean. Actually, I didn't even have to go through the office for this one. The Colombian guy who owns the auto body shop around the corner from my apartment thinks we are destined to spend forever together. He did this."

"Do you think asking him for favors is leading him on?"

"Maybe, but he's, like, seventy-five and has three of his sons working for him, and I think his wife is still in the picture, too. I'm not that great at reading people, but he doesn't seem like much of a threat."

What about me? Gabe wanted to ask, deliberately looking away from her. *Am I a threat?* He was surprised at the hurt he was feeling—hurt mixed with anger that she had lied to him more times in one day than Cinnie had over the entire length of their marriage.

"Ferendelli's place is in Georgetown, yes?" he asked.

"The far side from here—somewhere between a walk and a drive. How's your luck at finding parking spaces?"

"It was always pretty good in Tyler, but we only have three or four cars in town, and a lot of spaces."

"In that case, let's take this car." She flipped the keys to him. "Traffic's heavy, but I don't mind spending the extra time together if you don't."

Stop looking at me that way!

"I'll manage," he said, opening the door for her and receiving a smile of pleasant surprise in return.

"In my world, people worry that opening the door for a woman might offend her. I like your world better."

"So tell me. You dropped off the bullet at the lab?"

"I did."

"And did your handlers have any theories about who might have tried to kill me?"

If, in fact, the guy wasn't a Secret Service employee to begin with.

"I don't have any handlers, Doctor. I have department heads and a division chief. Was that snide tone on purpose?"

"Huh? Oh, no." He warned himself to be more careful. "I'm on edge about this, that's all. Someone tried to kill me, and the police show up a minute later, and at your urging I end up not telling them anything—or anyone else for that matter."

"Well, believe me or not, it was the right thing to do. I did speak to my superior about what happened. He doesn't have any idea who could have done this or why. Is there anything going on surrounding Dr. Ferendelli or the president that you haven't told anyone about?"

"Absolutely not." *Nice delivery,* Gabe thought. *Not too rushed, not too forced. A little bit of incredulity thrown in. You pick up on things quickly.* "Is this supervisor you spoke to the same guy who has no idea why Ferendelli might have disappeared?" he asked.

"Pardon me for suggesting it, but you're sounding snide again. You're upset because I didn't tell you I was Secret Service when we first met. Is that it?"

"Sorry. Let's drop it for now."

"Go left at the next light."

Except for finishing the directions, there was no other conversation.

Ferendelli's place was a three-story brownstone on a small, tree-lined street off MacArthur. A parking place materialized just three doors down, but with the tension between them more or less out in the open, there was no comment about Gabe's luck.

"Thirty-seven hundred a month furnished," Alison said as they paused on the short front walk. "Dr. Ferendelli and his wife both came from money. In addition to that, he invented something and got a patent on it—some sort of electronic gizmo that can pinpoint even small veins and arteries through the skin. I may not be completely right about what it does."

"I'll try to find out, but it sounds like such a thing might have some practical uses."

"Their place outside of Raleigh is for sale for two and a half million."

"I hope he's alive to spend the money."

"I've been here twice," she said, opening the front door and then deal-ing with the alarm keypad in the hallway. "The place has been thoroughly searched and dusted for fingerprints. I doubt there's anything left to find."

"I just want to get a sense of the man."

"I understand," Alison said coolly. "I can wait in the car or maybe in the kitchen. There's a neat view of the woods from there, and a little bit of the river. The views from upstairs are much more striking."

"That would be fine," he replied, matching her tone.

"And Gabe?"

"Yes?"

"I'm sorry we seem to have gotten off on the wrong foot."

"Me, too," he replied as much to himself as to her. "Me, too."

The house had a wonderful feel—heavy, rough-hewn beams and fire-places in both the kitchen and the living room, dark, rich wainscoting in the dining room, leaded glass in many of the windows. There was so much money in the world concentrated with so few, Gabe mused as he made his way up the ornate staircase. In one day, he had been aboard *Aphrodite* at the Potomac Basin yacht club, in the Watergate condominium residences, and now here.

So much money.

He thought about his small place in the desert on the outskirts of Tyler. Unlike his best friend and roommate at the Academy, he was never cut out for the life of brownstones and yachts. Even if the accident at

Fairhaven had never happened, he would have eventually found his way to someplace like the ranch.

The Ferendelli master bedroom had two tall mullioned windows that overlooked the tops of shade trees and beyond them the Potomac. Spectacular. Set up beside the window was a professional-grade artist's easel with the rough sketching on an eighteen-by-twenty-four-inch canvas for an oil painting and evidence that someone—Jim Ferendelli, he supposed—had begun painting the piece. Gabe expected it to be a rendering of the view he was seeing, and in fact it was a landscape. But instead of the scene outside the window, it was one of vast, rolling hills surrounding, in the distance, some sort of structures, perhaps the house, barn, and other outbuildings of a farm.

Physician, inventor, artist. Gabe had always felt that the term *Renaissance man* was overused, but it certainly seemed that in his predecessor he had found one.

Not the least bit certain what he was searching for, Gabe flipped through the clothes hanging in the two closets, checked the floor beneath them, and scanned the contents of the bureau and the bathroom medicine cabinet. There were the usual salves and over-the-counter analgesics, but no prescriptions. A healthy Renaissance man at that.

In no particular rush, Gabe checked the two smaller bedrooms on the second floor, then entered the exquisitely appointed office and library. The room, perhaps a thirteen-foot square, featured a mahogany desk, oxblood high-backed leather chair, and matching love seat. Finely framed prints, both Renoirs, graced two of the walls.

The drawers of the desk held nothing of interest except three portrait sketches that confirmed Ferendelli's skill as an artist. Two of them, both rendered in charcoal, were of a lovely younger woman with a narrow, intelligent face and large, widely set eyes—Ferendelli's daughter, Jennifer, perhaps.

A third portrait, again in charcoal, again neck-up, was of a somewhat older woman, also quite attractive, with short hair and eyes that seemed almost luminescent even when done in char—

Gabe stared intently at the work. Then he carried the sketch over to the room's only window. The early summer evening light was quite enough to confirm his initial impression that the subject of the drawing had to be Lily Sexton, the woman destined in the event of a Stoddard/ Cooper victory in November to be the first Secretary of Science and Technology.

The wall across from the desk and the window was the library— neatly aligned volumes, nearly all of them hardcover and many leather bound—ten feet across and extending up nine feet to the ceiling, the collection was impressive. There were classics: Chaucer, Dickens, Hemingway, Tolstoy, Fitzgerald; coffee-table art books: French Impressionists, Picasso, Winslow Homer, and a number of others; plus several volumes dealing with WW II.

In addition, there were groupings of American and European history, world history, philosophy, and politics—mostly conservative. Gabe opened several volumes, but there were no bookplates and no other indication as to whether the books belonged to the owner of the brownstone or to Renaissance man Dr. Jim Ferendelli.

Having learned more than he had expected to about his predecessor and having found one surprise—the portrait of Lily Sexton that the FBI and Secret Service may have missed—Gabe was about to head downstairs when his attention was drawn to book spines at the far right end of the very lowest shelf. A set of six or seven volumes, all paperbacks with colorful covers. He pulled out the largest, thickest of the volumes: *Nanomedicine,* by Robert A. Freitas, Jr. Volume 1: *Basic Capabilities.* It was a highly technical treatise, 507 pages long, with an extensive table of contents and vast index. Meticulously block-printed at the top of the inside front cover was the single word FERENDELLI.

Gabe set the tome on the desk and brought out the others. *Understanding Nanotechnology, Nanotechnology for Dummies, Nanotechnology: Science, Innovation, and Opportunity, Nanotechnology: A Gentle Introduction to the Next Big Idea.* Each of the volumes had Ferendelli's name carefully printed inside the front cover.

Gabe reflected on the neatly folded underwear and carefully arranged socks in the bedroom bureau and added "meticulous" to the characteristics he had already attributed to the man. Then he took a few minutes to flip though the volumes expounding on this latest aspect of Ferendelli—a fascination with nanoscience, the study and manipulation of atomic and molecular-size particles, and nanotechnology, the construction of useful chemicals and machines built from individual atoms and molecules.

Nanotechnology. What Gabe read in just three minutes of flipping pages was already way more than he knew about the subject.

But, he decided, that would not be the case for long.

He brought a heavy garbage bag up from the kitchen and set the books inside. When Alison asked what he was doing, he was ready.

"There are a couple of up-to-date medical specialty texts in the library that I could use at the clinic," he lied. "I'm sure the doc won't mind."

"Terrific. Find anything of interest up there?"

"Nothing," he lied again. "Truth is, I really didn't expect we would."

Piece of cake, he thought as they headed back to the Buick. Once you got the hang of lying, there really wasn't much to it.

Taking a good medical history was much harder.

CHAPTER 18

*M*idnight.

It had been years—decades, actually—since Gabe had studied uninterrupted with such intensity. Perhaps back then it was a test in med school, maybe his internal-medicine boards. Whatever the exam, given where his life had taken him after Fairhaven, he always welcomed the chance to study where some sort of goal was involved. Tonight that goal was learning as much as he could about nanoscience and nanotechnology.

He had gotten himself up and running with the perusal of a few articles on the Internet and then chosen the most basic of Ferendelli's texts—an overview of the field in a small volume put together by the editors of *Scientific American.*

Next came *Nanotechnology for Dummies.*

Now he was approaching the other books by topic, rather than trying to scan each from cover to cover. Nanotechnology in your world. . . . Pathways to molecular manufacturing. . . . Building big by building small. . . . Making molecules into motors. . . . The fantastic voyage into the human body. It was possible, even likely, that Jim Ferendelli's study of nanoscience and technology had nothing to do with his disappearance, but it was fact that at the moment Gabe had precious little in the way of ideas, and it was also fact that less than twenty-four hours ago a man—a legitimate assassin or part of an ingenious charade—had tried to kill him.

Alison had offered to take a cab or the Metro home from Ferendelli's brownstone, and Gabe, anxious to start reading and not wanting to screen every word she said for underlying intent, had come close to agreeing. In the end, though, he acknowledged his ambivalence toward her and his reluctance to end their evening together and made the drive to her place, although in near silence.

She lived in a prim brick garden apartment complex in Arlington, Virginia, just across the river from D.C., although she shared with Gabe that she now suspected the residence would not be hers for long. It seemed quite possible that by exposing her identity as she had, she might have outstayed her usefulness and be facing imminent deportation back to the desk job in San Antonio. The Secret Service was as uptight as any branch of the military, she told him—maybe more so. A blown assignment was a blown assignment regardless of the reasons.

Once during the drive, he had risked a glance over at her. She was gazing impassively ahead, approaching headlights glinting off the dampness in her dark eyes. She really did have an unusual, expressive beauty, he acknowledged, as well as an energy he couldn't get out of his mind. Still, something else he couldn't get out of his mind was that she had been placed in the White House Medical Unit to get information from him, possibly about the president's medical situation, and she was willing—no, *required*—to lie and possibly to steal as well to get the job done.

At that moment, no amount of beauty or energy could make up for the lack of trust he was feeling toward her.

Too bad.

"Well," she said as she opened the car door and stepped out in front of her apartment complex, "see you around."

"See you around," he replied, barely looking at her.

She took a step away and then looked back over her shoulder.

"Gabe?"

"Yes."

"It's not like you think."

Before he could ask what she meant, she had turned and was gone. Hours later, thoughts of her continued to intrude on his studies.

Despite a load of caffeine from a splendidly rich Colombian blend, Gabe could feel the hour and lack of sleep beginning to overtake him. Still, he was fascinated by the material and reluctant to call it quits for the night. Carefully avoiding the bed, and keeping the lights on full, he rotated from the desk, to a not-too-comfortable easy chair, to the kitchen table, and then back to the desk again. As he read, taking notes on a yellow legal pad, he felt an increasing connection to Dr. Jim Ferendelli.

What had drawn the man to be interested in this still-arcane field? What was his connection to Lily Sexton? Gabe remembered the spark of interest he himself had felt at first meeting her. But the images and the scent and gentle touch of Alison Cromartie were fresh and powerful enough to keep any fantasies involving Lily at bay.

Ferendelli and Sexton.

Possible, he mused. *Very possible.*

He had heard the term *nanotechnology* before and knew that it had something to do with constructing various materials beginning with very small particles. But until tonight that was about as far as his knowledge went. Well, he realized as he continued to read, not totally. He had come across someplace—an article or novel or possibly something on public radio—the phantasmagorical possibility of nanotechnology eventually creating a new life-form: submicroscopic nanorobots, capable of reproducing themselves again and again until the resultant "gray goo" began to smother all living matter on Earth.

Gray goo and nanobots.

Gabe washed the grit from his eyes, returned to the Internet, and did a more detailed reading on the subject. The terms *gray goo* and *nanobots,* possibly first coined by K. Eric Drexler, often referred to as the father of nanotechnology, were pure science fiction—speculation depicting the ultimate end of the evolution of the science, of *all* science for that matter, decades or even centuries in the future. Interesting to think about and to debate over coffee, but hardly an impending threat.

According to Drexler's theory, a self-replicating nanobot, one of hundreds of billions created to help society in any of hundreds or even thousands of ways, could undergo a change similar to a biological mutation. That one mutant particle then would create another; then the two of them would each reproduce again. Two would become four, then four eight, then eight sixteen—two to the eventual power of infinity, so long as the raw materials, the substrate, necessary to feed and sustain the process remained available. Because of the mutation, like microbes suddenly impervious to antibiotics, the technology to stop the unbridled growth of the new nanobots would no longer be effective.

Gray goo.

"The president feels that the federal government needs to take a more proactive position regarding control of scientific research and development—stem cells, cloning, nanotechnology . . ."

They were Lily Sexton's words.

Nanotechnology last night in the Red Room. *Nanotechnology* tonight in Jim Ferendelli's library. In Wyoming, Gabe had encountered the word maybe once every few years, Now, in Washington, twice in a day or so.

Gabe returned to the books.

At Carol Stoddard's urging, the president was on the verge of appointing Lily Sexton to a new cabinet post that would, in part at least, oversee the evolution of nanotechnology—protecting the world, in theory at least, from Drexler's Armageddon.

Two A.M.

The bellwether muscles at the base of Gabe's neck were screaming for the relief that only sleep could bring. He had sacrificed two codeines to the ache with little or no effect and pledged to use no more—at least not tonight. The caffeine was still punching away at his nervous system, but connecting less and less. It was time to stop. Still, what remained of his willpower refused to quit. The scope of the new science was mesmerizing, and although the future of nanotechnology was in many respects as vague and ill defined as gray goo, the present was already intensely fascinating—and, in some regards, quite profitable as well.

Gabe studied the photo of an early computer, nearly filling the room it was in. Thanks to microprocessors, his ultra-thin laptop probably had more power. Now nano-size computer transistors were making even the sleekest PCs seem clunky. Disinfectants for killing specific germs without generating any human toxicity, lightweight bulletproof armor, and nonallergic cosmetics were just a few of the products of nanotechnology already on the marketplace.

Gabe's eyelids drifted closed and refused to reopen until he promised them a trip to bed—no passing GO, no collecting $200. Once under the covers, he eased into sleep through swirling images of Drew Stoddard and Magnus Lattimore, of Ellis Wright and Alison, of Tom Cooper and LeMar Stoddard and Jim Ferendelli, and, finally, of the charcoal portrait of the woman he hoped to spend at least part of the day ahead with—the elegant, eccentric mistress of Lily Pad Stables, Lily Sexton, Ph.D.

CHAPTER 19

*E*ven during the drinking years Gabe had never been a sound sleeper.

Later on in his life, the nurses at the hospital and the answering service operators at Tyler Connections knew that no matter what hour they called, he would answer before the second ring and would invariably sound as if he were sitting at the kitchen table sipping coffee. Not even the Xanax he took when sleep simply wouldn't come at all kept him from going on instant alert.

This morning, when the phone began ringing in his Watergate apartment, Gabe was enmeshed in a bizarre and bloody dream involving being trapped inside a slaughterhouse. The woman trapped beside him might have been his ex, or Alison, or possibly even Lily Sexton. It was impossible to tell. The desperate bellowing of doomed and dying cattle was terrifying and totally vivid and yielded only reluctantly to the telephone, so that it might have been the third or fourth ring before his fumbling fingers located the receiver.

The LED on the bedside alarm read 5:00—maybe two and a half hours since he finally walked away from his nanotechnology notes.

"Dr. Singleton, it's Magnus Lattimore. I hope I didn't wake you."

At the sound of the man's voice, Gabe went cold. All he could think was that he had screwed up big-time in letting Lattimore and the Stoddards talk him out of initiating the Twenty-fifth Amendment. Why else a call at five in the morning?

"Is Drew in trouble?"

He doused the frog in his voice with water from the half-filled glass on his bedside table.

"No, no," the chief of staff replied quickly. "Everything's fine. Great. I guess I should have said that right away. Sorry. The president is doing fine. Fine. In fact, he just finished a forty-five-minute workout with his trainer."

"Terrific."

Gabe felt the tsunami of adrenaline begin to ebb. He remembered that at the Academy, Drew, like a number of the others—most of them private school kids with advanced study habits—often chose to wake up at two or three in the morning to do his work while distractions were at a minimum. Gabe also found himself wondering, in some corner of his mind, exactly what in the hell the slaughtered-cattle dream was all about.

"Believe me, Doc, you're doing a great job," Lattimore was saying.

"If he's okay, everything else is secondary," Gabe said, pointedly ignoring the praise.

"You've got that right, my friend. Well, I'm calling on his behalf with a request."

"Go on."

"There's a large meeting at the Baltimore Convention Center later this morning which the president was supposed to address. Some major political allies and donors are running the show, and one of them called quite upset that the Secretary of the Treasury had been written in to take the POTUS's place. You see, after the gastroenteritis attack the other night, you said we should stick close to home, and so we—"

"I know what I said, Magnus. Go on."

"Yes. . . . Well, although we still have a decent lead over Dunleavy, there has been a significant slippage in a couple of the important polls. The president is feeling great, and he thinks he should go speak to these people in person. It can be a very brief address."

"And what do you think?"

"I think we have made a deal with you and we are going to keep that deal."

"But you want him to go and make this speech."

"More importantly, *he* wants to go."

"Can the decision wait for twenty minutes?"

"Not too much longer than that. Our advance teams are on the way to Baltimore just in case we get the green light from you, but there are some other logistical problems that need to be worked out."

Gabe glanced down at his wrists, half-expecting to see the strings of a marionette.

"In that case," he said, "give me time for a quick shower and I'll be right over. I'll decide for certain after I have seen him."

"That's all we can ask for. You're in charge, Doc. You're always in charge."

"Yeah, thanks, that's good to be reminded of."

"A car will be waiting for you outside the main entrance."

"Magnus, tell me something."

"Yes?"

"That car—where is it right now?"

There was just enough hesitation so that Gabe knew the chief of staff was deciding if there was anything to lose by telling the truth.

"The car. . . . Yes. . . . Well, actually, the car is waiting out in front of the Watergate right now."

"Thanks. It looks like I'm going to have to work at being a little less predictable," Gabe said.

He set down the receiver wondering if any of those ill-fated cows being herded down the chute in his dream had looked like him.

"Three sets of forty, Gabe. That's a hundred and twenty push-ups. Do you think the President of North Korea can do a hundred and twenty push-ups?"

"How old is he?"

"I don't know, maybe eighty."

"I think you've probably got him. Drew, believe me, I'd be the happiest man alive if all the world's political problems could be solved by which country's leader could do the most push-ups. I'm going to look inside your eyes again. Pick a spot over there on the wall and just stare at it."

"Dilates the pupils, right?"

"You got it. Good. Looks fine in there. Now, touch my finger with your right index finger, then touch your nose. Do it five times fast. Okay, now the left index finger. . . . Good. . . ."

The president, sitting beside his bed, looking boyish and utterly fit, submitted to a physical and neurological examination. Nothing amiss. Absolutely nothing. Gabe tried once again to match the frightening display he had witnessed here thirty-six hours ago with any specific diagnoses—a frantic, manic, disoriented, hallucinating, hyperactive episode with cardiovascular acceleration that had come about with little warning and resolved after a couple of hours without apparent residual effects. MRI negative, CT scan normal—at least according to the coded records at Bethesda Naval. Blood work normal, although the samples were drawn eight weeks ago during his brief hospitalization, hours after his attack.

Most recent bloods, drawn by Gabe *during* an attack . . . missing.

It seemed logical that Jim Ferendelli had also drawn blood work during one of the episodes he observed, but neither the president nor Magnus Lattimore could recall any tubes being obtained until Gabe drew them.

Track down any blood chemistry results.

Gabe made a mental note and filed it with what seemed like an infinite number of other mental notes.

"Well, Doc? How'd I do?"

"You seem fine."

"I feel fine."

"If you go to Baltimore, I go."

"I wouldn't have it any other way. You're my shaman . . . my healer. Gabe, I know you want to treat me very conservatively until you know what's going on, but I have this sort of demanding job and—"

"I know, pal. I know. I'm doing my best to work around that demanding job, although I'll grant you, it is a bit like redecorating the bathroom with an elephant in the tub."

"Nice image. I like it. Although we really should think in terms of donkeys rather than elephants."

"From now on, donkeys in the tub. Drew, there was a message waiting for me in the office. The consultant I sent for—the psychologist—is going to be here this evening. I want him to do an interview and complete battery of what we call neuropsychiatric testing on you—intelligence—probably beginning tomorrow."

"What did you say his name was?"

"Blackthorn. Dr. Kyle Blackthorn. He's a little . . . um . . . eccentric, but he's also incredibly insightful."

"I revere eccentric *and* insightful. Bring him on."

"I will." Gabe fixed his gaze on the president. "Drew, do you remember the tubes of blood I took from you the other night?"

"Not really."

"Well, I did. Three of them."

"For what?"

"For whatever tests I decided I wanted."

"Fine with me."

"Except that they're gone."

"What?"

"Gone. Missing. They disappeared from the medical clinic refrigerator sometime during the day after I drew them. Any ideas?"

The president looked genuinely nonplussed.

"I have no clue what could have happened, but I'll get Treat and my staff on it right away. It would seem that quite a few people have access to that office—the doctors, the nurses, the PAs."

"Plus a couple of paramedics and one admiral," Gabe added.

"Ah, yes, Admiral Ramrod. Well, I think if taking tubes of blood isn't in the Officer's Manual of Right and Proper Things to Do, Ellis didn't take them."

"Okay," Gabe said, virtually convinced from his patient's reaction that the man had no knowledge the tubes had vanished, let alone any responsibility for the theft, "for the time being, why don't you just let me keep my eyes and ears open. I don't think there's anything to be gained by making a big deal about it—at least not yet."

"Maybe they got thrown out by accident."

"Anything's possible. So, when and where for today's deal?"

"I think ten thirty. Someone will come by your office to get you. Admiral Wright and whoever's covering today have put together the medical team. From now on, when we're going on the road, I'll have you do it. Either way, they'll all know that so long as you're around, you're in charge."

"I like the way that sounds, Drew."

"Yeah, I kind of enjoy hearing that one myself."

"It's good to be the king."

The president immediately picked up on the line from Mel Brooks's *History of the World.*

"You said it," he replied. "It *is* good to be the king."

The two friends shook hands and Gabe headed through the foyer toward the elevator. He was nearly there when his radio crackled on.

"Wrangler, Wrangler, do you read me. Over."

Wrangler was the radio name he had chosen with the help of the Secret Service. It wasn't used all the time—more often he was referred to as Doc—but Gabe liked it when it was. He threw the switch on the speaker attached to the sleeve of his jacket and spoke into it.

"This is Wrangler. Over."

"Wrangler, this is Agent Lowell—are you available to see a patient in your clinic? Over."

"I'm headed there now from Maverick's quarters. Over."

Maverick, the flamboyant, fearless Tom Cruise character in *Top Gun,* was the name given to the president in honor of his war record as a pilot. In accordance with White House Communications Office protocol, then, all of the First Family's call names began with the same letter as the president. Carol was Moondance, Andrew Jr. had chosen Muscles, and Rick had picked Mindmeld from *Star Trek*. Scotsman Magnus Lattimore was Piper after the instrument he allegedly played quite well, though seldom when he was sober.

"We'll be there in ten minutes. Do you copy? Over."

"Ten minutes. Roger that. What's the problem? Who's the patient? Over."

"The problem is a foreign body of some sort in the eye. The patient is Bear. He has specifically requested you. Do you know who Bear is? Over."

"I do. Tell him I'll be there to see him in ten minutes. Over."

"Over and out."

Curious.

Bear, named, Gabe figured, for his physique, or maybe his home state of Montana, was the vice president.

"He has specifically requested you."

Gabe stepped into the small elevator replaying yesterday's luncheon conversation with LeMar Stoddard and Stoddard's warning regarding Thomas Cooper III.

Now what? he wondered as the gears engaged. *Now what?*

CHAPTER 20

The clinic was being covered by a physician's assistant from the Army. Gabe dismissed her for an hour and then checked the fridge again for the tubes of blood. Nothing, except an Army lunch box and a Dr Pepper. It had to have been Alison. Motive . . . opportunity. He knew he was stretching the facts to fit his theories about the woman, but he was on edge—about her and in fact about almost everyone else he had met since arriving in D.C.

One main question about the missing tubes refused to go away: If Alison was, indeed, responsible for the theft, how had she known they were there? His plan had been to determine, through Lattimore and one of the senior docs on the White House staff, how to send the blood off for routine chemistries and hematology, along with some toxicology, without giving any hint as to their source.

How had Alison known about the samples?

If she had been planted in the office to gain his confidence and learn about the president's medical status, who was pulling her strings? The questions far outstripped their answers.

"Gabe? . . . It's not like you think."

Her words rattled around in his head. His coolness toward her was hardly subtle, but did she understand where it was coming from? He warned himself against letting her oblique comment affect his judgment. As far as he could tell, no one—not the president, not the First Lady, not the chief of staff, not Alison—had been absolutely straight with him since he stepped off the plane at Andrews AFB. Now it was time to see what LeMar Stoddard's warning was all about.

"Tom Cooper is a Brutus, and as things stand, he's just waiting until after the election to begin to assert himself and to take credit for Drew's achievements."

"Wrangler, Wrangler, are you on? Over."

With all the things Gabe had found difficult about his new position, one of those things he had absolutely enjoyed was being part of the intricate Secret Service radio system, with its jargon, monikers, and code words.

"This is Wrangler. I'm in my office. Over."

"We'll be by with your patient in two minutes. Over and out."

During his first week on the job, Gabe hadn't said ten words to the man who was a heartbeat away from the presidency. What Gabe knew about him was pretty much what he had heard in the barbershop in Tyler and on the car radio while headed into work.

Cooper, once the junior senator from Montana, was in his second term when Drew selected him from half a dozen or so possibilities to be his running mate. From what Gabe remembered, the selection was more political than ideological. Northwest joins Southeast; impoverished backwoods upbringing joins privilege and vast wealth; laconic, Lincolnesque country music musician joins slick, charismatic war hero; moderate pragmatist joins intellectual visionary.

Together, Drew and Cooper overcame a double-digit deficit to nip Bradford Dunleavy and VP Charles Christman at the wire. Now, from all Gabe could tell, Drew had kept his campaign promise to revitalize the office of vice president and to use it in such a way that every day and every mission better prepared Cooper to step in and lead the country. The two men met together regularly, and Cooper was encouraged to be active and visible, especially in the areas of preservation and enhancement of natural resources, conscientious improvement and updating of the country's infrastructure, and issues involving immigration and illegal aliens.

In some circles, in fact, Cooper was viewed as more effectively conciliatory than Drew, who at times could have a hair-trigger temper. One recent poll actually suggested that the VP, who everyone assumed was a lock for the head of the ticket in four years, might be as electable as his running mate, even in this campaign.

"Tom Cooper is a Brutus . . ."

"Dr. Singleton, your patient's here," Heather announced through the intercom before Gabe could complete the thought.

"Have him come on in," Gabe said, curious as to why a man with his own medical team would have specifically asked to be treated by him.

With a soft knock, the Vice President of the United States entered the office. He was six-foot-four or so and carried an extra twenty or thirty pounds without looking all that out of shape. He was wearing a black eye patch over his right eye and was carrying a thin, black leather folio, which he set down on the corner of the desk before he shook hands.

"So, Doctor, thank you for seeing me on such short notice."

His voice was low pitched and his speech measured. Totally presidential, Gabe decided.

"Your timing was perfect," he replied. "In another hour or so I'll be off for—"

"Baltimore. I know."

Of course. Here in D.C. land, everyone knows everything . . . except for those of us who don't. Gabe flashed on something LeMar Stoddard had said over lunch. *"In this town you're nobody if you know nobody. But if the only person you do know happens to be The Man, you're still a major somebody."*

"Yes, that's right," Gabe confirmed, with more flatness than he had intended. "Baltimore."

"President Stoddard originally asked me to replace him, but I have a speech scheduled myself."

Cooper settled into the chair opposite Gabe. There was a softness to Cooper's face that seemed to engender trust—especially backed up by the steely manliness of the eye patch. Still, whether it was LeMar Stoddard's Brutus warning or the as yet unexplained reason Bear chose Gabe over the medical people assigned to his care, there was tension between the two of them.

"Well," Cooper said, "we haven't had much chance to talk since you arrived here. Everything okay?"

"I'm still picking my way through the tulips and the buffalo chips, but all in all things have been pretty uneventful."

A totally political response. Lattimore would be proud.

"Good to hear. . . . You're from Wyoming, right?"

"Tyler."

"That's southeast?"

"Precisely. Eighty or so miles north and west of Cheyenne."

"Ever come up north to Montana?"

"From time to time. The fish there always seemed a little bigger and a little more gullible than the ones around where I live." Gabe had never had much patience for hidden agendas cloaked in small talk, and he felt certain he was confronting one now. He also had his medical bag to check over for the trip. "So," he pushed, "what's the deal with your eye?"

"Ever since I woke up this morning, I've felt as if there's something in it—maybe a lash or something."

"How about we go in the examining room and I'll take a look."

"Actually," Cooper said, removing the patch to reveal none of the redness that would have quickly developed had a lash or any other foreign body made contact with the eye, "I think whatever was in there may have washed out. There's been a lot of tearing."

"I see."

Gabe felt himself understanding more and more the concern expressed by LeMar Stoddard. Thomas Cooper III was not only oblique; he was unsubtle and oblique—hardly what Gabe expected.

"The truth is," Cooper went on, "the lash probably washed away pretty quickly, but I've had trouble with corneal abrasions before and wanted to have things checked."

"No problem."

"And," the VP went on as if Gabe hadn't interjected the words, "I decided to seek you out because there's another matter I wanted to discuss with you. Two birds and all that."

At last the other shoe falls.

"I've got to get some things ready for the trip to—"

"This won't take long. Doctor."

Just that quickly, any softness there seemed to be about the man vanished. Gabe's internal alarm sounded a strident warning. For all his country upbringing and easygoing, disarming manner, Tom Cooper was, in fact, a seasoned politician, who had risen to the second-highest office in the land not long after he turned forty-six. It seemed probable that he never spoke—obliquely or not—without knowing precisely what he was saying. There was no sense examining his eye, even though at some point well past there may have actually been something in it.

"Go on," Gabe said.

"President Stoddard never made it to the state dinner the other night."

"We had a press conference about that."

"I know. Migraine headache and gastroenteritis, complicated by his asthma."

If there was facetiousness in the man's tone, Gabe couldn't hear it.

"Mr. Vice President, I had written permission from the president to speak about those aspects of his medical condition to the public. I would never share any information about him otherwise—to anyone."

"I understand, and I completely support you in that regard. Tell me something, though: Did you know that at least twice in the past Dr. Ferendelli and the president withdrew from the public eye for an extended period of time?"

"That's not a question I can or will answer."

"For a city of almost six hundred thousand, Washington is like a small town. Rumors start. Rumors spread. Rumors vanish. Rumors refuse to die.

Some are total fabrication, some have a grain of truth, and some much more than that. Those of us who have been around here for a while have learned that when a rumor surfaces and then resurfaces, there is often something to it."

"Mr. Vice President—"

"Please call me Tom. It'll save time."

"Tom, I really have to get going soon."

"Dr. Singleton, the hot rumor in town at the moment—the one that doesn't seem to want to go away—is that the president is having problems other than migraine headaches and gastroenteritis and asthma. No one is speaking out about it, at least not yet. Magnus Lattimore and the rest of the president's spin people have done a remarkable job of keeping the rumor under wraps, but it keeps resurfacing—and from more than one direction, too, which I have learned over the years is something worth paying attention to. There are those who believe President Stoddard may be mentally ill in some way. For the moment, the rumors are just whispers. But I assure you, Doctor, the whispers are getting louder."

Gabe tried for a reaction of bewildered amusement but wasn't at all certain he succeeded.

"As the president's physician, I will not discuss his health in any way," he reiterated, "including to comment on whether he has or has not any mental or other medical problems. I'm sure you expect that same sort of professionalism and respect from your doctor. If you're that concerned about rumors you have heard, perhaps you should speak with Magnus, or even with the president himself."

"When I have translated rumor into fact, I intend to do just that. Meanwhile, Dr. Singleton, you need to know that I have supported Drew without hesitation or reservation since the day he chose me to run with him. After we won, he could have buried me in the political backwater like so many presidents have done with their vice presidents, but he chose to make me an important part of his administration. He is my friend, just as I am his, and I would do anything to ensure that his legacy is that of one of the most effective, significant leaders our country has ever had. His policies and vision for America are mine, and when I get my chance, I intend to continue them."

"Okay then," Gabe said, feeling ill at ease before Cooper's emotional outpouring of fidelity. "What can I do for you?"

The vice president opened up the leather folio and slid a document across the desk. Gabe sensed without looking what it was.

"There is a great deal at stake here, Doctor, and you have a significant role in the drama that may be unfolding."

As the president's frantic, frightening episode was beginning to resolve, Lattimore had mentioned that locked within The Football, along with the electronics and codes necessary to unleash Armageddon, was an agreement signed by Drew and Thomas Cooper III outlining those situations in which there was to be a transfer of power from president to vice president according to the provisions of the Twenty-fifth Amendment. At that moment, Gabe had made a mental note to ask the chief of staff for a copy of the document. Over the ensuing, chaotic hours and days, he had simply forgotten to do so.

Now, on the desk before him was that agreement, headed by the four impressively brief sections that made up the exceedingly complex Twenty-fifth Amendment—the statement believed by many to be the most comprehensive road map of political succession ever put to paper. Gabe had read the amendment at least half a dozen times during the hours he was caring for the president in his residence. Now he scanned the first of the two paragraphs composing section 4:

> Whenever the Vice President and a majority of either the principal officers of the executive departments or of such other body as Congress may by law provide, transmit to the President pro tempore of the Senate and the Speaker of the House of Representatives their written declaration that the President is unable to discharge the powers and duties of his office, the Vice President shall immediately assume the powers and duties of the office as Acting President.

Following a glance at his watch, meant more as a reminder to Cooper than to himself, Gabe flipped through the pages. Listed in outline form, more than described in detail, were the scenarios in which the vice president, head of the White House Military Office, White House chief of staff, chief legal counsel, and physician to the president could act in concordance in deciding whether to proceed with the political process of replacing the president against the president's wishes.

Sixth on the list was "Mental Illness." Gabe was careful to scan the entire document slowly and evenly, so that it wouldn't seem to Cooper as if he had spent any extra time on this one scenario. Though there was no specific delineation of qualifying diagnoses, the agreement did state that the president should, if possible, be medically evaluated by his own physician and also by a qualified doctor of psychology or psychiatry. The mandate of these caregivers was to determine whether or not the POTUS's condition was affecting his ability to do his job without impairment.

Gabe set the pages aside and was about to ask what the vice president wanted from him when Cooper saved him the effort.

"I can't give you any specifics yet, Dr. Singleton, but as I alluded to, there are persistent rumors that the president may be mentally ill. And if I have heard these rumors, you can bet the opposition in the upcoming election has heard them as well. There has been a significant slippage in our standing in the latest polls. No one is blaming the rumors for the drop in our lead—in fact, the pattern was more or less expected for this time in the campaign. But I don't believe Drew and I are strong enough at this point to withstand every challenge to our lead."

Again Gabe checked his watch.

"Mr. V—*Tom,* I don't want to sound rude, but I think you've got to get to the point."

Cooper sighed.

"The point is," he said, "that our polls suggest that as things stand, it is early enough in the campaign so that if Drew were to drop out now for health reasons and I became the candidate, with a carefully chosen running mate, I would still be a slight but significant favorite over Dunleavy and

Christman. But the closer we get to the election in November and the more confusion there is in our camp, the less time the American public has to get used to me and to appreciate the similarities between my political philosophy and Drew's. In other words, the later in the campaign we make a change in which Democrat is running against Brad Dunleavy, the less chance we have of coming out on top."

"Meaning?"

"Meaning, Doctor, that if there is something wrong with President Stoddard, the sooner he confronts it and does what's right—the sooner *you* confront it and do what's right—the better for the party . . . and for the country."

CHAPTER 21

*W*rangler, Wrangler, do you copy? Over."

Treat Griswold's gravelly voice resonated through Gabe's earpiece. Gabe clicked on the microphone clipped to his sleeve, raised it to his lips, and spoke in the purposeful tone he had learned to use. During his first day of orientation to the White House, Griswold had given him a radio and a detailed in-service on its use. Rule Number One, Griswold said, was never turn the transmit switch on or leave it on by accident. The humiliations resulting from an "Open Mike" had become the stuff of Secret Service lore. Rule Number Two was never to forget who the system was in place to protect.

"This is Wrangler. Over."

"Everyone, Maverick is on the move from the residence elevator to the West Wing exit. Wrangler, do you have your medical bag? Over."

"Right here."

"The FAT kit with all necessary resuscitation equipment and supplies will be on the van with the medical team. Over."

"Wrangler copies. First Aid and Trauma kit on board."

"Roger that. Maverick has requested Wrangler ride in Stagecoach with him. Stand by your location and we'll get you loaded. Over."

"No problem," Gabe said. "Will Moondance be accompanying us? Over."

Gabe was still somewhat disconcerted over the odd exchange during which the First Lady had intimated she might be just as happy if her husband dropped out of the race. He would be more at ease at the moment if she weren't with them. As it was, he had been looking forward to his first trip with the chief executive, but the session with Tom Cooper had severely dampened his enthusiasm. More and more he was feeling like a man sitting on a keg of dynamite while passersby kept flipping lit matches at him.

"That's a negative," an agent other than Griswold said. "Moondance will be staying here. Liberty, too. Over."

"Roger that. I'll be waiting for you. Over."

Gabe double-checked that he had turned off his radio, then glanced outside to where the motorcade had formed. From his vantage point, he could see two black limousines parked by the steps leading up to the North Portico. Beyond them, on Pennsylvania Avenue, he could make out two of what he knew would be many vans. Communications . . . counterassault . . . press corps . . . White House staffers . . . medical unit . . . photographers . . . military aides . . . Secret Service. He remembered some of the groups Lattimore had told him the fleet of vans would be carrying, but not all.

"Attention all posts, Maverick moving toward West Wing exit. Maverick moving. Over."

Staccato footsteps echoed down the corridor toward Gabe just before the first two of the president's Secret Service men appeared, one of them expertly cradling a submachine gun. Seconds later, Drew came into view, surrounded by four more agents, each one looking as if he took his job very seriously. From the moment the entourage appeared, Gabe's attention became fixed on his patient—not without reason.

Though smiling and waving to those White House employees standing back against the wall, Drew Stoddard looked strained and slightly gray. Gabe moved toward him, but almost on cue, a petite makeup artist materialized and, with the skill of a master conjurer, performed a remarkable thirty-second makeover.

And just like that, Drew was the rosy-cheeked picture of health. As he moved to Gabe, the Secret Service agents fell away to give them space and something approaching privacy.

"Hey, cowboy," Drew said cheerily, "ready to join the Donner party for a little wagon train ride?"

"Don't even joke about that. You okay?"

"You examined me this morning. You tell me."

"Actually, I thought you looked a little gray around the gills just now, but your makeup girl fixed that problem right up."

"Amazing, huh? When she goes home and washes off her own makeup, she's actually a three-hundred-pound Samoan football player."

"Having seen her work, that's not so surprising. How about your breathing? You seem to be going a little faster than I would expect."

"I've had a little cough for about an hour or so, but it's almost gone now. Maybe I'm getting a cold."

"Not on my watch."

"Even you can't do much about a virus. Did Admiral Wright talk to you about the medical team?"

"Not a word, why?"

"I guess he went ahead and put the team together himself. From now on, if you want to select the team to accompany us for travel in the States or overseas, you just go ahead and do it. I'll make sure ol' Ramrod doesn't get in your way."

"Mr. President," Treat Griswold called out, "I think we'd best get a move on."

"Gabe, on the ride up to Baltimore I've got to go over the speech that's just been written for me. I thought there might be time for us to gab during the trip, but no such luck. You can still ride in Stagecoach with us, or you can go in Spare, that's the other limo, if you want."

"Attention all posts," Gabe heard Griswold say from close by and also through his earpiece, "Maverick moving to Stagecoach. Departure imminent. Over. . . . Okay, Doc, Mr. President, ready to roll?"

As Gabe stepped out into the bright sunlight, he couldn't help but be awed by the clutch of photographers and reporters lining the short walk to the motorcade, as well as by the motorcade itself, which, minus two limousines, was parked along the recently renovated stretch of Pennsylvania Avenue, closed to motorized traffic at all times except on occasions like this one. A dozen or more huge vans waited—nine- and twelve-seaters, Gabe guessed—along with eight D.C. motorcycle police on Harleys, with blue strobes flashing. In baseball, the glitter and crowds and private jets and plush clubhouses of the major leagues were often referred to collectively as The Show. At that moment, those words were the only description Gabe could think of.

The Show.

The two identical black Cadillac limousines were parked on the driveway that arced to the steps of the White House.

"Stagecoach is number one today," Griswold said, hurrying his party of three—Gabe, the president, and a young, lanky, bespectacled speechwriter introduced by Stoddard simply as Martin—to the lead limo.

As they reached the bottom of the staircase, over the roof of the limo Gabe caught sight of Tim Gerrity, an Air Force physician's assistant, whom he had gotten to know fairly well over the short time since his arrival at the White House and who seemed to know more medicine than most physicians but was unassuming enough not to show off. Gerrity was standing in front of what Gabe assumed was the medical van. Today the medical support team had been selected by Admiral Ellis Wright, but from now on, if Gabe so wished, the president had decreed he could pick his own team.

The notion led irrepressibly to thoughts of Alison Cromartie. Maybe somewhere down the line, if she managed to stick around and if things ever got straightened out with her, they could do one of these trips together. At that moment, as if on cue, Alison appeared beside Gerrity, talking amiably and gesturing to the van. Even at a distance, wearing a conservative navy blue pants suit, she stood out.

From the moment she pulled out her Secret Service ID after apparently saving his life, Gabe had gotten used to feeling bewildered and unsettled around her. Now, even at a distance, he felt awkward. Despite Ellis Wright's rant at her that evening in the medical office, the man apparently had enough regard for her to assign her to The Show.

Curious.

"Doc, come on. Duck on in here," Griswold ordered, standing by the open door to Stagecoach.

The last sound Gabe heard before he slid onto the seat across from Martin was the President of the United States coughing softly.

The last thing he saw, turning back toward the White House for one final look, was Vice President Thomas Cooper III, flanked by two Secret Service agents, looking down at them intently from the portico.

CHAPTER 22

*S*ignal depart. All posts: We have a departure of Maverick. Over."
Treat Griswold lowered the sleeve transmitter and turned next to him
where Gabe was sitting. "You doin' okay, Doc?"

"Aside from being a little afraid I'm going to stretch my legs and blow
my foot off, I'm fine."

He gestured to the submachine gun that was lying on the floor of the
limousine.

"I told them we should build a gun rack in the limos for these things,"
Griswold said.

"Or else make your shoulder holsters a lot bigger."

Martin Shapiro, the young speechwriter, glanced up from the passage
on which he and the president had been working.

"I'm always looking for crisp, punchy lines, Doctor," he said. "Okay if
I appropriate that one? If not for this speech, then for something down the
road."

"I want to see it when you do," Gabe said.

"Here," Drew said, pointing to a spot in the manuscript. "Why make
him wait? Right here where I'm talking about our Korean friend, President
Jong, and his goddamn obsession with nuclear reactors. Let's say something
like having him persistently claiming that the massive towers on our surveillance photos are for sewage treatment and not nuclear production is a

little like our maintaining that the three-foot-long shoulder holsters we have just issued to the Secret Service—"

"Have nothing to do with submachine guns." Shapiro grinned as he finished the thought. "Give me a minute or two to get the wording and the timing right and I think we can use it."

"There you go, cowboy," Drew said. "Just like that, you're immortal."

"Just like that," Gabe said, genuinely impressed.

In spite of his long-standing friendship with the president, and the secrets he knew about Drew's mental imbalance and attacks of irrationality, throughout the ride from the White House to the Baltimore Convention Center, Gabe could not help but bask in the true greatness of the man.

Maverick.

Gabe knew the moniker had been chosen because Drew had been a stellar pilot. But now Gabe found himself thinking about the original meaning of the word—the meaning everyone from Wyoming understood: a range animal, usually a calf or steer, who had left the herd and would belong to the first person who could manage to capture and brand it. Over time, the meaning had been expanded to include people—specifically, a dissenter, who refused to abide by the dictates of a group.

It was an awesome privilege to watch and listen as Drew and his writer sculpted a speech that would be delivered to only two hundred or so well-heeled supporters but would be heard, instantly, around the world. The main focus this day was foreign relations, but over the course of the thirty-minute presentation Drew would touch on a number of the accomplishments of his first term in office, the progress that was being made in his Vision for America program, and several failures of the Dunleavy administration, which had preceded his. He would even manage somewhere along the line to comment on the evolving miracle of the Baltimore Orioles and Washington Nationals, local teams still leading their respective divisions in baseball and possibly headed to a million-to-one long-shot World Series match-up.

By the time the motorcade turned off Route 395 and headed into Baltimore, Gabe felt more committed than ever to get to the bottom of

Drew's bizarre breaks with reality and to keep him in office if at all possible. A good deal of Gabe's resolve still depended on the findings and conclusions of Kyle Blackthorn, but as things stood, invoking the Twenty-fifth Amendment and effectively elevating Tom Cooper from running mate to presidential candidate was not a move he was going to make.

It wasn't as if the vice president had made that terrible an impression on him, although it did seem a bit naïve for a man of his stature to expect the president's doctor to share any information about his patient's medical condition. It was more that Cooper was just . . . eager. That was the most descriptive word Gabe could think of at the moment. *Eager.*

Drew Stoddard's dry cough quieted down for a time but then picked up again as they entered the outskirts of Baltimore. It was minimal and would not have been the least bit alarming had it been occurring in someone other than the President of the United States. Because of the makeup, it was impossible for Gabe to evaluate Stoddard's color, but his respiratory rate was no more than slightly elevated at eighteen per minute and the beds beneath his fingernails looked reasonably pink—a decent sign that he was getting enough oxygen into his circulation. Gabe felt comfortable speaking about the president's asthma in front of Griswold, but not the speechwriter.

"You okay?" Gabe asked after a brief volley of hacking.

"Maybe a little wheezy, but no big deal," Stoddard replied.

"You have asthma?" Martin asked, ending whatever concern Gabe had about making the disclosure.

"Low-grade for years," Drew replied matter-of-factly.

"I have it, too. Used to be bad when I was a kid. But it seems to have gotten pretty much better as I get older. Now, I don't think I have it anymore."

"Burnout of childhood asthma is quite common," Gabe offered, not taking his eyes off his patient. "You feel able to go through with this speech, Mr. President?"

"Of course. I'm really fine. You brought an inhaler for me, right?"

"Actually I have several of them—both bronchodilators and cortisone. They're in the FAT kit in the medical van."

"Griz," Stoddard asked, "do you have one of my inhalers with you?"

"Right here, as always."

The Secret Service agent patted over the inside breast pocket of his suit coat.

"Okay, then. If I feel like I need a puff of that stuff, I'll get it from you until the doc here unlocks the medicine case in the van and gets me whatever he has there. That okay with you, Doc?"

"I . . . um . . . guess so," Gabe said, reflecting on his conversations with the chief executive's father and the vice president and wondering if he should find a way to warn Drew to be a bit less cavalier with information regarding his medical status. "I would like to have a listen to your chest before we do anything, but somehow this doesn't seem to be the place for that."

"We have a screened-off prep area backstage," Griswold said. "A place for the president to sit down, get his makeup refreshed, and get ready for his speech."

"Good," Gabe said. "That'll probably be fine. Mr. President, grab a water bottle from the fridge there and drink at least half of it. You want to stay well hydrated."

"Got it."

"Doc, I'll get you and the president up to the screened-off area as soon as we arrive. Meanwhile, Mr. President, if you need any of this Alupent inhaler just ask."

"Roger that. Mr. Shapiro, I think we've done as much as we can with this puppy. You've done a great job as usual. Stanford, right? What was your major there?"

"Creative writing."

Before anyone could comment, the limousine stopped in front of a side entrance to the Baltimore Convention Center.

"Attention all posts," Griswold said to his sleeve, "Maverick moving toward BCC entrance. Over. . . . Okay, sir, Doc, we're going in that door, then up to the third floor. Stairs or elevator?"

"Stairs will be fine," Stoddard said.

"Let's do the elevator," Gabe countered before he had even processed the significance of overruling the most powerful man on the planet.

There was a moment of absolute quiet.

"We're going to head directly for the elevator," Griswold announced through the radio, scooping the submachine gun off the floor with his free hand. "Over."

The limousine doors were opened simultaneously, and the four occupants stepped out to be immediately engulfed by a buffer of Secret Service men. Griswold, ever observant, remained positioned next to the president, sunlight glinting off the balding area of his pate and the perspiration on the fold of his thick neck. Gabe flashed briefly on an image of the man, looking a bit like the mutant comic book hero the Thing, exploding through a massive cement and fieldstone wall to get at the source of danger to the president.

When they were inside, Gabe switched on his transmitter, pleased again to be playing the radio game.

"This is Wrangler to medical team, Wrangler to medical team. Over."

"We're here, Wrangler," Alison's satiny voice replied. "Unloading now. We'll meet you on three. Over."

"Be sure you have the FAT kit, an IV stand, and an oh-two tank. Over."

"Roger that. FAT kit, IV stand, and oxygen. Everything okay? Over."

"Better to not need it and have it," Gabe said, feeling the comfort and security of being a practicing doc once more. "See you on three. Over."

"Three."

"Breathe in . . . now out. . . ."

Cloistered behind a ten-by-ten-foot barrier of dark blue velvet drapes, Gabe conducted as thorough an exam of his patient as he could manage in the twelve minutes that had been allotted him. He wasn't all that alarmed by what he was seeing and hearing, but neither was he totally at ease. The president was wheezing—the sine qua non symptom of asthma. The sound, in this case not audible without a stethoscope, was caused by narrowing of the man's bronchial tubes, the result of a combination of spasm in the muscular wall of the tubes and plugging of the tubes themselves with mucus.

"So, how do I sound?" Stoddard asked.

"The more important question is: How do you feel?"

"Not bad, really. Something like this happens every other day. I think it's mold. Mold in the limos, mold in the residence, mold at Camp David, mold in my cabinet."

"How did they let you fly jets with this?"

"I didn't really have it back then, but as far as I know, most properly treated medical conditions, including asthma, will still allow a pilot to get a license—even a commercial one. I'm not sure of the military, though."

"You need a puff or two from your inhaler?"

"Actually, that stuff makes me feel a little speedy. I'd prefer to avoid it if I can. There's a couple of million in potential donations to the cause sitting out there. That'll make me speedy enough as it is."

Gabe considered his findings and the situation.

"In that case, knock 'em dead, pal."

CHAPTER 23

*I*t is time, my friends. It is time we joined together with a vision for this country and its people. It is time the children of our poor and disenfranchised stop seeking out drugs as the only way to cope with the perceived hopelessness of their situations. It is time they seek out their teachers and advisors, and hopefully, even their parents. It is time they learn to use the computers that will be on every desk, and work through their fears and concerns and curiosity and dreams in classes that are of a reasonable size.

"It is time there were enough hospital and halfway-house beds for our mentally ill and addicted, and there were government-mandated insurance programs to pay for their treatment.

"It is time there were jobs for everyone and anyone who wants one, as well as incentives to keep individuals off of public assistance.

"Yes, my friends, it is time for the people of this country to come together with a vision. . . ."

Gabe had never had much interest in politics or much faith in politicians and their promises. Now, though, he stood off to one side of the third-floor hall in the beautifully renovated Baltimore Convention Center marveling at the skill, intellect, and charisma of the man who had once been his drinking and studying buddy—at the time, little more than just one of the guys at the Academy. In the limousine Gabe had sat quietly as the president and his bright young speechwriter reviewed the lines of this speech quickly and analytically. Now he listened to the words again—notes he had seen written on a page, now transformed by a virtuoso into a concerto—mesmerizing and very special.

"I believe him."

Alison Cromartie had materialized at Gabe's elbow.

"I've seen video of Kennedy speaking," Gabe whispered, still focused on the podium but well aware of the scent of her. "I'll bet the feelings in the audience back then were the same as here."

"We're all set up the way you wanted," she whispered.

"Good. Thanks. It doesn't look like we're going to be needed."

"Amen to that."

He and Alison had exchanged a few words during the fifteen minutes before the president headed up to the podium but no sentiments. Gabe still couldn't, or wouldn't, get past the lies she had told him on the evening they first met, her anxiousness to learn about the president's health, and especially the fact that she was on duty in the office around the time the tubes of the president's blood disappeared.

During Gabe's time backstage with her, there had been no mention of the visit to Jim Ferendelli's place or her cryptic statement that things were not as Gabe thought, and this was clearly not the time or place for him to ask her about it.

"I want to say a few words," the president was saying, "about the Middle East peace proposal of ours that's currently being considered by—"

A brief volley of coughing cut the sentence short. Gabe instantly went on high alert. Stoddard drank from a glass of water, then started speaking again. More coughing. Gabe looked across to where Treat Griswold was standing, and instantly they connected.

"This may be trouble," Gabe whispered to Alison. "Go ahead back and make sure the FAT kit is unlocked and the IV and oxygen are ready."

"Got it," she said.

Stoddard apologized. Muttered something about a little cold and began speaking again. This time Gabe could almost hear the wheezing.

"Wrangler, Wrangler, are you on top of this?" Griswold's urgent whisper asked.

"I'm not going to let it get any worse before I pull the plug," Gabe replied.

He noticed that several of the attendees were watching him as he spoke into his sleeve, and sensed an instant change in the mood of the room.

". . . Our envoy, Mr. Chudnofsky, is in Amman at this . . ."

The president took a sip of water and glanced over at Gabe. Without hesitating Gabe crossed over to him.

"Mr. President," he whispered, "let's go backstage and sit down before we have a big problem. Excuse us, please," he said to the deathly silent audience.

"All of a sudden," Stoddard whispered hoarsely as Gabe led him away, "my chest just got real tight."

Griswold motioned to the presidential aide to take over and helped Gabe guide Stoddard off the slightly elevated stage and back around to the chair behind the velvet drapes. By the time the aide had begun to tell the attendees to hold their seats, a cordon of Secret Service agents, facing outward, had formed a ten-foot circle from the edges of the curtains. Inside the circle, Alison had opened the FAT kit and was readying equipment. Gabe had already started his evaluation. With Griswold's help, the president removed his shirt.

"Oh-two by mask," Gabe ordered, setting his stethoscope in place, "six liters. Griz, you have that Alupent inhaler?"

"I do."

Stoddard's chief Secret Service agent passed the inhaler over to Stoddard.

"Mr. President, go ahead and take a couple of puffs from this," Gabe said. "In fact, make it three. Alison, as soon as you have the oxygen in place, please hook him up to the pulse oximeter. Tape it to the IV pole if you have to so that I can see the readings. Then get out the cortisone inhaler from the FAT kit. We have Alupent right here, so we won't need any more of that. Mr. President, you're doing fine. It's not too bad. Just take nice, slow breaths. Nice and slow."

"I . . . I couldn't catch my breath . . . for a moment there."

"You're moving air fine now," Gabe said with steady reassurance. "Probably just some mucus plugs in a couple of your bronchial tubes. Nothing to be worried about. I'm good at this."

"I'm . . . glad."

"All that prairie dust keeps people in Wyoming wheezing all the time. Alison, as soon as you can, let's give him a couple of puffs of the cortisone. Then wheel over that IV. We'll use—a twenty intracath. I'll put it in, so I'll need a tourniquet, Betadine, and some tape. If we can get him hydrated and bronchodilated quickly, this little attack should break in no time . . . Alison?"

"Huh? . . . Oh. Oh yes. . . . Sorry. Here's the cortisone inhaler. Check the security seal to make sure it's intact. And here's the IV pole and IV. Same thing with the seal on that. We have backups for everything if there are any questions. I'll get the intracath ready."

"Thank you," Gabe replied, surprised by her brief but striking lapse in focus. Considering who their patient was, it was hard to believe she would be even the least bit inattentive.

Well, he thought, at the moment *he* was attentive enough for both of them. He felt the familiar sensations of confronting a medical emergency. His vision and hearing seemed much sharper than usual, and he was processing information rapidly—correlating at beyond computer speed what he knew about asthma and about Drew Stoddard. Although Gabe was definitely keyed up, he suspected his pulse might actually have slowed.

From his very first days in medical school, this was the sort of situation he enjoyed the most. It was what all those countless hours of study and training and practice were all about. Now, if he could just keep the identity of his patient out of the equation, there shouldn't be any problems.

To his right, Magnus Lattimore had worked his way through the

Secret Service agents and asked the big questions of Gabe with his eyes. "Mr. President," Gabe went on, speaking as much to the chief of staff as to the man himself, "what we're going to do is to try and break this asthma attack right here, right now. That would mean no ambulance and no trip to the hospital, although we're completely ready for both."

"You fix me up, Doc. . . . I don't want any hospital. . . . You know . . . how they are. . . . I'm sure they'll keep me hanging around in the waiting room forever."

"Yeah, you're probably right about that. Okay, here's the deal. Are you comfortable in that chair? Otherwise we can have the paramedics bring us a stretcher from the ambulance."

"I'm fine."

"You always were tough." He tightened a tourniquet around the president's arm, located a suitable vein at his wrist, and after the obligatory, "Just a little stick, now," slipped the catheter in easily.

"That didn't even hurt," Stoddard said. "You are damn good."

"Told you I was. You run the country, I stick needles in people."

"In my America, everyone's got to do something."

"We're getting this IV going to improve your hydration and loosen up some of the mucus that's causing you trouble. As soon as I'm comfortable things have settled down, I'll pull it. In addition, we're giving you bronchodilator and cortisone to widen your tubes and let more air in, and to reduce any inflammation. On a scale where ten is the worst asthma attack imaginable, you're maybe a three-point-five."

"I think my breathing's already a little easier."

"Good," Gabe said, confirming that air movement was certainly no worse. "That's a definite possibility. Alison, let's go ahead and give him zero-point-three of epinephrine subcutaneously."

This time, she was totally present.

"Epi, zero-point-three. Check the security seal on the box and I'll open it up and give it. Sub-Q."

Gabe verified as he had with the cortisone inhaler that the packaging was intact. Then he unwrapped it and passed it over to Alison. Except for her brief episode of distraction, she engendered confidence and was as much of a pleasure to work with as she was to be around.

"Gabe? . . . It's not like you think."

What in the hell had she meant by that? he wondered now.

Five minutes passed. Gabe stayed focused, constantly checking the president's blood pressure, pulse, respiratory rate, oxygen level, and air movement.

Lungs clearing . . . respiratory rate down from 26 to 18 . . . BP 130/85 . . . oxygen saturation up to 95 from 92.

Five more minutes. Half a liter of IV fluid in. . . . *Color good . . . wheezing almost gone . . . O2 saturation 96 . . .*

Lattimore had returned to the audience. Gabe could hear him speaking through the microphone but couldn't make out the words. Whatever he said brought about a healthy round of applause. Moments later, the chief of staff reappeared.

"I just told them you were doing well," he whispered to Stoddard. "The vultures want to know if you're coming back."

"No!" Gabe snapped. "He's not."

"I'm breathing much better," the president said. "Plus that shot—what is it, like adrenaline?"

"It's exactly adrenaline."

"Well, it's really pumped me up. I feel like I'm about to take off from the deck of a carrier."

"Mr. President, you need to just stay put. You were this close to an ambulance ride to Johns Hopkins."

"If I can pull it together and reappear, think about what my press people can do with this. The world will love it."

"The world will think you're an absolute nut with no regard for his health and a total incompetent for a doctor."

"Listen, Gabe. I can't help it if you happen to be really really good at what you do."

"You've got an IV running."

"All the better. I'll drag it out there with me. Just a minute or two, for closure . . . and a couple of photos."

"No!"

"Gabe, we're talking about a presidential election—my last shot at really making a difference in this country and the world. Your doctor's head will always opt for the conservative approach—well, almost always. But please try and look at the big picture. You've broken the asthma attack for me. You did it! I can feel it. Look, I don't even have to gasp for breath between sentences. Let me just go out there and say thank you and good-bye and show the people that I'm all right and I'll be back in this chair before you know it."

Exasperated but at the same time exhilarated, Gabe turned to Lattimore.

"How long have you been working for this guy?" he asked.

"Long enough to know what the outcome of this one's going to be," Stoddard's chief of staff replied.

CHAPTER 24

*I*t was a bad dream.

Alison kept telling herself that as she and the paramedics packed up the FAT kit and got ready to head for the medical van.

What she had witnessed, the conclusions she was considering—they had to be nothing more than a bad dream.

But she knew otherwise.

Treat Griswold, the legendary Treat Griswold, number-one Secret Service agent to the President of the United States, had reached into his jacket pocket, withdrawn an asthma inhaler, allowed the president to administer the contents to himself, and then put the inhaler back in his pocket. It sounded innocent enough and probably looked like no big deal to anyone else who observed the incident—although there were few, if any, in a position to do so.

The problem was that drugs of any kind, when destined for the president, had to follow a strict, immutable chain of custody. The prescription was given by the White House doc or nurse to the administrator of the medical unit, who then called it in to a specific high-clearance pharmacist, using any of half a dozen fictitious names. The pharmacist knew the drug was destined for the White House but had no idea if it was for the POTUS, another patient, or even the medical clinic in the Eisenhower Building next door. The pharmacist formulated the prescription and, if necessary, prepared multiple sealed containers, which were picked up by a White House driver. The driver signed for the drug and turned it over to the nurse in the White House medical office, who signed for it and put it in a locked medicine cabinet. The president's physician then retrieved the drug and administered it himself.

In the case of an inhaler, the president might be given one to keep in his residence bathroom. Other inhalers would be secured on Air Force One, on Marine One, in his personal physician's bag, and at Camp David. The president might use the inhaler on his own, but otherwise, its contents should be dispensed only by his physician or the doc covering for him.

The chain of custody would probably not stand up in a court of law, but it was a chain nonetheless, based in large measure on the assumption that none of those intimates handling any of the sealed packets would want to harm the president.

Alison had learned the unwritten protocol from a physician, who was both showing off and possibly flirting with her, but after just a few days in Washington it appeared that Gabe Singleton had yet to be brought up to speed on it. Admiral Wright had been away when Gabe arrived on the scene, so it was possible that during Gabe's orientation whoever took Wright's place had simply forgotten or neglected to cover the handling of meds. Perhaps the other medical office docs hadn't thought to mention it, either. It made sense, then, that having Treat Griswold produce an inhaler would have seemed quite natural to Gabe, who had yet to learn that no one except the president's physician should be dispensing meds of any kind to the man.

Perhaps, she thought, she should try to break through Gabe's fortress of mistrust and tell him, although it probably would be better if one of the other docs did it.

"Come on, Alison," Gerrity, the physician's assistant, called out. "I've got the rest of this stuff. We have to get down to the motorcade or we're going to be left here searching for a cab so we can get home and start searching for jobs."

Alison surveyed the area one final time. At the base of the high velvet curtain was a plastic Baggie—the one, sealed and signed by all who had touched it, that had originally contained a cortisone inhaler, which was also sealed and signed per the chain-of-custody protocol. The final step, the loop closer, was that once the seals had been broken and the medication used on the POTUS, regardless of what that medication was, it was to be disposed of immediately and a new chain of custody implemented.

It was most likely no big deal that Treat Griswold had control of the president's inhaler. Griswold had been a loyal, even heroic guardian of presidents for two decades at least. The best thing she could do was probably let the matter drop. Still, Dr. Jim Ferendelli had vanished, and she had been placed undercover in the White House Medical Unit specifically to keep her eyes and ears open and to report to the head of internal affairs anything out of the ordinary—anything at all.

The notion of blowing the whistle on anyone, let alone Griswold, was chilling. She thought about her horrific experience in the hospital in L.A. She had been in the right then—totally in the right. The incompetent surgeon had killed a patient and destroyed a good, caring nurse. The proof Alison had of that was solid, if not absolute. At least that was what she believed before her life was methodically undermined and sent crashing down around her.

Not this time.

Even if her job was to observe and report, there would be no whistleblowing on Treat Griswold without irrefutable, undeniable proof that rules had knowingly and willfully been violated. Instead, she would learn what she could about the man, searching for a chink in his armor of competence and devotion to office or else affirming that he was beyond reproach and worthy of the honors bestowed upon him over the years.

"Alison, this is it. We go now or we don't bother!"

She hurried to the elevator and rode down with the PA. The career military men who served as White House valets were mess specialists—trained to observe the preparation of the POTUS's meals and personally serve whichever plate he wound up getting. They watched every bit of food he was served and from time to time would taste the meal as well.

Would any of them tolerate a Secret Service agent showing up in the kitchen carrying and then serving the president's dinner?

No chance.

She had to proceed to look into this situation, but to do so cautiously. The likelihood was that the president himself had chosen to bend the rules for the sake of convenience and that Griswold was simply complying with his commander's wishes.

When they arrived at the medical van in the motorcade, the Secret Service agents were poised to take off. Alison glanced up ahead at the lead limo. Gabe would be settled in next to the guy who had once been his drinking buddy in school and now was the most influential, potent person on Earth. She wondered whether the founding fathers, had they known about nuclear weapons and drug abuse, homelessness and health insurance, space exploration and runaway science, would still have chosen to cede such awesome responsibility to just a single individual.

From the president's point of view, the day had been an incredible success. Thanks to Gabe Singleton's quickness, clinical judgment, and quiet competence, his asthma attack had been aborted before it could evolve into a full-blown medical crisis. Once broken, the bronchospasm and mucus production abated, and within less than half an hour Stoddard had tucked his shirt in (leaving the collar and cuffs open), taken hold of his IV pole, and bravely wheeled it out to the podium. He stood there, bracing himself on the pole just a bit as boisterous applause filled the hall. Then he explained that his doctor had easily broken what he described as a mild asthma attack and would be removing the IV as soon as the last of the solution had run in. Stoddard then spoke ad lib for two minutes or so—more than enough to gain closure with the donors, exposure before the reporters and cameras, and, Alison guessed, smiling to herself, control of at least 90 percent of the nation's asthmatic vote.

The move to return to his supporters was blatantly theatrical—Ringling Brothers all the way. But given the potential danger of his asthma attack, there was nothing bogus about it. And judging from the prolonged, enthusiastic response of the audience, what could have been something of a body blow to his campaign—increased concern about his health—had instead become a war cry signaling that he was fearlessly ready to move forward with his Vision for America.

Down the road, it seemed as if Andrew Stoddard might point to this day as one in which the many facets of his run for reelection were triumphantly brought together.

Still it seemed possible—just possible—that within the ranks of his supporters, specifically in the person of his favorite, most trusted Secret Service guard, there was potential trouble.

CHAPTER 25

There was no one who passed the blind man, making his way through the throngs at Reagan National Airport, who did not take notice of him. He was tall and broad shouldered, with a long ebony ponytail protruding from beneath a white cowboy hat that featured an ornate band of turquoise medallions linked by hand-tooled silver. He strode ahead with surprising confidence, his thin white cane tapping away at the tiled floor like an insect's antenna. His face, high cheekboned and powerful, was the reddish brown of the clay that for centuries had been the bedrock of his people, the Arapaho.

As the man emerged from the security zone, Gabe quietly fell in stride beside him.

"Dr. Singleton, I presume," Dr. Kyle Blackthorn said after just a step or two, though there had been no physical contact between them.

"How'd you guess?"

"It was no guess, my friend, I assure you of that. And I really don't think you want to know which of my senses were at work."

"No. No, I suppose I don't. Luggage?"

"Right here. One night's worth of clothes and my testing materials. I'm due back to teach at Wind River the day after tomorrow."

"You still go out to the reservation every week?"

"Just one of the tribulations of being a role model."

"Those kids are lucky to have you."

"I am the lucky one, just as are you for the work that you do when you don't have to."

"Well said. Thank you for dropping everything and coming so quickly. I know how busy you are."

Gabe smiled as one traveler after another turned to watch them pass. He had wondered how easy it was going to be to sneak the six-foot, three-inch Indian into the president's residence at the White House. Now Gabe found himself searching for another place the two men could meet for a three- or four-hour evaluation. As difficult as Blackthorn was to hide, the President of the United States was even more so. Their session was simply going to have to be in the White House residence.

"You ready to go to work?" Gabe asked.

"The president?" Blackthorn asked in a near whisper.

Gabe nodded.

"Good guess," he said.

"Not too difficult. You were front-page news in the local rag when you left. Everyone was talking about it. Before this, they were proud of the things you have done with the children. Now, they are absolutely in awe."

With no prompting from Gabe, Blackthorn turned toward the stairway leading down to the parking area. Perhaps it was some telltale sound from the roadway below, perhaps an increase in the foot traffic heading in that direction or maybe just a slight gust of breeze. Whatever senses he was reacting to, the psychologist responded with certainty, his cane confirming more than directing.

As far as Gabe knew. Blackthorn had been blind since birth. No one in Tyler spoke about it very much. It was as if no one really saw it as a disability—at least not in him. Certainly it was a drawback to be overcome, but rather as an inescapable fact of the man's life—something to work with rather than around, almost like being left-handed.

On the way into town from the airport, Gabe recounted in detail the bizarre and remarkable episode he had observed in Drew Stoddard before learning from his wife and chief of staff that it was at least the fourth one.

Blackthorn, his trademark hat resting on his lap, dark glasses shielding whatever there was of his eyes, listened quietly, but Gabe could tell he was processing every word. In the courtroom, The Chief, as he had inevitably come to be called away from the stenographers, was a forensic expert witness to be reckoned with. He was equally adept at exposing defendants attempting to hide behind a plea of insanity, and championing with irrefutable logic the defense's claims of diminished capacity.

"You have a sense of how these episodes began?" he asked when Gabe had finished his detailed description.

"I wasn't there, but his chief of staff tells me it was quite sudden. He reports a twitch or a tic at the corner of the president's eye—the right one, I think—then some disjointed, word-salad sentences, then suddenly, boom, a full-blown, manic craziness with hallucinations, motor irritability, and pressured speech. By the time I arrived at his bedside, he was really quite mad—disoriented, hyperkinetic, sweating, blood pressure and pulse headed off the charts."

"Then just as quickly it all began to resolve."

"Exactly. Over about twenty or thirty minutes, the mania and hallucinations gave way to profound fatigue and, soon, exhausted sleep."

There was a prolonged silence, eventually ended by the psychologist as they cruised over the George Mason Bridge and into the city.

"We shall see what the testing blots and the blocks have to tell us," he said, "but off what you've told me, it sounds toxic."

"Some kind of drug reaction?"

"Or something that's being secreted in his body."

"Like from a tumor? I thought about that. He's had a normal MRI and a CT scan, but they were just of his head. A chemical-secreting tumor could be anywhere."

"So what have you chosen to do about all this?"

"Do?"

"Well, the man does have a fair amount of—how should I say it?—responsibility."

"He's been a hell of a president."

"I agree. So do most of the minorities in the country."

"And over the next four years there's no telling how much he can accomplish."

"Provided he doesn't go off the deep end and push the shiny big red button."

"I need to find out what's wrong with him, Kyle."

"I'll say you do. You sure you're not the one who needs help?"

Gabe risked a glance over at the man, but The Chief was facing stoically ahead.

"I wish I were back home," Gabe said.

Blackthorn set a hand on Gabe's shoulder.

"When it's time, you'll come home," he said. "Meanwhile, the president has the right doctor taking care of him. Of that I am certain."

With help from Treat Griswold, Gabe had surprisingly little trouble getting Blackthorn into the White House and then to the medical clinic, which had been closed since before the motorcade to Baltimore. Then, after ensuring that there were no reporters or other surprise visitors wandering about, Griswold stood guard as the two doctors crossed to the elevator and rode up to the president's residence, where the chief executive waited with his wife.

After brief introductions, Gabe took advantage of the situation to confirm that Stoddard's lungs were still clear and that he was, in fact, ready and able to undergo extensive psychological and neurological testing. In case of any problem, Carol would remain close by in another room and Gabe would be in the clinic. Neither the president nor the First Lady showed any particular reaction to Blackthorn's appearance or his blindness, although Stoddard did ask the man if he was Democrat or Republican.

"Arapaho," was the reply.

CHAPTER 26

*B*ack in his office, Gabe fished out Lily Sexton's card and called her at Lily Pad Stables. The secretary-designate answered on the first ring, prompting Gabe to wonder what the caller ID read for calls originating in the White House.

"This is Lily."

Gabe flashed on the woman, elegant, alluring, and stately in her tuxedo—clearly one of a kind. Despite the drawing in Ferendelli's desk and the notion that Lily and the man were involved with one another, the idea of spending some time with her, especially on horseback, held definite appeal.

"Lily, it's Gabe. Gabe Singleton."

"Well hi. After the other night I was hoping I might hear from you. Everything all right with the president?"

Gabe focused on what he and Lattimore had told the world after Stoddard missed the state dinner. It was no surprise, really, but the list of those anxious for information on Drew's health kept growing.

"He's doing fine."

"Excellent. After we spoke the other night, then you rushed away on your mission of caring, I decided you needed Serious Therapy, so I've been anxiously waiting to tell you."

"Are you that perceptive? Half the people who know me think I could use a good shrink."

"Not a shrink, Doctor, *Serious Therapy.* He's my best trail horse—an absolute hunk."

"And here I thought you had brilliantly diagnosed me after just a few minutes together."

"Maybe I have. We'll see what you need after you spend some time on S.T. I hope you'll agree this is some horse. The president's ridden him twice."

"Before he became the leader of the free world, Drew and I rode several times at my ranch in Wyoming. For a Navy man, he knows his way around a horse pretty well. Serious Therapy sounds perfect for me."

"Name the day."

"Tomorrow if possible. Sometime in the late morning or early afternoon?"

"Serious Therapy tomorrow at, say, one. You'll love him."

"I suspect I will."

"Some tea and maybe a little lunch first?"

"That would be perfect. One other thing, Ms. Lily. Do you know very much about nanotechnology?"

There was a hesitation before her reply—just a beat, but definite.

"At this point, before answering, I'm supposed to ask you why you want to know. But instead I'll just tell you that among certain circles I might be considered something of an expert on the subject."

"That's terrific. Do you mind if we make our lunch and ride sort of a nanotechnology in-service? I've done some reading, but I want to know more."

"I'll do what I can. Do you want to tell me why the sudden interest?"

"Sure. It's probably nothing, but one of the other docs here told me that my predecessor, Jim Ferendelli, had a rather large medical library in his house in Georgetown. I thought I might borrow some of his basic medical textbooks to use in the White House medical office. I'm sort of famous back home for looking things up in front of my patients. I figure that if they know I'm not afraid to admit I don't know something, they might lower their expectations a bit.

"Anyhow, I mentioned the book thing to Drew, and he had a key to Ferendelli's place. So I went there. In addition to just the sort of books I need, the doctor had a number of volumes dealing with nanotechnology. I brought them home with me and just started reading. Fascinating, fascinating stuff. But educating myself has been a slow-going process. I thought maybe you could give me a bit more grounding."

"I'll be happy to try," Lily said. "It's impressive that he should be interested in such an arcane subject."

"Did he ever mention that interest to you?"

"Hardly. In fact, except for maybe one brief introduction, I've never spoken to the man."

Gabe felt himself go cold.

The drawing in Ferendelli's desk drawer, quite well done, with obvious caring, was clearly of Lily. It seemed possible, albeit remotely so, that he could have done it from photographs, but why? How could the two of them not have known one another, and quite well at that?

Gabe struggled to remain calm and to come up in tempo with just the right words.

"Well," he managed, "it sounds like you would have had something in common with him."

"Probably so. In addition to industrial manufacturing and communications, medicine is probably the most promising area of nanotechnologic research."

Gabe's mind was swirling through the possible reasons that Lily would deny knowing Ferendelli. He felt desperate to get off the phone before he somehow gave his concern away.

"So then," he said, "tomorrow it will be nanotechnology and Serious Therapy."

"And tea," Lily Sexton said. "Never forget the tea."

CHAPTER 27

*L*ate afternoon shadows stretched across the esplanade as Treat Griswold, driving a two-year-old silver Jeep Grand Cherokee, maneuvered through light traffic. Half a dozen car-lengths behind, Alison followed warily. There was no reason for Griswold to suspect he was being tailed, but he was a pro and he had seen Alison on several different occasions, including just that morning in Baltimore.

After her return by motorcade from the Convention Center, Alison had spoken to Secret Service director of internal affairs Mark Fuller, who had originally sent her undercover into the White House medical office. Careful not to allude to Griswold in any way, she explained that while she was waiting for something, *anything,* to break regarding the Ferendelli disappearance, she had decided to do background checks on a number of White House employees, including several agents. Fuller considered her request for access to personnel files and then somewhat reluctantly gave her the passwords she needed.

Alison took pains to review the files of a dozen randomly chosen men and women. The last thing she wanted anyone to know was that she had a particular interest in any one of them—especially the president's number-one protector. It was frightening to know that she was dealing with perhaps the most thorough, effective, efficient investigative agency in the country. If she had been asked to keep an eye on the White House, there was no reason *not* to suspect that someone had been given the task of keeping an eye on her. Mixing her subjects and keeping meticulous records as to how long she spent on the files of each, she began to piece together the story of the man who had been decorated three times for his service to three different presidents but who also seemed to have surprisingly little life outside of his job.

Griswold, a state high school wrestling champion, born and raised in Kansas and educated in criminal justice at K State, had turned fifty-one this past month. He had been married and divorced twice before he was thirty-two—the first time after four years, the second after just two. No children. No subsequent marriages. He lived in what sounded like an apartment complex in Dale City, Virginia, thirty miles south of the capital. There was really remarkably little else to be learned about the man.

He earned a better than decent salary, approaching $175,000 with Senior Executive Service and SAIC—Special Agent in Charge of detail—pay factored in, but didn't seem to live up to his means. He was right up to the minute in terms of using his fairly generous allotment of vacation time, but as far as she could tell, he had never taken a day of sick time. Never.

As part of her training, Alison had taken courses in single and team surveillance. Keep slightly to the right of the car ahead. No sudden lane changes. Anticipate the moves of the quarry, and be ready to react smoothly. Employing every rule she could remember, she followed Griswold across the Potomac and onto I-95 leading south into Virginia. On paper, and indeed in real life, Treat Griswold seemed almost too good to be true. To this point, in addition to his not being among the most physically attractive men in the world, the only chink in his highly polished armor seemed to be the inhaler he carried in breach of regulations, or at least in violation of tradition and unwritten protocol.

The likely explanation, hardly a thrilling one, was that the president had simply found it more convenient to do things that way, rather than having to scout down the doctor on duty each time he felt wheezy while away from the medicine cabinet in the official residence.

Griswold was driving in no particular hurry, but now, for the first time, something curious had happened. He had passed the exit to Dale City and was continuing south on the interstate. Alison pulled her road map up and smoothed it open over the steering wheel. There was no doubt about it. Griswold wasn't headed home. Five miles . . . ten . . . twenty. . . .

Alison fished two sticks of bubble gum–flavored Trident from her purse and began working them over with vigor. She had been a serious gum chewer since grammar school, having made her way from Fleers Dubble Bubble, through Juicy Fruit, to Wrigley's Spearmint, and finally to Trident sugar-free, with an occasional jawbreaker thrown in. It wasn't the most attractive habit in the world, she knew, but she was hooked. Over the years, she had come to chew mostly when she was tense, and like a ventriloquist of sorts, she had mastered the art of chewing, when she had to, without visibly moving her jaws.

They were entering Fredericksburg when Griswold eased off the highway. Alison slowed and managed to keep a car between them, but the situation was getting dicey. Still, there was no hint from ahead that she had been spotted. She risked dropping back half a block.

According to her map, the city was located on the Rappahannock River, fifty or so miles south of Washington and the same distance north of Richmond. If her memory was right and Richmond, the capital of the state, had also been the capital of the Confederacy, then Fredericksburg must have been in a hell of a tense spot during the Civil War.

They crossed the river and entered a tangle of streets with rows of minimally maintained buildings. Alison was a block away when Griswold suddenly pulled into a short drive in front of a two-bay cinder-block garage, with separate pairs of doors. She ducked down and peered over the dash as he surveyed the street. Finally, apparently convinced that it was safe, Griswold pulled open the doors of the nearer bay and quickly drove inside.

The street, totally deserted at the moment, had a few duplexes and triplexes but hardly seemed like the sort of place where people paid much attention to their neighbors' business. Five minutes passed. Alison was about to drive past to determine where the man might have gone when he emerged, having changed his black suit for a sporty dark windbreaker and tan slacks and his business shoes for a stylish pair of loafers—European, she guessed. His bulk actually seemed somewhat transformed, although there was little he could do about his thick, stubby neck and bald spot.

He locked the doors behind him and again warily scanned the street. Hunched low behind the wheel, Alison breathed deeply and exhaled slowly, trying to calm herself.

At that moment, again apparently satisfied that he was unobserved, Griswold unlocked the second set of doors. Hinges badly in need of oiling screeched as he swung the doors open and disappeared again into the garage. After a few seconds, the subdued thrum of an engine cut through the still air. Alison slid down even farther, until she could just see up ahead from beneath the top of the steering wheel. The engine noise continued— a low, even, powerful growl. Finally, the agent rolled backward out of the garage at the wheel of a pristine silver Porsche 911 Cabriolet convertible— eighty or ninety thousand at least, Alison guessed.

Clearly anxious to get away as quickly as possible, his pate reflecting the sun, Griswold closed and locked the garage doors, swung out of the drive, and sped back down the street in the direction they had come, passing just a few feet from where Alison was huddled under the wheel.

By the time she dared to sit up and turn her Camry around, the Porsche was gone. Pessimistic about her chances of reconnecting, she guessed that Griswold must have headed toward the interstate. Doing eighty, she weaved through traffic back across the Rappahannock. At the last possible instant, she caught sight of the Porsche—a bullet streaking onto I-95, headed south away from D.C. and toward Richmond. It took a while to catch up, but she strongly sensed she had done it without being spotted. By the time they reached the outskirts of the capital of the Confederacy she had written down the license number.

The car, the clothes, even his swagger—it was as if Treat Griswold had driven into the rickety garage in Fredericksburg and emerged a different man. Now that man was easing off the interstate into the low-rent district of Richmond. Comfortable with the pattern of his driving and his lack of attention to the road behind him, Alison pulled over nearly a block away from where the Porsche had stopped. They were on a street of aging gabled houses that had probably been very special during the Civil War but were now all in need of scraping, paint, and carpentry—all, that is, but one.

Griswold turned right into the driveway of that house—an immaculately restored Victorian, painted gray with maroon trim and white mullions on what had to be at least two dozen windows. It was at once massive and elegant, perhaps half-again larger than the other homes on Beechtree Road. The rooflines of its two street-side spires were gracefully curved, and the lower two of three stories featured broad, circular porches. The curtains on most of the windows were drawn, although, like the street in Fredericksburg, Beechtree seemed like one where the residents kept to their own business.

By the time Alison risked cruising slowly past the drive, Griswold was gone and the 911 was locked in the garage.

Out of nothing, something.

An asthma inhaler had led her a hundred miles from the White House to . . . to what? A brothel of some sort? Her instincts said no, but her instincts had led her astray more than once over the years.

She noted down the address of the house next to the license plate number of the Porsche. There was no way to check on the owner of either without giving away information Alison needed to keep to herself. She would just have to wait until she got back to D.C. The day might come when she would need to blow the whistle on Treat Griswold for something illegal, but when and if she did, her case would be a hell of a lot better documented than the one at the hospital in Los Angeles had been and she would be a hell of a lot more prepared for the counterattack that was sure to follow.

Now she would just have to settle in, be patient, and wait for something to happen.

With the late afternoon sluggishly giving way to dusk, she parked down the street, replaced her Trident with two fresh sticks, and settled in. Three hours, she decided, sliding in a best of Sting CD and seeking out "Fields of Gold." If nothing happened after three more hours, she would head back to the city and resume her one-woman stakeout another day.

Not surprisingly, as the time passed she found herself thinking more and more about Gabe Singleton. There was a sweetness and vulnerability beneath his rugged cowboy exterior that had drawn her in immediately. The men in her past had been, well, slick, she acknowledged—smart, self-assured, ambitious, and, almost to a man, not totally forthcoming. Gabe had lost his faith in her honesty the first night they had met when he caught her in the lie she was forced to tell by being undercover. Still, there was no way she could have let him be killed to preserve her status as an undercover agent and no way she could explain her actions that early morning other than with the truth.

He was even wondering if the whole assassin thing was a setup to gain his confidence and lead him to share some presidential medical secrets. Those suspicions were totally off base, but confronting him and denying his concerns would only strengthen them.

She also had chosen not to share the rumors she had heard that the president was not mentally well. They were grossly unsubstantiated—questions from medical unit personnel, whispered in dim, late night taverns—hardly the sort of thing she would expect Gabe to share with her. Where her attraction to the man might lead, if anyplace, was a total mystery at this point. What she did know was that there was something special she felt when she was around him—an almost little-girl musing of what it might be like to curl up with him on a chilly winter night. But she also wondered why a man as bright, handsome, and caring wasn't married . . . or a father.

What secret are you hiding, Gabe Singleton? she asked herself now. *Why do you seem so vulnerable?*

An hour passed.

Inside the house, lights appeared behind a few of the windows that weren't covered by drapes. The two functioning streetlights remaining on

Beechtree Road, neither of them near where she was parked, winked on. Then, just as Alison was considering limiting her time there from three hours to two, the front porch light came on, the front door opened, and two people emerged. Alison brought her field glasses up and focused on their faces. One was a statuesque woman with a face about the color of her own. Latino, Alison guessed.

The other was younger—much younger. Possibly ten or eleven at the oldest. Like the older woman, she was mocha skinned and dark eyed, and also like her, she was pretty. No, not pretty, Alison suddenly realized, stunning, with perfect, gentle features, an incredibly sensual mouth, a lithe body—still more girl-like than woman, but with breasts that were already well beyond nubs. Such things were almost always a matter of personal taste, she acknowledged, but the girl was as beautiful as any young woman Alison had ever seen.

What was Treat Griswold doing with such an attractive woman and a spectacularly beautiful girl? It seemed as if the only ones who could supply the answer to that question were the woman and girl themselves. The pair, arm-in-arm, descended the stairs and began to walk leisurely in the direction away from where Alison was parked.

Alison waited, sorting out her options. Then she set the binoculars down, turned off the CD, and followed.

CHAPTER 28

*A*nother liar?

An hour had passed following Gabe's conversation with Lily Sexton—a conversation in which she denied knowing a man who possessed a beautifully and accurately rendered charcoal drawing of her in the drawer of his desk. The questions came far faster than their answers. Was it possible the drawing wasn't of her? If it was, could it have been done from a photograph—perhaps one in a magazine? Given her style, poise, unusual beauty, and acknowledged intellect, it seemed that if Jim Ferendelli was obsessed with her from afar, he wouldn't have been the first.

Could she simply have been frightened about being connected to any scandal when she was so close to being the subject of a major confirmation hearing in Congress? That possibility made more than a little sense.

Was it worth confronting her with the drawing and asking for some sort of explanation?

And finally, would it be possible to trust anything that she said?

Questions without answers.

Gabe massaged the sudden throbbing in his temples, pulled out the vial of painkillers in his desk drawer, then just as quickly put them back again. His headache was real enough, but the solution lay in getting at the causes—diagnosing the president, finding Jim Ferendelli, and getting the hell back to Wyoming, where, most of the time at least, hidden agendas weren't a way of life. Maybe the headache would help Gabe stay sharp. It was a reasonable guess the codeine wouldn't.

A floor above, in the presidential residence, his friend Kyle Blackthorn was administering the neuropsychological tests that would go far in determining whether or not the man entrusted with the safety of every being on the planet was fit to continue in that role. Blackthorn was a person of great character, passion, and intellect. He had never, as far as Gabe knew, come to a forensic decision regarding a patient or defendant that had proven to be inaccurate.

Vice President Cooper, Magnus Lattimore, Admiral Wright, LeMar Stoddard, Lily Sexton, and of course Alison—were any of them someone Gabe could truly rely upon? Probably not. Certainly not in the way he could rely upon The Chief.

Gabe sat at his desk, biding time by shuffling papers, wondering if it was worth contacting Alison to arrange a repeat trip to Ferendelli's brownstone. No, he decided, not with her, anyway. She was far too eager to learn about the president's health—at least that was the way it appeared to him. It would be terrific, absolutely wonderful, if he was wrong about her. She had never been far from his thoughts since the drive back to her place from Ferendelli's.

During the president's asthma attack, she had functioned with quickness, medical knowledge, and, except for a brief moment when she seemed oddly distracted, composure. Cinnie had the same qualities. Alison seemed to be telling the truth about her role as an undercover agent for the Secret Service, but she might have been forced to improvise after her quick thinking saved his life—or at least *seemed* to have saved his life. If the shooting wasn't something she had orchestrated, she needed an immediate explanation for why she had been following him from the White House in the early morning hours. If it weren't true, the undercover assignment story was brilliant. But brilliant improvisation or not, it would still have been a lie.

Then there was the matter of the missing tubes of blood. How would Alison explain that? Could anyone but she possibly have been responsible?

Another hour passed. Gabe's brain felt as if it were being squeezed in a vise. His headache—tension, he felt certain—failed to respond to some Tylenol, but still the codeine remained in the drawer. *I never took a drug that I didn't have a pain for,* he had once heard a recovering addict say at an AA meeting.

I never took a drug that I didn't have a pain for.

It had been a long, long while since he last went to a recovery meeting, Gabe thought now. A couple of years at least. Maybe it was time he started going again. The AA program taught not only how to stay away from a drink or a drug for a day but also how to do the right thing when it came to making difficult decisions. Maybe it was time. Why in the hell had he stopped going in the first place?

Grateful that he had closed the medical office for the day and diverted all traffic except the president to the Eisenhower Building clinic, Gabe returned some routine phone calls, then leaned back in his chair and dozed off—one of the perks of having such a truncated practice. The ringing telephone intruded on a hazy scene in which he and Alison were riding across the desert together, bareback on what looked to be Condor. Her arms were locked around Gabe's waist and her cheek was pressed against his back. Blearily he checked his watch. Blackthorn had been with the president for four and a half hours.

"Dr. Singleton," he answered, the words reminding himself of that fact.

"Yes sir, Doctor. Agent Blaisdell here. I'm upstairs in the residence. Your man has finished with the president, sir. We're checking to see if the coast is clear; then we'll bring your man down."

"Everything all right?"

"As far as I know, sir. Agent Griswold signed out a few hours ago, and just asked us to contact you in the office when the president was done with his visitor."

"Well then, bring him down, but be very careful he isn't spotted by anyone."

Gabe hurried to the small bathroom and splashed cold water on his face. From the moment Magnus Lattimore had led him into the president's bedroom, from the moment he had seen his onetime roommate thrashing about, sweating profusely, and babbling incoherently, Gabe had felt isolated—alone with his sensibilities and his emotions; alone with what *seemed* right and what *felt* right; alone with the awesome pressure of the Twenty-fifth Amendment. Now he would at least have an ally he could rely on in the struggle to sort things out—a friend with no hidden agenda and nothing at stake except getting to the right diagnosis.

Gabe had just toweled off when, without a knock, the outer door to the medical office opened and closed. Hat in hand, looking none the worse for his lengthy ordeal, Kyle Blackthorn stood alone in the center of the waiting room. He set his valise of testing supplies on the floor by his feet. It looked to Gabe as if Blackthorn were quietly invoking the senses available to him, hypertrophied from overuse like the muscles of a weight lifter, to get the lay of his situation. After just a few seconds he turned directly toward the small bathroom.

"So, Doctor," he said, "you were napping in my absence."

Gabe stepped into the waiting room.

"Actually, I . . . what I was doing was . . . okay, yes, actually, yes, I was. But how did . . . ?"

"If you hadn't been napping you would have been out here to welcome me back, not in there toweling off your face."

"Well, at least you didn't begin your explanation with, 'Elementary, my dear Singleton.'"

"I thought about it. Ready to talk?"

"Almost five hours. That must have been quite a session."

"For an incredibly impatient, kinetic man, your friend Mr. Stoddard displayed remarkable restraint and a deep desire to get to the bottom of things."

"I'm not surprised."

"Your office the best place?"

Gabe flashed on Alison working undercover for the Secret Service. Was it possible she had somehow managed to bug the medical office? It seemed highly unlikely, but his trust in anything or anyone had been pulled perilously thin.

"You hungry?"

"I can always eat."

"And I could use some fresh air. Let's go have an early dinner at the Old Ebbitt Grill. Magnus Lattimore, the chief of staff here, took me there. The food's excellent, and at its quietest the place is noisy enough so that the only person anyone can hear is the one sitting directly across the table or right beside them."

"I am aware that you are in a hurry to come to an understanding on this matter," Blackthorn said, "but I assume you know that my final conclusions will have to wait until I have gone over all the test results and my notes and correlated them."

"Notes?"

"I have written nothing down, but I have used an electronic, Braille typewriter."

"Just hold on to it tightly."

"The moment someone tries to get into my notes without using the right password, the machine erases its contents."

"So, you want to review your notes and correlate them with the test results. Makes sense. But you have formed some preliminary opinion?"

"I have."

"And you'll share that with me?"

"I will."

The two men left the White House through the East Wing and headed up Fifteenth Street through fading afternoon sun.

"So," Gabe said, "thanks again for doing this. I know how busy you are and how much you don't like leaving home—especially for government work."

"I've never been one to hold a grudge," Blackthorn said. "Whenever I'm troubled about the genocide of my people, I just think about all those big, shiny casinos and how reassuring it is to have organized crime on hand to help take care of us."

Gabe sympathetically patted him on the back. He had heard the man eloquently decry the subject of Indian genocide in any number of speeches and forums over the years.

"So," Gabe said, "over and above the testing, what did you think of my patient?"

"What do you want me to say, Gabe?"

"I don't know. I guess I want you to tell me that as a psychiatrist *and* a psychologist you found him to be a man of magnificent character, who has the potential for true greatness as a leader."

This time it was Blackthorn who patted Gabe on the back.

"My dear friend," he said, "to make that pronouncement, I would have to be with the person in question for a good deal longer than the few hours I spent with your Mr. Stoddard this afternoon. Besides, if nothing else, this is a time for objectivity."

"Objectivity," Gabe echoed as they entered the Old Ebbitt Grill.

The restaurant, refurbished from a mid-nineteenth-century saloon, still featured dark-stained wood, marble-topped bars set in brass, and a Beaux Arts facade. According to framed pictures and documents on the walls, the place had been a favorite of Presidents Grant, Cleveland, Harding, and Teddy Roosevelt. Gabe wondered how many times issues affecting the future of a presidency and the country had been discussed at its tables. Certainly, few would guess that the tall blind man and his wind-worn companion were about to become part of that particular history.

The Old Ebbitt was neither as crowded nor as noisy as it would probably be in another hour, but the young and beautiful movers and shakers of the capital, along with the young and beautiful mover-and-shaker wannabes, were already two to three deep along the length of the bar.

"I don't think we have a place quite like this back in Tyler," Gabe said as they were waiting to be shown to a booth.

Blackthorn inhaled deeply through his nose.

"Smells like success," he said.

He folded his cane, took a seat opposite Gabe, and asked only for water. Later, after they had talked about almost everyone of interest in Tyler and ordered fish, Gabe could wait no longer.

"So?"

"Let us not use names at all," Blackthorn suggested.

"Agreed."

"First of all, on the surface at least, the man really seemed to be trying. He certainly had important things to do, but he never made me feel as if I were an intrusion on his busy day. He was never curt or condescending, and as I said before, he sincerely seems to want to get to the bottom of what is going on.

"In addition to the actual testing, I took an extensive history from him, stressing what he remembered from each of the episodes, and also an exhaustive history from his wife, stressing exactly what she had witnessed. Allowing for the fact that the husband remembers little of the details, their descriptions of each of the events were similar, but there were differences in what they described from one event to the next."

"Explain."

"I really can't, Gabe. At least not until I put all the test results together, but these episodes aren't behaving with the consistency of, like, a seizure with a specific focus in the brain, or a tumor."

Gabe glanced around to ensure there was no one he knew or who seemed to be paying undue attention to them. The place was filling up, but none of the faces were familiar.

"So, at this point, what's your guess?"

Blackthorn leaned forward.

"Toxicity," he said in a gravelly whisper.

"Drugs?"

"Some kind, yes."

"But—?"

"Don't ask, Gabe, because I don't have the answers. Right now, though, that's the only thing that makes any sense to me. The man is taking something that's causing this, or someone is finding a way to get something into his body."

Gabe sighed and exhaled slowly. The implications of what the psychologist was suggesting were staggering.

"I don't even begin to know what to do with that."

"Those blood samples you drew would be a good place to start. I would find the best forensic chemist you can find and have the specimens tested for anything that's not normally found in the human body—anything and everything."

Gabe felt sick about having allowed the samples to vanish. He should have had the presence of mind to take them back to his apartment.

"Will do," he said, wondering if there was anything to be gained by drawing blood from Drew in between the attacks. Certainly, a negative report would prove nothing.

"There's more," Blackthorn said, smoothing a few errant wisps of long gray and black hairs from his forehead.

"Go on."

"I don't quite know how to say this, Gabe, so I'm going to start by telling you that you can accept what I'm going to share or reject it. And other than to say that I believe my lack of eyesight since birth has everything to do with what I'm going to tell you, I have no real explanation. But I have had enough experience with my unusual ability to believe with certainty that it exists."

"Unusual ability?"

The psychologist hesitated, perhaps to emphasize that what he was about to disclose was personal and private.

"Most but not all the time," he said finally, "I can tell with some consistency when someone is lying. Call it a sixth sense if you wish, although in my case it would be the fifth. But I get a strange, almost indescribable feeling deep in my thoughts when a person isn't telling the truth, or even when they are withholding information and telling a half-truth. There's a word that I believe is from Zen—*shingan.* It means 'mind's eye' and refers to the ability to sense a person's thoughts or feelings. I believe that I am in touch with my *shingan.*"

Over the years, Gabe had encountered enough examples of the power of the mind-body connection not to be surprised by anything in that regard. But that was the mind-body connection within a person. The notion that there were individuals who could read the auras or minds of others still had not taken root for him. Now a man he respected to the point of reverence was claiming to be something of a living polygraph—a psychic of sorts.

Shingan.

"What does this ability have to do with the person in question here?" Gabe managed, finally.

"Well," Blackthorn said, "I am not sure I can completely answer your question. But I can tell you that the subject is lying about something, or withholding information."

"Lying about what?"

"I don't know. But whatever it is, is powerful. I felt it almost every time he spoke, regardless of the subject. There is more to your man than we know or he lets on. Perhaps much more."

"But—"

"It may be that in decoding and interpreting the tests I administered something will become clearer. For the moment, what I have told you is all there is."

"And you feel pretty strongly about this *shingan* . . . this ability of yours?"

Kyle Blackthorn lifted his head so that he was facing Gabe directly. The lights behind Gabe reflected eerily off Blackthorn's dark glasses.

"I feel as strongly about my ability," he said, "as I do about the fact that you have chosen not to tell me that the blood samples you drew on our patient have disappeared."

CHAPTER 29

T^{he} attractive woman and her striking young companion wandered down Beechtree Road in no particular hurry, speaking nonstop and animatedly, often punctuating their conversation with laughter. Alison had grown up around both Spanish and Creole French and was competent, if not fluent, in both. From a distance, unable to hear distinctly even through the open car window, she sensed that they were speaking Spanish.

At the fourth or fifth cross street, Foster, the pair turned right. Alison cruised past them for two blocks, checking their progress through the rearview mirror, then turned onto a side street, drove half a block down, and waited. If she had blundered by assuming the pair were going to stay on Foster, she would have to decide whether it was worth driving around to find them again. Perhaps she should call off the stakeout for the time being, determine the owner of the Porsche and of the elegant Victorian home on Beechtree, and try again another time. Two tense minutes later, the women crossed the side street where Alison was parked and continued down Foster. She left her notes and field glasses on the floor of her Camry and headed after them.

Foster was a busy commercial street, though still with a small-neighborhood feel. The facades of the bistros, specialty stores, and other merchants had been refurbished for a number of blocks, giving the area a surprisingly quaint charm. Walking briskly, Alison followed the pair from across the street until they turned into A Place for Nails, a small salon, one door from the corner of Foster and Coulter.

Half an hour for the manicure and polish, Alison figured, followed by fifteen or twenty minutes in the drying chair or whatever they used. Fifty minutes—an eternity for someone like her, cursed with the patience of a gnat. It was doubtful the two would go anyplace that would shed light on who they were and how they were connected to the president's number-one protector. The only option seemed to be to speak to them directly.

WALK-INS WELCOME, a sign in the window encouraged. Alison examined her nails, which she kept in decent shape for work but did not feel comfortable covering with any color.

As she approached the girl at the counter—Southeast Asian, as were all the manicurists in the salon Alison had gone to shortly after her arrival in D.C.—she realized that she had caught a huge break. There were four manicurists in A Place for Nails. Two were starting work on the woman and the girl, and one was chattering in badly broken English with a blue-haired woman in her eighties. The fourth was at the counter, welcoming Alison with a cheery smile.

"You have time for me?" Alison asked, holding out her nails.

"Oh, bad, very bad," the woman said, her speech nearly identical to that of the girls at the salon in D.C. "What you do? Wash dishes? Build houses?"

From her spot in the first chair, the girl from Beechtree Road peered up to check out the newcomer. Clearly Hispanic, she was even more stunning than Alison had appreciated through the binoculars. It was difficult to tell if she wore any makeup, but there was certainly no need. Her light mocha face was smooth and stress free, with dark, doelike eyes, long lashes, and full, sensual lips. Beneath her ochre tank top, her breasts were already diverting, though not, Alison guessed, nearly as exciting to men as they would be in another year or so.

The girl's older companion was seated with her back to the counter and so missed the brief connection that was taking place. Her charge, if, in fact, that was their relation, smiled somewhat demurely, then lowered her wonderful eyes and turned her attention back to the manicure.

"Actually," Alison said to the manicurist, still totally uncertain as to what was going to follow the word, "I run a day care. Children."

Alison could tell by the woman's expression that she was not the least bit interested.

"Choose color," the woman said, motioning to a rack of perhaps eighty small bottles. "Choose, then come."

Alison noted that the chair in which she would be done was catty-corner from the older of Griswold's females. Funny, she mused, that she should think of them that way, even though she had absolutely no clue as to how they and the legendary agent were connected. She hurried over to the rack and quickly selected Marooned on a Desert Isle. She had only a limited time to insert herself into the lives of the two women, and if she made a poor choice in colors, there was always the salon back in D.C.

"Soak. . . . Soak here," the waiflike but clearly controlling manicurist ordered. "What you do to nails?" she mumbled to herself, shaking her head in utter dismay. "What you do?"

Alison risked a glance over at the woman across from her. She had probably been too lost in the girl to notice, but this woman, probably in her early twenties, was, by anyone's standards, nearly as striking. Thin and open in her manner and expression, she was a bit darker skinned than the girl. The woman's eyes were wide and innocent, and her high cheekbones and sensuous mouth were the stuff of cover girls.

Okay, Alison thought to herself. *Be careful, but not too careful. . . . It's showtime.*

"What color did you choose?" she ventured as the icebreaker.

The woman was clearly used to people starting conversations with her and didn't seem to mind.

"I always use Red Anything Good Lately?"

Her English was excellent, with just enough of a Latino edge to make clear that Spanish had once been her primary language. Alison checked the bottle.

"Great name. Great color. I work with kids, so I'm happy when my nails make it for a week."

"Nails bad," the manicurist muttered. "Very bad."

"You run a day-care center. I heard when you were at the counter. Is it near here?"

"No. Actually, it's outside of Fredericksburg. I came down to meet some friends for dinner, but I'm early."

Actually. Alison decided that as often as not, the word introduced a lie—at least in her world it seemed to.

Actually, I'm an astronaut. . . . Yeah, that's it, an astronaut.

Lying had never been pleasant for her and, in fact, she had never been very good at it, but in preparing to go undercover she had been trained in the art and had proven to be quite educable. She wondered if, when this assignment was done, she would be able to undergo some sort of debriefing to reconnect with the honesty she had packed away.

"Oh, I love children," the woman said. "I look forward to having some, myself, one day."

"I'm sure you will. My name's Suzanne."

Error! Alison realized. *Fredericksburg . . . child care . . . Suzanne.* She had already offered way too much information. As facile as she had become at bending and even mauling the truth, she had lost sight of the fact that if the woman reported on their adventure at A Place for Nails, Griswold had all the resources he needed to assure himself that, in all probability, no such combination existed. Having established that fact, he might be much more alert than he otherwise had reason to be. If nothing else, from now on he would be paying much more attention to his rearview mirror.

"And I am Constanza . . . Connie."

"Pleased to meet you, Connie. You two are together?"

She nodded toward the girl.

"Yes."

"Is she your sister?"

The smallest cloud passed over the woman's upbeat expression, then vanished.

"No," she said benignly. "Beatriz is . . . just a friend. I am her . . ." She paused, searching for the right word. "Tutor."

She hadn't prefaced her explanation with the word *actually,* but she might as well have.

Alison decided to push things just a bit.

"Hello, Beatriz," she said to the girl. "I'm Suzanne."

The remarkable beauty smiled over at her.

"Hello, pleased to meet you," she said, her English densely accented. Then she lowered her eyes again to focus on her nails. Her response was packaged, as if she had learned it from a tape . . . or from her tutor.

Hello.

Hello, pleased to meet you.

"Goodness, but she is very beautiful," Alison commented.

"I know," Connie said. "Her English is improving, but she is still embarrassed by it."

"Yours is nearly perfect. Are you both from the same place?"

Keep digging! Alison exhorted herself. *Keep searching for some sort of opening you can begin to probe.*

"Yes, Mexico," Connie said, "but not the same city."

"Oh, I should have been able to tell. I spent years as a child living with my grandmother in Chihuahua. *Beatriz, ¿dónde vas a clase?*"

Where do you go to school?

The girl looked up, nonplussed.

"She is tutored at home," Connie said, quickly and somewhat uncomfortably.

The blue-haired lady had repaired to the small drying area, and the pair were nearing the end of their manicures. They might choose to sit in the drying area as well, or they might simply leave. They didn't seem like the type who would risk smudging, but Alison worried that her question about school may have made the tutor willing to take the risk. She could back off and hope to learn more another time through surveillance, or she could push on and risk further alerting the woman or, worse, having her inadvertently alert Griswold. As things were,

Alison's manicurist was in overdrive, and she had nearly caught up with the others.

A young mother wheeled her sleeping infant into the salon and entered into an animated discussion with the available manicurist. Alison decided to risk a little more probing.

"¿Vives con familia?" she asked, hoping that Beatriz might perk up and join the conversation. *Do you live with relatives?*

"No, well, yes," the woman replied in terse English. "An uncle."

Beatriz stood up at that moment, extending her glistening, wet nails in front of her and turning toward the dryers. She was surprisingly tall, Alison realized—and unselfconsciously regal in her bearing. Her lithe body, highlighted by her designer jeans and tank top, was absolutely arresting. A surpassingly lovely pubescent Mexican girl . . . a beautiful, young tutor . . . no relatives in Richmond except a probably bogus uncle . . . residence in a magnificent old home that almost certainly belonged to some secret incarnation of Treat Griswold. Alison felt queasy as her mind spun through the possibilities.

More information, she thought. *Try for more.*

"What does her uncle do here in Richmond?" she asked in English.

"Beatriz, just a few minutes of drying, then we leave," Connie said in Spanish, gingerly carrying her cell phone to the seat next to the girl. "He is a salesman," she said over her shoulder to Alison.

"There, nails were ugly, now perfect," the bellicose manicurist announced. "Now, go dry."

The drying stations were three opposite three. Alison took one across from Beatriz and Connie, trying to frame a question that would further elucidate Griswold's relationship to the two of them while also gauging when she could ask it without seeming too curious.

"I just broke up with my boyfriend," she tried, in English. "He turned out to be a real jerk—you know, all he cared about was himself. Your uncle wouldn't by any chance be single, would he?"

Beatriz clearly understood, because she looked down and was unable to fully stifle an impish grin.

"He is single," Connie said, "but he works very hard and has no time for any women . . . except for his niece."

Again, the sly smile from Beatriz.

Alison's queasiness intensified. Something was going on between Griswold and the girl. The deepest parts of Alison's intuition were telling her so.

"Ah, well," Alison said. "A man wrapped up in his work is not exactly what I had in mind. I want one who will be all wrapped up in me."

It was time to stop. She had been luckier than she could have ever anticipated being. Now she could drive back to D.C. and ponder the big question: Was there any possible connection between what she had learned about the man today and his misuse of the president's inhaler?

The ring of Connie's cell phone—"La Vida Loca"—burst in on Alison's thoughts.

Expertly careful of her nails, Connie answered it, speaking in a polite half whisper that it was still impossible for Alison not to hear.

"Yes? . . . We are doing fine. . . . She's perfect. Very happy. . . . She chose Scarlet O'Hara, your favorite. . . . Yes, she misses you. . . . Well, we'll be home soon. . . . It is still early. If you wish to go for a ride in the country with her, that would be fine. You know how she loves riding with the top down. . . ."

Again, a restrained smile from Beatriz.

"*Dígale que venga a buscarme*," the girl said softly.

Tell him to pick me up.

CHAPTER 30

Shingan.

Blackthorn was registering at the front desk of the airport hotel when he first became aware of the man, standing not far away to his right. It was his heartbeat that first caught Blackthorn's attention—less than forty a minute, with startling power in every contraction. The man was standing virtually motionless, taking eight or ten deep, even breaths each minute.

Power, Blackthorn thought. *Power and danger.*

Blackthorn picked up his overnight bag and briefcase and headed toward the elevator. The man followed but stopped as Blackthorn knelt and fumbled with the latch on his briefcase until an overweight man and his equally overweight wife moved past him, both breathing heavily from just the simple act of moving.

"How're you doing?" the large man muttered to the dangerous one, who grunted irritably in reply.

The four of them entered the car, with the man taking a position far enough to Blackthorn's right not to make contact. He was five-foot-ten and wore no cologne or other scent. Blackthorn's mind's eye conjured an image of dark hair and dark eyes that were constantly focused on him.

On the third floor, the doors glided open to let the large couple out. Blackthorn waited until the last instant and followed, even though his room was 419—a floor above. The doors closed completely and didn't re-open. Eschewing his cane, Blackthorn followed the couple to where their room was and then passed them and found the staircase at the end of the hall. Perhaps he had misread the man and the situation, he was thinking. His instincts weren't always perfect.

Trying to envision where his room might be located, he entered the corridor of the fourth floor and felt the numbers on the first two rooms— 430 . . . 428. He took his electronic key from his pocket and crossed the hall. 425 . . . 423 . . . 421.

"One more," the man's voice said quietly and calmly, in a pronounced southern drawl. "Four-nineteen, that's what the registration girl said. Four-nineteen. Move naturally or you're dead. You know I'll do that, don't you."

"I do."

The soul of the man was as cold as death.

Blackthorn felt the muzzle of a gun press into his side. He felt stunned that he hadn't detected the man in some way when he opened the stairway door. It was as if he were made of ice.

"Slip the key in the lock, open the door, and go on in. Quickly now."

The man's smooth speech belied his power. Blackthorn sensed that unless he took action, he was not going to live through this encounter.

He set his briefcase down, widened his stance, and began nervously attempting to insert the key in its slot. The man was a professional; he felt certain of that. Not a professional thief—a professional killer.

"Please, please," Blackthorn whimpered as he positioned the key. "I don't have much money, but you can just take what I have. And . . . and my watch. Take my watch."

"The door, open it!"

Blackthorn knew that in the cluttered hotel room he would be totally at the gunman's mercy. Whatever he did had to be now, right here, in the corridor. He had taken years of martial arts—karate for a time, then aikido, the way of spiritual harmony. He had the skill to reverse the situation against most men, but this one, this man of ice, was different.

179

The only advantage he felt certain of was that the man with the slow, measured speech couldn't know Blackthorn had no intention of allowing them both to enter the room. Before he engaged the key, the psychologist stiffened his body. Then, as he felt the muzzle of the gun move slightly away from his side, he spun, swinging his overnight bag in a sharp, vicious arc against where he knew the gunman's hand and wrist had to be. The gun clattered against the wall, and Blackthorn sensed the man diving for it.

In one movement, Blackthorn jammed the key down into the lock, opened the door, and pulled it closed behind him. Two bullets snapped through the wood next to the door handle, but the bolt held.

"Hey, what's going on?" a man's voice called out from down the hallway. "Barbara, the guy's got a fucking gun! Get back inside and call the desk!"

Blackthorn crawled from the doorway into the bathroom and locked that door. If the killer blasted his way into the room, it might take a few more seconds for him to get into the bathroom. Otherwise there wasn't going to be much he could do.

But there were no more gunshots.

Blackthorn stayed where he was. A minute passed, then another. Finally, he heard a pounding on his door, and voices. He had just opened the bathroom door when two security men, both with guns drawn, burst in.

"You all right?"

"I'm fine. What about my briefcase?"

"Jesus, he's blind."

"My briefcase and my glasses," Blackthorn snapped.

"Your glasses are right here," one of the guards said, setting them against Blackthorn's hand, "but there's no briefcase."

"Damn."

"The police are on their way."

"What's he ever gonna be able to tell them?" the other asked. "He can't see a thing."

CHAPTER 31

Five ten, maybe five eleven. Deep southern accent. I'd bet Alabama or Mississippi. It would seem that he followed us when we drove from the White House to the hotel."

Stunned, Gabe listened to Kyle Blackthorn's account of the assault in his hotel.

"A professional killer? How could he have known about you?"

"Somehow, I don't think that White House of yours is a bastion of safe secrets."

"I'm just glad you weren't hurt. And I'm sorry about your briefcase."

"They're not going to get much useful information from it. Besides, my memory is a lot better than my eyesight. I'll get back to you very soon with my conclusions, although you can start with what we spoke about."

"I'm really sorry, Kyle. Do you want to stay here tonight?"

"They've put me up in their VIP suite. And since the guy missed, it seems like a fair trade to me. I'll tell you, though, he's the coldest human being I've ever encountered who wasn't on a slab in the morgue. If you're up against him, you've got problems. Not me, though. First thing tomorrow, I'm off for Cheyenne."

"I wish I were going with you, Kyle. I really miss the plains. I haven't even fully unpacked and I already want to go home."

"You'll do fine. Just watch your topknot, Doc. Not much scares me, but this guy did."

"Count on it, Chief."

Gabe set the phone down and paced the apartment. The circle was wider than he could ever have imagined. Now there appeared to be a professional killer involved. Everybody seemed to know or sense that something was wrong with the president, but gratefully, to this point at least, no one had a handle on precisely what it was or how serious. Meanwhile, the POTUS himself seemed to be doing fine.

After dropping Kyle at the airport hotel, Gabe had driven back to the White House and stopped by the residence. Largely as a result of Drew's heroics at the Baltimore Convention Center, his poll numbers had crept upward for the first time in weeks. Stoddard himself was feeling fine, and Magnus Lattimore assured Gabe that the commander in chief had never been sharper.

Still, it seemed like wishful thinking to believe the episodes of altered thinking and bizarre behavior were finished or that there would continue to be ways to cover them up. Gabe needed answers and he needed them before the Twenty-fifth Amendment once again reared its massive head.

First things first. . . . One day at a time. . . . Accept the things you cannot change; change the things you can. . . .

Funny how in difficult times the old AA slogans kept creeping into his mind. More and more lately. Maybe, he thought now, a couple of meetings wouldn't hurt.

He fixed some decaf and padded over to the dining room table where Ferendelli's nanotechnology library was spread out. A little studying would help take his mind off the attack on Blackthorn. Somehow, someone knew who he was and what he had been doing in D.C. It seemed like only a matter of time before rumor and speculation would turn into headlines.

He pulled a chair up and turned his attention to preparing for the woman who claimed to barely know a man who had a well-rendered sketch of her in the drawer of his desk. In the morning Gabe would be driving out to Lily Sexton's horse farm not far from Flint Hill and the

Shenandoah National Park, eighty miles or so west of the city. If nothing else, she should help him understand Ferendelli's fascination with the science of atomic-size constructions and nanomachines.

The decaf he chose from LeMar Stoddard's stash was a Brazillian blend, so rich and aromatic that it was hard to believe it wasn't high-test. Probably, like everything else in this city, Gabe decided, the coffee was a sham—loaded with caffeine.

Nanotubes and fullerenes.

It took time for Gabe to shuck frightening thoughts of a professional killer and Blackthorn's attack from his consciousness enough to concentrate on the material before him, but finally he was able to begin taking notes and making some drawings.

Nano came from the Greek for "dwarf" and in scientific terms meant one-billionth, as in a billionth of a meter, 1/75,000th the diameter of a human hair. Nearly incomprehensible for a layman—even one with a background in science.

Nanotubes and fullerenes.

At the foundation of nanotechnology were carbon atoms, the basis of life, found ubiquitously in millions of different molecules—solids, liquids, and gasses. The building blocks of the nanomanufacturing process were carbon atoms bound together in submicroscopic tubes of varying lengths and thicknesses, and also in soccer ball–like molecules containing precisely sixty carbon atoms. These molecules, perfect spheres, were named fullerenes and nicknamed buckyballs after architect Buckminster Fuller, designer of the geodesic dome, which the fullerene resembled. Remarkable. Absolutely remarkable.

Most of the science was more than Gabe wanted to or even could handle. But the potential of nanotechnology was as apparent as it was limitless, made possible in large measure by the chemical ability of carbon to bond with other atoms and by the invention of futuristic machines such as the scanning tunneling microscope and the transmission electron microscope, capable of actually visualizing nanotubes and fullerenes. Remarkable.

Already there were more than seven hundred commercially available products as varied as cosmetics, golf club shafts, and bullet-resistant shirts all built with nanomaterials. Nano toothpaste containing nanohydroxy apatite was able to bind to the protein in plaque, making it easier to loosen and remove, while at the same time it was filling scratches on dental surfaces. Nanosilver coatings on flatware, doorknobs, wound dressings, water faucets, makeup implements, and socks impeded or eliminated bacterial growth. The list and variety of products were stunning.

This was not the science fiction of gray goo. This was the real deal, making its way into the fabric of society on an incredible number of fronts and with a speed that had to be astounding even to those brilliant and visionary Nobel laureates who originally created the field.

Somewhere around one in the morning, Gabe had fallen asleep on his notes. At one thirty, still seated, facedown at the table, he was awakened by the ringing telephone.

"Dr. Singleton?"

"Yes."

"Sorry to call you at such an hour, sir. This is McCabe at security downstairs. There's an envelope for you that was just dropped off here by a messenger. It says to deliver it to you immediately. Would you like me to send it up?"

Gabe pawed at his eyes and combed his hair with his fingers.

"No, no. I'll be right down. A messenger?"

"Yes, sir. None of us caught what company he was with, and there's no indication on the envelope. Just the instructions to deliver it to you immediately."

"I'll be there in a minute."

The headache, a familiar electric pain behind his eyes, seemed to have woken up when he did. Before he had even fully processed his action, he had opened his bureau drawer and taken out the plastic vial of codeine and other pills.

"I never took a pill that I didn't have a pain for."

The notion stopped him short. From the moment his former room-mate had stepped out of Marine One at the ranch, Gabe's rather straight-forward, comfortable, and uncomplicated life had been transformed to one enmeshed in half-truths and outright lies. Now, according to Kyle Blackthorn at least, it appeared that Drew's withholding the fact of his mental illness was not his only deception. Whether the psychologist's *shin-gan* sense was right or not, time would hopefully tell.

It was becoming increasingly clear to Gabe that there was little he could do about those around him except trust none of them. There was, though, something he could do about the deception he had been working on himself. There were thousands in AA recovery, maybe tens of thou-sands, who managed to deal with routine headaches without leaping for a mind-altering painkiller.

For years, the fallout from the deaths at Fairhaven had been a smol-dering depression that had cost him in many ways, including his marriage. He had tried to overcome the feelings by starting Lariat and by going on medical missions to Central America, and he had successfully sworn off booze. But the reliance, if not dependence, on pills was a constant re-minder that the depression was always lurking and never very far below the surface.

He flipped the vial back into the drawer and washed down some Extra Strength Tylenol instead. For the time being, the motion to give up on the pills had been tabled. But at least he could watch himself more carefully. As the twelve-step book so eloquently stated, recovery was a matter of progress, not perfection.

The five-by-seven manila envelope was completely unadorned except for DR. GABE SINGLETON, neatly block printed in black ink, and the instruc-tions that the envelope was to be delivered immediately, printed in the same way beneath it. Curious more than apprehensive, Gabe questioned the man who had accepted the delivery and assured himself that he had no informa-tion that would be of any help. Then Gabe brought the envelope back to the condo and opened it on the table.

We must meet.

Tell no one.

Come alone.

Go to the office we both have occupied.

The meeting time is to be exactly twenty-four hours from now.

In the office there are four framed photos taken by me. Examine the third photo from the right. I will meet you beneath that structure.

The nightmare must end.

J.F.

CHAPTER 32

*D*onald Greenfield.

    With each passing hour, thanks largely to the Internet and courses on its use that she had taken during her training, Alison grew to know more and more about the man.

Donald Greenfield, owner of a one-year-old Porsche 911, Virginia registration number DG911, garaged on Lido Court in Fredericksburg. Apparently paid for.

Donald Greenfield, owner of the forty-one-hundred-square-foot Victorian house at 317 Beechtree Road, Richmond. Purchased ten years ago for $321,000 and recently assessed at $591,000. Refinanced five years ago. Shared with at least one beautiful Mexican woman, Constanza, and one stunning Mexican girl, Beatriz. Previous residence, 14 Collins Avenue, Salina, Kansas; home owner there for fourteen years.

Donald Greenfield, occupation: self-employed; Social Security number 013-32-0875; mortgage $2,139.00 a month; no other mortgages; no credit card debt; no dependent ex-wives, no children; no criminal record. Checking account—Bank of America, Richmond. Credit rating 650. (*Why so low?* she wrote beside the number.)

Alison flipped through her notes, both pleased and dismayed with the results of her first day of investigation. She wondered in passing who Donald Greenfield had been before Treat Griswold appropriated his name and identity. Of all the hundreds—probably thousands—of federal agencies, there was still none coordinating births and deaths. Griswold had probably searched the cemeteries for an infant or child who had been born around the same year as had he. For a person with his understanding of the workings of the federal government, obtaining a Social Security number in the dead child's name would have been easy, and from there fleshing out an identity would have been even easier still.

Questions remaining to be answered included where Griswold was getting the money to support his double life and whether there was any connection between what she had uncovered about him and his practice of toting around an inhaler used regularly by the president.

Another gnawing question needing resolution soon was when she was going to share the burden of what she was learning and with whom. That was the most perplexing question of all.

It was after one in the morning. Her jaws ached from hours of vigorous gum chewing. The tension of the day had left her more wired than tired, but a glass of Merlot was usually all that was needed to nudge her toward sleep. She uncorked a new bottle—medium priced with a label she liked, from a California vineyard she had never heard of. She poured one glass, drank it slowly, then decided on a second, which she dispatched quite a bit quicker.

St. Boniface's Winery. Good label, good stuff.

She wrote down the name and terse evaluation in the small spiral notebook she always carried in her purse. No need to specify Merlot. It was rare that she drank at all and, as she was a creature of habit, even rarer that she ventured to another grape.

"Griswold . . . Griswold . . . Griswold," she murmured, settling back in her desk chair. "What's with you, Griswold? Are you really into what I think you're into?"

Kidnapping? Illegal alien trafficking? Pedophilia? Statutory rape?

She reached across her notes to the corner of her desk and extracted a letter from its envelope. It was the second time she had read it that night but possibly the twentieth since she had received it about a year ago.

Dear Cro,

Do people still call you Cro? I used to think that was the coolest nickname in the world.

Surprise! It's me, Janie, this time coming to you from beautiful downtown Bakersfield, home of The Driller Diner, where I am currently employed waitressing tables. The only thing here less appetizing than the patrons is the food.

It's been a few years, so I hope this address in Texas is still a good one to get this to you. As for me, this is like the tenth city I've lived in since I got shoved out of my job in the ICU at Shitcan General Hospital, and onto the street for doing exactly nothing wrong. Needless to say, since the hammer fell I never have gotten my nurse's license back. I've had a lot of lousy jobs like this one, but that's okay because I've never been able to hang on to any of them for very long. You know, depression, meds, worse depression, more meds.

The reason I'm writing is that my sister sent me the obituary on Dr. Numbnuts Corcoran, the incompetent bastard who started it all. Two columns and a photo in the L.A. Times. *No mention at all of the lives he took or the one—mine—that he and his cronies in the Cognac and Cuban Cigar Club ruined. Well, at least it was cancer. I hope it was a slow and painful kind. I hope it for all of us.*

Thank you for trying to fight them, Cro. At least you tried. That's more than anyone else can say, and plenty besides you knew I didn't do anything wrong. Thank you for trying. I don't blame you for bailing in the end. I never did. I hope you know that. You tried.

Take care. I hope whatever you're doing, you're happy. Me? I get to go into L.A. every few months and see how much my kids have grown. I was always a good mom and I still love them no matter what.

Keep fighting the good fight.

Janie

Keep fighting the good fight.

By the time Alison had finished reading, the Merlot had kicked in. Good thing. Sleep wasn't going to come easily. Now, as she padded unevenly to bed, she was grateful that fade to black was only minutes away.

She was in over her head—maybe way over. In the end, if she kept pushing, she might well end up in Janieville, waiting tables or working at Wal-Mart and wondering what in the hell had happened to her life. Had Treat Griswold been an L.A. surgeon, he most certainly would have been a member of the Four Cs. In the Secret Service, he was The Man—respected, even revered. Now, she was contemplating trying to take him down.

There was still time to just drop the whole thing and take the low road out of town and back to the desk in San Antonio. There was still time. . . .

■

"Baby, I want to spend some time upstairs with Beatriz."

"Donnie, honey, it is one o'clock in the morning. She's sleeping."

"So, she'll wake up. I'll be gone all day tomorrow. There'll be plenty of time for her to sleep then. I've been working really hard lately, and I need a back rub."

"I can give you one. I know just how you like them."

"I want her to know how I like them. I want her to know how I like everything. You know the rules. Your time with me is coming to an end. It's your job to help me get her ready. Then it is your job to manage things until Beatriz is ready to take over for you with whoever follows her."

"That is what I'm doing, yes?"

"Yes, baby. You're doing a good job as long as you understand the way things work here."

"I do. When the time comes I will be ready to leave."

"That time's still a ways off. Now go and wake Beatriz and bring her upstairs to the room. I'm going to shower. Then I'll be up. I want her showered, too."

"Her hair also?"

"If you think so."

"I understand."

"Excellent. I love it when you understand."

"I did good telling you about the woman in the nail place, yes?"

"You did good . . . maybe very good depending on what fingerprints we find on that bottle of nail polish I bought from Viang."

"Marooned on a Desert Isle. That is what she chose. Women notice things like that."

"Marooned on a Desert Isle," echoed Donald Greenfield, running his hand over Constanza's firm breasts and down her lean, cocoa body to the smoothly waxed mound between her thighs. "We shall see what tales our little bottle has to tell us."

CHAPTER 33

The nightmare must end. . . .

It was everything Gabe could do to keep from racing over to the White House at 2:00 A.M. to inspect the third photo from the right on his office wall. He had enjoyed looking over at the black-and-white studies but was embarrassed now that he had never examined them in any detail and had no idea that Jim Ferendelli was the photographer. Given the quality of the sketch of Lily Sexton and of the landscape by the upstairs window at the physician's house, little about the man's creative abilities was surprising.

More exciting than being contacted by Ferendelli, though, was the knowledge that he was alive. It would be difficult to keep such good news from the president.

Ultimately, Gabe accepted that after yet another long, emotionally grueling day what he needed more than anything else right now was sleep. As excited as he was to be moving closer to the end of the Ferendelli mystery, learning what meeting place his predecessor had chosen could hold until morning. Gabe already had plans to check the president over first thing in the morning and to make an item-by-item approval or rejection of his typically overloaded schedule. He also had to sign out to the covering doc and to get Drew's approval to travel "out of range" to Lily Pad Stables from late morning until what would probably turn out to be early evening.

Heavy-lidded, he read Ferendelli's urgent note one more time.

We must meet.

Tell no one.

Come alone.

Go to the office we both have occupied.

The meeting time is to be exactly twenty-four hours from now.

In the office there are four framed photos taken by me. Examine the third photo from the right. I will meet you beneath that structure.

The nightmare must end.

J.F.

Gabe managed four dreamless hours of sleep, after which it looked as if he hadn't once shifted position. He awoke wondering if the man who had tried to kill him and the one who had attacked Kyle were one and the same. The notion made little sense, but until he and Jim Ferendelli stood face-to-face, Gabe knew that nothing much was going to.

Two sets of thirty push-ups sandwiched around a hundred sit-ups, followed by some fresh-squeezed orange juice, a prolonged shower, and a travel mug of a startlingly rich Sumatran blend and he was totally ready for the day.

Something was going to give, he told himself as he headed to the garage. Whether it was news from Kyle Blackthorn, or insight into Lily, or resolution of the mystery of Ferendelli's disappearance, or even some hint as to what the president might have been holding back during his neuropsych testing, before much longer things were going to begin to come together.

Before being summoned to work in the heart of the White House, Gabe had never even visited the place—not as a tourist, not as a student, and not even as a midshipman at the Academy. He wondered how long it would take, if ever, for him to get used to walking up to the security station, being recognized by the guards, and, after a brief check of his credentials, strolling into the seat of the country's executive power. Now he smiled inwardly at the notion that, with Jim Ferendelli alive and at least making contact, he might be back on his ranch before he ever found out the answer.

Surprisingly, the outer door to the medical clinic was unlocked. He eased it open and stepped into the reception area. From behind the closed door to the bathroom and examination room a woman was singing steamy blues.

"This world ain't always tasty like candy. . . ."

Her tone was velvet, rich and husky—a captivating voice made to sing the blues. Gabe slowed his breathing and listened.

"That's what my mama once told me. . . ."

Ferendelli's photographs were just through the door to his office, but Gabe stood there, transfixed by the incongruity of hearing such a voice in such a place.

"Sometimes it'll shake you and bend you, try to upend you. . . ."

Probably someone from housekeeping, he decided. Someone who had pulled herself up from the wrong side of the tracks and was doing janitorial work to help support her family. A woman who would have made it big on *American Idol* if the show had only been airing when she was younger. Maybe even now friends and family had told her to audition . . . but she just smiled and shook her head. These were her blues, not something she wanted to share with the world.

"Knock you right off of your feet. . . ."

Gabe moved slowly through the doorway of his office. To his left were the photographs. To his right, the angle made it impossible to see the woman, who was cleaning either the bathroom, the cabinets, or the countertop. The song was too special to interrupt, so he moved silently to the wall and Jim Ferendelli's art. Gabe was hardly a connoisseur of photography, but this set, each picture labeled on its frame with a small engraved brass plaque, was pleasing and in some respects fascinating—studies in light and shadow, in angles and shapes and shading. A scene across the reflecting basin. A striking close-up of a portion of the Capitol. The blues he was listening to seemed to fit the grouping perfectly.

"So when those hard times come a calling, remember you've got to take the bitter with the sweet."

The third photo, more somber than the others, was titled: *Anacostia from the Benning Street Bridge.*

Anacostia.

He had heard the section of D.C. mentioned from time to time and thought he remembered that it was a poor part of the city—mostly blacks and Hispanics. But he had no idea exactly where it was. There was a map in his desk. If there was time after examining Drew, perhaps he could take a ride there and familiarize himself with the bridge and the area beneath it. A final examination of the photograph and he turned toward the examining room.

Alison Cromartie, dressed for work in slacks, a light blue blouse, and a navy blazer, was leaning against the door frame, wearing a pair of rubber gloves.

"Hi," she said.

Until he heard his voice, Gabe wasn't certain he'd be able to speak. It felt as if his heart had stopped.

"Hi yourself," he managed. "I . . . loved your song."

"Thanks. When I was younger, and thinking about a career in show business, I used to moonlight singing in various disreputable places—sort of a low-rent lounge lizard. Now, I still love singing, but mostly it's in the shower."

The image of that was almost more than Gabe could handle. He struggled to remind himself that this was someone who had been placed in the medical unit to spy and to deceive, and who had almost certainly stolen the bloods he had drawn.

"You're here early," he said.

"Not really. I always come in about now to straighten up and see if anything needs ordering. Speaking of straightening up—" She went onto her tiptoes and adjusted his tie. "My daddy wore ties all the time—all kinds."

"Well, it's pretty obvious that I don't," he replied, dizzy as he had been that first night from the closeness of her.

She moved back to survey her handiwork, but only half a step.

"I didn't think you were on duty today," she said.

"I . . . I'm not. I have an appointment that will take up most of the day. I just came in to . . . pick up some papers and check in on The Man and the First Lady before I leave."

Alison lifted her hands between them, slowly pulled off the gloves, and flipped them into the leather waste can by his desk. Although there was no sense that she meant it to be, the mundane gesture was at once sensual and incredibly sexy. Even more sensual were her dark eyes, which never left his.

Gabe felt an exquisitely unpleasant fullness in his throat. This wasn't like the other instances when they had been together—not even the first time. The connection he was sensing between them was far more intense and mesmerizing. He felt at once consumed by the need to touch her—to hold her—and as awkward as a teen at his first dance.

"You want to sing some more?" he ventured.

"Some other time, maybe, you can have a command performance."

Gabe closed what little gap remained between them, eased his arms around her, and set her cheek against his chest. Her hair smelled like summer, and he buried his face in it, his lips pressed against her.

Thoughts of her as a spy or even a thief vanished. All he wanted was to hold her.

He ran his hands inside her jacket and up to her shoulders. Her hold on him intensified. She worked her fingers into the muscles of his back.

"I haven't been able to stop thinking about you," she whispered.

He reached under her blouse and ran his fingertips over the silky hollow of her back. In that moment, nothing else seemed to matter—nothing but her touch and the feel of her skin.

It had been so long since sex was special, he was thinking—so long since a kiss really mattered.

"Gabe," she whispered, "tell me there'll be time for us."

He set his lips on the base of her neck. "I can't believe this is happening. There'll be time. I promise you there will—as much time as you need, as much time as you want."

She eased herself back, never taking her eyes from his.

"I knew you were out there, Gabe. A smart, kind, gentle, funny man. I knew it."

"I don't want you to stop touching me."

"I intend to redefine the term. But any moment now the covering doc will be strolling in. I'm not sure this is the way we want him to find us."

"I love that it's happening," Gabe said, holding her tightly, one last time. "And I really do promise you there'll be time. But what's his name up in the residence and his wife are expecting me, and I think maybe I should show up there since they are my only patients."

Alison straightened up and tucked in her blouse.

"You're not afraid of me anymore?"

"Do you mean afraid, or mistrustful? Because I was never afraid."

She kissed him under his chin and then adjusted his tie once more and smoothed his jacket.

"So, what do you want to know?" she asked suddenly.

His gaze fixed on hers.

"Did you really save me that night or was that whole car thing a setup to gain my confidence?"

"There was no setup, Gabe. That was the real deal, just like this is."

She rose to her tiptoes and kissed him lightly on the lips.

He gently moved her away from him, keeping his hands on her shoulders, knowing that if she was lying, he was hardly in a position to be able to tell. Still, he desperately wanted to ask one more question—provided he could ask it without giving away privileged information.

"The bloods I drew on the president," he suddenly heard himself asking, "why did you take the tubes from the refrigerator? You were one of the few besides me who had access to them."

Alison looked utterly dismayed; then suddenly she nodded her understanding.

"Gabe, I need your trust here. I need you not to ask me anything more about the blood."

"But why?" he insisted. "Did you take the tubes or not?"

"I need your promise. No more questions about this. At least not for now."

"I'm at the point where I don't trust anyone. But if we're headed together to where I hope we are, I'm going to promise, so long as I have your word—no more lies."

"No more lies, baby," she whispered.

"In that case, no more questions."

"Okay, then," she said. "I absolutely didn't take the blood. But I believe I know who did."

CHAPTER 34

The drive to Lily Pad Stables, Route 66 west to 647, took ninety minutes. The zip code of the place was probably Flint Hill's, but according to Lily, the house, barn, other outbuildings, and white-fenced pastures stood alone, nestled in the foothills of the Blue Ridge Mountains, several miles from the actual town.

After carefully checking over the president and, much to the chagrin of Magnus Lattimore, reducing his appointment schedule by half on general principles, Gabe changed clothes in the Lincoln Bedroom, signed out to the physician on call for the day, spread his city map out on the seat of the Buick, and headed out Pennsylvania Avenue to Anacostia. Somewhere, Jim Ferendelli was mentally preparing to meet with him.

Without requesting an explanation for why he wanted to know, Lattimore and the president had filled Gabe in on Anacostia, which encompassed the east and southeast portions of the city, primarily occupying the land east of the river for which it was named.

Anacostia was, according to both of them, an area badly in need of a renaissance, and soon to get it if the joint federal/municipal commission they had instituted had its way. For the time being, they said, as in any inner city, it was best to be cautious walking the streets of that neighborhood at night.

Gabe felt virtually certain from the photo and the geography that

Ferendelli planned to meet him beneath the east end of the bridge. His mission, before heading off for Flint Hill, was to familiarize himself with the area and to find a place to park that was reasonably close to the base of the bridge, and also reasonably close to a streetlight.

It took only minutes for him to locate a spot with which he was comfortable. Mid-morning was certainly not 1:00 A.M., but he found Anacostia to have a pleasant, vibrant, neighborhood charm. The parking place he selected, on Clay, seemed like it would be safe enough. After a brief stop to reconnoiter the space beneath the bridge, he worked his way back through the city to pick up Route 66 at the Roosevelt Memorial Bridge and headed west.

There was no need to put on the radio for the drive to Lily Pad Stables. The memory of Alison's voice kept him company enough. It had been so long since a woman had him feeling as fascinated, optimistic, and excited as she had—a natural antidepressant, well beyond the equivalent of all the Prozac and Welbutrin he had taken over the years.

Lily's directions were perfect. They had to be because the roads quickly became narrower, windier, and less well marked. If she didn't already have a pied-à-terre in D.C., she would certainly need one after her appointment to Drew's cabinet. Gabe checked the trip odometer. Her place had to be close. The land along the road was densely wooded, with occasional broad pastures and narrow dirt roads that were marked only by a mailbox or handmade sign and immediately disappeared in the summer forest.

". . . So when those hard times come a calling, remember you've got to take the bitter with the—"

Gabe stopped singing and slowed, completely awed by the picture-book vista that had opened up before him. The woodlands had given way to vast, rolling pastureland, crisscrossed by pristine two-rail whitewashed fencing. Scattered among the meadows were horses, at least two dozen of them, grazing contentedly. To his left, a professionally made sign read:

LILY PAD STABLES
MAIN ENTRANCE

An arrow pointed straight up. On the other side of the paved drive, a second sign, with an arrow pointing to the right, read:

LILY PAD STABLES
REAR ENTRANCE
STABLES 0.5 MILES
ALL DELIVERIES THIS WAY

Gabe swung the Buick to the left, drove up a short rise, and this time stopped altogether. Nestled in a verdant valley, set against the breathtaking mountains, still in the distance, was the main house of Lily Pad Stables— a sprawling white farmhouse with black shutters that would not have done the term *mansion* any discredit.

But it wasn't the incredible beauty of the place alone that had stopped him short. He had seen that exact view—mountains, outbuildings, pastures, and main house—before. It took a moment for him to connect with how that could be, but only a moment. It was the scene depicted in the oil painting sketch awaiting completion on the easel by the upstairs window of Jim Ferendelli's Georgetown brownstone.

Gabe gripped the wheel until his knuckles were white, then remained parked on the rise for several minutes, composing himself and wondering how he could possibly get at the subject of Lily's connection with his predecessor without arousing her suspicion that he might know more than he was letting on. Finally, having failed to come up with any specific plan other than to improvise, he eased his foot off the brake and rolled slowly down the first of several gentle grades.

The driveway to the main house was more than a quarter of a mile long. As he approached the broad, finely landscaped turnaround, the dark blue Taurus that had been following him since he pulled out of the Watergate garage drove past the main drive and toward the rear entrance to the farm.

CHAPTER 35

A lison spent a sluggish morning in the White House clinic, wondering if it was metaphysically and psychologically possible to be absolutely obsessed with two men at the same time.

Her attraction to Gabe had been smoldering since the moment they first met. Now she had trouble focusing her thoughts on anything else—anything, that was, except for Treat Griswold or Don Greenfield, or whoever the Secret Service icon was today.

Actually, this was a Griswold day, or at least a Griswold morning. She had seen the man take the elevator up to the residence and return soon after with the president's widely beloved dog, a handsome, powerful pit bull terrier, following dutifully at his heel. The two of them had gone into the Rose Garden for a time and then returned. It all seemed so typically normal. But nothing involving that man would ever be normal again.

Restless and feeling scattered and distracted, Alison ran meaningless errands and made two trips to visit with friends in the clinic on the first floor of the Eisenhower Building next door. It was a blessing that, to this point in the morning at least, nothing medical had happened to the president or to any of the visitors to the White House. There was no predicting how she might have responded.

The physician on duty with her, a humorless Army major, who looked too young to be a doctor, let alone a White House doctor, kept his nose buried in journals most of the morning.

Her thoughts about Griswold inevitably included memories of L.A., her friend Janie, and the 4Cs surgeons. She was hardly prepared yet for the fallout that was sure to accompany any effort to expose the agent. And in fact, his perversion, assuming that was what Beatriz represented, might well have nothing to do with the president or the bronchodilator inhaler, in which case there was really nothing to expose. But then again, because of her refusal to accept what seemed like a fairly minor break in protocol, a path had opened. Now it would be foolish not to follow that path to the end.

As the morning had worn on, Alison had became more and more fixated on the consideration, however remote, that the inhaler Griswold was using might have more inside it than simply Alupent. At this point, the notion made little sense, but it had moved in and taken up residence in her mind. Rumors—the very rumors that had led her chief to send her into the White House undercover—had been whispering that Drew Stoddard was mentally unstable. True or not, it was her job, quietly but quickly, to investigate anything related to that possibility. If nothing else, she decided, in addition to fleshing out Donald Greenfield and his relationship to the women of Beechtree Road, she had to examine the contents of the inhaler Griswold carried in the inner breast pocket of his suit coat.

Piece of cake, she thought, grinning sardonically as she checked supplies and certified that the defibrillator was ready and waiting. If Treat Griswold wasn't the toughest and sharpest of the president's protectors, he was close. Short of coming on to him in a manner she was absolutely averse to, there was no way she was going to get near that inhaler, let alone switch it for a duplicate.

In his transformation from Treat Griswold to Donald Greenfield, he had either left his suit coat locked in Griswold's car in the Fredericksburg garage or placed it in the luggage compartment of Greenfield's Porsche. It seemed like somewhere in that transformation there might be a moment, but no approach was lighting up for her. She considered and discarded several other possibilities, each time coming back to the one scenario she had absolutely rejected, an all-out come-on, taken far enough to get Griswold's jacket off.

No way! she decided emphatically. As a Secret Service agent, she had vowed to sacrifice all for president and country. But allowing a beast like Treat Griswold to—

Her thoughts were interrupted abruptly by the germ of an idea. For several minutes, like an enophile with a new wine, she did nothing but explore the possibility from every aspect. Then she began to savor it. At that moment, the idea was still a remote possibility—nothing more. To make it work would require a number of pieces falling into place, followed by a hell of a lot of luck. But the best alternative she had been able to come up with to this point was unacceptable.

She approached the studious young physician in his office and asked to take the rest of the day off to deal with a nearly incapacitating migraine.

"Need anything for it?" he asked, barely glancing up from his *New England Journal of Medicine.*

"No, no. I have exactly what I need at home."

In truth, what she needed was right in her purse, her address book, and in her jacket pocket, her cell phone. Somewhere in that book was the initial step in converting a remote possibility into a plan—the phone number of Seth Owens of San Antonio. FBI agent Seth Owens.

CHAPTER 36

*W*ell, Doctor," Lily said, "I can't begin to tell you what a pleasure this has been, getting to drink tea and break bread with the most talked about man in D.C."

"The most talked about man in D.C.? Now that's a little hard to believe."

"Well, it's true—not even a contest. In Washington it is all about proximity and access to the president. Nothing more, nothing less. Proximity and access. In lesser cases, it becomes proximity and access to the ones with proximity and access. You, sir, are not only the new man on campus, but you are handsome, unassuming, and have total access to the big guy. Now, if that doesn't get you talked about, I don't know what does."

She shrugged matter-of-factly and held her hands out as if to say, *That's the way it is.*

No, Gabe thought. *The way it is, is that you have a relationship with Jim Ferendelli that you're willing to lie to protect.*

The two of them sat across from one another on fine leather sofas in Lily's richly paneled den, sipping tea from ample Oriental mugs and sampling a variety of tiny pastries and wafers.

"Remember, we still have tuna steak and salad waiting," Lily said. "Save some room."

"No problem. I'm ready for lunch and I'm very ready to feel a saddle beneath my butt. I'm grateful to you for this day, Lily. I haven't felt this at ease since the president showed up at my place with the suggestion that I come out here."

"Why, Doctor, what a very kind and very gracious thing for you to say."

"Okay, no more 'Doctor,' unless you want me to start calling *you* that. I'm sure you know it, but a Ph.D. in just about any field is much harder to get than an M.D. anyway. If anyone deserves to be called Doctor, it's you guys."

"More tea . . . Gabe?"

"I guess one more cup. I don't usually love tea, except iced, and then only outside on the hottest days, but this is really delicious."

"It converted me from coffee. I discovered it on a trip to western China, and now I have it shipped in regularly. From what I've been told, it's a variety of *Camellia sinensis* that doesn't grow anywhere else in that country, and maybe in the world. The closest I've encountered to it is Keemun black tea, but they really aren't that similar."

She picked up a small bell from the coffee table and shook it once. In seconds, the smiling, robust black woman who had been serving them materialized with another cup of the remarkable brew. It was a rich, translucent rusty brown, with an aroma and taste that reminded Gabe of . . . of what? Cinnamon? Honey? Some sort of nut? All three guesses were good ones, he acknowledged, but none of them was quite right.

He breathed in, then exhaled contentedly—almost a sigh. It had been his intention to move any conversation to the dual subjects of interest to him—Jim Ferendelli and nanotechnology. But now he realized that his sharp sense of urgency was gone.

He took another sip of tea, then forced himself to sit more upright and to push back against the euphoria and complacency that seemed to have overtaken him. Helping to bring him back on task was the realization that the unique turquoise necklace Lily was wearing today was precisely the one Ferendelli had drawn in the charcoal rendering of her. Why was she lying?

"Ready for some lunch?" she asked, reaching for the bell.

"In a moment."

"Are you okay? You look a little glassy-eyed."

"No, no. I'm fine. A little tired is all."

"Would you like to postpone our ride for another time?"

"Hardly. I've been looking forward to it. What was the horse's name? Intensive Care?"

"Close. He's named Serious Therapy. You'll love him."

Gabe was beginning to feel a bit more in control.

"So, here's what happened," he managed. "Ever since I arrived at the White House, I've been trying to piece together the life of Jim Ferendelli—to try and get some clue as to what might have happened to him. Did you know that not only has Ferendelli disappeared, but his daughter as well? She was going to school in New York."

"Oh, I didn't know. That's very frightening."

"You said you had met him?"

"Just once. We didn't have time to get to know one another."

"From what I can tell, he seems like quite a guy—sort of a Renaissance man, into art, photography, medicine, music."

"Fascinating."

"Yes. Well, I know that both the FBI and Secret Service investigators are very involved in the search for him, but I decided to walk through his place looking for anything that might have meant something to me as a doc, but that the investigators might have passed by. And believe it or not, I found something on his bookshelf—at least I might have."

"Go on."

"Jim Ferendelli had become fascinated with nanotechnology—especially the medical aspects of nanotechnology. He has a collection of books on the subject in his library, from *Nanotechnology for Dummies* to some fairly sophisticated scientific texts. I thought I remembered you mentioning the field when we spoke, so I figured I might kill three birds with one stone by seeing you, going riding, and picking your brain on the subject."

"Well, I assure you, Gabe, while I may have mentioned nanotechnology as one of the interests of the administration, I am far from an academic expert on the subject." Lily surprised Gabe at that moment by once again ringing the tiny bell, as if she was dropping the subject altogether. "Maddy," she said to her servant, "is lunch ready?"

"All set, Ms. Lily."

"Good. We'll be there in just a minute. I know you've got business in town. You can leave for the day as soon as you've taken care of the dishes."

"Thank you, Ms. Lily."

"And Maddy, please call William at the stables and tell him we'll be ready to ride in thirty-five minutes."

"Yes, ma'am."

Gabe tried quite unsuccessfully to imagine himself so at ease dealing with servants. He couldn't even deal with his horses on anything but a strictly even basis. If Lily Sexton wasn't born into the role of mistress of the manor, she had certainly succeeded in the adaptation.

It wasn't until they were settled in at one end of her impressive dining room table that she finally brought the subject back to nanotechnology.

"I suppose if you've been studying, you have some grounding in the field," she said.

"Well, I know about the Eric Drexler talk that sort of started it all. And I know some of the very basic chemistry and a bit about the potential of the science and how it stands to impact all of our lives. But I really still don't know where speculation and potential stop and reality begins."

"Well, neither does the president, or any other government agency for that matter, from Capitol Hill down to the smallest town. It's one thing to be excited that nanosilver shoe disinfectants is becoming a new industry. It's another to try and determine what the effect of aerosolized or ingested nanosilver particles would be on human organs."

"So you think new public health laws are needed?"

"The president does, and that's what counts."

"But what happens if every governmental agency from Congress to the East Podunk City Council starts drafting control legislation—especially when they're operating with outdated or little or even no scientific information?"

"That's exactly what the president is trying to head off at the pass by forming this new cabinet post, centralizing control of the new sciences, and drafting well-thought-out, comprehensive legislation, with curbs on unbridled research. We know that industry and especially big pharma would always rather ask forgiveness than permission. We'll be trying to circumvent that without stifling creativity and without smothering what will probably be the most important development in our civilization since fiberoptics, and may turn out to be the linchpin of science for the next several centuries."

"The ability to construct beginning with atoms. That's some power," Gabe said, as much to himself as his hostess.

"The truth is, I don't particularly want the sort of clout and responsibility that would go along with being the Secretary of Science and Technology," Lily said, "but the other truth is, I don't want anybody else to have it, either."

"Any ideas why Jim Ferendelli would have developed such an intense interest in the field?"

Lily shook her head.

"He never contacted me about it. But you should know that except for maybe understanding the organic chemistry surrounding fullerenes and nanotubes, I am no expert, and if Dr. Ferendelli had been studying as hard as you say, I may not even know as much as he did—I mean does."

"I certainly hope *does* is right," Gabe said.

It would have been great to have Kyle Blackthorn there to help him sort out how much of what Lily had been saying was a lie. The meeting tonight in Anacostia would surely help straighten things out, but as his euphoria gradually abated and his focus sharpened, Gabe found himself wishing more and more for an unencumbered hour or two to look around Lily's mansion for any evidence that she knew Jim Ferendelli more intimately than she claimed.

"Want seconds?" Lily asked, gesturing to Gabe's empty plate.

"Um . . . no, thanks. I'm done."

She rang one of the ubiquitous little bells and Maddy materialized to clear the table.

"I'll tell you what, I'll answer any questions that occur to you during or after our ride. Maddy, just leave the house open when you go. We'll be back in an hour—two at the most."

The servant smiled cheerily, nodded at her boss, then at Gabe, and quietly receded to the kitchen.

Gabe wondered in passing if Maddy was as content with her life as she seemed to be. One thing he strongly suspected was that the woman wouldn't be able to remember the last time she caught someone in a lie as monumental as the one Lily Sexton seemed to be caught in now.

Maybe Lily had a man in her life, Gabe mused, and was having an illicit affair with Ferendelli. He followed her downstairs to a lower level that didn't exist on the front side of the house, then out a back door to the stables. An illicit affair would fit most, if not all, of the facts.

As Lily had ordered, the horses were ready and waiting. Serious Therapy was a sturdy bay quarter horse with a distinctive blaze along his nose from high on his forehead to his muzzle.

"I like him already," Gabe said, checking the tightness of the cinch and the length of the stirrups before swinging easily onto a hand-tooled saddle that might have cost as much as his car.

Lily eschewed the offer of a leg up from William, the stable man, but did use a low step to mount Belle Starr, an elegant steel gray mare. Side by side, Lily and Gabe began a slow walk past the corrals and out along a slightly shaded trail heading toward denser forest and the hills. For five minutes, perhaps even longer, little was said between them. As advertised, Serious Therapy was special—powerful, alert, and responsive. Later, when Gabe had the chance to reflect on these qualities, he concluded that they might well have been responsible for saving his life.

Lost in the perfection of the moment and in thoughts around the mysterious, unfathomable woman riding a few feet to the left and in front of him, he wasn't certain whether or not he had seen movement ahead of them and to the right, quite far into the woods. The possibility triggered a small jet of adrenaline—enough of a rush so that, when the threat became clear, his reaction was quick.

The horses had slowed as they headed up a modest rise. The man dressed in black and wearing a black ski mask materialized from behind a tree, twenty-five yards or so to their right. His rifle, with what might have been a hunting sight, was aimed directly at Gabe.

"Lily!" Gabe barked.

He reflexively pulled his reins back and sharply to the left. Serious Therapy went straight up on his hind legs and pirouetted like a ballet dancer, spinning to the left.

At the same instant, the rifle spit off one shot, then another. Gabe heard the second bullet snap into a tree somewhere to his left.

Belle Starr reared, as had Gabe's horse, but Lily was totally unprepared. She lost her seat and was airborne before she could respond, twisting ungracefully, then landing heavily on her left side, crying out in pain as she hit the hard-packed dirt.

Gabe clambered to the ground, thinking that she had been shot. Hunched low and weaving, he raced to where she lay, groaning and in obvious pain. Belle Starr stood dutifully nearby. The gunman was gone. Far to his right, Gabe thought he saw movement through the distant trees, but then there was nothing. Cautiously, his eyes still fixed on the forest, he turned to Lily.

She was conscious but in severe pain.

"Are you shot?"

"I . . . I don't think so. My shoulder. I think it's broken or—"

"Easy, Lily. Your neck hurt?"

"No . . . not really."

"Well, try not to move it anyway."

Her face was ashen, and already she was showing the early signs of shock. Careful to keep her left shoulder as stable as possible, Gabe checked her quickly for any gunshot wounds, then had her move her legs and left arm and finally turned his attention to the shoulder that, if she was lucky, was fractured just below the head of the humerus and, if she was quite unlucky, was both fractured and dislocated. Either way, she was shocky and in need of attention.

He slipped off Belle Starr's saddle and used it to elevate Lily's legs. Then he stabilized her shoulder with the saddle blanket. Finally, he eased off her boots and slid them, toe first, one on each side, under her neck. When he was certain there was at least some splinting action from the boots he warned her not to turn her head or move unless she absolutely had to.

Then he swung up into the saddle, with Serious Therapy galloping the moment his feet were firmly in the stirrups, and bolted back down the trail.

CHAPTER 37

Alison stood on the walk at the base of the Lincoln Memorial, alternately pacing impatiently from one side of the broad stairway to the other and gazing up at the profoundly moving statue of The Great Emancipator. With a mixed heritage, she had always revered the man, his accomplishments, and the heart-wrenching decisions he had to make.

Seth Owens's man was late—fifteen minutes late to be exact.

Most days Treat Griswold went off duty at four, some days, it seemed, at three. Soon, even the remote possibility of moving on him today would be gone.

Yet another group of children, from yet another summer camp, jostled past her and up the stairs, followed by yet another trio of weary, perspiring counselors. Alison checked her watch, cast about again, and decided to wait five more minutes before calling Seth. Three years ago, the two of them had managed to make the difficult transition from being lovers to being just friends. At the time, Seth was on the rebound from a failed marriage and was still very much in love with his ex-wife, although he wouldn't admit it. Alison, still smarting from a failed relationship in L.A., had hoped for an uncomplicated physical connection with no expectations and periodic good times and great sex together. Quickly, though, she realized that as therapeutic and adult as such a relationship sounded in principle, in practice she was simply not cut out for it.

Alison hoped things with Gabe would turn out to have more substance. Meanwhile, it was good to know that the witty, intelligent, resourceful Owens was on her side—especially in situations like today, when the only one who might rapidly be able to fill her needs was an FBI agent. Owens had been happy to hear from her but made no promises at first. However, within half an hour he had called her back with a single name, Lester; a time, two thirty; and a place, right where she was standing. She reached into her jacket pocket for her cell phone at the moment it began ringing.

"Yes?"

"Alison, it's Seth. Everything okay?"

"Well, not exactly. It's, like a hundred degrees out here in front of the monument, every ounce of love I once had for schoolchildren has been ripped from my bosom by one stampeding horde after another, and your man Lester has failed to appear."

"Are you sure?"

"Of course I'm sure."

"Very sure?"

"Uh-oh."

"I did mention that Lester had a flair for the dramatic, didn't I?"

"I think you might have said something like that, yes."

"So Alison, my flower, what did you call and ask me for?"

"I asked you for the best pickpocket on the planet—the man you guys would send out to pluck a prime minister's speech out of his jacket before he got to deliver it."

"That's exactly what you said. So, why don't you take a look inside your purse."

"Inside my—"

The moment she touched her shoulder bag, she knew something was wrong. She opened it up. Her wallet was gone. So were her notebook, her lipstick, at least four packs of Trident, and a mini-size copy of *A Walker's Guide to Washington*. In fact, the purse was empty, completely empty. Well, not exactly. Lester—she had to assume it was he—had replaced the weight of what he had taken from her with plastic packs of Tic Tacs, at least a dozen of them.

"Your right earring?"

"Gone," she said, realizing even before she felt for it that it was.

"Like you, Lester is very good at what he does."

"I guess. Okay, Owen. I'm a believer. Where is he?"

"See the group of kids at the far end of the stairs?"

"Yes."

"See the guy entertaining them?"

"The one juggling?"

"Lester."

"He just waved to me without dropping a ball. I owe you big-time, Owens. When I get back to San Antonio, dinner at Paloma Blanca's on me."

"I thought you didn't want to come back," Seth said.

"If I screw this up, I may be shipped back to wash the urinals. Gotta go. Lester just waved to me again, this time with an Indian club while he was juggling two more with his other hand. I think he and I will be able to do business, provided he doesn't get busted by the park ranger heading toward him. Thanks, pal."

CHAPTER 38

*T*he laconic stable man, William, tall, gaunt, and in his seventies, handled the news of the gunman and Lily's injury with anxious composure. He called 911 and ordered the police and ambulance to Lily Pad Stables, while Gabe loaded up with water, bandages, anything that would pass for a splint, and blankets.

"Is there any easy way a man with a rifle could have gotten as far into the forest as he did?" Gabe asked, swinging back onto Serious Therapy.

"They's a number a ways, actually. These hills're crisscrossed by old logging roads and old mining roads and even old military roads from the war—the Civil War, that is. The bastard couldda taken the one right at the base of that hill over yonder. Ends up at an abandoned coal mine 'bout six miles in. Runs right alongside the Yellow Brick Road—that's this trail here that you was on—for three, four mile before cuttin' away."

"Send the rescue people right out," Gabe said, urging his horse to a full gallop with just a tap of his heels.

Lily was essentially as he had left her, eyes closed, moaning in pain, and looking as if her blood pressure was still quite low. For more than half an hour Gabe ministered to her, replacing the splints protecting her shoulder and neck, keeping her warm and as hydrated as she would allow, and whispering steady encouragement. Her injury was severe—probably a fracture dislocation with significant hemorrhaging—and as likely as not she would be in the operating room before the night was out.

Having done everything he could think of, Gabe knelt beside her and peered into the woods toward the spot where the shooter had stood. It would be worth taking the police there against the remote chance the man had left anything behind. The more Gabe thought about the episode, the more convinced he became that the gunman who had nearly killed him on the street near the White House and this assailant were the same or at least were working for the same people. It was nearly impossible to believe otherwise.

But why target him? Trying to come up with an explanation that fit the facts was a shortcut to a migraine.

"Hang on, Lily," he said. "Help should be here in just a few minutes."

"Can I make it to a hospital in D.C.?" she asked, her voice weak and raspy.

"In the shape you're in, I wouldn't chance it. You've probably lost a significant amount of blood into your arm and back into your chest. At some point you're almost certainly going to need anesthesia and a procedure to fix your shoulder. Maybe after you're stabilized, you can arrange to be transported to a university medical center for that."

"Thanks, Doctor."

Her eyes closed and again she drifted off, breathing sonorously. Moments later Gabe heard an approaching siren, and within a minute two cruisers came jouncing up the deeply rutted Yellow Brick Road, followed by an ambulance.

The paramedics, as was the case almost everywhere Gabe had ever watched their brothers and sisters work in the field, were confident, efficient, and damn good. The two of them, a young man and an older woman, were kind enough to compliment Gabe on his makeshift first aid as they immobilized Lily's neck, started an IV, put some oxygen in place, did a quick, competent check for other injuries, and expertly immobilized her shoulder. Gabe reminded himself of what he already knew well. If he was ever injured outside of a medical center, he would take a paramedic's care over that of any but the most exceptional trauma physician.

On the way in, the team had noted a place to turn around, and after loading Lily in the back of the ambulance and again praising Gabe's thoughtful work, they backed up toward the spot, with one of the Flint Hill cruisers following.

Not surprisingly, there was nothing in the woods or on the road beyond to suggest the identity of the shooter, although there may have been a few cracked branches in the area where Gabe thought the man had been standing. Gabe felt obligated to disclose to the policemen the nature of his connection to the president but chose to say nothing to them about the previous attempt on his life. He would contact Alison as soon as he got back to D.C. Then, unless she had strong objections, he would speak with Magnus Lattimore and probably with the president himself. With two attempts on Gabe's life in less than a week, it seemed like time for him to get some Secret Service protection of his own.

First, though, he had some business to attend to—a search of Lily Sexton's home. She had left the house open. If her housekeeper was gone, as it seemed she would be, he would have some time to search for any information regarding Jim Ferendelli and then head for the hospital to check on Lily.

Gabe led Lily's horse back to where the stable man was waiting. Then, after muttering something about picking his briefcase up from the den, he returned to the house and let himself in.

He began at the master suite, a massive carpeted bedroom and elegant bath located at the rear of the house. There was a small desk but no papers of interest on top of it or in the drawers. The closets, however, were more interesting. There were two of them, one a walk-in, the other much smaller. The walk-in was filled with the gowns and casual clothes of a woman who took pains to dress well. The smaller closet was taken up with clothing belonging to a man—a man who dressed as tastefully as did the mistress of the manor. Business suits, several tuxedoes, worn work clothes, riding attire, and casual shirts and slacks. Thirty-three waist, thirty-two leg, sixteen-thirty-three shirts. The man, Gabe estimated, was about five eleven, one hundred and seventy pounds, and in shape. Gabe had no idea if these were Jim Ferendelli's clothes, but he wouldn't be the least surprised later on to find that they were.

What amounted to the back staircase led down to three guest bedrooms, each comfortably apportioned with its own bath. With his enthusiasm for finding anything else of significance waning rapidly, Gabe did a walk-through of the guest rooms, pulling out a drawer here and there and checking the closets, all of which were empty but ready for guests, with extra blankets and towels.

He was about to head upstairs to retrieve his briefcase when he stopped in the center of the guest room farthest from the back staircase and directly under the den. Behind the antique oak bureau and tall mirror was a door in the wall, visible from either side of the bureau but only at an acute angle. Gingerly Gabe slid the bureau aside. A typed half page was sealed in plastic and tacked to the door, which rose no more than five feet from the floor.

LILY PAD FARM AND THE UNDERGROUND RAILROAD

The construction of the central house of Lily Pad Stables took place between 1835 and 1837. Sheep rancher Thaddeus Boxley and his sons were the first owners. It is unclear whether the family died out or moved away. By the mid-1840s, the farm became the property of Abolitionist James Sugarman. It also became an important cog in the Underground Railroad—a series of way stations for slaves trying to make their way from bondage to freedom in the cities of the North and in Canada. The small room behind this door often held as many as ten men, women, and children for as long as a day. Feel free to look inside, but please touch nothing.

The low, narrow door, constructed of three skillfully conjoined planks, slid into the wall on a pair of tracks. Gabe wondered if the bureau had been there from the beginning. It made sense, especially given that there was barely room for the furniture in any other arrangement. The concealment of the door wouldn't survive anything more than a cursory exam, but he could imagine situations where it might have been overlooked.

Gabe opened the drapes to let in more light and switched on the bed-side lamp. Then, with extreme care, he hooked two fingers into a north–south groove that had been carved into the right-hand margin of the door and pulled. The door slid across into the wall with surprising ease, revealing a dark, somewhat dusty space, about eight feet square, with a packed red clay floor. There were three rough-hewn benches against the walls, an old straw broom, a wooden water bucket and ladle, and a second, larger bucket with a cover, which Gabe surmised was to aid in the disposal of bodily waste.

There was no source of light, but if someone stood back from the doorway, enough flowed in from the guest room to illuminate most of the space. Three of the four walls were constructed of the same packed red clay as the floor. The fourth, to Gabe's left, was some sort of rough-hewn wood panel. That was all there was to it—a way station for slaves, virtually unchanged for over 160 years.

Frustrated, Gabe turned to leave, then turned back to be certain he hadn't left any telltale footprints. The heels of his boots had, in fact, made several gouges in the earthen floor. The rest of the floor had been brushed smooth, possibly with the old broom.

Careful not to track clay back into the small guest room, he pulled his boots off and set them aside. Then he got down on his knees and was smoothing out the defects when he noticed small bits of loose clay around the bases of the legs of the bench leaning against the paneled wall. It appeared as if the bench had been dragged forward and then pushed back again.

He crawled cautiously to the bench and pulled it toward him. It was fixed to the wall, with just enough space at one end to admit his fingers. A stronger pull and an invisible low doorway opened on almost invisible hinges, revealing a tunnel, similar to the room itself, supported every ten yards or so by upright railroad ties and a crossbeam. The tunnel was quite dark but was faintly lit from somewhere in the distance. Electing not to put on his boots, Gabe crossed the small chamber with one step and entered the tunnel with the next.

In total silence, his senses keyed up, he moved through the deep gloom toward the faint glow in the distance. He had traveled perhaps a hundred yards when he began to hear the thrum of machinery. The faint light, he now realized, was coming from beneath a heavy drape of some kind. Cautiously, he eased the drape aside a few inches. Just beyond it, a brushed-steel door, with glass in the upper half, separated him from a gleaming, tiled, brightly lit corridor. Along the corridor on the right-hand side were five doors identical to the one before him. Each was identified by a letter and number painted just above the glass. In addition, there were name plaques in brass just below several of the panes.

Gabe inhaled, held his breath, opened the door, and slipped inside. The steady, mechanical humming was coming from the far end of the corridor. Otherwise, there was neither sound nor movement. He angled himself to be able to see through the glass of the first door, labeled B-10. Below the glass, a bronze plate read: DR. K. RAWDON.

The room, gleaming beneath white fluorescent lights, was clearly a lab of some sort, devoid, at the moment, of people. There were several computer terminals set alongside a complex apparatus that was a tangled arrangement of thick and thin highly polished metal tubes, connected by numerous rivets and bolts and constructed around a series of lenses and eyepieces. The effect was as if he were looking at the inner workings of a nuclear submarine.

But Gabe knew better.

His study of the materials borrowed from Jim Ferendelli's library had disclosed a number of images of equipment nearly identical to the apparatus in Room B-10. The instrument was, he felt certain, a scanning tunneling microscope, capable of mapping the surface of materials atom by atom. It was this instrument, more than any other, that was elemental in the design and construction of nano-scale systems. It had become, in essence, the basis of the entire field of nanotechnology.

CHAPTER 39

*L**ester*, how're you doing?"

Grateful for her hands-off headset, Alison worked the wrapper off a stick of Trident and slipped it into her mouth to join the two sticks already there. From the moment she spotted Treat Griswold heading for his car, she knew this was going to be a three-stick operation. Three at least.

"I'm just passing Dale City," Lester said. "Is he out yet?"

"He's out. Just getting into his car. Lester, listen, are you sure you want to go through with this?"

She already knew the answer. Everything about the man said that the greater the challenge, the more he welcomed it. He was slightly built, with bright dark eyes that suggested he was up to something even when he was just sitting still. After connecting with him by the Lincoln Memorial, Alison had treated him to some coffee from a kiosk and found a bench where they could talk. The deal to move ahead was consummated after just a few minutes.

Lester had told her not to worry about his last name, only the three-hundred-dollar fee they had agreed upon—this after she had offered him five hundred. He was a busker, he said—a street performer with simple tastes. Nothing more, nothing less. Alison strongly sensed there was much more to the man, but he admitted only to being an entertainer, who did contract work from time to time for the FBI to keep his juices flowing.

"Why would I not want to go through with it?" he said now.

Alison waited until two cars had inserted themselves between her and Griswold's Jeep, and then eased into the flow.

"Lester, this is not any normal man. He's built like a small ox, he's trained to kill, and he's armed. I know you're the one who's putting himself in harm's way, but I'm getting cold feet."

"In that case," Lester said, "let's make it three twenty-five."

"Okay, okay, three twenty-five it is. Well, traffic's not bad. We're almost out of the city. As soon as our man passes the exit to his place up here, we'll know he's headed to Fredericksburg. You dressed appropriately?"

"Just like you wanted. Plus a little Jack Daniel's cologne to heighten the effect. I know a good idea when I hear one. This is going to work, Alison. Piece of cake."

"Lester, who *are* you?"

She could almost see him grinning.

"Like I told you in the park, just someone who needs a little danger and excitement in his life every now and then, and who owes your friend Seth a favor—make that a *couple* of favors. He said you were the real deal and wouldn't be setting this up if it weren't important. That's all I have to know."

"Your call."

"Now we're talking."

"In that case, I would think Seth's glowing recommendation would qualify me to learn how you did that thing with the Tic Tacs."

"A Congressional Medal of Honor wouldn't qualify you for that one. How's it going with our man?"

"We're coming to the exit he'd be taking to his house up here . . . and . . . and . . . he's driven past it. We're on, my friend."

"Okay. I have the Fredericksburg street map spread out right here. I'm going to find a safe place to leave this jalopy of mine not too far from the garage. Then I'll walk over there and practice looking like I'm picking the lock until he gets there."

"The right-hand door. He's not as likely to take you apart for trying to open that one rather than the one with the Porsche behind it. Just don't get busted by any of the local police. I'll call and let you know when he's getting off of Ninety-five."

"Good enough. But then I'm going to leave my cell phone under the seat. You just relax and have a Tic Tac."

Despite the gum. Alison's mouth seemed dry as she followed the Jeep from three car-lengths behind. Traffic was perfect—not too dense, not too light. As they approached the Dumfries exit, Griswold suddenly broke with the pattern Alison had anticipated he would be following. At the last possible moment, he whipped the Jeep to the right and down the exit ramp. She could almost see him scanning the rearview mirror for any sudden movement from any of the cars behind him. If she duplicated his move, she would be giving herself away. Helpless, she tapped the brake once and continued down the highway as she dialed Lester's number to warn him something was wrong and they should consider backing off and trying another time.

There was no answer.

With a dreadful sinking in her gut, she accelerated and pulled out into the passing lane.

CHAPTER 40

*T*reat Griswold had no idea why he suddenly turned off at the Dumfries exit except that he had been feeling edgy since an unknown, exotic-looking woman with light copper skin had struck up a conversation with Constanza and Beatriz in the manicure parlor. They had strict instructions to avoid prolonged conversations with anyone and to report any unusual contacts to him. This they had done.

He swung onto the exit ramp too rapidly and felt the Jeep's center of gravity lurch to the right. But even though the years had been somewhat unkind when it came to the muffin top overlapping his belt, his coolness in crisis and his reflexes were as sharp as ever. There was no rollover, and from all he could tell through the rearview mirror, there was no one following him, either.

He was a little paranoid, he told himself. That's all. Just a little paranoid . . . not that he didn't have every reason to be.

Whoever had tailed him last year—a hell of a thorough private eye, he guessed, or maybe someone from one of the other agencies—had mapped out his secret Richmond life in agonizing detail, complete with photos and video. The night the phone rang for him at the Beechtree Road house, the man on the other end had his ducks in an absolutely perfect row.

There was to be no debate, no arguing, no denying, no protesting, the voice said. Griswold was to go along with what was being demanded of him or he would be finished—exposed, suspended from his job in the Secret Service, and, in all likelihood, prosecuted. On the other hand, if he did as he was told, there would be more than enough cash to ensure that in a few years, when Beatriz had grown old and tiresome, he would have the resources to recruit and develop her replacement.

Griswold maneuvered the Jeep through back roads he knew well and rejoined I-95 at Garrisonville.

A little paranoid, that was all.

The lab had promised him a report on the prints retrieved from the Marooned on a Desert Isle nail-polish bottle as soon as today. Suzanne . . . child care . . . Fredericksburg. . . . That was the information he had to work with. He had already begun a discreet inquiry into the woman, but as yet, none of his sources had come through with anyone who fit the description. They would, though, he assured himself. If she was for real, they would.

In all likelihood, though, he was making mountains out of molehills. Nothing more than that.

Griswold settled back and relaxed with vivid images of what his evening with Beatriz held in store. She was a quick learner, and easy as hell to program with the use of selected drugs, CIA brainwashing techniques, and, of course, Constanza. Another six months and the girl would be providing him with the most sensual, devoted, custom-made companionship imaginable. In fact, in many ways, she already was.

A final glance in the mirrors suggested nothing out of the ordinary. Griswold slipped in a Grateful Dead CD and dialed up "Truckin'," his all-time favorite cut. By the time the song was done, he was nearing the garage. He licked his lips at the prospect of getting behind the wheel of the Porsche again. The Jeep was serviceable and predictable, but the Porsche was . . . well, Beatriz.

He turned onto Lunt Street and immediately spotted a man with a pry bar, trying to open the lock on the empty right-hand side of his garage. The man, not impressively built, looked like a derelict, with sneakers, shabby pants, a worn tan windbreaker, and a nondescript blue baseball cap.

Over the years, the government had treated Griswold to a variety of courses and refresher courses in defensive and offensive driving, most given in conjunction with firearms training at a reconditioned racetrack in rural Virginia, informally referred to as Crash and Bang.

He had practiced the maneuver he reflexively chose a dozen times, and accelerated into it without hesitation. Engine roaring, he barreled directly toward the man, who stood as if transfixed, staring wide-eyed at the fast-approaching grille. At the last possible moment, Griswold slammed on the brake and spun the steering wheel hard to the right. If he handled the maneuver correctly, the rear end of the Jeep would spin around and the thief would be virtually pinned to the garage door. If he missed, even a little, the man's lower body and the heavy wooden door would become one.

The spin was perfect. Tires screeching and smoking, the Cherokee spun just over 180 degrees, tapping gently to a stop against the garage and cutting off the derelict from any escape except to his left. That route vanished before the man could react as Griswold, pistol in hand, leapt from the Jeep, raced around to where the grimy intruder still stood, grabbed him by the front of the jacket, and slammed him against the garage door. The pry bar clattered to the pavement.

The look in the man's eyes was unmistakable panic. He smelled densely and unpleasantly of alcohol and hard times.

"P-please don't hurt me."

"What in the fuck are you doing?"

"Everything all right?" a woman's voice called from somewhere down the street. "Do you want me to call the police? I saw everything."

"No!" Griswold snapped over his shoulder. "I can handle this. . . . Well?"

"I . . . I was just lookin' for somethin' I could sell," the man managed, his speech thick and clumsy. "These are hard times, you know."

Griswold jammed the barrel of his pistol up under the intruder's ribs.

"You lying to me? You lie to me and I swear I'll blow you away. Why'd you pick this place?"

"I . . . I couldn't get into the one over there. I was just workin' the street. Honest, mister. I was just workin' the street."

At that instant, Griswold's cell phone began ringing. With his gun still pressed firmly against the man's gut, Griswold released the windbreaker, checked the caller ID, and set the phone against his ear.

"Griswold here."

"Griz, it's Harper at the lab. I think we've found a match for those prints on the nail-polish bottle."

"Can you hold on for a minute?"

"Sure, but hurry up. I think you're going to want to hear this."

"Just hang on."

Griswold turned his attention back to the thief, who now was beginning to cry.

"P-please. I'm living on the fucking street. I'm sorry. I'm really sorry. It won't happen a—"

"If I see you around here again, you're dead. Got that? Dead!"

Griswold stepped back, opening a way out for the man. Tentatively, the derelict moved forward a few steps. Then, in an awkward, stumbling gait, he headed down the street, waiting until he was around the corner before cracking a smile.

"Okay," Griswold said, again pressing the phone to his ear. "What gives?"

"What gives," the crime lab specialist said, "is that the prints match a Fed."

"A what?"

"A Fed. In fact, if I'm not mistaken, she's Secret Service. Just like you."

CHAPTER 41

*A*stonished and bewildered by what he had discovered, Gabe stood beside the recessed doorway to Lab B-10 willing his pulse to slow and his sense of what was smart to take over.

Get back to the house. . . . Get back and regroup!

He was alone in the brightly lit corridor of an underground laboratory that had at least one tunneling scanning microscope—the pricey, highly technical, sine qua non centerpiece of nanotechnology research. The facility, carved into the foothills of the Blue Ridge Mountains, not far from the Shenandoah Valley, was reached from one direction through a little-used hidden entrance in the guest wing of Lily Sexton's opulent country home. There had to be one or more other entrances as well, but how far they were from this one was anybody's guess.

Go back!

Two things were all too clear at this point. The brilliant, elegant, beguiling Ms. Sexton had far more than a passing interest in nanotechnology—one of the sciences she was slated to try to place under government control should she become the country's first Secretary of Science and Technology. In addition, she quite probably had more than the passing acquaintance she claimed to have had with Dr. Jim Ferendelli.

Gabe was equidistant between the door back to Lily Sexton's house and the next doorway on the corridor, which he could see was B-9. His best approach would be to head back and, as soon as possible, check some real estate ledgers and maps involving the area. But the part of him that had always caused trouble was urging him on—at least to the next room.

This is dumb and risky, he warned himself, as he inched along the wall toward B-9.

Risky and dumb.

He felt the adrenaline rush that had long ago stopped being a significant part of his life but had led him to any number of dangerous decisions along the way. The last thing he needed, just seven hours before he was scheduled to meet Ferendelli, was to get caught down here.

He moved ahead several more feet.

The recessed B-9 doorway was identical in every respect to B-10—brushed steel and high-tech, with thick glass filling the top half. He peered into the brightly lit room, which was another deserted lab, featuring another research apparatus he recognized from his studies of nanotechnology—a scanning electron microscope. The SEM was capable of creating remarkably well-defined images of invisibly tiny nanotubes and fullerenes by bombarding them with a stream of electrons.

The brass plaque beneath the glass read simply: ELECTRON MICROSCOPY. No nameplate. Gabe speculated that Dr. K. Rawdon of the tunneling microscope lab was probably the head of this unit as well.

Distracted, Gabe was a step slower than he might have been in reacting to the voices and footsteps echoing down the hallway from someplace ahead and to the right. He held his breath and flattened himself within the recessed doorway of B-9 just as two men in security guard uniforms emerged from a corridor, chatting and laughing. They each wore sidearms.

"Did you understand a word they were saying in there?" one asked.

"No, but that's why they're eggheads and earning the big bucks and we aren't."

"I did love the stuff Dr. Rosenberg was showing, though. Real, living brains without bodies. Could you believe that? I heard he was keeping them in his lab on A Wing, but that's the first time I actually saw them."

"Yeah, I wonder what they're thinking. Maybe something like 'Gosh, it's dark in here.'"

"Yeah, and 'Hey, I can't hear a damn thing, either. Where in the hell is everybody?'"

Both men laughed roundly. If either of them had turned to his left, he would have been looking directly at Gabe, who was just thirty feet away and unable to conceal himself fully in the recessed doorway. Instead, they turned to their right, away from him, and exited Corridor B through a pair of swinging steel doors.

Gabe's desperate need for answers again began doing battle with his common sense.

The silence that followed the guards' departure was not complete. Gabe could still hear the low, machinelike hum and also some voices.

Real living brains without bodies.

Fascinating.

There was no way he could retreat now without trying to get even a little more information. His common sense had been routed. Just a little more information. . . . Just a little more.

Hanging on pegs near the scanning electron microscope were two knee-length lab coats. Gabe tested the knob to the room and the heavy door swung open. Seconds later, he emerged wearing one of the white coats. With his boots back at the beginning of the tunnel, his dark socks protruded from beneath his jeans, looking rather foolish but at the same time making it easier to move silently up the corridor. Still, it seemed as if anyone within earshot would be able to hear his heart slamming against the inside of his chest.

Room B-8, fiefdom of a Dr. P. Wilansky, was another empty lab filled with sophisticated equipment. There was a branching corridor ahead and to the right—the hallway from which the guards had come. The low machine hum was more pronounced, as was a man's voice, loud enough now to make out some words.

"Note . . . brain . . . stained . . . immunofluorescence . . ."

Gabe inched around the corner and peered down the corridor. At the end were two more doors, identical to the others. The right one was closed and the left one open. Pressed against the wall, every muscle tensed, he moved ahead. If someone came through the doors behind him now, there would be no retreat and, in all likelihood, no meeting with Ferendelli. Still, he had to see.

". . . This slide is a photo taken two months after the subjects were dosed with ten micrograms of fullerenes coated with antibodies specifically coded to hypothalamus neuroprotein. Administration in this subject was oral, but the results for intravenous and aerosolized fullerene administration were virtually the same. As you can see, there has been virtually no change in the location and concentration of immunofluorescence, even after thirty days. When these little fellows attach, they stay pretty well attached, although there is a very gradual leeching out."

Gabe thought the line about the "little fellows" and the way Rosenberg delivered it might have engendered at least a chuckle or two, but the assemblage remained stonily silent.

Five more feet.

Gabe was just a few steps from the closed door now. Through the glass he could see seven white-coated scientists—five men and two women—their backs to him, standing shoulder to shoulder at the far end of a carpeted room that was about a twenty-five-foot square—probably a conference room with the chairs removed.

Turn around and leave! Leave while you have the chance!

A slide was being projected on a screen before the small gathering. From what Gabe could see, the image was a cross section of brain, with the jade green glow of an immunofluorescent marker dye scattered over an area that apparently was the hypothalamus. At his very sharpest in neuroanatomy, which would have been a few minutes after finishing the course in med school, he could have easily identified the structures in the brain slice. Now, though, those days were long past and he would have to take Dr. Rosenberg's word.

A grainy slide with fluorescent marker was hardly the real living brains without bodies that the security guards had talked about. Gabe inched closer. At that moment, as if on cue, one of the scientists at the center of the line stepped back, turned to her left, and coughed deeply several times.

Through the opening she had created, Gabe saw three large glass cylinders, four feet high and a foot in diameter. They were filled to near the top with a translucent golden liquid—serum or some other form of nutrient, he guessed—which was being aerated by a bubbler built into the base, the source of the mechanical hum. A large number of monitoring wires snaked over the lips of each cylinder, connecting outside them with elaborate monitoring equipment, at least one of which was an EEG—an electroencephalogram—that was showing continuous brain-wave activity.

The other ends of the wires were implanted in brains—one in each cylinder, suspended by some sort of transparent Lucite frame. Each brain included not only the cerebrum and cerebellum but also the brain stem and eight inches of spinal cord.

Gosh, it's dark in here indeed!

Functioning, metabolizing brains! *Living, thinking brains!*

They could have been human, but Gabe's knee-jerk assessment was that if they were, they weren't the brains of fully grown humans. Before he could further assess their nature or any other aspect of the macabre setup, the woman stopped coughing and stepped back into her slot in the chorus line of white-coated scientists.

Now, go!

This time he began a slow, measured retreat back to the B corridor and out of the laboratory. There would be time to sort out what he had just seen and heard, but for now his focus had to be on getting out of the lab and back to D.C.

His attention still fixed on the conference room doorway, Gabe moved backward, checking over his shoulder with every step, anticipating the return of the security guards. Instead, the danger came from the room itself. With little more than a brief, perfunctory round of applause, the scientists turned and, without much conversation, filed out through the already open door and directly toward where he was standing, not more than twenty-five feet away.

Gabe had, at best, a few seconds to react. His instinct was simply to turn and run, but even if he made it back down the tunnel to Lily Sexton's, there was a good chance the armed security guards would catch up to him before he had gone too far. If he did manage to get away, there were bound to be repercussions when Lily learned what he had done.

Still, fleeing seemed like his only option, and he was set to do that when he flashed on his first cellmate at MCI Hagerstown, Danny James, a canny jewel thief, who had entered a mansion during a lavish party wearing a tuxedo, marched up to the master bedroom, located the family safe behind a mirror, cracked it, pocketed what jewels the hostess wasn't wearing, and then stayed for a round of hors d'oeuvres before strolling out to his car. He would have made an absolutely clean escape had he not taken the jewels from his pocket and set them on the passenger seat to admire only moments before being accidentally rear-ended by a police cruiser.

"Everyone with even half a life is always wrapped up in his own business," James said one evening after final lockdown. "The trick is to be bold and to look like you know what you're doing, so they can continue to think about their two favorite topics—themselves and their work."

The next day, dressed as a garbageman and, Gabe assumed, acting like a garbageman, James managed to ride a waste disposal truck out of the prison and into the sunset. When Gabe was released at the end of his year, to the best of his knowledge Danny James had still not been caught.

The trick is to be bold and look like you know what you're doing.

Almost instinctively, ignoring his stocking feet, Gabe stopped preparing to run. Instead, he strode forward toward the first of the group, a gangling, stooped-shouldered professor with thick glasses and an unruly thatch of pure white hair that looked like the product of an electric shock.

"You all done in there with Dr. Rosenberg?" Gabe asked cheerfully.

The man, perhaps sixty, glanced at him momentarily, mumbled something about the session taking far too long, and walked past him, followed lemminglike by the others. It was not at all clear if he or any of the rest no-ticed that the man threatening to intrude on their thoughts and their con-cerns about the run-over session was wearing no shoes and had no identification badge hanging from his neck.

It was all Gabe could do to keep from continuing his spontaneous per-formance by marching into the conference room to question Dr. Rosen-berg about his research and whether the brains were, in fact, human. But it seemed unlikely that any of the security team would be as self-absorbed as the scientists or as accepting that anyone in a lab coat had to be one of the good guys, shoes or no shoes.

The extensive underground laboratory, devoted at least in part to nan-otechnology research and to neurobiology, made no sense yet, but cer-tainly it had to be connected to the books he had taken from Jim Ferendelli's library. For days, questions had been piling up like autumn leaves. Now, in just a few hours, there would finally be answers—provided, of course, that he could get out.

Cautiously, he made his way to Corridor B and then to the swinging door back to Lily Pad Stables. As he passed Laboratory B-10, he could see Dr. K. Rawdon hunched over the oculars of the scanning tunneling mi-croscope. On the wall above the scientist was an ornately painted sign, in a simple black lacquer frame, which Gabe had missed on his first pass by the lab.

THINK SMALL, the sign read in lowercase letters.

THINK SMALL.

CHAPTER 42

*T*his is the pharmacist."

"Your name?" Alison asked.

"McCarthy. Duncan McCarthy."

Alison checked the list of qualified pharmacists pasted innocuously in the back of the White House clinic patient ledger. McCarthy's name was there.

"Please fill the full Alupent inhaler prescription that's on file for Alexander May."

May was the code name for a prescription that was going to the White House, and *full* meant seven identical inhalers.

"The name of the driver who will be picking it up?"

"Cromartie." Alison spelled the name. "Alison Cromartie. I'll present my ID when I come."

"Time?"

"Tonight. No, no, wait. Tomorrow. I'll stop by the hospital to pick it up tomorrow morning."

"Very well," the pharmacist said. "I'll be here."

Alison set down the receiver on the examining room phone and entered the doctor's office—Gabe's office. It was nearing seven and there was no sign of him. She wished that somewhere along the line she had thought to get his cell phone number. There was much for them to talk about. Still, it might have been for the best that she hadn't called him yet. She had time now to think over how much she wanted to disclose—to him or to head of internal affairs Mark Fuller. She had evidence that Treat Griswold was probably involved in a perversion involving young girls—or at least one particular young girl. That in itself made him an easy mark for extortion.

In addition, she had hard evidence that Griswold had broken with unwritten White House law by repeatedly handling the president's medications—specifically his inhaler. Whether or not there was a connection between the inhaler and any psychiatric problems the president might be having would depend on what a sophisticated analysis of the contents revealed.

What she had at this point might have been enough to present to Fuller, but there was no way she was going to put her career on the line and go up against the most powerful and respected agent in the Secret Service without more than indirect evidence and speculation. She needed proof of his relationship to the girls on Beechtree Road, and she needed a positive analysis of the contents of the inhaler he had repeatedly given the president to use. Lester had done his job well, although according to him, his life may have been spared by a fortuitous call on Griswold's cell phone.

If she was to move at all against the president's number-one Secret Service man, she needed absolute proof of wrongdoing. Los Angeles had taught her that having unsubstantiated knowledge, good intentions, and the willingness to engage in a she said/he said confrontation simply wasn't enough to blow the whistle on anyone with clout.

Her plan was to have the contents of several Alupent inhalers analyzed, including the one Lester had taken from Griswold. But there was no way she could risk going through Mark Fuller or anyone else connected with the Secret Service to do so. It seemed Fuller had done a decent job of protecting her identity until now, but despite what he had told her, it was hard to believe no one except Fuller knew that she had been sent into the White House undercover. The Service was very closely knit, and with a man of Griswold's stature involved, sooner rather than later there were bound to be leaks.

Lester had guarded his words closely when they first spoke. If he was actual FBI, would she be giving him up by asking him to come forward and speak to Fuller? Using an FBI operative to trap a Secret Service agent wasn't going to sit well no matter what. Was there any way around doing that?

At the moment, the inhaler was wedged beneath the seat of her car. Was there any lab outside of the government with sophisticated analytical capabilities that she could trust for both reliability and discretion? The answer was most certainly yes, but she had no idea how to locate such a lab or how to approach the people working there.

The Internet? she wondered.

Possibly. She could probably get some idea of the reliability of a place from a phone call to whoever was in charge, but with so much at stake and only one sample, she wanted to know that whatever place she chose was the best.

A better idea would be Gabe.

It was time she trusted someone, and he was the obvious choice. She had already blown her cover to him. Sharing her concerns about Griswold would probably be safe, and with luck Gabe would have had experience in his practice with just the sort of blood chemistry lab she needed.

She took an envelope and a sheet of Gabe's stationery from the desk.

> Important stuff to talk about, big fella. Please call me. Anytime, day or night.
>
> A.

She added her home and cell numbers, sealed it, wrote his name and title on the envelope, and set it carefully on the corner of his desk blotter. At that moment, she heard the door to the reception area softly open and close.

"Gabe?" she called out.

Nothing.

Alison checked the placement of the envelope one more time and took several steps toward the outer room. Through the doorway, the room looked empty. Had she really heard something? She felt her pulse accelerate.

"Gabe? . . . Is somebody out there?"

She stepped through the office doorway into the reception area. Directly across from her, the door to the outside corridor was closed. At that instant she sensed movement from her right. She started to turn, but far too late. A thick, powerful arm locked across her throat, tightening with dizzying force, cutting off her breathing and making it impossible to scream. A cloth saturated with some sort of liquid was pressed over her mouth. The arm across her neck loosened just enough for her to inhale.

"Griswold!" she tried to say, thrashing against his cinder-block body and ineffectually pounding backward at him with her fists and feet. "Griswold, no!"

"What do you think of this stuff, Cromartie, huh?" Griswold asked in a coarse whisper. "State-of-the-art liquid inhaled anesthesia—tasteless, odorless, rapid onset, long acting. Invented by our own people just for us field operatives. If you could get it over a water buffalo's mouth and nose, he'd be on the ground in half a minute. You don't know about it? Oh, sorry. I guess they don't tell snitch nurses, just the *real* agents. We're kept up on every new drug. As you'll see."

Quickly Alison's terror gave way to impotence and then to a strange detachment. She tried to hold her breath, to continue kicking backward against Griswold's shin. She drove her elbows against his barrel chest. She attempted to bite the hand that was forcing the cloth even tighter against her mouth, crushing her lips against her teeth.

Waves of dizziness and nausea made it impossible to continue struggling. She was going to throw up . . . throw up and aspirate and choke to death. She was . . .

The fear, helplessness, and intense nausea gave way to a giddy lightheadedness and ennui, then, moments later, to blackness. The last things she heard, from the lips beside her ear, were Griswold's grunting breathing and guttural speech.

"They gave you up, Alison. . . . All I had to do was make one phone call and they gave you up. How's *that* for respect?"

CHAPTER 43

*S*o, enter the hero."

The President of the United States, wearing a white terry-cloth robe and matching flip-flops, greeted Gabe in the living room of the White House residence. Even though it was only ten in the evening, two or three hours before Stoddard's bedtime, the weariness enveloping his eyes seemed even more pronounced than usual.

"Hero?" Gabe asked.

"Evon Mayo, Lily Sexton's assistant, called and told us what happened. She said the doctors told her your treatment in the woods might well have saved Lily's life. Apparently, in addition to her broken shoulder, she punctured a lung and was in danger of bleeding to death."

"There really wasn't that much I could do out there, but I make it a policy never to dissuade people from thinking I'm a hero."

"For some reason, I don't think I believe either part of that statement," Stoddard said.

"I stayed at Fauquier Hospital in Warrenton with her until they had inserted a chest tube, given her a unit of blood, and she was stabilized. For a small place—or even a big place for that matter—that hospital's really quite terrific. Reminds me of ours back home. If you could send out a presidential something or other to them, I know they'd appreciate it."

"Done," the president said without even writing a memo.

And Gabe had no doubt it would be.

"Good hospital or not," he said, "Lily wants university people to take care of her shoulder, and they have a helipad right next to the ER, so tomorrow morning if she's ready to travel, she'll be flown to Georgetown."

"So, what happened out there? Lily's a hell of an experienced rider. I've been out on those trails with her myself, and she's come riding with me and Carol from the stables near Camp David a couple of times as well. Makes me look like a tenderfoot."

Gabe had been preparing for this moment throughout the drive from Warrenton back to the capital. It was time Drew learned some of what was swirling around him. Not all yet, but some.

"A man shot at us from the woods. A rifle. Black ski mask, black clothes. Wasn't much of a marksman—certainly not by Wyoming standards. From the distance separating us and him, he should have at least hit one of the horses, but he hit nothing except a tree trunk eight or so feet from us. Lily's horse reared and threw her. I suppose mine was already worn-out from lugging me up the trail. He just stayed put."

"Black ski mask, black clothes, out there in the woods where you two just happened to be . . . doesn't sound like a whacko to me."

"I don't think he was."

"So, was he trying to kill Lily?"

"Me," Gabe said simply.

Stoddard's look of surprise was fleeting.

"You sounded sure it was a he," he said. "I had the feeling you had more to tell me."

Gabe paused as he prepared to pull his finger from the dike. To say his onetime roommate had more than enough on his plate was a gross understatement, but now it was time to pour on a little more.

"This is the second time since I arrived here that someone has tried to kill me," Gabe said finally. "I think they were the same guy."

Eyes narrowed, Stoddard listened impassively as Gabe reviewed the botched shooting on G Street. He saved his questions until Gabe was done.

"You said this man would have killed you if you hadn't been rear-ended at that exact moment?"

"That's correct. Assuming it's the same man, after watching him with a rifle I don't think he's any kind of a professional hit man. But even he couldn't have missed me from five feet."

"And the collision was a fortuitous accident?"

Stoddard, as usual, was right on top of things. Gabe was prepared for the question. First Alison, then the call from Ferendelli, and finally the bizarre finding off the lower level of Lily Sexton's home. He was beginning to buckle under the weight of the secrets he was keeping from the man who had brought him to Washington. During the ride back from the hospital in Warrenton, he had worked out what he was going to share with the president and where he was going to draw the line—at least until he had more information.

"The person who banged into me and probably saved my life was following me purposefully," he said. "Tailing me."

"To hurt you?"

"No. I think to protect me."

"Do you want to tell me who that was?"

"I don't, Drew. I sort of promised to think carefully before I told anyone. But I'm prepared to now."

Again, Gabe could see Stoddard's intellect rapidly processing the information as it had been presented so far.

"Whoever this is was tailing you from the White House at two in the morning?"

"Yes."

"Secret Service?"

Gabe wasn't surprised at how quickly the president put things together. This was a man who, after the accident at Fairhaven, had gone from being a middle-of-the-pack student at Annapolis to first in his class, to a governorship, and finally, to the presidency.

"Working undercover," Gabe replied.

"To what end? At whose order?"

"I can answer the second question, but I'm not so certain about the first. The head of internal affairs sent the agent in. I think the goal was to learn how much truth there was to—"

"To the rumors that I was going nuts," Stoddard said.

"Yes, sir, plus maybe to search for information that might shed some light on what happened to Jim Ferendelli."

Again, Gabe could almost feel the president working through the facts, reasoning out the possibilities.

"It's that woman, isn't it," he said suddenly, "that nurse my pal Mike Posnick in California called me about, asking me to set her up in the Secret Service."

"Alison Cromartie. Yes, Mr. President, it is."

"And she was in Baltimore with us, right? I thought I knew her from someplace else. I'd only met her once, maybe a couple of years ago. Interesting looking."

"I have to agree."

Stoddard glanced over at Gabe with something of a glint. He grinned momentarily. Then just as quickly his expression darkened.

"They're closing in, Gabe," he said. "Like goddamn hyenas smelling the rot, they're closing in."

He took a computer printout from the floor next to him and passed it over. It was a nationally syndicated column from the *Montgomery Mirror*, based on the latest Gallup Poll numbers, which indicated a drop in the Democrats' lead from 12 to 8 percent—the smallest gap since shortly after the Republican Convention.

WHERE THERE'S SCHMUCK, THERE'S FIRE

Question: What chief executive risked his health and the leadership of this country in a grandstand play at a Baltimore meeting of big-bucks liberal supporters? You see, the chief executive in question was in the midst of an asthma attack severe enough to cause him to break off his speech in the middle. And we all know how severe that must have been. Was it the behavior of a rational man to return to the podium after just a few minutes of treatment?

I think not.

Perhaps the rumors swirling about the nation's capital have some truth to them—maybe a lot of truth. The rumors are telling us that a good deal of the time the man in the golden chair, with the golden boy looks and the liberal, suck-gold-from-the-workingman philosophy, is showing an irrationality that can only be called Nixonesque. That's right, that's right, Tricky Dick was a Republican and here I am bashing him in a way most foul—by lumping him in with he who should not be named.

Well, crazy is nondenominational and apolitical, and if our chief executive, the man with his pointer finger on the BIG BUTTON, is losing it, I don't care what party he is. So, Prez, I say be afraid of these latest poll numbers. Be very afraid. The American public is getting concerned about what I have known all along—namely, that you are not all there. You're not the first chief exec to try and keep big secrets from us law-abiding wage earners, and you undoubtedly won't be the last. I suspect that by the time your poll numbers and Brad Dunleavy's cross for the final time, we'll know the truth.

Gabe set the printout down and exhaled audibly.

"*Hyenas* is the word," he said.

"We've got to get to the bottom of this before it blows up in our face."

"I'm working on it, Drew; I really am."

"And?"

"I need another day; then we'll talk."

"Have you heard from your psychologist friend?"

Gabe stiffened at the question. Among the many things he had decided to keep from Drew, at least for the time being, was the attack on Blackthorn at the airport hotel, and especially the missing briefcase.

Hopefully, as Blackthorn had promised, there was no accessible information in there.

"I haven't spoken to him since he returned to Tyler," Gabe said, "but his initial impression was that somehow a toxic chemical was intermittently entering your body."

"Like poison?"

"Not necessarily. There are other explanations. Drew, you're the boss here, but I really would rather get some more data before telling you what I've been able to learn."

"You're the doc. But make it quick, Gabe. You read that column."

"I understand; believe me, I do."

"Just tell me a couple of things. Do you think the guy who tried to kill you killed Jim?"

Tomorrow, Gabe had decided. Tomorrow after he and Ferendelli had spoken, he would bring Drew up to speed on the situation. For the moment, as Ferendelli had requested, he would tell no one.

"It's possible," he said. "But if he was as inept at Jim's assassination as he was with mine, there's a good chance Jim's still alive."

"And the woman, Alison?"

"I'm hoping to speak to her tonight or tomorrow. As far as I know, she hasn't uncovered anything."

"But she's sharp?"

"I think very sharp."

"You falling for her?"

"Too early to tell."

Stoddard's expression grew steely.

"Just remember who you're working for, okay? I have to know that I come first."

"You come first, my friend," Gabe said. "Now, I have a question."

"Go ahead."

"Is there anything of importance that you're holding back from me? Anything at all?"

Stoddard momentarily looked at him somewhat queerly, then shook his head.

"What's that all about?" he asked.

"Kyle Blackthorn told me he has like a sixth sense about people—whether they're being totally on the level or not. He wondered if you might be holding something back or maybe not telling the whole truth about something. I mean, when we first talked in Wyoming, you did manage to hold something rather big from me."

Again the flicker of that odd look.

"Well, not this time," Stoddard said. "If I know something of any importance, you'll know it. Now, keep me posted, and if you need resources that are at my disposal, just say the word and they'll be at yours."

"The closer to the vest we play this, the better," Gabe replied.

"I'll see you tomorrow, then."

The friends stood and shook hands.

"Tomorrow," Gabe said, before heading to the office to prepare for his rendezvous with Ferendelli.

On the ride down in the small elevator, he acknowledged two things. One was that it was very unlikely that he had any heightened or additional senses as did Blackthorn. But the other was that almost certainly, despite Stoddard's protestation to the contrary, the president was either holding something back from him or lying outright.

CHAPTER 44

Important stuff to talk about, big fella. Please call me. Anytime, day or night.

A.

*T*here was something wrong.

With Alison's note propped up against his desk lamp, Gabe dialed her home and cell phone numbers again. Nothing.

How long ago had she been in the clinic? What sort of important stuff
did she mean? *Big fella* made it sound as if she was enthused and in a good
space. Why couldn't he reach her now?

It was nearing eleven fifteen. An hour and forty-five minutes before,
hopefully, the mystery of Jim Ferendelli's disappearance and his relationship to Lily Sexton would be unraveled for Gabe.

Between the events earlier in the day at Lily Pad Stables and now his
strong feeling that the president was either lying to him or holding something back, this had already been a hell of a trying day. Now Alison wasn't
answering either of her phones.

Where in the hell was she at this time of night?

As often happened in stressful situations, Gabe's temples were beginning to throb—one howitzer shell burst for each heartbeat. What possible
sanguine explanation could there be for Alison leaving the note she did,

then not being available on her home phone or cell? It had to be something simple like a low battery or other malfunction of her damn phone. Back in Wyoming, he carried a cell phone because every doc on the hospital staff was expected to. But he didn't trust them—not in Tyler and not here. That had to be it, he tried to convince himself—her cell phone.

His jaws clenched against the frustration and concern.

Without any rummaging in his desk drawer that he was aware of, suddenly the vial of various pills was in his hand. It was like a number of patients with weight problems had told him over the years—the sad, recurrent tale of finding themselves standing in front of the open refrigerator and having absolutely no recollection of how they got there.

What in the hell was he, a supposedly sober alcoholic, doing with pills in his hand every time the going got difficult for him? He needed to face the fact that just as some people were functional active alcoholics, managing to hold down a job and maybe keep a marriage going despite their drinking, he was functioning despite the smoldering depression that had stunted his spirit for decades, since the nightmare of Fairhaven and the inestimable horror of having taken the lives of a woman and her unborn child.

One Valium. Five milligrams would take the edge off. It wasn't really that much. The manufacturer *made* a damn ten milligram.

He dialed both of Alison's numbers for a third time, leaving a concerned message with each. It was right there beside where he was sitting that she had tied his tie—right there where she had stood on her tiptoes, kissed him softly, and pleaded to let there be time for them. Now she was missing and he was preparing to respond to the crisis by taking yet another pill.

She deserved better. She deserved better, and so did he.

He took his secret stash into the bathroom, poured the pills into the toilet, and flushed them away.

■

Darkness . . . duct tape . . . and rats . . .

For some time after she regained consciousness, all Alison was aware of was the duct tape pulled tightly across her mouth and binding her wrists, elbows, ankles, and legs to some sort of heavy chair. Then, as the fog lifted from her senses, she became aware of the feet, scurrying from one side of the space she was in to another, and at least twice, she felt certain, brushing against her.

With time, her vision was able to make use of a small amount of light slipping beneath a door. She was in a cluttered room—a storeroom of some kind, it seemed. The air, which she had to work to draw in through her nose into her lungs, was cool and slightly musty. Across from her, she could discern the distinctive outline of a harp . . . then of a hat rack . . . and finally, behind them, a large sign that read: HAPPY BIRTHDAY, MR. PRESIDENT.

She was still in the White House—a prisoner in a storage room in the basement or even the subbasement if there was one, held there by the number-one guardian of the president.

Being uncomfortably bound and having to strain for each breath were distracting enough to keep her from being as frightened as she might have been, even with the rats. She should have written more in the note to Gabe, she chastised herself now—at least mentioned that there were problems with Treat Griswold. She had been too paranoid to do so.

One by one, she tested her restraints. No chance. Even the tape over her mouth had been wrapped tightly around her head and then reinforced in front with something firm to keep her from biting through. At the moment only two things were clear—she was absolutely helpless, and she wasn't dead.

She wondered how Griswold could have caught on to her. The answer was elusive. What was clear, though, was that unless Griswold was satisfied that she had told him everything she knew and why she had been prying into his life, in all likelihood she was going to get a lesson as to how much pain she could endure.

Would Griswold risk holding her here in the White House? However unlikely, it had to be unpredictable when someone might happen to need something from this room. There was a light outside the door. That meant her prison wasn't all that isolated.

An hour or so later, her questions were answered. With a soft click, the door opened, flooding the room with light from a concrete corridor outside. Treat Griswold slipped inside, flicked on the single bare overhead bulb, and eased the door closed behind him.

"Time to hit the road, lady," he rasped, his lips beside her ear. "But first, a little something to keep you from getting carsick."

Without another word, he stepped around behind her, buried a needle to the hilt at the base of her neck, and injected the contents of a syringe into her muscle. After just a minute, the room began to spin viciously.

CHAPTER 45

*O*n the way into D.C. from the hospital in Warrenton, Gabe had taken a half an hour detour and driven into Anacostia for a second time, then across the Benning Street Bridge. Once a sought-after middle-class section of the city, according to sources on Google and, of course, Wikipedia, Anacostia began its evolution from 90 percent white to over 90 percent black in the mid-1950s. Even though parts of the area had seen much better days, certain blocks still featured neatly maintained homes and yards and a distinct turn-of-the-twentieth-century charm.

Dr. John Torrence, a black major in the Army and part of the White House medical team, had grown up in Anacostia and still had family there.

"White or black," he told Gabe, "walking around Anacostia after midnight isn't something I'd recommend doing on a regular basis. But if for any reason I absolutely had to, I would. Like most inner cities, there are some gangs and drug crazies, but mostly, there are very good people there."

The evening was moonless and unseasonably cool. On his earlier reconnaissance, Gabe had identified a place to park that was as close as possible to the area beneath the Benning Street Bridge. He arrived at the spot twenty minutes before one. It was a narrow street running alongside the Anacostia Reservation, a broad field that just a few hours ago was alive with picnickers, softball and touch football games, soaring kites and

Frisbees. The lighting around the park was far from optimal and may have been at least one of the reasons Ferendelli chose the place to meet.

Ten minutes.

Gabe lowered the window of the Buick. There was almost no one about. Twice he heard voices, and once he saw the shadows of three or four people—boys, he thought—making their way across the field. Up on the bridge itself, there was a steady rumble of traffic.

As his eyes adjusted, he could easily make out the river, a tributary of the Potomac and the centerpiece for what was to be a rejuvenation of this part of the city. Just a mile or so to the south, East Capitol Street crossed the river, its westbound lanes headed into Capitol Hill, the Mall, and, of course, the White House.

Just a mile.

Gabe managed a thin smile at the irony. A meeting was about to take place in these hardscrabble surroundings that could affect the world as much as any that had been held in those staid and hoary buildings. It wouldn't be long now.

For a time, the attack on Blackthorn nagged at him. How could the killer have known where Blackthorn was staying? At the psychologist's urging, Gabe had asked Treat Griswold to have his condo checked over for listening devices. Reportedly, none had been found.

Two minutes.

The field remained deserted. There was no movement that Gabe could discern anywhere underneath the bridge. He wondered what he would do if Ferendelli failed to show. Perhaps he would pay a visit to Lily Sexton and offer to set her broken shoulder without anesthesia should she hold out on him anymore.

It seemed as if Ferendelli had carefully chosen the photograph in the medical office to ensure that Gabe would know with certainty that the meeting was with him. Still, Gabe was regrettably learning not to trust anything or anybody when it came to the president.

Careful to keep the interior light from going on and wondering if he had been unwise not to bring along a blunt weapon of some sort, Gabe locked the Buick, left it, and headed across the field toward the blackness beneath the bridge. Overhead, the whoosh of passing cars grew louder as he approached. Headlights flashed by. From his left, the scent of the river grew stronger.

As he neared the bridge, he suddenly found himself picturing the desert, and Condor at a full gallop, bearing him effortlessly across the parched ground, toward a burnt orange setting sun.

Soon, he thought. *Soon it will be over.*

The field itself seemed to be in excellent shape and reasonably free of debris, but the underside of the Benning Street Bridge smelled of stale beer, river muck, and urine. Broken glass crunched beneath his boots. Gabe stepped into the dense shadow just under the edge of the bridge. Then he turned toward the field and waited for the man he had succeeded in the White House—the Renaissance man who many felt was dead.

"I have a gun," a soft, cultured voice said from behind him. "Lift your hands where I can see them. Don't turn around. What's your name?"

"Singleton. Dr. Gabe Singleton."

"How do you get up to the residence from the office?"

"The elevator across the hall."

"Could you have been followed?"

"I didn't see anyone, but I didn't take any special evasive precautions, either."

"You should have."

"I'm sorry."

"Walk over there to that support. Keep your hands up."

Gabe did as he was ordered.

"Turn around slowly with your hands up."

Again, Gabe did as he was asked. The gaunt, unshaven man confronting him carried no gun. Instead, he extended his bony hand and gripped Gabe's with surprising force. His hair was unkempt, and at that moment he looked considerably older than fifty-six—the age Gabe had read in his personnel file. What Gabe could discern of his expression was grim. He was jittery and badly in need of a shower. His tension was nearly palpable.

"I can't tell you how relieved I am to find that you are alive, Dr. Ferendelli," he said.

"We are in a crisis of immense proportions, Dr. Singleton. Our president is under attack. His life is in danger every day."

"Then his psychiatric breaks are—"

"If by *psychiatric* you mean a disease of some sort—a spontaneous malfunction in his brain—his problems are not psychiatric at all."

"But—"

Even through the gloom, Gabe could see the intensity glowing in Ferendelli's eyes.

"President Stoddard is not insane," Ferendelli said. "He's being poisoned, dosed with a psychoactive drug—no, no, make that a number of psychoactive drugs."

"I wondered about that when I witnessed one of his episodes," Gabe said, "so I drew some blood for analysis. But the tubes were stolen from the refrigerator in our office."

"Stolen? Do you know by whom?"

"No. Do you?"

"I have some ideas."

"Dr. Ferendelli—Jim—are you all right right now? I mean are you ill?"

"I have not slept for more than two hours at a time in weeks. I'm in as much danger as the president is. They could kill me just as they could kill him, with . . . with the push of a button." Ferendelli looked furtively about. "Are you sure you weren't followed?"

Something about the question was bothersome to Gabe, but he could not discern precisely what.

"No, I'm not sure that I wasn't followed," he said. "I told you that. Listen, I have a car right over there. Let me take you to a hospital or . . . or to my place."

"Just talk to me," Ferendelli said. "Talk to me and listen to me.

They've poisoned me, Doctor. Just like the president, they've poisoned me. I haven't come in because I don't know precisely who they are, and I haven't run because I owe it to my president and the country not to."

"Is your daughter all right?"

"Yes. She's fine as far as I know. When all of this began to happen, I feared they might use her to get at me, so I had her go away to stay with friends. So long as she stays where she is, no one will find her. Now please, listen to me."

"I'll listen, Dr. Ferendelli, but try to stay focused. Who're they? Is one of them Lily Sexton?"

Mention of the woman's name hit Ferendelli like a sucker punch. For some time he said nothing. When he finally did speak, there was a noticeable tremor in his voice.

"I pray, sir, that you have had no contact with that woman."

"I'll tell you of my connection with her when you finish. Please, Jim, please. From the beginning?"

"Oh, this is bad," Ferendelli said. "Very bad. You've seen her, haven't you—been with her?"

"I have. But please, compose yourself and tell me what's been going on."

Inventor, physician, artist, intellectual. The Renaissance man Gabe had heard so much about was a nervous shell.

As if reading Gabe's thoughts, Ferendelli took a calming breath.

"I have a friend named Wysocki," he said, "Zeke Wysocki. He's an analytical chemist and owns a small lab just outside of Durham. He's a loner, with not one whit of social skills, but he is a wizard of a chemist, and a hell of a poker player. That's how we met—playing poker at a small, private game. He liked to talk about some of the contract work cases he did for the police and the FBI—cases that no regular labs could handle. So, on a lark, when the analysis of the president's blood came back negative, I sent one of the split samples I had kept to Wysocki."

"He found something."

"A number of things, actually. I drew bloods after two of the president's attacks. There were traces of several different hallucinogens in each sample, only not the same ones."

"Go on, Jim. You're doing great."

Ferendelli was again becoming jittery. He pulled a small bottle of spring water from his jacket pocket and managed a shaky, prolonged swallow. Gabe wondered if the bottle might contain vodka but didn't ask. Ferendelli wasn't intoxicated, just frightened—frightened and totally spent.

"You sure you weren't followed? I've been getting bad vibes about this place since you arrived."

Gabe glanced out at the empty field.

"I don't see how, but if you want to go someplace else, or maybe just drive and talk, we can do that."

"I . . . I guess we can stay here."

"Go on, Jim. Tell me what your friend found. This is all beginning to come together for me. We're going to get to the bottom of things. I promise you we are. And whatever you and the president need to be okay, we're going to get it for you. I've got a friend in the Secret Service we can trust."

If we can find her.

"I . . . hope so."

"You did the right thing to contact me, Jim. You're safe now, and I assure you, you are not alone. Now please, go on."

"I'm not alone," Ferendelli said, marginally more calm. "I like the sound of that."

A block away, a nondescript white van, lights off, rolled down the street, the antenna on its roof rotating slowly.

CHAPTER 46

*A*lison knew the pain was coming but was helpless to stop it. She lay
on her back, her gaze transfixed on the syringe in Treat Griswold's
hand. In horror, she watched as once again he slid the needle attached to it
into the rubber port on the IV tubing.

"I know you're not particularly fond of this stuff, Nurse Alison," Griswold said, "but I really have to know what's going on, and frankly, to this
point, I haven't been all that satisfied with your answers."

"What I told you was everything," she pleaded, aware of the sudden
wash of perspiration beneath her arms and across her upper lip. "*Everything.* Please, I have nothing else to tell. Please don't do that again."

She was on a creaky metal military cot, with her wrists and ankles uncomfortably bound to the frame. The thin, sheetless mattress reeked of
mold. The room—clearly for storage—was brightly lit from a bare overhead bulb and was less cluttered than the one in the White House. At
some point, she had been dressed in light blue surgical scrubs, possibly
taken from the clinic. Her clothes were neatly folded nearby with her bra
and panties carefully laid on top—Griswold's not so subtle reminder of
her helplessness. Almost certainly, she had decided, the two of them were
in the basement of the house on Beechtree Road in Richmond—Donald
Greenfield's house.

This would be the third injection Griswold had administered to her over what might have been two hours . . . or two days. The thought of having to endure the spasms and the pain again brought bile percolating into her throat. He had told her the name of the chemical in the syringe, but it was not one she recognized. In fact, he had mentioned that it was still somewhat experimental, developed by friends of his in the CIA.

After she was allowed to awaken from whatever anesthetic he had given her in the White House, Griswold listed the questions he was going to ask her, and then, without waiting for answers, he injected what he called a "quarter-strength" amount of the drug into the rubber port of the tubing draining intravenous fluid into her arm. In less than a minute, the muscles in Alison's body began to twitch. Then, suddenly, they cramped, every one of them, as brutal as any cramps she had ever experienced.

With her movement restricted, there was no position she could get to that would make the spasms go away. Her quadriceps muscles tightened into rock-hard balls. Her hamstrings pulled just as viciously in the opposite direction. The contractions in her abdominals were especially merciless. Her jaw was clenched so firmly, she was unable to open her mouth to scream.

It was possible—likely, even—that not long after the second injection she had passed out from the unremitting pain. She awoke, chilled from evaporating sweat, feeling as if she had been beaten with a two-by-four. Now Griswold was about to dose her for a third time.

"Griswold, Treat, listen. Dammit, please listen," she pleaded, her speech rapid and forced. "I was placed in the White House because Mark Fuller in Internal Affairs wanted to know what might have happened to Dr. Ferendelli. He also asked me to see if the rumors they had heard about the president's mental problems had any element of truth. Also, I was to keep my eyes open and follow up on anything unusual that I encountered. Fuller never mentioned any Secret Service agent specifically—certainly not you. Now, please, don't use that stuff on me again. I'm begging you."

"Why did you follow me?"

"I already told you. You were the only one I've encountered who did anything even the slightest bit unusual."

"Carrying the inhaler against regulations."

"Exactly. It may or may not be a specifically written rule, but in the clinic we all know that no one except us and the president himself is supposed to handle his meds, and certainly you've been around long enough to know the same thing, too."

Alison had said nothing about the pickpocket, Lester, or about having successfully switched inhalers. If Griswold got even the slightest scent of that one and if there was, in fact, anything unusual about the inhaler he had been carrying, she was in for more pain than she could possibly endure.

She stared up at his massive head, framed by the aurora of the overhead light, and at the deep fold in his truncated neck, and she hated him more, even, than she had come to hate the surgeons in L.A. Silently, she chastised herself for being too cautious and scarred from her prior experiences not to say something about the legendary agent to Gabe or even to Fuller himself.

For a time, neither of them spoke. Griswold just stood there, looking down at her with no particular emotion. Alison felt a glimmer of hope. It seemed to her as if he might be considering her responses.

Please, she thought. *Please, please don't do it again.*

She tried, unsuccessfully, to get a better read on his intentions. In her life, she had shown some courage and some pain tolerance but not, she guessed, much more than average.

Please, please . . . don't.

Finally, Griswold shook his massive head and shrugged his buffalo shoulders.

"I don't know why, Nurse Alison, but try as I may, I just can't shake the notion that you're holding out on me."

He lifted up the IV tubing and gazed at the rubber injection port as if it were some sort of precious, delicate blossom. Then he sighed and quickly emptied the contents of the syringe into Alison's body.

At the first sight of his thumb tightening on the plunger, Alison began to scream.

CHAPTER 47

*K*etamine . . . psilocybin . . . LSD . . . methamphetamine . . . DIPT . . . atropine . . . mescaline . . . PCP.

Jim Ferendelli's chemist had found traces of eight different mind-altering drugs in the blood of President Andrew Stoddard.

Eight!

"Zeke likes to say that performing analytical chemistry is similar to doing a differential diagnosis on a patient," Ferendelli said. "If you don't look for it, you'll never find it."

"I totally agree with that," Gabe replied. "Presumptions and assumptions are as dangerous in a physician as arrogance and ignorance."

"Well, Zeke took things one step further. Once he started getting positive results, he anticipated the obvious question as to how these drugs could have gotten into the president's blood in such minute concentrations. He decided that the amounts administered would be far too small to have any neurological effect unless they were delivered to precisely the part of the brain where they were the most effective. The best he could come up with was a theory summarized in several articles he gave me."

"Nanotechnology," Gabe said, almost breathless at the way the pieces were at last dropping into place. "I didn't find any articles, but I found your books on the subject while I was searching through your place for clues about what might have happened to you, and I've been studying them. I'm still an amateur on the subject, but I'm a lot more knowledge-able than I was when I started."

For the first time, Ferendelli managed a smile. He reached out and patted Gabe approvingly on the shoulder.

"I would bet you are an excellent physician," he said.

"I feel the same way about you. Initially you went to see Lily Sexton to learn about nanotechnology, didn't you?"

This time, at least, mention of the woman's name didn't provoke as much agitation.

"From what I read," Ferendelli said, "it seemed as if using molecular-size nanobots to deliver drugs directly to cancers or to specific sites in the body was still very much on the drawing boards and in the minds of futurists. I went to her to see if there was something I didn't know about the status of the field. I also needed to develop some sort of possible explanation—a hypothesis—to answer the question: If the president was being dosed with micro-amounts of psychoactive drugs, how were the chemicals being introduced into his body? How were the drugs able to seek out the area of his brain where they would be most effective? And perhaps most urgent and frightening, how could their release be triggered on cue?"

It's not in the future! Gabe wanted to shout, flashing back to the disembodied brains in Dr. Rosenberg's glass cylinders and the immunofluorescent deposits on his slides. *It's here—right now!* But first Gabe needed to learn how his predecessor—and Drew—had come to be in such danger.

Already it was clear to Gabe what a hero Jim Ferendelli was. In an incredibly short time, he had accumulated an astounding amount of information in trying to save the presidency of his patient and longtime friend. In the process, Jim had placed his own life in jeopardy. At this point, the man should be standing on a golden pedestal in front of Congress and the American people, awaiting the highest honors this country could bestow, not skulking in the shadows here amid the beer bottle shards and fetid odors, emaciated, unkempt, and fearful.

"What happened, Jim?" Gabe asked softly, picturing the lovingly drawn portrait in the man's desk. "What happened with Lily Sexton?"

"When I contacted Lily about picking her brain regarding nanotechnology, she invited me out to her stables for a ride. In fact, I went out there several times. It was difficult, because I had to speak to Lily in generalities, and not mention the president in any way, even though I suspected she had quickly put two and two together. We both know that my only patients are the president and his family. There have been a growing number of rumors over recent months regarding the state of Drew's mental health, and Lily's a very perceptive person."

"You'll get no argument from me there," Gabe said.

"Well, she didn't have that much to add to what I already knew about the field of nanotechnology. It's advancing at an incredible pace, and the high rollers are beginning to speculate, throwing incredible sums of money at the possibilities. But the field is still much more theoretical and potential than actual. Lily arranged for me to visit a research and manufacturing site in New Jersey and to speak with several of the scientists and even two major investors."

"Manufacturing?"

"It's a company that manufactures nanotubes of various diameters and lengths, and several different sizes of fullerenes. There's a huge demand for them right now in industries and laboratories all over the world. The people in New Jersey sell them by weight, like bananas."

"You're doing great, Jim. Can you go on?"

Ferendelli stepped out of the shadow of the bridge and scanned furtively through the gloom.

"They can kill me, Dr. Singleton," he said, a note of shrillness returning to his voice. "With the push of a button, they can kill me almost anytime they want. And they can kill the president, too. Anytime they want to they can kill him, just like that."

Gabe reached out and gently guided Ferendelli back into the darkness.

"Who are they?" he asked.

"I have some theories, but they are no more than that. I . . . I continued to visit Lily at her place. We never saw one another in D.C., only at Lily Pad Stables."

Gabe knew what was coming next.

"You fell in love with her, didn't you?" he said.

"I feel so stupid."

"Nonsense. I don't know if I've ever met a woman more interesting and attractive."

"Nothing ever happened between us—sexually, I mean. She kept encouraging me to visit her and ride with her, but each time I tried to advance our relationship, she alluded to being in a relationship that needed resolving before she could move on to another. Meanwhile, I kept doing research, speaking with experts, and secretly running tests on Drew's blood. I refused to believe that my relationship with Lily had no future, and she still wanted to see me. Now I know *she* was the one who was pumping *me* for information, not the other way around."

"I'm sorry, Jim," Gabe said. "I'm so sorry."

"I was a fool not to see the truth long before I did. My judgment and my ethics were warped by the feelings I had for her. I had been so lonely since my wife passed away . . . I . . ."

Gabe put his hands on the man's shoulders.

"It's okay, Jim. You did what was best for your patient. No one could ever fault you for that."

"Well, finally, in a last-ditch effort to win her over, I decided to take her into my confidence. I mean she was a friend of Drew's, and he was going to nominate her to be in his cabinet. So I told her what I had learned and what I was theorizing, and what I planned to do about it."

Again Ferendelli crossed to the edge of the bridge shadow and peered at the scene he had photographed so sensitively. The white noise and vibrations from traffic speeding overhead were in sharp contrast with the emptiness of the field and the stillness of the river. Feeling the connection between them strengthening, Gabe moved forward and stood shoulder to shoulder with his predecessor, the two of them silhouetted in the strobes of passing headlights.

"How did she respond to that?" he asked.

Ferendelli glanced over at him, his fear and sorrow nearly palpable.

"She told me I would be doing nothing of the sort—that I'd be doing exactly what she told me to do, nothing more, nothing less. She said it was in the tea she served each time before we went riding. Now it was in me—locked in place in my brain."

Gabe felt himself go numb. *The tea.* Lily had been so proud of her tea—so excited when he wanted another cup.

"What do you mean, *it?*" he asked, barely able to get the words out.

"Fullerenes—hollow nanoball molecules carrying drugs. She told me her tea was laced with just enough narcotic to make me love it, relax, and want to drink more."

"Oh, God," Gabe murmured, almost inaudibly.

"So that's how she got the fullerenes into my body. I don't know how she did it with Drew, and I don't know how the fullerenes with their microdoses of drugs end up exactly where they would have the most devastating effect."

"I'm afraid I can answer that one," Gabe said, not bothering at this point to recount his experience with the scientists in Lily's nanotech laboratory. "The fullerenes are coated with antibodies specific to neuroproteins or neurotransmitters—maybe those in the thalamus, the basal ganglia, and the caudate nucleus. Maybe other places in the brain as well. The fullerenes float through the bloodstream until they encounter those specific proteins; then they just latch on until some signal or other tells them to open up by breaking the chemical bonds that had kept them perfectly round."

"But the state of the science isn't remotely close to that level of sophisticated biotechnology," Ferendelli said.

"It is. Trust me. It is. Jim, listen, do you have any idea how the fullerenes are commanded to open?"

"Sound. They have a transmitter of some sort that must send out a specific frequency—the signal for the fullerenes to open up. Perhaps the transmitters send out different frequencies for different drugs. Lily said that chemicals had been placed in my brain stem over time and also the president's brain stem as well that could stop our heart or our breathing, or both, with just the press of a button from a transmitter. Like opening a garage door or—or changing a television channel. She actually showed one to me. Then she said I should just go about my business and nobody would be hurt—especially not the president."

"But you didn't buy that."

"Once I began to sense what she wanted, I couldn't believe the president wasn't going to be harmed anymore. So I took off. At the very least I knew what she had done. I didn't think Lily and her people would do anything to harm the president as long as I was on the loose and hadn't said anything to anyone about her."

"What did she want you to do?"

"I don't know for certain, but from pieces of what she said, I had the feeling that at some time in the near future they were going to ask me to invoke the Twenty-fifth Amendment and spearhead the movement to replace Drew because of his mental illness."

"Oh, man. But why? Do you think Bradford Dunleavy could be behind this?"

"Possible, I suppose."

"How about Tom Cooper?"

"I don't know. He seems sincere enough, and he's been a loyal vice president, but I also know he's very ambitious, and we're talking about the presidency of the United States."

"Very folksy, but very smart. I agree. A couple of days ago he came by the office and pumped me for information on Drew's mental health."

"Did you tell him anything?"

"No, no, I certainly didn't. Jim, why did you stay around D.C.?"

"I've been waiting."

"For what?"

"For you—for this meeting. I don't trust anyone, Dr. Singleton—anyone, that is, besides you."

"Explain."

"Someone close to the president is involved in this. I mean someone very close—closer to him than Lily. I have no reason to believe Drew has been having tea with her—certainly not enough to account for all the attacks he has had. According to Lily, the chemicals have to be delivered over time—multiple doses. That means somebody has been dosing Drew continuously with the drug-loaded fullerenes, and also has been causing them to break open and deliver their payload, probably on cue. Someone has to trigger the transmitter to do that."

Gabe couldn't bring himself to tell the man that there was every reason to believe that, like Ferendelli and the president, he was now a walking time bomb, too, at least to the extent that a couple of cups of Lily's tea could deliver.

"What people are you talking about? Who might be in a position to do this to Drew?" he asked.

"The list is an imposing one. The president's wife and children, the twenty-five or so people in the kitchen, the chief of staff and his office, the staff secretary and her office, the cabinet, the Military Office."

"That would be my pal Ellis Wright."

"Ah, yes, the admiral," Ferendelli said. "I hope your relationship with him is cheerier than mine."

"No chance," Gabe said. "He clearly can't abide anyone he can't control. This list of yours is getting quite long."

"Oh, I'm just getting started. There are thirty or so in the medical office, and think of the dozens of housekeepers and other servants—people who just come and go virtually unnoticed."

"And the Secret Service."

"I don't know any exact numbers for them, but probably a few hundred have direct access to the president at one time or another."

"And of all these people you just listed, it only takes one."

"It only takes one," Ferendelli echoed sadly. "And I think he or she has got to be pretty close for the transmitter to work."

"How do you know that?"

"A man has been after me—a professional hit man."

Gabe felt a chill.

"How do you know he's a professional?"

"He uses a silencer. A week or ten days ago, I stopped by my place in Georgetown for some papers. I hadn't been there for twenty minutes when I heard him opening the front door with a damn key. Probably one Lily had made. I managed to get out the basement and down to the Potomac, where I hid along the bank. Then, just a couple of days ago, he showed up at a hobo village where I was hiding while I figured out how to contact you. He killed one of the guys there. Shot him in the face just like that. Again I got out before he found me. Later, I went back. The guys told me he used a transmitter. I couldn't have been more than fifty or seventy-five yards away when he did, but nothing happened."

"Fifty yards," Gabe said, now consumed by a sense of foreboding. "Jim, is there anything else you can tell me about the man? Anything at all?"

"I only saw him in the tunnel—not in the house. And it's pretty gloomy down there. But there was one thing—he was southern. No doubt about that. Heavy accent. Georgia maybe, maybe Alabama. I'm not good at those things."

Trouble. The same man had gone after both Ferendelli and Blackthorn.

Instinctively Gabe scanned from the river across the field to the street and back.

At that instant, from somewhere far behind them came a soft, almost inaudible, crunch of glass.

A homing device! Gabe thought suddenly. The killer had to have fixed some sort of homing device to his car.

"Jim," he whispered urgently, "he's here—somewhere behind us. Get ready to run toward my car. It's way to the left, near that streetlight."

"But—"

Gabe could wait no longer. He grabbed Ferendelli by the arm and pulled him out into the field.

"There they are!" a southern voice behind them called out loudly. "Over there! Right over there!"

CHAPTER 48

There they are. Over there! Right over there!"

There were at least two of them, Gabe thought as he half-guided, half-dragged Ferendelli across the field of the Anacostia River Basin. *A homing device on the Buick!* That had to be it. That explained how the killer had found Blackthorn's hotel. And if the shooter on the trail by Lily's stables didn't directly tail him to Flint Hill, he could have easily followed Gabe using some sort of GPS device.

Gabe couldn't clear the notion from his mind of the mess he had made of things by not being more vigilant.

Although Ferendelli was just a few years older than Gabe was, his weeks of hiding seemed to have broken him physically. His reaction time was delayed, and he was gasping for air after just a few strides.

"I see them!" the southern voice from behind them yelled. "They're headed across the field toward you."

"Toward you!"

Gabe peered ahead to where the Buick was parked. Coming around the rear end of the car was a man, a gun in his right hand—or maybe, Gabe realized, it was the ultrasonic transmitter Ferendelli had told him about, the transmitter that could end either or both of their lives. He glanced over his shoulder. Just emerging from the darkness beneath the bridge was the professional killer Ferendelli had told him about, also holding up something in his right hand.

"Oh, God," Gabe muttered. "Jim, let's head this way, toward the river. It's our best chance."

"Can't."

"Come on, you *can*! You've got to!"

Ferendelli was staggering now, almost deadweight, grunting and lurching from side to side. Gabe risked another check of their pursuers. Both men were gaining on them. He could feel himself beginning to flag and to panic. A severe stitch in his right side had materialized and with every breath began slicing into him like dagger thrusts.

"Go!" Ferendelli gasped. "I . . . can't . . . do . . . this."

"Come on, Jim. Dammit, come on!"

They were still perhaps fifty yards from the river. *Then what?* Gabe asked himself. What if they made it? Again he glanced back. There was still some distance between them and each man, but the one coming from the bridge, the hit man, was far closer than the other and closing fast. If it was a pistol in the killer's hand, they were already near being in range. Either the men had instructions not to draw attention to the field with gunshots or they were intent on capturing him and Ferendelli alive.

Of course, there was another possibility. If the range of the transmitters was thirty yards or less, both pursuers would be in range soon.

Ferendelli stumbled, tried to recover with his extended arm, and then fell to one knee, totally spent.

Gabe, operating on a rush of adrenaline, grabbed the man's other arm and jerked him unceremoniously to his feet. Their run was awkward and uncoordinated, but they were definitely closing in on the river. Suddenly Ferendelli threw his hands up against his temples, cried out, pitched forward, and fell heavily, facedown, emitting a dreadful gurgling sound.

Gabe dropped down and checked his carotid pulse. If there was any, it was so faint as to be nearly undetectable. Ferendelli was still breathing, but not effectively. In any other circumstance, Gabe would be initiating CPR. But there was only a second or two to make a decision.

The hit man coming from the bridge, the one who had two near misses trying to kill Ferendelli, had stopped about twenty yards away. He had been aiming something at them that was clearly not a gun. Then he lowered his arm. Even through the gloom, Gabe felt certain he could see the man smiling.

"Stop, you bastard!" Gabe screamed. "Stop it!"

There was nothing to stop. The lethal weapon, undoubtedly a transmitter, had done what it was supposed to.

Ferendelli, facedown on the summer grass, was twitching. His agonal, liquidy breaths had quickly grown totally ineffective. The pulse in his neck was gone. On all fours, knowing that he might be moments away from death himself, Gabe moved several feet away, then scrambled to his feet. To his left, he could see the second man, egg-bald, still sprinting across the field from the Buick. He looked taller and more athletic than the one confronting him.

"Go ahead," the taller man cried out. "Go ahead and do it!"

The killer raised the transmitter once more.

Gabe whirled and, in a half crouch, bolted ahead toward the river, weaving from right to left to right again like the running back he had once been.

"Did you do it?" he heard the man behind him cry.

"I did," the one with the drawl shouted back. "It may need to recharge, or . . . or he may be out of range."

"I don't think so."

At that instant, Gabe became aware of an odd, not totally unpleasant aroma that seemed to be coming from deep within his nose, and a corresponding taste on the back of his tongue. His body felt lighter and more responsive. Head down, he charged ahead, weaving when he managed to remember to do so. The two voices seemed far away now . . . the sound garbled and unclear. Ahead, the lights from across the river were blurred and in motion.

He was an athlete, an Olympian, sprinting ahead faster than he would ever have thought possible, his feet barely touching the ground. The terror at Ferendelli's apparent murder, and his own mortal fears, had all but vanished. He felt euphoric and was getting more so every second.

Suddenly the moonless night exploded in color—streaks of red and gold, orange and green and white, shot across the sky, then burst over the river like fireworks. Pinwheels of light, now with sound, skimmed across the top of the water.

There were no voices now, only the rich, even sounds of his breathing—in . . . out . . . in . . . out. He was flying—running on air. Invincible. He was Hercules . . . Batman . . . Indiana Jones. Splashing through the dark, chilly water, then diving ahead.

Even with his eyes shut tightly, the colors blazed, bathing the inside of his lids and warming them. Shooting down his throat and into his soul, the water was his home. He pulled through it effortlessly, drawing it in through his nose and spitting it out his mouth. He was a fish . . . a shark . . . Aquaman. He was immortal.

He was a god.

CHAPTER 49

*M*ister . . . hey, mister."

The words were an annoyance, penetrating the void, prodding at Gabe's consciousness until it finally responded.

"Hey, mister, wake up. Are you hurt? Are you drunk? Do you want my momma to call an ambulance?"

Heavy-lidded, Gabe groaned, rolled to his back, and blinked until his vision began to clear. The first thing he saw was the gray-blue sky of early morning. The second was the concerned face of the young black boy who was kneeling beside him. Fragment by fragment, shards of the nightmare with Ferendelli drifted into place.

"Wh-where am I?"

The boy, perhaps ten, had an expressive face that featured huge, dark eyes. He wore a thin navy blue windbreaker and a Redskins cap with the brim pulled forty-five degrees to one side.

"You're up against the fence in the vacant lot at the end of my street."

Gabe pushed himself up onto one elbow and began to take stock. His clothes were sodden and his shoes were gone, as well as his radio, cell phone, and wallet. The lot that the boy had described as vacant was hardly that. It was more the "before" in a commercial for urban neighborhood reclamation—strewn with junk, trash, and garbage. Halfway across to a row of ramshackle two-decker houses Gabe saw a squirrel-size rat scurry from one hiding place to another.

"Is this Anacostia?"

He was sitting now, light-headed and nauseous, with a terrible, dirt taste in his mouth and his pulse pummeling the inside of his eyes.

"A course it's Anacostia," the boy said. "What'd you think it was? Man, I thought you was dead for a while. I cut through this lot on the last half of my paper route. I seen some wild things at this time of day, but never a dead white guy all pressed against a fence."

"I'm not dead."

"Not now, you ain't. But how was I supposed to know?"

Gabe pawed at the filth grating in his eyes.

"What's your name?"

"Louis. What's yours?"

"Gabe. Louis, do you know what time it is?"

"About five. A little after, I guess. I ain't supposed to talk to strangers, you know. You drunk or what?"

"Good question," Gabe said. "I think the answer's 'or what.' "

He sighed deeply and remorsefully as more details of the attack by the Benning Street Bridge drifted into place. Almost certainly, Jim Ferendelli was dead—killed in the exact way that the president would be killed at the whim of whoever was holding the appropriate transmitter; killed by Lily Sexton and by two thugs who would have never found them if Dr. Gabe Singleton had been more cautious and vigilant and had taken the time to try to work out an explanation for an event—the assault on Kyle Blackthorn—that most certainly demanded one.

Now there was another question that needed an answer: Why wasn't Gabe dead, too?

From what he could remember, the ferocious psychedelic response he experienced to having the chemical time bomb in his head set off was not anything like the virtually instant cardiac death induced in Ferendelli. It was far closer to what Drew had probably been experiencing. One explanation was that, like the president, Ferendelli had been dosed a number of times, while Gabe had only been inoculated with the drug-carrying fullerenes during that one session. Other possibilities crossed his mind—higher chemical concentration; more variety of pharmaceuticals; different target organs in their brains; perhaps such sophisticated controls built into the fullerenes and the transmitters that different frequencies triggered the specific release of different drugs.

God damn them!

Gabe tried to haul himself to his feet, but a wave of dizziness and nausea drove him back onto the dirt. He pushed to his hands and knees again and then, without warning, threw up—a mixture of river water, bile, and bits of undigested food.

From Louis's reaction, it was clear he had seen worse.

"That's gross, you know," he said clinically. "My uncle Robbie throws up all the time. Momma says it's because he drinks too much."

"Louis, how far are we from the river?"

"Few blocks. Three maybe."

"And how far from your house?"

"It's just down the end of the street."

"Can you take me there?"

"My momma would kill me for bringing a stranger home—and a bum at that. Besides, I have to finish my paper route. I hardly have enough customers to make any money as is."

"You're right, Louis. Go ahead and finish your route. I'm fine. If I'm still here when you're done, we'll talk."

The youth started away, then returned.

"Oh, heck. I ain't got school anyway. My friend Omar doesn't even start his route until seven."

Avoiding the small pool of vomit, Louis helped Gabe to his feet, then let him brace against the fence until he was ready to take a step. Finally, arm-in-arm, with Louis taking some of Gabe's weight, they made their way up the block.

"I think Momma's still in bed," Louis whispered as they tiptoed through the front door of a modest clapboard duplex with peeling gray paint and a dirt front yard.

"I'll try not to wake her," Gabe said, speaking softly and following Louis into a small, neatly kept kitchen with chintz curtains and a Formica table. "I just need to wash my hands and face in the sink, and then I need a minute to think."

"Think about what?"

"About how to get ahold of my boss."

"You got a job?"

"In a manner of speaking."

With no ID and no phone numbers that he could remember, contacting the President of the United States wasn't going to be easy. It was possible to cut some sort of a deal with Louis for cab fare, but he would not have been at all proud of the boy if he agreed to part with his paper route money, no matter how good the deal sounded. Besides, the best he could do would be, filthy and soaked, to approach one of the uniformed Secret Service agents at one of the White House checkpoints and beg to be let in.

He took the phone from the wall and dialed information. As soon as he could, he would make up the cost of the call and then some.

"City and state, please?" the electronic operator asked.

"Washington, D.C."

"Say the name of the business you want, or just say, 'Residence.'"

"The White House."

Gabe could see Louis's eyes widen as he was patched through to an automated switchboard with another automated operator, giving him a menu of six choices, none of which was to speak with a flesh-and-blood operator, much less to the president.

"What's going on here?"

Startled, Gabe whirled. Louis's mother, in bare feet, wearing a thin, tattered robe, arms folded across her chest, was staring at him from the doorway to the hall. She was a dark, expansive woman, who probably looked quite engaging when she was smiling, which at this moment she most certainly was not.

"He's calling his boss at the White House," Louis gushed. "The White House!"

"And did you reach him, Mr.—?"

"Singleton," Gabe said, smiling sheepishly. "*Dr.* Gabe Singleton."

The woman had already heard enough. She fixed a glare on her son.

"Louis, it's five thirty in the morning and you haven't finished your route. And how many times have I told you—?"

"Never to talk to strangers. I know. I know. But he was lying by the fence in the lot down the street and . . . and I thought he was dead or at least drunk. He's neither, just someone who throws up and needs help to call his boss."

"In the White House."

Gabe could see the woman softening and knew that she had probably never stayed angry at her son for very long.

"In the White House," Gabe echoed. "Can I explain?"

The woman studied him for a few moments; then, without a word, she turned and walked back down the hall, returning with a pair of sweatpants, a towel, and a black long-sleeved T.

"These belong to Louis's brother, Shaun," she said. "He's working nights stocking shelves until he goes away to school in the fall. They should fit, even though Shaun's taller. Sorry, we got no extra shoes. You can change down the hall in the bathroom. Put your clothes into this plastic bag. Then we'll talk about just who you are and how we might be able to help you."

Once in the bathroom, Gabe headed to the sink, then took a quick look at himself in the mirror and chose to shower instead. He absolutely had to connect with Drew. It seemed clear that at some point Lily Sexton or whoever she worked with, employing scientific techniques that Drew was planning on placing under strict government controls, was going to either end the president's life or ruin his career.

Ironic.

The question now was whether or not Ferendelli's death and Gabe's escape would alter some sort of timetable. If so, Drew might be in immediate danger, quite possibly from someone close to him, and Gabe, having exchanged information with Ferendelli before his murder, was now undoubtedly considered a serious threat.

He toweled off and put on Shaun's clothes, which weren't at all the mismatch his mother had predicted. Probably unkempt, filthy, and sodden Gabe was unimposing enough to appear smaller than he was.

"Now that's better," Louis's mother said, surveying Gabe.

She handed him a mug of coffee, determined that he drank it black, and introduced herself as Sharon Turner.

"Mrs. Turner," Gabe said, "I'm very grateful to Louis and I can't tell you how much I appreciate your trust and all you've done. It must have been quite a shock seeing me like I was. Now, what do you want to know?"

"I want to know the name of the man you recently replaced at the White House," she said, with some mirth in her expression at his surprise.

"Ferendelli. Dr. James Ferendelli."

"My sister's husband, Herman, works in the laundry at the White House. I called and asked him about you. He said he never met you, but that you just came on board. He couldn't remember the name of the doctor you replaced, but you answered me quickly enough to seem genuine."

Immediately Gabe's mind began to race.

"Is he home now?" he asked.

"Herman? Actually, he's just getting ready to head into work."

Gabe could barely conceal his excitement.

"Do you think I could speak with him?"

Sharon Turner picked up the phone, dialed, then handed it across to him.

"Herman," Gabe said after introducing himself, "can you get a piece of paper and a pencil or pen? . . . Great. I need you to get a short note to the president. Do you think you can do that?"

"We have people that bring the linens up to the residence. I help sometimes."

"I'd rather have you deliver the note personally if it's possible. Okay, you ready? The note should read: 'The man who rides Condor needs you to call him.' Then I want you to write down Sharon's number at the bottom of the note. If for any reason your supervisor won't let you go up to the residence, see if you can get one of the Secret Service people to deliver the note. But it would be much better if you do it. Any questions?"

Herman said there weren't, and Gabe set the receiver back on the wall. Then he settled back with his coffee, trying to conjure up a way to separate the president from all those who might be a threat to him, including his Secret Service protectors. By the time the phone rang, in just over forty-five minutes, an idea had germinated and begun to grow. It was an idea that would take some quick planning and some incredible luck, but given what was at stake, it was an idea that had to be made to work.

Sharon answered the phone, listened for a few moments, and then, rather shakily, handed it across to Gabe.

"It's for you," she said. "Man on the other end says he's—"

"That's who he is," Gabe said, managing a grin at her reluctance to give the caller a name or a title.

"What's the address here?" Gabe asked.

Sharon grabbed a piece of paper and wrote it down.

"That you, Gabe?" the president asked.

"In the flesh."

"I've been trying to reach you all night. Where in the hell have you been?"

"Long story. I'll tell you when I see you."

"Roger that. Good move with that Condor note. I never forget a horse."

"Mr. President, I need you to send someone out to get me."

"I'll send a car right out."

"Terrific."

Gabe read the address.

"Twenty minutes," Stoddard said.

"And send along a couple of photos—one signed to the Turners and one a thank-you to Louis Turner. Sometime soon I want you to have Mrs. Turner here and her family over for dinner."

"Done. Any friends of yours are friends of the Stoddards."

"Great. Hey, what were you trying to reach me about?"

"Something bad," Stoddard said. "Very bad. A few hours ago we got notified that your patient Lily Sexton was found dead in her hospital bed."

CHAPTER 50

The two friends sat across from one another enveloped in a somber silence. Twenty-five years ago, they might have been in their room in Bancroft Hall at the Naval Academy, chatting about women or an upcoming exam. Now they were alone together in the presidential study in the White House residence, mulling over the significance of frightening and deflating news—the deaths of former White House Physician Jim Ferendelli and the Secretary-designate of Science and Technology, Lily Sexton.

"The police and Secret Service investigators don't report finding anything unusual or suspicious below the Benning Street Bridge," Stoddard said finally.

"I'm not surprised. These people, whoever they are, are organized and professional."

"You're certain Jim's dead?"

"I'm as sure as I can be without a body to examine. I don't know much, but after all these years as a doc, I know dead. It was really quite horrible. We were running, and suddenly he grabbed the sides of his head, uttered a cry straight out of Edgar Allan Poe, and went down. When I knelt to check him, he wasn't reacting at all. He was not breathing effectively, and he didn't have any pulse that I could discern. It only took, like, ten or fifteen seconds. I think they stopped his heart either directly or through the connections in his brain. The two men were coming at us fast. That's when I took off. Running away from Jim like I did was a reflex reaction, but I'm certain that if I didn't, one way or another, either from some chemical they put into me or from a bullet, I'd be dead now. I'm sorry, Drew. I really am."

"I'm sorry, too. Jim was a very good man. Sounds like he went through hell these past weeks. And he said Jennifer was someplace safe?"

"He wouldn't tell me where, but yes. That's what he said."

"I hope we find his body. Except for Jenny he didn't have much family, but especially for her sake, I want to find it."

"An autopsy might help us answer some questions about you, too."

Autopsy. The word hit Stoddard like a slap.

"This is terrible, Gabe," he said, "just terrible. Listen, I want you to go over things one more time, just to be certain I have it all straight."

Patiently, Gabe again reviewed the events leading up to the meeting in Anacostia with Ferendelli, starting with the note that had been left for him at the Watergate. For the moment, he only alluded to his ill-fated ride with Lily Sexton and the remarkable search of her house that followed. The details he would fill in when it was clear the president had come to terms with the certainty of Ferendelli's stunning and horrific death.

As Gabe proceeded, Stoddard stopped him frequently, asking for clarification of the half hour or so that Gabe spent with Ferendelli and the man's unrequited love for Lily. After Stoddard was satisfied he knew all there was to know, he listened attentively to the account of the arrival of the two killers, the chase to the river, Ferendelli's collapse, the explosion of hallucinogenic drugs in Gabe's brain, and finally the moment Louis Turner found him unconscious in the vacant lot.

When Gabe felt comfortable that the president had processed the death of his friend and physician as well as he was going to, he took Stoddard step-by-step through the discovery of the underground passageway and the nanotechnology laboratory. It took most of an hour and a number of diagrams of drug-carrying fullerenes and brain sketches to bring Stoddard up to speed on how his irrational episodes, Gabe's powerful hallucinations, and Ferendelli's death were related.

At last, the president sank back in his high-backed leather easy chair and stared out the window, breathing deeply and slowly through his nose—a calming exercise Gabe remembered from their days at the Academy.

"Sorry about the car," Gabe said. "On the way back here we drove by where I had left it, but it was gone."

"I think my father has insurance," Stoddard quipped. "Gabe, who could it be? Who's doing this to me? And why?"

"As you and every other president and president's physician knows, there are no limits to the number of 'whys.' All I can tell you, Drew, is that Ferendelli felt that in order to dose you with drug-carrying fullerenes, and then to fire off the transmitter that causes them to open up, at least one of the people responsible had to be someone close to you—possibly someone in the background of your life, like an aide or a valet or a secretary; possibly someone quite visible, like one of your advisors, a Secret Service agent, or even a cabinet member."

"I'm getting a damn migraine just thinking about this."

"Speaking of Secret Service agents, there's another problem I'm really concerned and frightened about. Alison Cromartie, the undercover agent working in the medical clinic, may have vanished. She left me a note saying to contact her at one of two numbers, but she wasn't answering either before I left for Anacostia."

"Lord. Can you try again now?"

"I'm afraid her note was in my pocket when I went for my little swim. Maybe whoever rolled me took it. But I have a staff list in the clinic. I can get her numbers from there."

"Good. I'll contact Mark Fuller at the Secret Service offices right away and get people on this."

"Thanks. I'd appreciate that."

"I'm sorry, Gabe. I hope she's all right. First Jim, now Lily."

"And Alison's disappeared. I've been thinking the same thing. What happened at the hospital with Lily?"

"I don't have much to tell. She was transferred sometime last night to the medical center here in D.C. From what's been reported to me, she was perfectly stable. At some point today she was due to have her shoulder operated on. Then, a few hours after she was admitted, she was found dead in bed. So far no one's been reporting having seen a thing."

"I told you, these guys are professionals."

"You think she was murdered. Magnus was told they were thinking embolism—the sort that happens sometime when bones are broken or operated on."

"Fat embolism," Gabe said. "It's the fat in the bone marrow. Pardon me for my skepticism, but two people who are connected to you and knew each other well are dead within a few hours of one another. I'm just not big on coincidence. With an IV line and a chest tube in place, there were plenty of ways to see to it she didn't talk."

"There's an autopsy scheduled for later today."

"Don't bank on its finding too much. These people are good."

"I just don't believe this. Gabe, what should I do?"

For a time, Gabe studied his hands. The filth from the river and the vacant lot, still embedded under some of his nails, seemed to underscore the direness of the situation. Someone physically close to the president, at least intermittently, had the virtually unstoppable capability of either driving him insane or killing him.

"The problem is," Gabe said, "we don't know if Ferendelli's death has changed the rules—maybe caused whoever is behind this to alter their goals or their timetable."

"Do you think it could be Tom Cooper? It would seem he's got a lot to gain if I go bonkers, or worse."

"Or Dunleavy, or the Koreans, or the psycho terrorists, or the drug lords, or . . . or . . . or."

"If you're right, Gabe, than you might be in danger, too."

"I might. But I'm not the President of the United States. And to tell you the truth, Drew, at the risk of hurting your feelings, I wouldn't want to be."

"It requires a special kind of madness."

"You're making a difference, my friend. There's a spirit of optimism throughout much of this country. We've got to keep you healthy and in the game."

"I knew I brought you here for a reason—it's to remind me of stuff like that."

"The way I see it, we need to start grilling the scientists and administrators in that lab attached to Lily's place—find out who they're working for other than Lily, and what they might know that will help get those fullerenes in you neutralized or eliminated. But before we do that, I really think we should find a place to hide you away from anybody who might possibly be behind this."

"What do you mean by *anybody*?"

"Just that."

"My wife? My Secret Service protection? My staff? The country?"

"Drew, you're no good to any of us dead. At the moment, virtually everyone connected with you in any way is a suspect."

"Excuse me, my friend, but haven't you seen what life is like for me? Except for here in our little temporary apartment, I'm not able to go to the bathroom without a phalanx of agents standing by. It's their job, and they do it well."

Gabe tapped his fingers together and worked through the idea that had taken root in his mind.

"I have an idea for a way we might be able to get you separated from everyone—everyone except me, that is."

"Pardon me for *my* skepticism, but I've seen the Secret Service in action. I don't believe you can do that."

"I didn't say it was going to be easy."

Gabe stared out the window and again played through the scenario he had concocted.

"You have figured out a way to kidnap the President of the United States?" Drew said.

"It's not kidnapping if the president goes along with it—more like borrowing. What we need is a place to go—a place where you might be able to hide out for a few days."

"We would have to notify Tom Cooper that he's about to become president."

"Nonsense. It's his job to be ready to become president. That's why you picked him. Besides, as you suggested, he might be the last person we want to tell anything to. Drew, the Constitution and the laws of the land have been put together to handle situations involving you having to take a break from running the country."

"I suppose. I can't believe that my ratty ol' cowboy pal is lecturing me on constitutional law."

"Believe me, sir, your ratty ol' cowboy pal has been busy making himself something of an expert on this. Now, if we're to succeed in separating you from the world, it will have to be soon. Should be today, but I'll need time to get some things together. So tomorrow."

"I'll try and stay in here alone or with Carol as much as possible until then."

Gabe flashed on the unsettling exchange with the First Lady the night of Drew's psychotic episode.

"With Carol would be better," he managed. "I don't want you to be alone. If you can, I'd appreciate it if you make your main priority mobilizing people to help find Alison. I'm really worried about her."

"Count on it."

"Just keep the rest of the world as far away as possible. And please, tell her as little as you can get away with."

"Gabe, our marriage just doesn't work like that."

"I understand. Do what feels right. Remember, the person we need to be frightened of could just as easily be one of Carol's connections as one of yours. Now, what we need most of all is a place we can escape to where the minimum number of people, if any at all, will get a look at you. Specifically, I'm looking for a place within, say, a hundred miles of Camp David."

"What?"

"Camp David. Tomorrow afternoon or maybe evening, we're going to escape from Camp David."

"It can't be done."

"Maybe not, but maybe so. I'll go over the details with you and then see what you think. But first, we need a place."

"Within a hundred miles of Camp David."

"More or less. I'm actually wondering how Sharon Turner's house would work out, back here in D.C."

"I don't want to put her or her family in harm's way," Stoddard said, "and as neat as that woman sounds, there aren't many who could go without saying to some friend or relative, 'Oh, by the way, guess who's staying over at the house for a couple of days?' "

"Ferendelli's brownstone?"

"That would be one of the first places the Secret Service would look. As investigators those guys are the best. Hopefully you'll see that when they set out to find Alison." Stoddard hesitated, a resigned expression on his face. "I know of a place we can go to," he said almost reluctantly. "It's in Berkeley County in West Virginia about thirty miles west of—"

"Hagerstown," Gabe said. "I know the area. I spent a year of my life there, much of the time studying maps against the day when I reached the end of my rope and decided to make a break for it."

"Oh, God, I'm sorry for not being more sensitive, Gabe. I'm really sorry."

"No need to be. There just happened to be a prison there, and I just happened to be in it. What have you got in mind?"

"The place is called The Aerie. It's a castle, a real medieval castle, complete with moat, set on the top of a high hill, or maybe you could call it a low mountain, right in the middle of some of the wildest, densest forest this country has. It was built by my grandfather—my father's father."

"So it's secluded."

"Nobody goes there anymore, but it's still in the family. There's like some sort of family trust, but it only meets every couple of years and hardly anyone comes. I think someone comes in every month or two to do battle with the cobwebs and dust off my grandfather's collection of armor and weapons. I don't know for sure. But I am a trustee, and I do have a key."

"Electricity?"

"As far as I know. Either way, there's a generator."

"Sounds promising."

"Gabe, are you sure this is necessary?"

"Are you sure that it isn't?"

"Okay, okay. And try not to worry too much about Alison. I'm sure there's a simple, logical explanation why you haven't been able to connect."

CHAPTER 51

*H*atred.

There were no windows in Alison's prison, only the unadorned concrete walls, the scattered pieces of junk, and the bare bulb hanging directly over her head, making it unpleasant to open her eyes. After four sessions of Griswold's droning interrogation, each followed by a dose of the unbearable, muscle-tearing intravenous drug, he had left and not returned. Alison had discerned from her own sense of time and some remark he had casually dropped as he was heading off that it was morning.

Now, she guessed, it was evening again. Thirty-six hours—maybe more. She remained strapped on her back, drifting in and out of wakefulness. Her wrists and ankles were expertly secured by rope to the metal frame of her cot. She was helpless and in throbbing pain throughout her body. With her arms stretched above her head and barely able to move, her shoulders were especially uncomfortable. When—*if*—she finally did get to lower her arms, she wondered if they might simply fall off.

At some point during the endless hours, or perhaps during the actual torture that had preceded them, she had wet herself. Griswold, if he was aware of that fact, had made no attempt before he left to change her or to help her change.

Beside her, two plastic intravenous bottles, hooked in parallel, drained saline into her arm, one crystal drop at a time. Why would Griswold ever want her to dehydrate to death and deprive him of his sport?

During the time she was conscious, Alison was consumed by a hatred for Treat Griswold more powerful than any other emotion she had ever known. Being a quarter black, she had encountered racism from time to time, but never had it taken the form of overt hatred. In Los Angeles, there was no question as she watched her friend Janie's life be decimated that Alison hated the arrogant, self-serving surgeons who were master-minding the onslaught.

But never enough to kill them.

This time, she wasn't at all sure.

The president's number-one protector was a master at torture—at breaking his subject down until every statement, every revelation, was cer-tain to be the truth. Clearly, he did not yet feel he had reached that point with her. The doses were progressively larger and more excruciating. By the end of the all-night session, the muscles throughout her body were no longer able to relax fully between injections. The persistent spasms of her jaws threatened to pulverize her teeth, her scalp muscles to crush her skull.

"Who else knows about this?" . . . *"Why did you follow me?"* . . . *"Did someone specifically tell you to investigate me?"* . . . *"Tell me again about the inhaler. What was it I did that made you suspicious?"* . . . *"What did Con-stanza and Beatriz tell you?"* . . . *"Who else knows about this?"* . . . *"Who else knows about this?"*

Even now, in the dense silence, his voice was salt on the raw, exposed wound of her mind.

And yet with each passing second, each agonizing minute, she felt her power to resist grow.

If, as it seemed now, she was going to die, she was going to die victori-ous, with her secret and her self-esteem intact. Maybe sometime after her death Lester would come forward and the FBI would find and thoroughly search her car. . . . Maybe they would find the inhaler. . . . Maybe they would test it and determine that there was something out of the ordinary about it. . . . Maybe . . .

Alison smiled savagely at the notion that it was the very hatred Griswold had created in her that had kept her from disclosing what he wanted to know. It was the pain he caused that made her fight back. It was the knowledge that there was probably no way he could let her live that would keep her from ever telling him about Lester and what precious little she did know about the inhaler tucked beneath the driver's side seat of her car.

Still, she feared the pain.

When she needed to, she passed the hours by focusing her hatred on Griswold's visage—his basketball head, his balding pate, his pinched face, and his small, despicable eyes.

She tried lifting her head off the thin military pillow. The muscles in the back of her neck allowed the movement, but only at a painful price.

How could one human do this to another?

It was a stupid question. Humans had been torturing other humans for as long as there had been the means to do it.

And God made man in his own image . . . and God saw that it was good.

Not this time.

Mercifully, her eyes closed and sleep descended. As she was drifting off, she found herself focusing on why Griswold seemed so insistent on questioning her over and over regarding the inhaler. She had answered his questions not only plausibly but with the truth. Beyond the fact that Griswold had been handling the inhalers at all, she knew of nothing that he had done wrong. Now his persistence in not believing her had her wondering.

By the time she had been able to surrender and doze off, Alison had decided that no matter what she said about the inhaler, Griswold was unlikely to believe her. Sooner or later, regardless of what she divulged—truth or lie—he was going to kill her. By torturing her the way he had, he had more or less crossed the line and had left himself no other option. At the very least, she decided, with nothing to lose, she should do what she could to unsettle him—to drag things out and to make him wonder if she might not be the only one who knew about him.

When she opened her eyes again, the monster was there, staring down at her, still dressed in his shirt and tie and black Secret Service suit.

"Long day?" he asked.

"Go to hell."

"I don't know why, but for some reason I don't think you like me."

"Being a pervert pedophile and a sadist would be enough to accomplish that, but you're a traitor, too."

Nearly submerged beneath the fleshy folds of his brows, Griswold's eyes flashed.

"Why would you say that?"

"You know why."

"Tell me."

"Go to hell."

Griswold filled the large syringe with his torture drug.

"Tell me," he said sweetly, inserting the needle into the rubber port on the IV tubing.

"I've been workin' on the railroad," she sang as loudly as her stressed vocal cords could manage, "all the livelong day. I've been—"

Smiling in a most unsettling way, Griswold pulled the needle out and set the syringe aside.

"I've got a better idea," he said, suddenly looking very full of himself.

Theatrically he reached into the inside breast pocket of his suit coat and produced an Alupent inhaler.

The Alupent inhaler, Alison hoped edgily.

She pressed her lips together, testing how vigorously she was going to be able to resist.

"I think it's time," Griswold said, "that you and our fearless leader developed a common bond. I don't have the time or, frankly, the interest in explaining this little beauty to you, but it sure will be fun to see how you handle it—now and in the near future."

I knew it! Alison thought. *The inhaler! I knew it, I knew it, I knew it.*

"You are really slime."

"Actually," Griswold said, "I sort of like the big guy. I voted for him, and I never would have agreed to go along with this if I hadn't been—"

"Threatened with exposure because of this little baby-love peccadillo you've got going on here. That was your biggest sin of all—leaving yourself open to blackmail and extortion. Griswold, you are just *so stupid*."

"That's why *I'm* standing here and *you're* lying there," he said, seeming a bit rattled.

"What goes around comes around. You'll get yours. Who's blackmailing you? What's in that inhaler?"

"Call it a high-tech time release capsule. Certain chemicals in here enter your bloodstream and settle in throughout your brain, where I can set them off with a push of any of these little buttons. Some of them will make you act loopy in any of a number of amusing ways; one of them will make you act wild; one pair will kill you dead."

He produced a stubby black remote transmitter and held it up for her to see. It reminded Alison of an ice-cream sandwich and had seven or eight cream-colored diamond-shaped control buttons lined up in two columns along one surface.

At last Griswold had done it. At last she knew for certain what was going on, even if she had no idea how the chemicals got to where they were intended, or who was blackmailing the man to administer them, or why. She searched desperately for some way—any way—she could get free, at least long enough to get word to Gabe about what was happening.

"Treat, give it up. Give it up and no one's the worse for what you've done. Give it up and I can tell people how you cooperated. You—"

"Okay, lady," he said, pinching her nostrils closed until they hurt, "I've heard enough. Big breaths, now."

He rested his massive hand against her chin, pried her mouth open, and jammed the business end of the inhaler between her teeth. Then he sealed the opening in place with his hand and waited until she breathed in to send a jet of mist into her throat and lungs.

Alison was in no condition to put up much resistance.

The first jolt of the stimulant tasted like rusty water, the second made her dizzy, and the third made her dizzier still. Griswold's grip tightened. Another spray, then another. Her heart was pounding, sending shock waves through her head. Acid jetted up into her throat and she struggled to swallow it again, rather than to aspirate it and have it scald the inside of her lungs.

Instead of opening up her bronchioles, the repeated dosing now seemed to send them into spasm, smothering her. Another dose and she knew her nervous system was going to explode into a full-blown, grand mal seizure. She managed one final glare at her nemesis, hoping that image of his face might stay with her into the hereafter. Then she closed her eyes tightly and waited to die.

CHAPTER 52

*A*ny word about her?" Gabe asked.

Stoddard shook his head.

"Mark Fuller from Internal Affairs says it's too soon to be worried."

"That's nuts. Something's happened to her."

"He says tomorrow morning he'll start putting people on it."

"I don't want to wait any longer than that."

"First thing tomorrow. I'll check on it myself."

"Good enough. I hear you carry some weight around here."

"I'm counting on you to keep it that way. Now, what are we up against?"

It took most of two hours for Gabe and Stoddard to work out the details of the plan that would, in just over twenty-four hours, separate the President of the United States from a grave threat to his health and possibly to his life. In the process, he would also be separated from his wife and from the presidency itself. Vice President Tom Cooper, a major suspect in Gabe's eyes, would assume the duties of the office, though hopefully not for long.

Once Stoddard was ensconced in a place of absolute security and safety, Gabe would speak with the First Lady and tell her where her husband was. Gabe would also enlist her help in quickly mobilizing the force that would raid the nanotechnology laboratory adjacent to Lily Pad

Stables—the lab indirectly responsible for the death of her physician and the transient episodes of insanity that had been threatening to destroy her husband.

With luck, the scientists in the lab, once they were isolated and interrogated by professionals, would cooperate. With luck, investigators would quickly determine who had hired them and who was paying them. With luck, whoever was poisoning Stoddard and controlling the transmitter would be arrested. And finally, with luck, those ultimately responsible would be brought down.

"Two days," Gabe said. "Hopefully less. With the whole world looking for you, we need you out of sight for two days. Can The Aerie accomplish that?"

"You may have read or heard about my grandfather, Bedard Joe Stoddard. He made a fortune in mining, patents of all kinds, and manufacturing by being uncompromising in his business practices and in his opposition to the unions. Some would and did say *ruthless opposition*. Like many geniuses, B.J. was more than a little eccentric. And also like many geniuses, there were detractors who felt he often crossed over that invisible line between eccentricity and madness."

"Most of my family simply skipped the eccentric step," Gabe said.

"Well, at some point B.J. decided he needed a refuge that was both isolated and secure. That's why he built The Aerie—modeled stone-by-stone after a medieval castle in northern England he once visited and photographed. He brought in trainloads of foreign laborers—mostly the Chinese who had worked on the railroads. He designed the maze of dirt roads leading into the forest himself. Most of them simply stopped, or became endless loops. The roads that eventually would make it up to The Aerie were and are a closely guarded secret."

"But they're marked on the map you gave me."

"I don't think there are more than a half a dozen copies of that map in existence, so take good care of it."

"If the press finds out that's where you were hiding, there'll be more gawkers making their way up there than to the Grand Canyon."

"Hopefully, they'll all get lost in the forest. The whole project took eight years to complete," Stoddard went on. "Decades later, my father spent many more years upgrading the place, adding to B.J.'s bizarre collection of medieval weapons and instruments of torture, and increasing security there. He once told me that in the event of a nuclear attack, I was to eschew the bunker here at the White House and get the heck up to The Aerie, which he called the safest place in the world."

"Sounds like just what the doctor ordered," Gabe said, realizing only after he had invoked the platitude that it was actually funny. "How often does your father use the place?"

"Essentially never. He's much more into entertaining and wheeler-dealing on his yacht. It's been a long time since I was last there, but even then the place had fallen into pretty sad disrepair."

"Sounds perfect for us," Gabe said.

"It *is* perfect—especially if you get off on cobwebs plus the arcane and macabre. Wait until you get a load of it."

"I'm aimin' to do just that before it gets dark tonight. Now, I need two things from you."

"Name them."

"I want your promise to hole up here with Carol. For the time being, please, please tell her as little as possible. She may not believe that this business is as serious as it is, but she never got to watch Jim Ferendelli die like I did. Also, Lily Sexton was her friend. It may take some doing for her to believe Lily's involvement in all this. I don't know the range of those transmitters, but I don't want to take any chances on losing my only patient. I don't know what killed Lily, either, but if someone wants you dead, being a patient in a hospital is only slightly safer than sleeping on a firing range."

"You think she was a loose end?"

"As soon as Ferendelli made contact with me and I got away, I think the rules might have changed from 'make Drew look crazy' to 'make Drew be dead.' That's why I'm so worried about you."

"I appreciate that."

"Okay then, back to Carol. Clear everyone out of this apartment. No help, no valets, no Secret Service agents. Have her intercept anyone who makes it past the agents downstairs and watch them as they go back down in the elevator. Any argument from anyone, even someone like Magnus, and she needs to call the Palace Guards immediately."

"You have my word. What's the second thing?"

"Money. Cash. I'll need lots of it, and maybe a few wallets to stick it in. Can you do that?"

"I have a reliable banker at First Washington Trust. I'll give you a check and make a phone call."

"Just don't tell him why."

"I don't think I'll have to. Walter really belongs in one of those banks in Switzerland or Grand Cayman. He loves the chance to be discreet almost as much as he loves having people know how discreet he is."

"Then you're going to arrange for our evening ride, yes?"

"As soon as you leave, I'll set things up. We've got some damn fine horses out at the stables near Camp David."

"I want it to get dark an hour or so after we disappear. At first we'll need to see what we're doing, but then I want to make it as difficult as possible for the people who are looking for you."

"Now, why would they want to be doing that?"

"Beats me. You're only the president. Drew, I know this has got to be hard for you. It's tough getting bossed around when you're used to being the *capo del capo*. But please believe me, we're doing the right thing—the only thing."

"Why can't we just—?"

"Just what? Arrest everyone? It was horrible watching Jim collapse and stop breathing the way he did. He could have had a hundred Secret Service men around him, *a thousand,* and the outcome would have been the same."

Stoddard drummed his fingertips together, and Gabe could tell that he was scanning every possibility for how he might deal with the threat to his health and life and still remain president.

"You have the map I drew marking where you should leave the ATV?" he asked finally.

"Right here."

"Remember, I haven't been there for years, so there's no vouching for accuracy."

"I'm planning on making a trial run up there later today."

"Just call if you get lost."

"That reminds me. Do you have a cell phone I can borrow? Mine was in my pocket along with my wallet when I went for the big swim."

Drew padded to the bedroom and returned with a check and a cell phone.

"Careful now," he said, handing the cell phone over. "Push the concealed button by mistake and you wipe out Moscow."

The two friends stood quietly for a time, then shook hands and finally embraced.

"Where're you going to start?" Stoddard asked.

"I have some errands to run, but first I'm going to see just how easy it is to buy a car and get it on the road when all I have is cash."

"My money's on you. I just spoke a little to Carol and told her what's in store for us. She says she trusts you to do what's best for her husband."

"Thank her for me, Drew."

"I knew I did the right thing bringing you out here from Wyoming,"

"And I knew I did the right thing voting for you."

CHAPTER 53

*B*IG AL, THE CAR BUYER'S PAL.

The slogan, complete with a caricature of the man, was painted on a sign that rose from the top of a shacklike office, overlooking a lot of forty or so used cars, festooned with red, white, and blue balloons.

While Gabe was working over and over through the elements of the plan that was designed to save the presidency of Andrew Stoddard and possibly the man's life as well, Big Al Kagan was working over every cliché in his automobile buyer's Blue Book in an effort to sell Gabe a late-model Bordeaux red Chevrolet Impala, with CD changer, power sunroof, factory alloys, and cruise control.

"All you need to do," Big Al was saying, "is just take this baby out for a drive, just a quick spin around the block and out Sixty-six for a few miles, and you'll be belting yourself in for the long haul."

"What do you need?"

"Just your license and I'll hook a dealer's plate on this puppy and you're off."

"I . . . um . . . don't have a license right now. My wallet was stolen."

"ID?"

Gabe thought about the handwritten introductory note folded in his pocket from the president to banker Walter Immelman—a note he never even had to use to get twenty thousand dollars in cash.

"Nope."

"Do you have a trade-in?"

"No, I sold my other car."

"Well, then you must have the plates."

"I . . . well, yes, yes, I do have one."

"One is enough."

"If I get the plate, can I just take the car?"

"Of course, once I get a little paperwork done. But don't you want to take her for a little—?"

Stoddard's cell phone cut the bewildered dealer short. It was playing "Hail to the Chief."

"Give me a couple of minutes, Big Al," Gabe said, walking ten yards away to lean against a silver Infiniti with air, CD changer, low mileage, Bridgestone Turanzas, and a red balloon.

"Ellen?"

"Hey there, cowboy."

"Thanks for getting back to me so quickly."

Gabe pictured the trim, seasoned veterinarian seated in her pine-paneled office, just outside of Tyler, surrounded by photos and children's drawings and paintings of horses. Dozens and dozens of horses. In fact, her office chair and those in her modest waiting room were hand-tooled western saddles, transformed with backs and legs by the grateful owner of a patient.

"In no time at all, you've become a legend in these parts, Gabe."

"I promise to undo that misconception just as soon as I get back home."

"Before you go and do any undoing, my kids will want your autograph and a signed photo of your boss."

"Tell them if they want a legend, they don't have to look any further than their mom. . . . Okay, okay. Harry and—"

"Sarah, with an *h*. Harry and Sarah. Make it one for each."

"Done. You want one, too?"

"Only if he's on a horse. In that case it'll be to Dr. Ellen K. and

Gilbert F. Williams. Gilbert hates being left out. The middle initials'll make sure people know it ain't just any ol' Ellen and Gilbert Williams."

"Done."

"So, you mentioned your call has something to do with your patient. Now, pardon me for saying it, but that's intriguing. What can an ol' veterinary sawbones do for you and our esteemed president?"

"I need you to put a potion together for me and ship it out here so that I have it in my hands by noon tomorrow. Any later will probably be N.G."

"Exactly what's this potion supposed to do?"

Watching Big Al Kagan pace about his otherwise deserted sales lot, Gabe went over the details of his requirements. Seventeen hundred miles to the west, Dr. Ellen K. Williams listened intently.

"That's it," he said. "That's all I need."

"That's it, huh? Well, Doc, let me ask you something. What would you say to me if I called you long-distance and asked if you could do this to a bunch of humans?"

Gabe felt himself sink. He had been so immersed in the logistics and potential of his plan that he did not think for a moment that Ellen Williams, whom he had known professionally and socially for years and who was on the board of Lariat, would be morally unwilling to go along with a scheme that might end up killing horses.

Desperately, he searched his mind for alternatives. The best he could come up with on the spot was finding a large-animal specialist locally and opening one of the wallets full of cash he was carrying. He knew that there was no way a bribe of any size would work on Williams.

"You're right, Ellen," he said finally. "If I were even going to consider such a request, I'd want to know details—details and exactly what was at stake. Well, unfortunately, I can't tell you all the details. But I can say that the life of the man I am caring for may be at stake, and I am desperate enough to beg, but not desperate enough to ask you to compromise your professionalism and love of animals. As a physician, I completely understand why you would have misgivings."

A long silence followed.

"You'll be careful?"

"I promise. You've been out to my place. We've even ridden together. You know how I feel about horses."

"Okay, Gabe," she said finally. "I'll do the compounding myself and see to it that the mixture is at your D.C. address by noon. It will be a blend of ketamine, Nembutal, and maybe some fentanyl, although I'm not sure yet how much of each. I'll have to make my best guess as to when each drug will do what it does, and how they will work together. There's a couple of rescued animals here I might be able to try various combinations on. They could use some rest."

"I owe you, Doc," Gabe said, "and I think the country owes you as well."

He gave her the address of the Watergate, slipped the cell phone into the jeans Stoddard had lent him, and turned his attention back to Big Al, feeling not that pleased about what he had just coerced a very wonderful doctor into doing.

"Listen, B.A.," he said, "I'm going to run home and pick up my old plate. Then I'll be back. I'm glad I didn't throw it out."

"Me, too," Big Al called out as Gabe was leaving the lot.

When he reached the street, Gabe glanced about casually. Then he began the evasive action he had started the moment he left the White House. The lesson learned in Anacostia was an indescribably painful one, but it was a lesson nevertheless.

Except for what he had seen in the movies and read in some thrillers, he was a rank amateur in the cloak-and-dagger business. But he was logical and, in most circumstances, he wasn't dumb. Down uncrowded sidewalks; through stores and restaurants with back exits; into one cab, then another. With each move he fought against complacency and against allowing the pressure of time to make him careless. As things stood, with what he knew he might be as much a target as Drew.

Now, leaving Big Al's, he moved thoughtfully, ducking into a doorway from time to time and flagging down a cab for a zigzag five-minute ride to no place in particular. After a two-block walk, he stopped in a hardware store, emerging from the alley entrance with both slotted and Phillips head screwdrivers. Parked against one of the walls in the alley, looking as if it might not have been driven for a while, was an old Chevrolet—hardly a perfect match for the car he was about to buy, but a match of sorts nonetheless. He ducked behind the junker and in just a minute emerged with its plate.

If nothing else, he had just made Big Al's day.

Finally, after returning to the lot, screwing the plate on the Impala, paying Al off, and freeing the balloon, it was time to use some more of the president's hard-earned cash to brighten up someone else's day—this time, it would be Lily Sexton's stable man, William.

CHAPTER 54

*G**abe* had first seen the muddy four-wheel all-terrain vehicle parked outside the barn at Lily Pad Stables. It would be perfect for negotiating the rutted dirt roads up Flat Top Mountain to The Aerie, where it could then be easily concealed in the forest. But first it had to be trucked from Flint Hill to the mountain, fifty or so miles away.

Now, after an explanation that included the assurance that lending Gabe the ATV was what Lily Sexton would have wanted, he was in his newly purchased Impala, leading Lily's stable man, William, up I-81 toward the West Virginia border. Tied down in the back of William's Ford pickup was the ATV—a Honda quite similar to the one Gabe used on his ranch.

If things worked out tomorrow the way he and Drew planned, they would go from horseback to the Chevy and, after an hour's drive, leave the car concealed at the base of the mountain and head up to the castle on the ATV. At the least, as soon as word got out that the president was missing, the sky would be dotted with helicopters and fixed-wing aircraft and the roads jammed with cruisers. Sooner or later, some bright investigator might come across mention of The Aerie someplace and contact LeMar Stoddard, but by then, hopefully, Drew would be ready to come back out into the open.

Their best bet, Drew suggested, would be to stay off the roads as much as possible—even the tangle of dead ends and other dirt roads that his grandfather had built around The Aerie. Drew had owned off-road motorcycles and later ATVs from the time he was a child, and even though he hadn't been up to the castle since before his election, he still felt confident that he could negotiate the narrow hiking paths winding up through the forest and concealed from overhead by the dense canopy of foliage.

William, a laconic septuagenarian, had been born and raised in the Shenandoah Valley and had been working at Lily Pad Stables when Lily took it over nearly ten years before. He had no idea what, if anything, he should charge Gabe for the ATV, which Gabe promised to return when his use for it was done. In the end, the stable man settled for a thousand dollars, which he said he would send along to his niece in Harrisonburg. Gabe added an additional two hundred of the president's money after William promised to keep that amount for himself.

Just past Winchester, they crossed from Virginia into West Virginia. Now Gabe began using his trip odometer and consulting the map Stoddard had drawn. Somewhere off to the left, on a high hill named Flat Top Mountain, was The Aerie. Gabe slowed and took Exit Thirteen. William followed. At 1.2 miles, the narrow two-lane road curved off to the right. To the left, barely visible, a rutted dirt road cut off into the forest.

"Fifty or a hundred feet in on the right," Stoddard had said, "is one of those dead-end roads I told you about that my grandfather built. That's where we'll leave the ATV, covered with branches. Later, we'll leave your car there and put the branches on it."

Saying nothing to William of his intentions, Gabe stopped before reaching the dead-end spur. Together they unloaded the ATV. Gabe started it up, and with William squeezed in behind him, they made a quarter-mile test run down the paved road and then back. The machine seemed a bit sluggish at first but then rallied. Depending on the steepness of the paths up to The Aerie, Gabe decided, he and Drew ought to have a decent shot at making it.

After again expressing his regrets over Lily's sudden and tragic death, and having William refuse his offer of another hundred dollars, Gabe stood by the ATV and watched as the truck rattled back down the road toward Virginia. Then, amid lengthening shadows, he used the seven-inch blade of a newly acquired hunting knife to cut down the branches that would conceal the Impala tonight and again tomorrow. Finally, a bit winded from the effort, he leaned against the trunk of a mature hickory and listened to the noisy quiet of the West Virginia woods. It was time to familiarize himself with The Aerie.

Tomorrow he would buy a pair of western boots and then arrange for a messenger service to pick up the package from Ellen Williams at the Watergate and deliver it to him at their office. He would avoid the White House and his condo. Then the next time he would surface would be at Camp David in the Catoctin Mountains of Maryland, fifty-five miles from where he was standing now.

Through the gathering night, Gabe clutched Drew's map to the handlebars as the ATV jounced upward over rutted dirt tracks that were just wide enough for a car. The woods on either side of the road were truly the Forest Primeval of poets and songwriters, as dense as any he could remember, with the panoply of leaves overhead blocking what little daylight remained.

His love of fishing had led to a solid knowledge of the outdoors and in particular of trees. As he rumbled along, Gabe picked out cedar and black oak, white ash, beech, and cherry, basswood, aspen, and birch. Twice the surroundings and atmosphere overwhelmed his impatience to reach the summit, and he shut off the engine to stand by the roadside and listen, breathing in the cool, sweet air.

Tomorrow Drew would guide them to The Aerie not on these roads but along rooty paths through the thick foliage and undergrowth—a cinch, Gabe suspected, compared to floating a $20-million jet onto the deck of a pitching carrier. He accelerated and leaned into the sharp turns, getting more and more connected with the rhythm of riding the four-wheel stallion.

The forest began to thin as the summit neared. Rock formations grew larger and more spectacular. Suddenly the vegetation fell away completely, and as if born from the ground itself, The Aerie appeared—a massive brooding Gothic fortress of gray stone, rising to a height well above the surrounding trees. The footprint of the castle was nearly square, with towers at each corner and battlements running the length of the walls. The entire structure was surrounded by a ten-foot-wide moat, crossed by a drawbridge leading to a huge portcullis.

Eccentric, indeed!

Gabe left the ATV near the tree line and crossed the drawbridge. Through one of the narrow windows, he could see light. As the president had promised, the power was on and the lights on timers. Gabe used Drew's key and entered a musty, massive great hall supported by exposed post-and-beam trusses. The walls were lined with moth-eaten flags and mannequins in tarnished suits of armor, one of them sitting astride a sixteen- or seventeen-hand-high model horse, also in full armor, adorned by dense cobwebs. If, as Drew had said, a caretaker came in every month or so, the cycle had to be at its end.

Gabe made a brief tour of the place using a flashlight he located in the kitchen. Where he could easily locate a light switch, he used it. He inspected the ancient pipe organ in the great hall and then moved into the expansive dining room, with a long, dust-covered table that once might have seated twenty. Out the far side of that room, up a short flight of stairs, was an empty pool, hewn out of rock and at least ten feet deep. Moss was growing along the insides.

Each of Gabe's bootsteps echoed eerily off the stone and concrete walls.

Skipping a lot of exploring, he went down a dark staircase to the underground levels. In the basement was a security room with monitor screens, none of which seemed operational. There was also an intensely creepy hall containing seven or eight medieval machines of torture, many of them festooned with cobwebs.

But it was on the level beneath that one that he found what he had come down there to see—the bunker that he planned would be home to the president for as long as they needed it to be.

It was a room, twelve-by-twelve, that had only a minimal layer of dust and few cobwebs. There were two rustic single beds and a bookshelf containing several hundred volumes, a built-in television, dozens of movies, mostly old videotapes but some DVDs, and a stereo console. Along the base of the walls were large bottles of water and, in a small pantry, enough canned goods to keep a family going for weeks. The refrigerator was plugged in but empty, and the roomy bathroom was tiled and surprisingly homey.

Gabe found the switch for the air conditioner and turned it on as Drew had suggested.

"Reinforced walls, six feet thick," he had said, "with filtered air. Built originally by Bedard Stoddard himself and modernized by LeMar in the eighties. We've been told that anyone inside here during a nuclear blast will survive as long as the generators keep going, even if the warhead hit as close as Washington."

Gabe spent twenty minutes wiping down the space. Drew groused about having it be his room but in the end agreed that his safety was what their mission was all about.

Before he headed back upstairs, Gabe made one final survey of the quarters, three stories below the ground, surrounded by solid granite and six feet of reinforced concrete. His knee-jerk reaction was that despite serious efforts to make it comfortable and inviting, the space gave him claustrophobic jitters. Still, he acknowledged, it would be the perfect sanctuary for the president . . . or the perfect coffin.

CHAPTER 55

*T*he noise, from the stairway behind Alison, was faint—the opening of the door. A footstep on the top stair.

The sound was significant. It meant, in all likelihood, that she wasn't dead.

She had no idea how many hours it had taken for her cardiac, respiratory, and nervous systems to recover from having been overdosed with metaproteranol—the pharmacoactive drug in Alupent. She still felt jittery, sick to her stomach although she hadn't eaten for thirty-six hours or more, and profoundly ill at ease.

Her muscles ached terribly, even though she could not recall having been injected after the inhaler overdose. It was doubtful that Griswold had any idea of what dosage of metaproteranol a person could survive. More likely was that he had simply kept forcing the medication into her lungs and bloodstream until the apparatus had run dry. It was a miracle her body hadn't simply given in—her lungs exploding, her heart ceasing to beat, her brain shutting off altogether.

She had to find a way out—to cause Griswold to make a mistake of some sort.

The footsteps continued down the stairs.

The monster was back for another session. She had beaten him this far—even gotten him to boast that there were, in fact, various drugs adul-terating the president's Alupent—and somehow, she vowed, she would beat him again.

Or die.

Softly she began to hum, singing the words in her mind, preparing herself for whatever was to come.

"This world ain't always tasty like candy. . . . That's what my mama once told me. . . ."

Another step . . . then another. Alison tightened her eyes shut and clenched her fists.

"Sometimes it'll shake and bend you. . . ."

The footsteps ended on the concrete floor. Then she heard a woman gasp.

"*¡Ay, Dios mío!*"

Constanza came into Alison's sight.

"I can't believe he let you down here," Alison rasped through parched, split lips.

Constanza lifted the back of Alison's head and gave her a sip from a bottle of spring water. The jeans and black beaded sweater she wore looked elegant on her, but her gentle, exotic face was dark with anguish and concern.

"Donald doesn't know I am down here," she said. "He has forbidden it, but I know where the key is. I have lived here in this house for ten years. There is little I don't know. Beatriz and I heard you screaming last night and the night before from upstairs, even though this room is below the basement. It was very frightening."

"He has caused me terrible pain," Alison replied. "And he plans to continue torturing me until he is convinced I have told him all that he wants to know."

"And why won't you tell him?"

"Because then he will kill me. Sooner or later, he plans to kill me any-way."

"I can't believe that about Donald."

312

"Constanza, please, please listen to me. You must listen and help me. Help me or I will die. Donald works for the government."

"No, he is a businessman."

"Does this look like something a businessman would do?"

"Who are you? I remember you from the nail shop. What is your name?"

"Please. I won't last much longer. My name is Alison. I work for the government, too—just like Donald."

"I'm sorry he had to do this to you."

Alison studied the woman's face but could see no sign that she was lying—that she had been sent down by Griswold to accomplish what his muscle-tearing chemical and the Alupent overdose could not.

"He didn't *have* to do this to me, Constanza; he *wanted* to. Please untie me. I am in so much pain."

"Donald is sending us away," the beauty said, pointedly ignoring Alison's pleas.

"You and Beatriz?"

"Yes. There is a woman in Mexico City he knows. We are to leave to go there in just a few minutes, and wait until he sends for us. We are all packed. We have money. He is sending a car to take us to the airport."

Don't bother coming back to this house, Alison was thinking. *It's not going to be here. Soon—maybe as soon as tonight—your Donald is going to see to it that this place mysteriously burns to the ground. That is what people like him are expert at—covering up and then counterattacking.* It was one thing to blow the whistle and bring charges against such highly connected people. It was another to come up with the evidence to make them stick.

"What time is it now?" she asked.

"Almost nine in the morning. Donald has gone to work."

"Constanza, listen to me, please. Don't leave me like this. I know Donald has been good to you, but he has hurt me. He has hurt me badly. And he's not done. He will continue to hurt me until he is convinced I have told him all I know; then he will kill me."

"But Donald will be furious with me. He sometimes has a short temper, and he can get very angry."

Alison continued desperately fumbling for the right words.

"Think of . . . of how you would feel being tied down like this."

Constanza did think for a time. Then she shook her head, turned, and headed back toward the stairs.

"I'm sorry," she murmured over her shoulder.

Alison felt her heart sink.

CHAPTER 56

So far so good. . . . So far so good. . . .

As Gabe showered, the mantra flowed steadily through his head.

So far so good. . . .

He got no cell phone signal in the castle, but he did outside. He dialed both of the numbers he had for Alison, half-expecting—or was it praying—to hear her voice. No answer at either. The mantra slowed, then stopped.

Was there anyone he could call to report that she was missing? Anyone he could ask? He briefly wondered if he should try to reach the admiral. Possibly Ellis Wright knew something.

The third number he dialed was answered on the first ring.

"Yes?"

"Drew, it's Gabe."

"Hey! Calling from The Aerie?"

"By the moat. There's no signal inside."

"What do you think?"

"Charming little bungalow. A monument to benign neglect—sort of like me."

"Look at the bright side: You could have grown up there."

"Everything okay with my patient?"

"Never better. I've been up for an hour. Did a little stretching, drank

315

some coffee, did a few sit-ups, vetoed some bills. You know how it is with this job."

"You ready to ride?"

"I'm ready to put this whole business behind me. I feel so damn helpless. What good is it being president if you can't control everything and boss everyone around?"

"Not to worry. You'll be back martineting before you know it. Just remember, until we know who and why, everyone is a potential assassin, no matter how meek or innocent they might seem. Keep your eyes open and keep your plans guarded until the very last minute. I'll be coming into the city to run some more errands; then I'm going to find a safe place to stash my new wheels just off one of the riding trails."

"You going to be able to find the car again once we're galloping through the woods?"

"I intend to go to the stables as soon as I can and to convince the stable master—what's his name again?"

"Rizzo. Joe Rizzo."

"To let me go for a brisk solo ride to clear my head."

"I'll make a call and set that up for you. You have that map I drew showing where the stables are?"

"It's a break that they're outside the compound. Will they be bringing our horses to us?"

"Probably."

"Any special horses or should I pick?"

"You pick. I don't know them well enough. Meanwhile, everything's going okay, yes?"

"I'm not so sure," Gabe said.

"No Alison?"

"Nothing. It's been more than two days now."

"I promised to call Mark Fuller and get some people on this, and I will."

"Right now?"

"Right now. I'm sorry this is happening, Gabe. She's all right. Just wait and see. Some sort of misunderstanding."

"Thanks for doing this."

Gabe reiterated his plea for vigilance, then rinsed out a cup and poured the first of what would undoubtedly be a number of cups of coffee. He paced as he drank, mentally ticking off his to-do list. The most critical item was picking up the mixture sent by Ellen Williams. If for any reason the tranquillizer didn't arrive on time, he and Drew would have to find a way to delay everything for a day when every minute meant more danger, not just for the president but for Gabe as well.

Sunset would be at seven forty-five—later than he would have liked, but likely to be of some help before they reached The Aerie. The less daylight when they hit the riding trail, the better. If possible, he would find some way to communicate to Drew the need to stall for a few more minutes of dusk. Details. Details.

By six fifteen, he was back on the ATV, rumbling down the mountain to where the Impala was hidden. Not enough cover, he decided, easily picking it out from a dirt road that was virtually untraveled anyway. Using his hunting knife, he cut a dozen more branches, then pulled the car out and replaced it with the ATV, which instantly became swallowed by the forest when he covered it up.

With no idea whether or even why he might need them, he added the knife to some rope and tools and two bottles of water, stashed in a small backpack he had left on the seat of the Chevy. Also in the pack were some apples and sugar cubes for the horses. Details.

At ten forty-five, when the call came in to his cell phone from the front desk at the Watergate that a package had arrived for him via FedEx, he was walking the streets of D.C., breaking in a new pair of calfskin boots that needed no real breaking in and might have cost as much as the total of all the other boots he had ever owned. He had chosen a messenger service on L Street and had paid them well to have the messenger bring the package from the Watergate to their office and then have a different messenger take the package out the back door to the lot three blocks away where Gabe had parked the Impala.

On the way there, Gabe gave in to his fears and frustration and tormented himself by trying Alison's numbers again. Nothing. Once at the lot, he ducked behind a van and scanned the street for anything or anyone unusual. They couldn't have followed him here, he was thinking, at the same time he was picturing Jim Ferendelli collapsing to his knees, then pitching forward onto his face. They couldn't have followed him there, either.

The messenger arrived, and the exchange was quick and uneventful. Gabe tipped the man fifty dollars of the president's money and then added a second fifty for the one who had picked up the package at the Watergate. One final check of the lot and Gabe slid behind the wheel of the Impala and set the package on the passenger seat.

It was time.

Twenty-five miles outside the city, he was convinced enough that he wasn't being followed to pull off into a rest area on I-270 and open the package from Ellen Williams. The carefully wrapped box consisted of a Tupperware container with five sealed plastic Baggies, each containing two large gauze pads, soaked with liquid.

SPECIAL MIXTURE, the label on the Tupperware read. APPLY ONE OR TWO AS NEEDED.

Gabe's heart told him one, but his head insisted on two.

If things didn't work for him and Drew Stoddard, there would not be a second chance. Word would get out that the president had behaved irrationally, and within no time a button would be pushed by someone and the First Patient would suffer either a public episode similar to the one Gabe had witnessed in the White House or, worse, one identical to the episode he had witnessed in Ferendelli.

With that notion grimly dominating his thoughts, Gabe set the package aside and checked the map Drew had given him locating the stables. Then, staying well under the speed limit, he headed north to Thurmont, Maryland, and, just beyond it, Camp David.

CHAPTER 57

I'*m sorry.*"

The words had been spoken so softly, barely more than a whisper. Had Constanza really said them, Alison wondered, or was it the fallout from the drugs Griswold had forced into her? Could the woman have possibly just left her in such a horrible situation? The answer, of course, was yes. Ten years. That was how long Constanza had been under Treat Griswold's control. Ten years.

Battling to breathe and to keep her leg muscles from seizing up, Alison closed her eyes and drifted off. The pain was so much more tolerable that way.

When she awoke, after a few minutes or a few hours, she was still spread-eagled on her back, her wrists and ankles still tightly bound. The visit from Constanza had been a dream, she realized despondently—only a chemically induced dream.

Then she felt the knife resting in her palm. Slowly, painfully, she closed her fingers around the handle and craned her head to the right to see. It was a sturdy kitchen knife—black plastic handle, serrated six-inch blade. And it was almost certainly not a dream.

Why hadn't Constanza simply cut the rope?

The answer wasn't hard to discern. Alison had already experienced Griswold's power and lack of caring for human life and pain. He was a patient master at bending subjects to his will. In less than forty-eight hours he had all but broken her. What had ten years of manipulation, chemicals, and abuse done to Constanza? It seemed highly likely that the poor woman couldn't bring herself to go through with such an act of rebellion against the man who had taken her from her home before she had even reached her teens. Setting the knife in place was simply the best she could manage.

Now it was Alison's job to go the rest of the way.

For a while, she lay still and listened, preparing herself. There was only stillness—an intense silence. The house was empty. She felt certain of it. Constanza and Beatriz were gone. Slowly, desperate not to let the blade slip away, she turned the handle in her swollen, stiff fingers until the serrations lay against the rope. Then, no more than a fraction of an inch with each stroke, not worrying whether she cut rope or flesh, she began to saw. There would be no resting, she vowed, no taking the chance that sleep would overcome her. Her muscles ached terribly, and she had little strength. But Treat Griswold had given her the power to cut through the cords. He had given her the hatred.

Twenty minutes? Thirty? An hour?

Alison would never know how long it took. She would only know that she never stopped. A fraction of an inch with each awkward stroke. The blade cut through her skin, but the pain was nothing compared to what she had already endured. Her biggest fears were that she would saw through a tendon or hit an artery. At the moment when it felt like even her hatred for Griswold wasn't going to be enough to keep her fingers moving, the cord snapped apart.

She sat on the edge of the cot for a long time, waiting for the dizziness to subside and for her legs to give her some sort of a sign that they were ready to bear her weight. Then she cut several strips of pillowcase and stanched the blood flow at her wrist. Finally, using the bed frame for support, she pushed to her feet. Just as quickly, her legs buckled at the knees, her quadriceps muscles all but spent. A second try again dropped her awkwardly to the concrete floor. The third time, her legs wobbled, then held.

Her clothes were still neatly folded by the wall. Her pocketbook and wallet weren't there, nor was her ID lanyard. But there was one thing Griswold had not yet disposed of or hidden. One thing he hadn't counted on that she would ever need or use again.

With consummate effort, she sat on the edge of the tawdry cot and dressed herself. Then once again she stood. Her legs were stronger this time, more willing. She took a step toward the staircase, then halted. Her smile was vicious. The moment she had stopped believing would ever come was here.

"I'm coming for you, you son of a bitch," she rasped, testing the battery on Griswold's mistake, her two-way radio, then hooking it to her belt. "I'm coming for you."

CHAPTER 58

*T*hree hours to go.
So far so good.

The mantra had started up again of its own accord as Gabe adjusted himself in the saddle of a muscular black stallion named Grendel, opened the trail map that the stable head, Joe Rizzo, had given him, and headed off into the state forest to plan where he and the president might break away from his Secret Service guardians. Gabe had parked the Impala in town and taken a cab to the visitors' entrance to Camp David. Then, cleared for entry by the president, he walked straight through the 125-acre compound and out the guarded north entrance to the nearby stables.

There would probably be three agents accompanying them on their ride, Drew had said—all decent riders and armed with handguns that they knew quite well how to use. If things went as Gabe projected, by the time the agents realized that their mounts were not responding to their commands to speed up and the president and his doctor weren't responding to their commands to slow down, they would be too confused and too far out of range to risk a shot. If he was wrong about that, the first shot one of the agents did take would undoubtedly be at him.

So far so good.

His concern for Alison remained acute, but for the moment there was nothing he could do, and the task ahead was daunting. There were so many variables to consider—so much that could go wrong. In just three hours, if things went as he hoped, he would have become the second most wanted man on the planet.

The afternoon was cool and overcast. Grendel was anxious to pick up the pace but responded nicely when Gabe called for a walk. His first goal was to determine how far out on the trail they would be after twenty-five minutes. At that point, with luck, the Secret Service horses would be in no shape to match the speed with which he and Drew would take off. After their break from the agents, on the first acceptable trail to the left, the two of them would cut toward the paved road, which was smudged on the map but might have been Route 491.

Twenty-five minutes.

Gabe had subtracted five minutes from the thirty Ellen Williams had estimated in order to make up for the time it would take them to get back to the stables from where they would have mounted up at the rear entrance to Camp David.

Twenty-five minutes.

Gabe grinned at the notion of treating this operation as if this were some sort of science. The size of the horses minus twice the weight of the agents plus the rate of absorption of the Williams potion squared minus the angle of the sun equaled . . . twenty-five minutes. No problem.

At the spot on the trail, twenty-five minutes out, Gabe stopped Grendel, sharpened his hunting knife on a whetstone from his backpack, and marked several trees at horseman's eye level. They then proceeded at a careful walk, scanning along the left tree line for an opening. With luck, the next time he traveled over this portion of the trail, he and Drew Stoddard would be moving at a full gallop. He felt his mouth go dry at the prospect.

Is there any other way? he asked himself for the thousandth time. *Is there any other way?*

Now there were just three more pieces—a trail going off to the left toward the highway, a place to leave the horses where they would eventually be found, and finally a concealed spot just off Route 491 to leave the Impala.

Gabe's best guess was that the car would have to remain undiscovered by the park rangers for at least two hours. If they found it and had it watched or towed, some trucker would have a hell of a tale to tell about the two guys he picked up hitchhiking.

The first piece, a trail to the left, was a narrow track that had some dried hoofprints but didn't look as if it were used much. It was just a few minutes from where Gabe hoped he and Stoddard would be leaving their posse—closer than he would have liked, but far enough to work, and perfect in every other respect. The tree marks here were critical in that he would have to see them at a gallop. He made a few cuts, then dismounted and built a subtle cairn of stones on the right side of the main trail, ten yards before the path.

When the Secret Service men secured help—probably in the form of some sort of four-wheel-drive vehicle—he didn't want to make the pursuit too easy. Once he and Drew were in the car, every mile they could put between themselves and the end of the path would widen the circle of possibilities the agents and police would have to consider and make it that much less likely that one of the roadblocks would snag them.

The final two pieces were easier to find than Gabe had expected. A small clearing ten feet off the path and twenty yards from the paved roadway would be the perfect place to leave the horses, and a partially overgrown rest area just thirty or forty yards to the north offered some concealment for the Chevy without having it appear too suspicious. Now, there was just the matter of getting the car to the rest area from where he had left it in Thurmond, putting a sign on the windshield that it was disabled and awaiting a tow truck, and walking back to the stables to do what he could to help the stable man get ready for the president's early evening ride.

First, though, it was time to let patient Grendel have his head. Gabe swung up into the saddle, whispered a few words of encouragement into the stallion's ear, and then prodded him with a gentle nudge from his new boots. The horse hesitated for a beat, then shot back down the trail toward home like a missile.

CHAPTER 59

*A**lison* spotted the man parked half a block down from her apartment the moment the cabdriver from Richmond Taxi turned onto her street.

"Keep going!" she demanded, ducking down onto the floor.

She instructed the driver on a circuitous route around several blocks and watched to ensure they weren't followed. Then she had him pull over in front of an apartment on the next block. The man in front of her place was either Secret Service sent there by Gabe or, much less likely, someone put in place by Griswold as the result of a change of heart on Constanza's part. Either way, Alison wanted no part of him.

The driver took the hundred in cash they had agreed on for the trip and left the garden apartment complex by a different route. Alison had found the money—four hundred altogether—in the sock drawer of Griswold's bureau. As she had anticipated, when she made it upstairs from the basement Constanza and Beatriz were gone. Alison gave passing thought to a thorough search of the house but in the end decided that she had neither the strength nor the time for it. It sickened her even to touch his clothes. He had violated her in ways as vicious, dehumanizing, and unfeeling as rape, and somehow, soon, he was going to pay.

There was one room she did opt to visit before calling for the cab—the attic space where the bulk of the training of Donald Greenfield's girls had taken place.

The room, straight out of the sixties, she imagined, was repulsive enough so that she could only last a few minutes there. Circular water bed . . . red satin sheets . . . ceiling mirror . . . dense psychedelic curtains . . . various mood lights and lamps . . . sound system . . . and a huge HDTV with a large collection of video pornography, most involving older men and girls. Surprisingly, there were no cameras—at least none that she could see. She thought about the person who was blackmailing Griswold. If there had been a camera at some point, it seemed possible, even likely, that the blackmailer had the film.

She couldn't bring herself to open any of the drawers. If, as she expected he would, Griswold burned the place to the ground, the world would be the better for it.

During the cab ride up to Arlington, she tried to piece together everything she knew about the man. Griswold seemed once to have been a devoted, effective public servant, who had fallen prey to his own perversity and to someone with the intelligence to document that perversity and to force him to violate his oath as a protector of the president. Perhaps, as his Porsche, second home, and other activities suggested, there was a payoff involved as well. At this point, there was no way to know.

Griswold's mandate appeared to be the administration of psychedelic drugs to the president by way of his Alupent inhaler. Remarkably, though, the drugs remained inactive until triggered by some sort of handheld transmitter, thus making the commander in chief a marionette, who could be caused to go insane by the push of a button, ironically by another marionette.

It was incredible technology—well beyond Griswold's ken, she thought, even though, almost certainly, it had been Griswold who had stolen the blood samples Gabe had placed in the clinic refrigerator.

Unanswered at the moment was how could she provide proof of what she knew to be true, and exactly who was the master puppeteer pulling Griswold's strings. What she knew with certainty was that she was not going to go up against a man with Griswold's reputation and clout without hard, no, *impenetrable* evidence.

She assumed her car was in the White House parking area where she had left it. The inhaler beneath her seat might get the ball rolling, provided it was still there and was found to be contaminated by drugs and marked by Griswold's fingerprints. But she needed more than that—if there were any lessons to be learned from her L.A. experience, probably much more.

Meanwhile, she also needed to protect herself from becoming a victim once again, this time in every sense of the word. Griswold was no less powerful and respected, and probably even more ruthless, than the Four Cs surgeons in L.A. If she was going to bring him down and uncover the identity of his puppeteer, she was going to need to move quickly and keep Griswold worried and off balance. She also needed help from someone she could trust, and the list of people she could safely approach in that regard was short—very short.

As soon as possible, she and Gabe had to talk.

Alison crossed between two units and carefully approached hers through the backyard. Then she used her elbow and punched in a window panel in her rear door, reached inside, and turned the lock. The neat little two-bedroom had been expertly ransacked. Every drawer had been emptied onto the floor. The rugs had been pulled up, the cupboards swept clean, the pillows on the living room sofa slashed open. Broken glass was everywhere, and what few personal items she had brought up from San Antonio had been destroyed.

Could Griswold possibly have figured out the switch she and Lester had pulled off, or was he just being thorough—looking for anything she might have uncovered?

At first, Alison battled back tears as if Griswold were watching and she didn't want to give him any satisfaction. Then, shuffling to the bathroom to shower, she finally allowed herself a thorough, cleansing cry. The condition of her place didn't matter, she decided as she toweled off. From now until her war with Treat Griswold was over, she would not be staying here—not for a minute.

She found a clean pair of jeans and a navy long-sleeved T. Then she set about looking for the only two things she needed from the place. The first, a spare set of keys to her car, she found on the kitchen floor beneath a bowl. The second was right where she had hidden it—a short, efficient, 9mm Glock 26, tucked neatly in front of a knee-length nylon in one of a pair of four-inch spiked heels that she never wore for fear of breaking her ankles. Tucked in the other shoe, also behind a rolled-up stocking, were two full magazines of ammunition.

Finally, she remembered that she was now in range and turned on her radio. The first voice she heard was one she was listening for.

"Attention, all posts," Griswold was saying, "this is Special Agent in Charge Griswold. Prepare for Maverick departure on Marine One. Wheels up in two hours. Repeat, two hours before departure."

Marine One.

Griswold had said nothing about their destination. Andrews Air Force Base? Camp David? A speech somewhere?

No matter. When she was ready, she would find them. First, though, she needed to contact Gabe. The apartment phone was still working. Standing amid the wreckage, she took up the receiver and dialed the White House medical clinic.

CHAPTER 60

*R*otors.

Just a couple of weeks had passed since the president had dropped in at his ranch for a visit. Gabe had been on horseback then, and he was on horseback now, helping Joe Rizzo, the stable master, and Joe's ten-year-old son, Pete, lead four horses from the stable to the rear entrance of Camp David for the president's early evening ride with his physician. The difference between this ride and the many others that various presidents had taken along this trail over the years since 1942, when Camp David—or Shangri-la, as it was called before President Eisenhower renamed it after his grandson—officially became a presidential retreat, was that this time the president would not be coming back.

In just an hour or so, President Andrew Stoddard, among the true visionaries who had ever held the office, would confirm those rumors that he was mentally unstable by escaping his Secret Service protectors.

Totally pleased with the horse, Gabe had asked permission to ride Grendel again. Pete, with whom Gabe instantly connected, especially after he taught the boy a couple of neat rope tricks with the lariat he had brought in the backpack, promised he could make that happen with a rub-down, a cooling sponge bath, and an extra helping of oats.

Joe Rizzo, too, clearly enjoyed having a man around who was both a doctor and a cowboy. When Gabe checked out the horses and suggested the president might like a ride on a dapple gray thoroughbred named Mr. Please, the stable master readily agreed. The horse, Gabe saw, was long in the neck and legs—a mover if ever there was one. It was good money that Grendel and Mr. Please could beat the Secret Service horses in a straight-up race, to say nothing of a contest where their three opponents were floating on clouds of Nembutal, ketamine, and fentanyl.

"They've landed!" Rizzo exclaimed in his charming accent, as the distant thrumming slowed, then stopped. "It should be a very beautiful ride, Dr. Gabe. A little breeze, not too many bugs."

"They wouldn't dare to bite the President of the United States anyway," Gabe said.

There was a hitching post near the rear gate to the compound. Gabe helped tie the horses up and then made preparations for what would be the daunting task of slipping drug-soaked gauze pads beneath the saddle blanket of each one without being seen and without having even the slightest bit of white showing.

From his backpack he took a pair of riding gloves—something he would never wear if he weren't trying to keep himself from absorbing enough mixture through his palms to topple from his own saddle. While rummaging through the backpack, he eased the top off the Tupperware container, separated out three packets of soaked gauze—two pads in each—and replaced the top. At that instant, his radio crackled to life, actually startling him.

"Doc, this is Griswold. Are you there? Over."

"Griz, g'day, mate. I'm here at the rear gate. Got some mighty fine mounts for you. Over."

"We'll be there in five minutes, just as soon as the nurse and corpsman finish loading up the van. Over and out."

Gabe felt himself go cold.

"Joe, what kind of van is he talking about?"

"The medical van, of course. The president never goes out on the trail without three or four Secret Service agents and the medical van. Hey, wait a minute, aren't you the doctor?"

"The *new* doctor," Gabe corrected, his mind swirling. "I've never been out on the trail before."

So much for carefully contrived scientific formulas. *How in the hell could Drew not have mentioned that there was going to be a van tagging along?*

Gabe began rapidly flipping through what little he knew about disabling cars. The best he could come up with on the spot was dropping the sugar lumps he was carrying into the gas tank and hoping for the best. Ludicrous.

"Joe, what happens with the van if we go on a narrower trail?" he asked.

"The van waits where it can. A couple of years ago, one of the horses threw a guest and the man broke his leg. The agents had to carry him back down the trail to the van."

No help.

What a mess!

Gabe glanced at his watch. Even if he and Drew managed to disable the horses and take off, the van would be able to haul the agents back to camp in a matter of minutes. The two of them might not even be in the Impala before a massive pursuit began, with the Secret Service prominently represented in Marine One.

Why in the hell did he ever think he could pull this off?

"Doc, Griswold here. The van's all set. We're on our way. Over and out."

Damn!

"Joe," he said, handing over the two apples, "could you give these to Grendel and Mr. Please? I'm going to check the saddles one last time. I'm in no mood to play doctor out there."

Moving quickly, he crossed behind the horses, feigning a check of the blankets, stirrups, and cinches, while at the same time sliding the gauze as far up under the saddle blankets as possible. He was just easing the third pack into place when the president's entourage appeared and approached the guardhouse.

Gabe glanced at his watch and mentally started timing absorption of the drugs. Thirty minutes.

Trailing behind the three agents and the president as they reached the guardhouse was a small van—a Mitsubishi, with a nurse and corpsman inside. He had met each in the White House clinic.

The thirty minutes were down to twenty-nine, maybe even twenty-eight.

Stay cool, Gabe urged himself. *Just stay cool and think.*

He approached the president and shook his hand warmly.

"Why didn't you tell me about the van?" he whispered through nearly clenched teeth.

It took several precious seconds for the significance of the vehicle to register.

"In the heat of all that planning, I just never thought of it," Stoddard said. "Are we dead?"

Gabe glanced over at the van. From where he stood he could see the spare that was mounted on the rear.

"I need a minute alone by the van," he whispered suddenly. "Can you get me that?"

"Watch me."

Without hesitating, the president doubled over, grabbed his throat, and crossed unsteadily over to the entrance. Then, using a corner of the guardhouse to brace himself, he started to cough . . . and cough. The moment the agents realized what was happening, they raced to him. By then, Gabe had slid the hunting knife from his backpack.

"A bug!" one of the agents called out. "He says a bug or a bee went down his windpipe."

The racking cough continued—Academy Award quality, Gabe acknowledged. Now, completely concealed from the agents and the medical team, he set the knife handle against his chest and leaned against the sidewall of the spare with all his weight and all his strength. The powerful blade easily slid through the rubber and became buried to the hilt. He withdrew it and had it back in his pack when Griswold called to him from beside Stoddard.

"Hey, Doc, what's going on? Get over here!"

"I'm coming, I'm coming."

Without bothering to explain the delay, he raced over to the group, all of whom were standing helplessly around the hunched-over, distressed, sputtering commander in chief. Gabe set one hand on the front and one on the back of Stoddard's chest.

"It's okay now, Mr. President," he whispered.

He applied a slight, quick thrust with each hand. Instantly the hacking stopped. Stoddard sputtered once for effect, then stood up, smiling.

"Gone," he said. "Damn, but that was scary."

The entourage, amazed and totally impressed, turned to Gabe.

"Kind of a Wyoming version of the Heimlich maneuver," he said matter-of-factly. "Now, let's ride."

With six minutes gone, they mounted and headed up the trail.

One tire down, Gabe was thinking, *at least one to go.*

Quickly the Secret Service trio dropped back, allowing twenty or thirty yards to open between them and the two riders ahead.

"Nice acting job, Mr. President," Gabe said.

"Just like the olden days. Remember those coeds from Goucher?"

"This was better."

"Did you accomplish anything?"

"I disabled the spare. Now I have to get at one or two of the other tires and we've got a chance."

"Sorry I forgot about the van."

"Nonsense. Listen, Drew, I am just so grateful you are trusting me with all this. I know it isn't easy for you."

"I'm scared to death with what we're doing, and I'd be just as scared if we weren't doing it."

Gabe checked the time.

"With any luck, we've got fifteen or twenty minutes. The farther away we are from Camp David, the better. If nothing happens to their horses, I think we have to abort. But if the sedatives kick in, I'm going to go back there. I want you to keep steadily putting distance between us. I'll go back to check on their horses. That's when I'm going to try and take care of the van. Questions?"

"When do I take off?"

"Keep drifting ahead; then, when you see me move, you hit the gas. There's a trail to the left somewhere up there that'll take us to the car. I've set up a pile of stones on the right about thirty or forty feet before the trail. Keep an eye out for it. Also, I've marked the trees at eye level where we're supposed to turn. By then I should have caught up with you."

"I'd feel less frightened trying to elude my Secret Service people in a jet."

"You're doing fine."

For some minutes, the two rode in silence. Then Gabe leaned over slightly toward his onetime roommate.

"Drew, there's something I want to say. I don't know how to put this in any delicate way, but I want you to know that for years and years, even though I haven't had a drop of alcohol, I've been popping pills—never without a reason, mind you, headaches, insomnia, and the like—but you can probably guess that those reasons are more like justifications or excuses. I should have told you when you came to the ranch."

"Do you really think that would have mattered to me? Look at all the things you've done with your life."

"The funny thing is, since I had to watch Jim die, and focus on what was being done to you and to the country, and deal with Alison's disappearance, I haven't wanted to take a pill no matter how tense or frightened or sleepless I've been. It's like Jim's death was a slap of perspective for me—a shot across the bow of my life, telling me that I wasn't doing any justice to the lost lives of that woman in Fairhaven and her child by systematically destroying mine. I just needed to say it before we—"

"Doc, this is Griswold," his radio boomed. "You two slow down and get back here. There's something wrong with the horses."

"We're on!" Stoddard exclaimed.

"God bless Ellen Williams. Okay, Mr. President, just keep walking ahead, slow and steady."

Without bothering to respond by radio, Gabe gave Grendel's reins the slightest right-hand tug and then urged him ahead. The powerful animal spun like a seasoned rodeo performer and charged back down the trail. Gabe was pleased to see the size of the gap that had opened up between them and the agents. If they were paying as much attention to the president as they were to their horses, which wasn't likely, it would still be hard for them to realize, or to believe, that he was still moving away.

Confusion and distraction. Those were his biggest allies now. *Confusion and distraction.*

Even at a distance, he could see that the agents' horses were in no condition to keep going. Two were standing still, muzzles hanging down almost to the ground, their riders still sitting in their saddles, urging them forward. The third, Griswold's mount, was leaning against a hickory, contentedly rubbing his shoulder against the shaggy bark. Griswold was standing by the tree, looking into the horse's eye. But best of all, both the corpsman and the nurse were out of the van, checking to see if they could be of any help.

Be calm, Gabe urged himself as he dismounted and led Grendel toward the van. *Be calm and look like you know what you're doing.*

The handle of the hunting knife was in his palm, the blade concealed up along his forearm.

"Would somebody go after the president," Griswold ordered.

"This guy won't move," one of the agents said.

Gabe bent over and hammered the broad blade through the sidewall of the left rear tire. Soundlessly the van sank toward that side.

"Then get down and run!" Griswold was shouting. "Never mind, never mind. I'll get him myself. Hey, Mr. President. Stop!"

Of the three agents, Special Agent in Charge Griswold was carrying the most bulk. Exactly what shape he was in, Gabe mused, would be determined momentarily. Griswold threw off his windbreaker and started sprinting after Stoddard. With everyone watching Griswold, Gabe was able to take out the right rear tire with a single adrenaline-driven thrust. The van dropped to its rear end like a prizefighter who had just taken one to his glass jaw.

"I'll get him!" Gabe hollered to no one in particular. "I'll get him!"

He couldn't remember the last time he had done a running mount, but he never hesitated. With massive Grendel charging from standstill to full gallop in a single step, Gabe grasped the dense mane with his left hand and the saddle horn with his right and jammed his left foot into the stirrup. He went to push off his right foot, but he was already airborne, sailing along beside the powerful horse like a streamer. A second later, using strength he never would have guessed he had, he was upright in the saddle, thundering past Griswold.

"I'll get him," Gabe hollered.

Up ahead, the president glanced back at him and smiled. Then he gathered the reins and prodded the gray with a single brisk kick against the animal's flanks.

"Keep going!" Gabe shouted, pulling alongside.

They galloped that way, shoulder to shoulder, for another minute before Gabe spotted the marker he had built and pointed first to it, then to the woods on the left where the narrow trail would materialize.

The president pumped his fist.

Gabe tried to look as enthusiastic, but he knew he missed. He was consumed by a voice in his head that kept shouting one thing, over and over.

What in the hell have you done?

CHAPTER 61

*W*ith the lights off, the President of the United States driving, and his personal physician hanging on behind, the ATV negotiated the crooked dirt roads and trails up Flat Top Mountain to The Aerie. It was dark by the time they reached the castle and parked the four-wheeler in a concealed spot just inside the edge of the woods.

For a few moments, the two men stood by the drawbridge over the moat and watched what were probably three helicopters and a couple of fixed-wing aircraft circling off to the east.

"We made it!" Stoddard exclaimed. "I can't believe it. We made it! It must be absolute chaos back there in Washington."

"Like I said, this country is built to go from one leader to another at a moment's notice and with the minimum of chaos. If all that Twenty-fifth Amendment reading I did when I first arrived in D.C. taught me anything, it taught me that. The country is and always will be bigger than any one man."

"Maybe so. Still, I'd like to think I'm being missed right about now."

"I'm sure you are. You're doing an incredible job."

"Thanks. Speaking of missed, I've got to call Carol. I left her an envelope of instructions including the numbers of a chief with the Virginia State Police whom I trust and a federal magistrate judge as well. Carol can contact them, and they can get the warrants we need and some reliable officers to serve them. They'll meet you at Lily's place first thing tomorrow."

"Perfect. You've been a real hero, Drew. I can't imagine what it must be like to have to walk away from *your* job."

"I'm certainly hoping to get it back."

"As long as we keep you safe from those transmitters, I'm sure you will."

"Speaking of heroes, you've been one, too . . . and more. You've been a hell of a friend, Gabe. Better than I deserve."

What an odd thing to say, Gabe thought.

"Nonsense," he said. "Go reassure Carol that you're okay and I'm not a madman. Then I want to show you where Ye Olde Royal Physician has decreed you'll be spending the night."

"I already think I know."

For another minute, the two remained immersed in the noisy silence of the forest, trying to wrap their minds around the enormity of what they had just accomplished. Finally, Stoddard motioned Gabe to stay nearby and called his wife. In just a couple of minutes, he passed the phone over.

"You really think someone on our staff is behind this, Gabe?" Carol Stoddard asked.

"I think someone who regularly gets physically close to Drew is involved. That's the most I can say."

"And you think Lily is—was—involved, too?"

"I'm sure of it. I saw firsthand evidence when I was at her place, and Jim Ferendelli told me himself before he . . . was killed."

"But . . . but Lily was one of my dearest friends—like family."

"I'm sorry, Carol."

"And you think she was murdered, too?"

"I do. Alive she was a threat to someone. Once I discovered the laboratory tunnel from her place, she became a loose end."

"Gabe, this is an awful lot for me to digest."

"I understand. It would be for me, too, if I hadn't seen it all. Meet me tomorrow at Lily's farm at, say, noon, with the warrants and the men we need, and you'll see for yourself. For the moment, Drew is safe, and that's all that matters. I suspect we can keep him safe for another twenty-four or even thirty-six hours if we need to, but it's just a matter of time before someone figures out where we are. I'd rather get this business moving and over before anyone has time to react."

Gabe waited until the First Lady had nothing left to say, and then, mouthing the words *I don't know,* passed the phone back to her husband.

"I love you, sweetheart," Stoddard said. "Believe me, Gabe has done an amazing piece of work for us. You'll see."

Gabe felt certain that whatever Carol Stoddard said wasn't a ringing endorsement of his theories or their actions.

"Thank you, honey," Stoddard replied. "Thanks for trusting us this much. When you speak to the boys, just tell them I'm safe and I love them. Nothing else, though. Okay? . . . Okay?" He put the phone away and turned to Gabe. "That tunnel to the nanobot factory better be where you say it is, or like Ricky Ricardo says to Lucy, we're gonna have some 'splainin' to do."

The two men entered The Aerie.

"You're planning on putting me in the bunker downstairs, aren't you?" Drew said.

"Whoever murdered Jim and Lily and has been doing this to you is remorseless and resourceful. If anything goes wrong, I want you safe, that's all. I cleaned the place up last night."

Whoever murdered Jim and Lily . . .

The words reopened his fears regarding Alison. As soon as things were resolved tomorrow, he vowed to spend every minute searching for her for as long as it took.

"I think it's overkill," Stoddard said. "We pulled it off, Gabe. We kidnapped me right from under the nose of everyone. Now, how about a room with a view?"

"There are posters on the wall of the bunker."

"God, but I hate taking orders."

"Probably not as much as I dislike giving them. We've come this far,

Mr. President. Let's not risk screwing everything up by getting complacent. Your safety is what this is all about."

Stoddard sighed and allowed himself to be escorted downstairs to the bunker.

During the minutes that followed, Gabe felt himself hit a wall. The adrenaline rush of their escape was still churning, but it was merging with an intense exhaustion that his body had probably been storing up for days. It was a tribute to eleven-hundred-dollar boots that he was barely aware of having been in them, walking and riding, since early that morning. He trudged up the spiral stone staircase of the West Tower, hauling along the backpack of supplies that had served him so well.

The high-ceilinged circular bedroom was cool and comfortable. Gabe slipped off his boots, lay on the bed, and awaited the return of his exhaustion by flipping through the pages of a three-year-old copy of *Field & Stream*. A trout-fishing-in-the-Tetons article made him profoundly homesick, and he decided it would be worth petitioning the president for a replacement as soon as the warrants were handed out and the arrests began. Although they had never spoken about it, he strongly suspected that Alison would love pulling on a pair of waders and stepping into a crystal Wyoming river, fly rod in hand.

It was nearly midnight when he finally set the magazine aside and headed for the bathroom. On the way, the spiral metal staircase leading up to the battlements caught his eye, and suddenly he wanted one last view of the magnificent panorama that had contributed to giving the castle its name. Not bothering with his boots, he climbed up and opened the heavy door leading outside.

The sky was somewhat overcast, but the view from the tower might have been fifty miles on a clear day. He was looking mostly out to the distant west and north, although there was nearly a 360-degree panorama available. It was almost by chance that he gazed directly downward when he did. There, past the moat, at the edge of the forest, he saw a figure moving furtively among the trees.

In an instant, any fatigue he was feeling vanished.

"Stop right there!" he called out. "I can see you and I have a gun!"

His words seemed to be swallowed by the night.

Below, the figure vanished into the forest.

Then, from Gabe's right, he saw a second shadow, moving parallel to the first.

These weren't kids looking for mischief. Every fiber in his being said that whoever was down there was trouble.

For a minute, Gabe continued peering through the dark. Then he raced down the staircase, pulled on his boots, and crossed to the door. He was about to open it when he glanced down at his backpack. He removed the hunting knife and slipped on the pack with its rope and collection of tools.

Then, hefting the knife in his hand, he slipped out of the bedroom and moved cautiously, silently, down the stone staircase.

CHAPTER 62

*I*t had been stupid to yell out from the tower the way he had. Absolutely stupid.

Hunting knife in hand, Gabe reprimanded himself as he cautiously descended to the main floor.

What now?

He tried without success to get his brain around the answer to who could have found them within just six hours. Drew's belief that few, if any, outside his immediate family knew of The Aerie had to have been misguided. Someone else knew and had put the pieces together. Gabe had heard that of all the investigative services, including the CIA and FBI, the Secret Service was the most resourceful, efficient, and imaginative. It wouldn't surprise him to learn that The Aerie was in one of their files, along with its history and maybe even some blueprints.

Hopefully, Secret Service agents were the ones who were laying siege to the castle right now. In truth, although Gabe had chosen to suspect anyone and everyone as betraying Drew, the president's protective detachment would have been the ones he trusted first. One thing Gabe was certain of—the forms outside weren't his mind playing tricks. He envisioned a Secret Service SWAT team, or the equivalent, silently positioning themselves in the night.

It would take some serious work and preparation to breach the walls of the castle. Probably whoever was out there would take the more straightforward approach of simply setting aside stealth and blowing the massive portcullis to toothpicks.

What in the hell have I done? Gabe wondered once again.

The West Tower staircase opened into the far end of the dining room. To reach Drew, he would have to cross the great room to the basement staircase. Gabe frantically tried to reason out what there was to be gained by alerting Drew before he knew what they were up against. Would Drew agree to stay where he was until it was clear how much of a threat there was to him? At least for the moment he was locked in the bunker and reasonably secure. But he also had the cell phone. Gabe considered and quickly rejected the possibility of trying to sneak out and get down the mountain to ask for help.

Maybe whoever was outside would be unable to breach the walls or blow up the portcullis. Maybe they were just kids looking for mischief. Maybe . . .

Harsh whispers echoing from the kitchen, no more than twenty feet away, stopped him short.

How in the hell had they gotten in?

A siege tunnel! Gabe felt certain of it. Most medieval castles had one or more secret ways to go around or behind a besieging army to escape or to bring in supplies and weapons. It would have been a surprise if eccentric Bedard Stoddard had *not* built one.

"Crackowski, what in hell happened to you back there?"

The heavy southern drawl was one Gabe recognized immediately.

His heart stopped, considered remaining that way, then slowly started up again, missing every few beats.

"I smashed my fucking head in that fucking tunnel," the other man, Crackowski, said. "Shit, it's bleeding."

"That's what you get for shaving your head."

"Fuck you, Carl. When we've taken care of business here, I'm gonna shave your head."

"It'll be really hard to do that with a bullet through your eye. Now, let's get this over with."

"You take the front half out there, I'll take the rear. Any lights you find, turn them on. Whoever yelled knows we're here, so we're not going to take anyone by surprise. One alive, one dead."

"One alive, one dead," Jim Ferendelli's killer echoed.

Gabe silently backed away and into the great room, where there were some swords and a spear or two, plus a number of places he could conceal himself. If he understood the orders from the man named Crackowski, the other killer, Carl, would be coming his way.

"One alive, one dead."

Gabe had little trouble believing that he was the throwaway. With the nanotechnology at their disposal, it seemed that whoever was behind the transmitters could deal with the president any time they wanted. Of course, it was still possible that Drew was the real target and not just his presidency, as Ferendelli believed. But like Lily Sexton, Gabe had become a dangerous loose end.

The two killers knew about the siege tunnel. Did they know about the bunker as well? If Drew remained locked inside, getting at him would be a hell of a problem . . . unless they were able to shut off his air.

With the skipped heartbeats increasing again, Gabe pressed himself against the wall behind the huge armored stallion and rider and forced himself to calm down and focus, much as he had done over the years when faced with medical crises.

Chances were that he was going to die, but the two men were going to have to earn their kill.

At that moment, Carl moved cautiously into the great room, his heavy pistol ready. Gabe clutched his hunting knife and tried unsuccessfully to imagine any scenario where he might have even a slight advantage. He ducked down and moved deeper into the shadows behind the mannequin steed and its rider as the gunman approached.

Fifteen feet . . . ten . . . five . . .

Any second, Carl would be able to see him. Gabe braced himself against the armor covering the haunch of the horse and tightened his grip on the handle of the hunting knife, preparing for an overhand stab. Between horse and rider there had to be at least two hundred pounds of steel, probably more. He had to bring the setup down quickly and accurately.

One more step, just one, and . . .

Gabe drove his shoulder into the armor as if he were trying to take out an onrushing lineman. Carl's reaction, not unexpectedly, was to whirl and fire. The impact of the armor sent him stumbling backward, and he fell heavily, with much of the horse collapsing down on him. Gabe dove on top of the armor, slashing randomly downward with the heavy blade again and again until he felt it hit flesh and heard Carl's cry.

Then, an instant later, Gabe was shot.

The bullet, one of a volley of wild shots from Carl's pistol, tore through the tissue just above Gabe's right hip, spinning him backward and off the horse. Above the armor he could see the killer trying to set for another, more accurate shot, but through the gloom he also saw the hunting knife protruding from the man's thigh. Gabe managed to get his feet onto the mannequin and pushed it against the killer as hard as he could. Then Gabe rolled over and stumbled to his feet, gasping at the pain from his wound at the same moment Carl was screaming, "You fucker! You stabbed me! I'll kill you! You fucking bastard! I'll kill you!"

Several more shots exploded, echoing through the vast hall.

Dragging his leg, Gabe lurched toward the dining room and headed for the short stairway leading up to the second level, away from where he suspected the other gunman, Crackowski, would be coming. His jeans were rapidly soaking through with blood, and he felt blood dripping down into his boot. Still, no matter what, he had gotten one in for Jim Ferendelli.

The pain from his wound was intense but manageable. Using the stone banister, he hauled himself up to the second floor and around to the balcony surrounding the empty pool from twelve feet above. It was easy to imagine Drew, his father, and his grandfather, as well as family and friends, jumping and diving from the balcony into the pool, which included, Drew had told him, an overhead grid of pipes used to simulate a rainstorm on cue. In fact, the pipes were still there, illuminated to some extent by light reflecting off the clouds and coming through a glass canopy as large as the pool.

With the glimmer of an idea beginning to form, Gabe ignored the burning pain in his hip and managed to stand on the balcony wall, propping himself against one of the pillars that supported the glass canopy. Then he tested the main pipe, which seemed solidly anchored to a metal frame that came down from the roof. Whether or not it could hold more than double a man's weight was anyone's guess, but that was what he would be asking it to do.

The knife was gone, and he was hardly mobile enough to go foraging for another weapon. But he did have a weapon—at least a potential one—in his backpack, and he knew damn well how to use it. Carefully, he removed the rope he had used to entertain and educate the stable master's son, Pete—forty feet of excellent lariat cord, purchased in the store where Gabe had gotten his boots. Then he took one end and swung it over the pipe. Finally, he tied that end around his waist and used it and the descending length to test the pipe and lower himself back to the balcony floor.

No problem.

It would be a hell of a throw, but somewhere in a box in his basement were dozens of tarnished trophies that said he could make it.

Spent from the pain and the effort, Gabe sank onto the stone floor of the balcony and waited, trying not to gasp out loud with each breath. It seemed likely that when Carl was upright the two killers would separate again. The knife wound to Carl's leg would have them angry, anxious, and even a little shaken—a recipe for error. All Gabe could hope for now was that one of them didn't come up to the balcony.

He shifted his position and felt a daggerlike pain from his wound into his groin. He was about to check to see if there was an exit hole when he heard noise and sensed movement from below. Peering between the cement balustrades, he could make out a man's form, moving cautiously along the pool. No limp. Then, light through the canopy glinted off his shaved pate.

Crackowski.

Gabe shifted again, checked the knot that fixed the lariat around his waist, then the slipknot he had tied at the business end of the rope. A glance overhead to ensure everything was in place and he gathered in the slack, moved into an agonizing crouch, and waited as, a step at a time, the killer headed toward the spot just beneath where the rope looped over the rain pipe.

Under ordinary circumstances, Gabe knew he could make the throw ten times out of ten—but that was without walls behind him and overhead, and allowing for a few warm-up spins, and, finally, provided the subject to be roped wasn't holding a gun. This time Gabe would have one chance and only one. A miss and he would be trying to outrun a professional gunman on a leg that was barely functional.

He hefted the lasso and tried to imagine the moves he would make to close the loop as he was dropping over the balcony wall, using Crackowski as counterweight to keep him from smashing to the concrete poolside.

Just another Sunday hangin' in Dodge.

No mercy, he pleaded with himself. *No mercy. . . . No hesitation. . . .*

He took a step back, then leaned over the balcony, swung the lasso once to open a small loop, and floated it around the killer's head. Before Crackowski could react, Gabe toppled off the balcony, grasping the rope from the rain pipe with all his strength. The drop was rapid, the snapping neck sickening, and Crackowski's death instantaneous. Gabe hit the concrete floor with force, but only enough to stun him. He released the rope, still tied to his waist. The killer crumpled to the floor beside him, the stench of excrement already filling the air.

For most of a minute, Gabe stayed dazed on the floor, trying to orient himself from what he knew had to be a concussion. Finally, thoughts and images of Carl worked themselves into his hazy consciousness, intermixed with images of Gabe's high school coach, kneeling over him, administering smelling salts, and asking if he knew where he was and if he was able to go back into the game.

He had to move. Carl was painfully wounded, but he was mobile and

he had a gun. For a moment, Gabe became excited about finding Crackowski's pistol. Then he vaguely remembered seeing it clatter down into the
empty pool. Had that really happened?

Groaning with every movement, he crawled to the edge of the concrete hole and peered down. He could barely make out what he thought
was the bottom and could not discern anything else.

Perhaps he was wrong. . . . Maybe the gun was still nearby. . . . Maybe
it was under Crackowski's body.

Gabe knew he wasn't thinking clearly, but he was unable to focus any
better. His head was pounding, and the wound beside his hip made turning especially unpleasant. He crawled over to Crackowski's body. The
killer's eyes were bulging nearly out of his head and his protruding tongue
looked like a plum. Blocking out the odor, Gabe rolled the corpse over
once, then again. No gun.

Still trying to shake the fog from his brain, he tried to rise, then fell
back to his knees. When he turned back to the pool, Carl was standing
there, watching him curiously, his heavy pistol resting loosely in his hand.

"Now this here's a scene you just don't see every day," he drawled.

The jolt of adrenaline dispelled Gabe's fogginess like sunlight.

"That knife in your thigh hurt?" he asked.

"Not nearly as much as you're going to."

"Such a wit."

From time to time, Gabe wondered what his patients might have been
feeling at the moment of their death. Now he acknowledged that it really
wasn't all that bad. Carl whatever his last name was, was going to pull the
trigger and Gabe Singleton wasn't going to exist anymore. It was as simple
as that.

"Stand up!"

I'm not going to make it easy, Carl, Gabe was thinking. *I promise you
I'm not.*

"Do I look like I can stand up?" he said.

"Stand up or I swear I'll shoot through every joint in your body starting from the toes up."

Gabe had heard enough.

Let it end here, he was thinking. *Let it end here for both of us.*

Without hesitation, he planted the right toe of his boot and drove his head with all his remaining strength into the man's groin. Carl went over the edge of the pool backward, with Gabe clinging to him like a chimpanzee to its mother. Somewhere during the fall there might have been a gunshot. Gabe felt another tearing pain—this one through his shoulder. Then there was a fearsome impact, with air exploding from his lungs.

Then there was nothing.

CHAPTER 63

Stilettoes of bright light penetrated Gabe's lids and pierced his eyes. He felt himself coming to like a patient in the recovery room following major surgery, only without any analgesia. Bit by bit, he was able to catalogue the pain. His right hip was throbbing, but no less than his left shoulder. The top of his head and space behind his eyes were like cardiac monitors, recording every heartbeat with a totally unpleasant pulsation. Bile and acid grated across the back of his throat.

He opened his eyes a slit, squinting at the glare, and was surprised to see the chandeliers and tattered pennants of the great room. Bit by bit, visions of his struggles with the two killers came into focus. He forced his eyes to open wider.

"Quite a mess you made in there, Doc. You should have seen ol' Carl's brains splattered all over the bottom of that pool."

Gabe stiffened but made no attempt to turn toward the voice. There was no need.

"Do you think you'll be in line for another performance citation for this, Griswold?" Gabe asked.

"We each gotta do what we each gotta do."

"And you just gotta destroy the life of the man you've sworn to protect."

With no small discomfort, Gabe rolled over and managed to get up to his hands and knees—actually, his *hand* and knees. His left shoulder simply refused to bear much weight. There was a high-backed dark wood chair not far away. He crawled to it and pulled himself up with no help from Griswold. Blood was congealing in Gabe's jeans and shirt.

"Don't tell me about destroying lives," Griswold snapped. "Two kills before you went to prison, another two kills here. You're like a death machine. I'll bet you're murder on your patients."

"Enough, Mr. Griswold," a familiar, authoritative voice said from the shadows of the columns at the end of the room. "I'll take over from here."

Carrying a large, thin case, LeMar Stoddard stepped into the light.

Gabe stared at the man in utter disbelief, his mind unwilling to accept the magnitude of what he was witnessing. First the hit men, then Treat Griswold, and finally, at the top of the pyramid, the First Father.

"I assume the president is downstairs in the bunker," LeMar said.

Gabe shook his head in utter disgust and dismay.

"Unless I'm missing something," Gabe replied, "that *president* you speak of is also your son."

Stoddard, wearing khakis and a nautical windbreaker, strode regally across the hall, set the oddly shaped case down, and positioned himself to Griswold's left, six or seven feet in front of Gabe. His eyes were a piercing, electric blue, and Gabe felt slightly unsettled before their power. He also felt confused and on edge. The list of people he had been worried about did not include Drew's father, although strangely, at this moment, especially after spending some time with the man, Gabe wasn't finding the notion all that hard to believe.

"I assure you, Doctor, no one knows that fact better than I."

"Then why are you trying to kill him?"

"Not kill him. Why would I ever want to do that? I love him. I just can't have him spend another four years imposing his version of communism on the people of this country."

"So you want us all to believe that he is going insane."

"In a manner of speaking, yes. In another manner of speaking, he is. Kurt Vonnegut once wrote: 'We are what we pretend to be.' "

"So your son behaving as if he were insane means that he is."

"Precisely."

"Oh, that's just sweet. But Dad, Vice President Cooper shares almost all of Drew's political philosophy. And the polls say he would probably beat Dunleavy if the election were held today."

"Ah, but the election is not being held today," Stoddard said, as if the obvious were a revelation. "By the time President Stoddard's mental instability is exposed and he is forced to drop out of the race, the election will be almost upon us. In the resultant chaos, I feel certain that the American voters, led by the resurgent religious right and others in the silent majority, will cast their lots heavily with President Dunleavy."

"So these episodes your son has been having are merely experiments—"

"—to work out the most effective combination of medications," LeMar finished the sentence.

"Drugs," Gabe corrected. "Not medications, drugs—hallucinogenic, debilitating, deadly drugs that you have been feeding into the body of your only child. And just because he went and changed parties and politics on you. That is really disgusting."

"Politically expedient, yes," LeMar said, "but hardly disgusting. We have been playing political tricks on our candidates for as long as there have been candidates."

For the first time, his speech seemed somewhat pressured, as if his own rhetoric was getting more and more difficult for him to believe and to express.

Gabe forced himself to meet the mogul's imperious gaze.

Something isn't right, Gabe was thinking. The man seemed perfectly capable of vindictiveness. That was a given. But the extent to which he was taking revenge on his son seemed out of proportion to the hurt Drew's political metamorphosis had probably caused LeMar. It was as if he had chosen to retaliate against a fly with an elephant gun.

Something isn't right. . . . Something—

In that exact moment, Gabe took note of the way the man was dressed—his shoes, his slacks, his designer shirt, his carefully pressed windbreaker.

They were the sort of clothes Gabe had seen recently—very recently. Thoughts that had been free-floating suddenly began dropping into place.

"Those were your clothes I saw in the closet at Lily's farm, weren't they," Gabe said suddenly. "Or should I say *your* farm."

"I don't know what you're—"

"You were her lover—her sugar daddy. You were the one who pushed the president and your daughter-in-law to nominate her for the new cabinet post, just in case, for any reason, your scheme failed and your son got elected."

"Nonsense," LeMar said, but his lie was a weak one.

"But why?" Gabe went on. "Why? No, wait . . . wait, I'll tell you why. Because you own that underground lab, that's why. The greatest medical nanotechnology scientists the world has to offer, all brought together in secrecy and under one roof. If the scientific world is still at alpha in the area of nanodrug delivery, you and your operation are approaching omega. You've lapped the field, Dad. Monopolies Are Us."

LeMar moved to deny the conclusion, then finally just took a step back, his arms folded across his chest, his expression proud.

"You've learned a great deal in a remarkably short amount of time, Doctor."

Gabe wasn't nearly done.

"How much did that underground bastion of science and all those geniuses cost you to buy and develop, *Dad*? It had to be, what, billions? Tens of billions? As I recall, *Forbes* doesn't think you have quite that much. What did you do to get the money? How leveraged are you, Dad?"

"Stop that!"

"You rolled the dice on this, didn't you? Being in the top ten or top twenty wasn't enough. You wanted to be numero uno—the czar of the largest pharmaceutical empire the world has ever known. And your liberal son's platform of government control of nanotechnology would have forced you and your lab out into the open before you were ready. How many years will be lost if his policies are implemented, LeMar? How much of your money will go down the drain? Most of it? All of it? How many secrets will you have to share with the scientific community if your son gets reelected? This was never about political ideologies. How foolish of me to think it was."

LeMar Stoddard seemed suddenly restless, his demeanor less confident. Was he squinting?

"I need you, Gabe," he blurted out suddenly.

"What?"

"I need you. I can make you rich beyond your imagination."

"Need me for what?"

"I need you to keep quiet about what you've learned, and I need you to tell the world when it's time that the rumors are true and the president and vice president have been deceiving the American public about the president's mental health."

"It was all about money," Gabe said, ignoring the plea completely. "Not one whit of political principle. Just money. Lily Sexton was your lover. Your confidante. Did you just pick up the phone and order her killed because she had become a liability? Which of those animals did you pick to do the job? Crackowski? Carl?"

"That's ridiculous."

"Is it, you arrogant sonofabitch? How many laughs have you gotten out of the irony that the very fullerenes and nanotubes that are going to make you rich beyond even your standards are the tools you and your stooge there used to deliver toxic chemicals to your son's brain?"

"You ungrateful little turd!" LeMar bellowed, his face suddenly flushed, his voice up half an octave. "After all I did for you when you were in such trouble—the money, the attorneys, the payoffs to reduce your sentence to the minimum. Yes, my naïve friend, there were payoffs. And . . . and now, too. Convincing the president to bring you to Washington. My apartment. My car."

The rhythmic squinting seemed more noticeable now, and his cheeks were nearly crimson. Gabe thought back to all the pills the tycoon was taking for high blood pressure.

"Take them back, LeMar," Gabe said. "The car, the apartment—the price tag is way too high."

"T-take it from me, Gabe, this president is not worthy of his office."

What is going on with his speech?

"The voters are supposed to decide that, *Dad*," Gabe said.

"You don't understand. I tell you, this presidency is not worth saving."

"Let me reason with him," Griswold cut in, brandishing his pistol. "I promise he'll come to understand."

"No, you creep!" a woman's voice cried out from the side of the hall. "I promise *you'll* come to understand."

From the corridor to the portcullis, Alison stepped into the room, her pistol leveled at Griswold from, perhaps, twenty-five feet away.

"Alison!" Gabe cried out.

"Set the gun down, Griswold. Set it on the floor and kick it away. Hard!"

Griswold seemed to be weighing his options; then, slowly, he did as Alison demanded.

"As you wish, ma'am," he muttered. "My, my, my, my, my."

"You should never have left me my radio, Griz. I caught up with you when you left all the others and flew back from Camp David to the White House. Seemed fishy then, seems fishy now."

"Those naughty girls," Griswold said, smiling in a most unsettling way. "They know perfectly well that insubordination will not be tolerated. I think a spanking is in order. Now, if you will be so kind, Agent Cromartie, it is my turn to demand that you put down *your* gun."

He lifted up his left hand to display a transmitter.

"What do you expect to do with that?" Alison asked.

"Expect to do? Well, for starters, I expect to push these buttons here and release the chemicals that my trusty inhaler deposited along your brain stem and other areas in your cute little noggin. Enough chemicals, I would say, to blow your mind—literally and figuratively. Many times more than what we've been giving to the prez."

"Drop the transmitter, Griswold or I swear, I'll put a bullet between your eyes."

"From there? In the heat of battle? With a dainty little, what have you got? A Glock? A Glock Twenty-six maybe? You must be kidding. At this range, with your hand shaking like a leaf, and death staring you in the face in the form of me, you'd be lucky to hit the wall behind me. Now, I'm going to count to three. Put your gun on the floor or I push these buttons—all of 'em at once. One . . . two . . . three!"

Griswold depressed the buttons on the transmitter. His narrow eyes widened. They widened even more when Alison held up the Baggie containing the president's inhaler.

"Guess what this is," she said. "You never should have let that pick-pocket at your garage in Fredericksburg get away. He made the switch, you pig. The Alupent you almost killed me with was nothing more than that—Alupent. I'm glad you pushed those buttons, though. That makes this self-defense."

"You fucking bi—"

Griswold, reaching for a pistol in his belt, got no further.

Alison dropped to one knee, extended both arms, aimed, and fired the Glock once—just once. Instantly a perfect hole materialized in the center of Griswold's expansive forehead. He stared at Alison in utter disbelief until life had faded completely from his eyes. Then he pitched face-first to the stone floor.

It's not going to come down to your word against mine, Griswold, Alison was thinking savagely. *Not this time. Not ever.*

She walked cautiously over to the agent and nudged his corpse with her foot. Then she turned to Gabe and quickly surveyed his wounds.

"Don't worry, honey," she said, embracing him. "I'm not always this disagreeable. We'll get you to a hospital right away. We'll get you put back together."

"Alison, meet LeMar Stoddard, Drew's loving father. He didn't have enough money."

"So I heard back there."

"Gabe, p-please, listen to me," LeMar said. "Miss, y-you listen, too. Listen and you'll both work with me. L-listen and you'll see that the . . . the president isn't fit for his office. I p-promise you will."

He bent down and retrieved the oddly shaped leather case from next to Treat Griswold's corpse.

Gabe sighed.

"I can't think of anything you could possibly say that I would want to hear, *Dad,* but go ahead."

The squinting and stuttering continued. Something was going on inside LeMar's head, Gabe was sensing. Something very bad. The man's blood pressure had to be off the chart.

"Okay then," Stoddard went on. "H-here's what I have to say. You weren't driving the car that killed that woman and her unborn . . . child that night in Fairhaven. The man sleeping downstairs in the bunker was."

"That's impossible."

But even as he uttered the knee-jerk response, Gabe knew that LeMar's statement was not only possible, it was true. Blackthorn had warned him and his own instincts had told him Drew was lying about something—something important.

"Your l-life has been ruined by . . . by an accident that the . . . the president was guilty of. Y-you were in an alcohol-induced blackout that night, but the president wasn't. H-he knew what had happened. H-he knew who was driving. The two of you were f-found down . . . an embankment in a muddy ditch, a h-hundred feet from the accident. You h-had a bad h-head injury and no memory whatsoever."

The stuttering, thick speech and blinking were worsening.

"I can't believe Drew would be aware of what happened and not say anything."

"He . . . he was f-frightened of the c-onsequences if he confessed. . . . He . . . he asked me to help. I couldn't say no. He was my son. I saved his life—his . . . his career. I took care of what policemen I had to. . . . And— and then look what Andrew did: He has made me look like a fool! . . . All these years, a f-fool. And now, he is threatening to t-take everything from me—everything!"

LeMar's speech was intensely rushed and pressured now, and the slurring of his speech was more pronounced. He was still animated and speaking with his hands, but Gabe could see now that his right arm was not moving nearly as much as his left. In fact, it was barely moving at all.

"LeMar . . . ?"

"Later, I did what I c-could to be certain it didn't go too h-hard for you. . . . I-I got you the best lawyers. I-I talked to the judge on the case and h-helped him with a little matter. . . . I-I got you the minimum sentence possible."

His stroke was clearly evolving now, his speech thicker and more forced. His arm was hanging limp.

"Mr. Stoddard," Alison said urgently, racing to support the man before he fell over.

But LeMar Stoddard ranted on, making his tongue and his lips form thick, clumsy words, it seemed, by the sheer power of his will.

"I have proof. . . . I have proof what he did." He began fumbling with the brass zipper on the case, all the while muttering, "I have proof. . . . I have proof."

His leg gave way completely, so that Alison could no longer bear his weight. Gently, she lowered him to the floor. Gabe was out of his chair now, kneeling beside the man. He checked the pulses in LeMar's carotid arteries. Both were present.

"I think hemorrhage, not clot," he said to Alison. "But I guess it could still be either."

"The case . . . the case."

Gabe slid back the zipper and removed a large, sealed heavy plastic bag containing the steering wheel from a car—an old car. There were smudges of powder in various spots.

"From the accident?" he asked.

"The car you b-borrowed . . . only his fingerp-prints. . . . None yours. . . . Kept in a safe all these years."

LeMar Stoddard could speak no more. His eyes closed and his head lolled to one side. Spittle appeared at the corner of his mouth. Alison took her jacket and folded it between his ear and the floor. His breathing became deep and sonorous.

Gabe slipped the steering wheel back into its case and stood up painfully. Then he held Alison closely.

"I was so sure something had happened to you."

"Nothing that matters now," she said, stroking his hair away from his forehead.

"Do you want to call the cops?" he asked.

"Will you be all right?"

"For now. I've got to go downstairs and have a serious talk with the man in the bunker."

CHAPTER 64

Gabe only had to push the electronic buzzer by the bunker door once. In seconds a narrow panel in the center of the door slid open.

"Hey, Doc," the president said, fully awake with the immediacy and clarity of an emergency physician . . . or a head of state, "why so early?"

"We've had visitors, Drew. But it's okay now. The threat's over."

The heavy bolt on the inside slid open. In the dim light, it took several seconds for the extent of Gabe's injuries to register. Stoddard quickly helped him inside and into a chair.

"Were they after me?" Stoddard asked.

"Not really," Gabe replied. "They were after me. I knew too much."

"And I slept through the whole thing?"

"Probably just as well."

Stoddard, wearing cotton pajamas and a light robe, poured some water for each of them.

"Tell me," he said.

Uncertain how much longer he could remain upright, Gabe gave a terse, though complete, account of the attack on The Aerie by two killers, employed to protect the secrecy of a massive scientific facility exclusively owned and run by Drew's father.

"The two men are both dead."

"You did that?"

"I don't even want to think about it. Treat Griswold is dead, too."

The president looked surprised but not shocked.

"You again?"

"Alison. She was following him. He tried to kill her."

"I'm glad she's all right."

"No thanks to Griswold. He tortured her, but she escaped. We can talk more about that later. Turns out Griswold was the one we came here to get away from—the one with the transmitter. Your father had found a way to blackmail him into poisoning you. Griswold kidnapped young girls from Mexico and kept them for his pleasure."

"Treat and my father," Stoddard said. "Who can you trust?"

"Well, clearly not them."

"I wish I were more stunned to learn it was my father. Is he still alive?"

"For the moment. Initially there's no way to know with strokes, and his is a big one."

"Dad had that heliport built on the roof. The Aerie was so well constructed that almost no shoring up had to be done. I'll call rescue."

"Do that. Tell them they may have to make two trips."

"How bad are you hurt?"

"For someone who's been shot twice and bashed around, not so bad."

"Will LeMar make it?"

"He might. No matter what, his life as master of all he surveys is over. Given the best he'll have to look forward to, I think he would opt for a quick end."

"I'm sorry. No matter what, he's still my father."

"It doesn't seem like he ever had his priorities straight."

"Well, my friend, you certainly have gone above and beyond the Hippocratic oath in this one."

Gabe shifted in his seat to find a position he could handle for a few minutes more.

"Drew, I'm not sure how much longer I can remain upright. But before we go upstairs, I want you to have this."

He handed over LeMar's case and the president opened it, peered in at its contents, then slowly pulled the zipper closed.

"From Fairhaven?"

"Your father got ahold of it after the accident. He says your fingerprints are all over it. None of mine."

"I was going to speak to you about Fairhaven after this business—the election—was over," Stoddard said. "It's been hard for me."

"Drew, it's been hard for *me!*"

"I . . . I was so frightened of my father that night, of what might happen. Turns out he knew all the time."

"He said you petitioned him to keep you out of trouble."

"I . . . well, maybe I did. It's been a long time."

"Gee, it's been just that long since I was in prison and I remember every detail of every day I spent there, Drew. I remember my father being too ashamed to speak to me right up until the day he died. I remember going to AA meetings and lying to everyone by saying I was clean and sober when I couldn't stop popping pills all the time. You're fortunate that your blackout seems to have been more selective and lasted much longer than mine."

"I tried to make up for what I did by the way I conducted my life."

"The country is grateful to you. You've been a hell of a president."

"Are you going to go public with what I did? You know I won't have a prayer at getting reelected if you do."

"I don't know, Drew. Right now, I don't know anything except that I'm almost fifty-three years old and more than half my life has been lived under the cloud of two murders I didn't commit."

Stoddard crossed to where his jeans were hanging and from the pocket pulled an envelope folded in half.

"This letter reached me soon after I was elected four years ago. I was going to give it to you when I told you . . . about the accident. Then, right before I left for Camp David yesterday I took it with me."

Gabe took the envelope and extracted a single sheet of plain typing paper, written in pen in uneven print.

Mr. President,

Irina Kursova and I were ready to get married when she was killed by a car you were in. My son Dimitri in her womb died also. I cannot find the man Singleton who was the driver with you that night. If I could I would kill him. I know you are protecting him, but if you send his address to Milton, care of 253 Nolan Street, Annapolis, 01409, I will do the rest.

"The man who tried to kill me—twice," Gabe said. "Someone must have showed him that article in the paper announcing I had joined your team. After all these years, suddenly there I was back in town."

"His name isn't Milton. It's Leon. Leon Uretsky. He works as a baker in Bowie. The address belongs to friends of his. The Secret Service found him pretty easily, but aside from a few threats, there wasn't anything they could do. I didn't know he had gone after you until you told me about the attempted shootings."

"You could have told me about this letter when you flew to Tyler, Drew," Gabe said wearily. "You could have told me a number of things that you chose not to."

"I'm sorry. Truly I am."

"More than thirty years. Such pain to want to kill even after thirty years. Did this man ever marry?"

"Not as far as I know."

"I want his contact information, Drew. I want it as soon as you can get it to me."

"Gabe, listen, I—"

"And you know what else I want? I want you to find him and go to him."

"But—"

"Tomorrow, Drew. I want you to find Leon Uretsky and go to him and tell him that it was you who was driving that night. Do that or I swear, you will have made the decision for me, and I'm going straight to the papers and anyone else who will listen."

"But you're going to see him, too?"

"Yes. If he'll let me. He and I need to talk. We need to talk about pain . . . and loss. We need to talk about you."

"It will finish me, Gabe. If this gets out, it will finish me and everything I have stood for."

"Maybe." Gabe pulled himself up and hobbled toward the door. "Maybe it will."

CHAPTER 65

*I*t was the first time Gabe had been in Fairhaven, Maryland, since the accident. Working off a MapQuest printout, he removed his sling and negotiated the streets through a steady drizzle. His mood was as somber as the evening. In the trunk of his rented Honda, his bags were packed. In the early morning he would leave Alison in the hotel room they were sharing and head to the airport for the trip home to Wyoming.

Three days had passed since the nightmare at The Aerie. He had not returned to the White House, nor did he ever intend to enter the place again. He had spoken to the president only long enough to ensure that he had honored Gabe's demand to personally visit Leon Uretsky.

It had required more than an hour in the operating room to debride the wounds in Gabe's hip and shoulder. Gratefully, there was nothing critical to repair, and he left the hospital twelve hours later. After that, he had spent as much time as possible with Alison when he wasn't giving statements to the investigators from the Secret Service and police. What Alison's plans were after everything was cleared up remained uncertain, but he was hopeful they would somehow include him.

The shot that had brought down Treat Griswold, she told him—the improbable, remarkable shot—was one she had made over and over in her mind as she lay tied up, humiliated, and in continuous agony in the basement of the house on Beechtree Road. During those endless hours, what little hope she hung on to became focused in that shot. None of the hundreds she imagined ever missed its mark.

Several times during the nights they had spent together, Gabe held her and dried her tears at the notion of having taken a life the way she did—even one as monstrous as Treat Griswold's. The story she shared of her battles in L.A. to clear the name of a fellow nurse, and also her subsequent torture at the hands of Griswold, more than justified her actions in Gabe's eyes. But there were tears nonetheless.

Gabe's own reaction to having killed the men sent to kill him was far more tempered—certainly less anguished than on the two occasions in his life as a physician when his decisions, forced during raging medical emergencies, contributed to the death of a patient.

Pine Grove Cemetery.

With a heaviness in his heart, and even some trepidation, Gabe left his car on the street and entered the small cemetery through a wrought-iron arch, using a cane for support. In his other hand he carried a single rose. Through the gloom and the persistent drizzle, he could make out the silhouette of a man, standing motionless by one of the stones.

Thirty years.

The man, about Gabe's height but thinner, had his head bowed. He looked up as Gabe approached. His face was narrow, his posture proud.

"Singleton?"

"Gabe."

"All right. If you wish, Gabe. I accept you calling me Leon."

Uretsky spoke with just the hint of a Russian accent and Eastern European phrasing.

"Thank you for seeing me like this."

"I have twice tried to kill you. Meeting you seems the least I could do."

"I'm glad you weren't so good with your guns."

"The truth is, Doctor, I am quite good. I was a marksman in the Russian Army before I moved here at age twenty-five. The weapons I used those two times were mine, bought some years ago for target practice . . .

to stay sharp. For all those years I thought about revenge. Then, at the last minute, both times, I just could not do it. Thirty years ago I could have, I believe. I tried to find you after you left prison, but I was a recent immigrant and had little means. Each trail took me no place and cost me money. Finally, I just gave up. But I never forgot. Then, when a friend showed me the article about you—"

He was unable to continue.

Gabe moved a step nearer to Uretsky, unsure whether the moisture on his own cheeks was from the drizzle or from his eyes. One thing was certain. In that instant, he felt an indescribable closeness to the man.

"You loved her very much," Gabe said.

"I was put on this earth to love her," Uretsky replied. He motioned to the headstone, which had both the names Irina Kursova and Dimitri Uretsky inscribed. "And I believed you took her from me. Her and my son."

"We had no right to drink like we did and no right to drink at all, then drive."

"No one does. You sent the president out to see me because you knew I'd never believe you if you told me he was the one."

"Do you believe me now?"

"I do."

"For thirty years I have had to live with Irina's and Dimitri's deaths if not as painfully as you have, then nearly so."

"Stoddard did you a deep wrong not to tell the truth from the beginning."

"I agree. I can't begin to tell you what getting kicked out of college and then spending a year in a maximum-security prison was like. In some ways, though, Leon, you have broken the spiral of tragedy by your unwillingness to take my life. There is nothing more wonderful you could have done for your Irina."

"Perhaps," Uretsky said. "Perhaps you are right. Are you still leaving as you said on the phone?"

"I am. First thing in the morning. I have had enough of Washington and politics."

"Do you think we should let the public know the secret of the man they have entrusted with their country?"

"I haven't really decided. You?"

"I need to think—to go back to baking my bread, and to think. Irina had only been in this country for six months when she died. She had already made great progress with her English."

"I think we should keep in touch, you and I—speak every week or two. I would like to get to know you better, and I wish to know what you decide. If you decide you need to go to the press, I will probably choose to support you."

"Andrew Stoddard has hurt us both."

"Badly. But for both of us there is still life. Now, I suppose, it is he who will suffer. Drew can be self-centered and callous, but he is also very human. Regardless of what we decide to do, he will suffer. Do we need revenge for what he has done? I don't know. I really don't know."

"Someone else can run the country."

"He's done a good job, I think, but yes. Someone else could run it and maybe do just as well."

"Maybe better. I need to think."

"I understand."

"I have the number you gave me in Wyoming. I promise to call."

"And I have yours."

"We need to talk some more—to share our feelings."

"I think so, Leon. I think we can be of help to each other."

"I could use that."

"So could I."

Gabe set the rose down at the base of the stone. He nodded toward Uretsky, acknowledging their bond, stood there for another silent minute, then finally turned and hobbled back toward the gate.

EPILOGUE

*T*he scene might have been an oil by Frederic Remington or a photograph by Bert Greer Phillips. The barn . . . the cabin . . . smoke curling from the fieldstone chimney . . . the hitching rail . . . vapor rising from the nostrils of the three saddled horses . . . the pure white rime, covering the ground for as far as the eye could see . . . the slate-colored sky . . .

Midwinter on the high plains.

Bundled against the deep chill, Gabe burst out the back door of his ranch, purposely leaving it ajar. He mounted Condor with fluid, experienced grace, wincing just a little at the stretching of five-month-old scar tissue near his shoulder and his hip.

"Come on, you guys," he called out. "I want to be as far away from civilization as possible when the clock strikes ten."

"Hold your horses, my friend," a man's voice called back. "The lady is helping me get my boots on. Hey, hold your horses—that is very funny, no? You really *are* holding your horses."

Finally, Alison emerged into the cold in a leather rancher's coat with a heavy fleece collar and a western hat with a rattlesnake band and eight-inch feather.

Radiant, Gabe thought, as he did every time he saw her. *Absolutely radiant.*

Behind her, Leon Uretsky walked gingerly in new boots. His borrowed western hat hung between his shoulder blades. His hair and eyes were raven dark, and his features were sharp and appealing.

"Left foot in the stirrup, Leon," Gabe said. "Then grab the pommel up there and swing your right leg over."

"This is your plot to get even, isn't it?" Leon asked.

"Come on, big guy," Alison urged. "You're going to love it. Besides, the doc here and I both work in the hospital. We're not going to let anything happen to you."

Uretsky swung his leg up and over like a seasoned cowboy. Then, for a few moments, the three riders remained motionless, breathing in the air and the spectacular silence.

"Beautiful," Uretsky murmured, "just beautiful. I have never been anyplace like this. Not even in Russia."

"I told you," Gabe said, turning Condor with the most subtle of movements. "I'm really glad you finally agreed to come out."

"Both of us are," Alison added. "Honey, is it time yet?"

"Not quite. We can still make it to Wizard's Ridge by ten."

The three horses walked easily away from the house and out along a trail marked only by a few tracks.

"What is so special about this Wizard's Ridge?" Uretsky asked.

"Nothing . . . and everything. I named it because, well, you'll see. The bread is in your saddlebag?"

"And butter and jam if they are not already frozen solid."

"Mmmm. I love fresh-baked bread," Alison said.

"You are going to have five whole days of it. I plan to bake a different kind of loaf each morning I am here, plus some other goodies."

"Wonderful."

At five minutes of ten they rode up a gentle slope and stopped on Wizard's Ridge. Beyond them, mile after mile of white-coated desert stretched out to the mountains.

"Remarkable," Alison said. "Doc, I really love it here. And in case I haven't told you enough times today, I really love you, too."

"And I love you," Gabe said, still amazed at how easily the words came out. "Leon, I told you after I left Washington last summer, you'd be welcome out to the ranch anytime. Now, here you are. I'm especially happy to be sharing all this with you of all people. Next time, bring that woman you've started seeing, if she wants to come."

"Dolores? Perhaps. I think she would like it here. You know, the better I get to know you, the happier I am that I didn't kill you."

"I'm glad you didn't kill me, too, my friend. The loss of the prison bakery at MCI Hagerstown, where you would have ended up, is our gain. Okay, everyone, it's ten o'clock on the dot. How about we break some fresh bread together."

The three passed a soft, oval loaf, one to the next, each ripping off a healthy chunk.

Seventeen hundred miles away, the Bible was being presented and the hand was being set upon it. The throng who had braved the chilly January day to witness history held their breath as loudspeakers sent out the words and the voice they had come to hear.

"I, Andrew Joseph Stoddard, do solemnly affirm that I will faithfully execute the Office of President of the United States, and will to the best of my ability, preserve, protect and defend the Constitution of the United States."

"Pass the jam, Leon, will you?" Gabe said.